Praise for the novels of
New York Times bestselling author Lynn Kurland

"One of romance's finest writers."   —*The Oakland Press*

"Both powerful and sensitive . . . A wonderfully rich and rewarding book."   —Susan Wiggs, #1 *New York Times* bestselling author

"Kurland weaves another fabulous read with just the right amounts of laughter, romance, and fantasy."   —Affaire de Coeur

"As always, Kurland does a spectacular job blending thrilling fantasy adventure with rich characterization—making sure readers are in for an exceptional ride!"   —*RT Book Reviews* (4½ Stars)

"[A] triumphant romance."   —Fresh Fiction

"Woven with magic, handsome heroes, lovely heroines, oodles of fun, and plenty of romance . . . Just plain wonderful."
          —Romance Reviews Today

"Spellbinding and lovely, this is one story readers won't want to miss."
          —Romance Reader at Heart

"Kurland infuses her polished writing with a deliciously dry wit . . . Sweetly romantic and thoroughly satisfying."   —*Booklist*

"A pure delight."   —Huntress Book Reviews

"[A] consummate storyteller."   —ParaNormal Romance Reviews

"A disarming blend of romance, suspense, and heartwarming humor, this book is romantic comedy at its best."   —*Publishers Weekly*

"A totally enchanting tale, sensual and breathtaking."   —Rendezvous

Lynn Kurland

THE
WHITE SPELL

BERKLEY SENSATION
New York

BERKLEY SENSATION
Published by Berkley
An imprint of Penguin Random House LLC
375 Hudson Street, New York, New York 10014

BERKLEY and BERKLEY SENSATION are registered trademarks and
the B colophon is a trademark of Penguin Random House LLC.

Library of Congress Cataloging-in-Publication Data

Names: Kurland, Lynn, author.
Title: The white spell / Lynn Kurland.
Description: Berkley trade paperback edition. | New York : Berkley Sensation, 2016. |
Series: A novel of the nine kingdoms ; 10
Identifiers: LCCN 2016012081 (print) | LCCN 2016018560 (ebook) |
ISBN 9780425282205 (softcover) | ISBN 9780698198753 () |
Subjects: LCSH: Good and evil—Fiction. | Magic—Fiction. |
BISAC: FICTION / Romance / Fantasy. | FICTION / Fantasy / General. |
GSAFD: Fantasy fiction.
Classification: LCC PS3561.U645 W48 2016 (print) |
LCC PS3561.U645 (ebook) | DDC 813/.54—dc23
LC record available at https://lccn.loc.gov/2016012081

First Edition: October 2016

Printed in the United States of America
1 3 5 7 9 10 8 6 4 2

Cover art copyright © Melanie Delon
Cover design by Katie Anderson

The White Spell

To the horses—and their staff, of course—
who have changed my life in such profound ways . . .

Prologue

Murder, mischief, mayhem. Those were the sorts of things that he dealt in. The business of do-gooding . . . well, it just didn't agree with his digestion.

Acair of Ceangail, son of the most powerful and, admittedly, most unpleasant black mage still darkening the doorways of the Nine Kingdoms, looked at the pair of do-gooders sitting across from him at a worn table in a rather less-seedy tavern than he was accustomed to frequenting, and decided the time had come to put his foot down. He fixed them both with a steely gaze.

"That was the very last one of these I am willing to do."

The men sitting there looked unmoved by his declaration, which he supposed shouldn't have surprised him. They were up to their necks in all sorts of noble activities he wouldn't have engaged in if his life had hung in the balance.

He paused. Very well, he had engaged in just their sort of rot, but that had been because his life *had* hung in the balance. He had agreed to a ridiculous bargain with those two there when they'd caught him in a moment of weakness further polluted by something another might have termed regret, but he'd done his part and now he had put any untoward and unsettling impulses to appease anyone but himself behind him. He was finished. It was past time they understood that his protestations weren't simply for show.

He leaned forward and gave them the coldest look he could muster. Considering the sort of year he'd recently endured he was afraid it had barely reached chilly, but there you had it. Too much spreading of sunshine and happiness had obviously done a foul work on him.

"That recent journey to Meith," he said, slowly, so they wouldn't misunderstand him, "was the very *last* of these ridiculous parleys I am willing to engage in with whichever insipid monarch, grossly offended head of state, or richly dressed underling you have selected for me to grovel before. I have spent months apologizing, smiling, and generally making a complete ass of myself. I will *not* do the like any longer."

The pair across from him exchanged a look. Acair was, he had to admit with as much modesty as he could muster in difficult circumstances, extremely adept at reading between the lines. Or between the looks, as it were. There was an untoward amount of amusement being shared, as well as something that spoke strongly of already-discussed, nefarious intentions. Both annoyed him, but he supposed he could have expected nothing less from the two fools huddled together there on the opposite side of that worn tavern table.

The fool on the left was his half-brother, Rùnach of Tòrr Dòrainn. Rùnach was the second eldest of a collection of impositions on the world his own father, Gair, had decided to produce with an elven princess several decades after Acair's birth. Why Gair had wed Rùnach's mother instead of Acair's own was a mystery . . . well, knowing his mother as he did, Acair had to admit there was no mystery to it at all, but that didn't solve the problem of his half-brother sitting across from him, smirking. Rùnach loved nothing more than a hearty bit of good cheer, something Acair had learned early on to dislike about him. Acair scowled at him, then turned his attention to his half-brother's companion.

Now, *that* one gave him pause and there wasn't another soul in the whole of the Nine Kingdoms who gave him pause. Soilléir of Cothromaiche was . . . odd. His magic was unsettling, his power staggering, and he had a way of looking at a body so the body being so observed felt as if it were standing there in its soul alone. Acair shook his head. Damned unnerving, that one. Soilléir wasn't so much smirking as he was just watching, as if he knew exactly what Acair intended to do before he did it.

As he'd said. Odd.

Rùnach cleared his throat in a way that bespoke serious business indeed. "The thing is, Acair," he said slowly, wrapping his hands around his mug, "we feel that you have one last bit of—" He frowned thoughtfully and looked at Soilléir. "What did we decide to call it, my lord?"

"Penance," Soilléir supplied.

"Penance," Rùnach repeated, nodding. "Aye, that was it." He looked at Acair with an expression of innocence he had likely not had to practice more than once. "We believe you have a bit more penance to do in order to make up for your past misdeeds."

"What past misdeeds?" Acair hedged. If they couldn't name them, he wasn't going to admit to them. That had gotten him out of more than one tight spot in the past, to be sure.

"Most recently you tried to drain the world of all its magic," Rùnach said. "There's a start to the list, wouldn't you agree?"

"I believe the important word there is *tried*," Acair said, "and thank you so very much for reminding me of my abysmal failure."

"Failure?" Rùnach echoed. "Acair, you toppled at least two thrones I can bring immediately to mind, as well as vexing several other very powerful members of the Council of Kings."

"True," Acair said with a light sigh. The list should have been longer, but again, it had been a difficult year and he'd been distracted by trotting out his best court manners and using them in ways he hadn't particularly cared for.

"It wasn't a compliment," Soilléir said.

"You can't say you wouldn't do the same thing," Acair said pointedly, "given the proper inducement."

Now, there was a piece of truth if ever there were one. Who

knew what that one there dreamed up as he sat in his private chambers in the schools of wizardry, contemplating that staggering amount of power he had that was no doubt simply lying about his chambers like so many unmatched socks.

"I *could*," Soilléir said, "but I never would."

Acair suppressed the urge to roll his eyes. When Soilléir of Cothromaiche started making a fuss about his nobler instincts, the conversation was doomed to head downhill very quickly. Best to head off any potential rhapsodic waxing about the health benefits of virtuous living before the man truly hit his stride.

He studied the two on the other side of the table and considered the lay of the land, as it were. He hadn't minimized the misery they had already put him through. It had been at least half a year that he'd been dragging himself from one tedious locale to another, forcing himself to smile politely, speak without threats, and keep his hands in his pockets instead of allowing them to linger in any visible coffers. It had been absolute hell, but he was nothing if not a man of his word and he had agreed to do the like.

That Soilléir had threatened him with life as a lawn ornament if he didn't comply had been a decent bit of motivation, but he'd done what he'd agreed to do and now he had other plans. He hadn't wanted to choke down a meal with the lads facing him, but the invitation had been less of a request and more of a summons. He had assumed he would be required to give some sort of recounting of all the things he had learned, promise never to behave poorly again, then be relegated to a distant if not fond memory. His life would again be his own and he would never darken either of their front stoops again.

He knew he shouldn't have been surprised to find that extricating himself from their clutches was going to be a bit more difficult than he'd anticipated.

He pointedly ignored Soilléir and turned to Rùnach.

"Very well," he said briskly, "tell me quickly what preposterous thing I must do in order to win my freedom from your presence and let me about it. Just realize I am only doing this to humor you. If I were a lesser man, I would simply leave you here at the table to pay for my drink yourselves."

They didn't look as alarmed by that possibility as they should have, but insults only went so far with men who obviously hadn't the wits between them to know when they were being insulted.

Rùnach looked at him seriously. "We want you to apologize to Uachdaran of Léige for disturbing his sleep with the rivers of power you set to running under his kingdom."

"I didn't do that," Acair spluttered.

Rùnach only looked at him in a way that was so reminiscent of Soilléir, Acair almost flinched.

"Very well, I *did* do that," he said, "but if you think I'm going to go prostrate myself in front of that feisty old curmudgeon and apologize for anything, you're mad."

Rùnach shrugged. "If that doesn't suit, then we'll take a century of your doing no magic instead."

Acair knew he was gaping but couldn't keep from it. He revisited his three favorite activities and wondered which one would be the most effective on the two sitting across from him. He sat up a bit straighter and smoothed his hand over his tunic. "What horrible fate do you have waiting for me if I tell you to go to hell?" he asked politely. "Or shall I simply slay you both whilst your noses are buried in your cups?"

Soilléir lifted a pale eyebrow. "I could turn you into something you wouldn't like."

"I can't think of anything I wouldn't like," Acair said promptly, ignoring any previous discussions he might or might not have had with the man sitting across from him regarding birdbaths. "Do your worst."

"You might want to reconsider," Soilléir advised. "Imagine the locales where I could put you, silent as stone, doomed for eternity to simply watch those around you living pleasant lives."

"You're bluffing," Acair said dismissively. "Your vaunted code prevents you from doing something that evil."

Soilléir only looked at him in that way he had. "For you, Acair, I might make an exception."

Acair almost shivered, which alarmed him more than anything he'd been faced with so far that evening. He didn't shiver; he made others shiver. He was accustomed to walking into a hall and having the entire company sink to the ground in a terrorized faint. It was just what he did, that terrifying the bloody hell out of everyone he met. He had to admit, with extreme reluctance, that he didn't care for it at all when that same sort of feeling tapped him on the shoulder and demanded his attention.

Damn that Soilléir of Cothromaiche and all his ilk. He should have drained the man's bloody homeland of all its power long before now.

It wasn't as if he hadn't considered the possibilities of that previously, and very seriously too. The actual execution of that sort of theft had turned out to be rather more daunting a prospect than he'd thought, which had forced him to shelve the idea for the time being. Perhaps 'twas past time he took the plan down and reexamined it. Soilléir had to sleep at least occasionally, surely. A wee rest for the man, a substantial bit of pilfering for himself, and then he would be saved from being turned into a lawn ornament for those damned faeries from Sìabhreach.

"The choice is yours, of course," Soilléir continued with a shrug. "No magic, or a visit to the king of the dwarves."

Acair rubbed his hands over his face. Damnation, would the torment never end? He had a drink of ale to purchase a bit of time for thinking, then decided there was no point. He should have been paying more heed to the chess game he'd become an unwilling part of the all those many months ago. As it was, he now found himself pinned into a corner of the board where the only way out was forward. He looked at his half-brother and wondered if a last-ditch bit of honesty might save him.

"I can't go to Léige," he said.

"Can't," Rùnach asked, "or won't?"

"Does it matter?" Acair returned shortly. "I've paid especial attention to that old whoreson over the years, vexing him at every opportunity, carrying on the long and glorious tradition of my fathers. He doesn't like me."

"King Uachdaran has a fair number of companions in that activity," Soilléir noted.

"I also may have spirited away one of his daughters for a fortnight of ale-quaffing," Acair admitted. "Several years ago."

Soilléir blinked several times—a sure sign of surprise. "Ale-quaffing?"

Acair shrugged. "She was beautiful and I have a weakness for handsome wenches. Decent ale too."

Rùnach looked at him, then laughed. Acair cursed them both but that didn't seem to leave much of an impression.

"He doesn't like me," Acair said stiffly, "and that is all you need to know. I will not set foot in Durial."

Rùnach was apparently having difficulty breathing. "Please tell me your dealings with that poor gel were limited to pub crawls."

"Hardly even that," Acair said grimly. "She called me a very unkind name at the first establishment, clunked me over the head with a chair, then scampered off with an elf from *your* mother's homeland, an opportunistic lad who will remain unnamed for his own protection."

"Though you would spew out his name in a heartbeat if you thought it would save you," Rùnach said, still grinning like the idiot he was.

"Well, of course I would," Acair said. "You would too—you can't deny it."

"Depends on the elf," Rùnach said, then he looked at Soilléir. "I had wondered what had happened to her."

"Middle child," Soilléir said wisely. "Trouble in the making."

"Apple of her father's eye," Acair corrected, "which is why Léige is the last place I will go. Perhaps your memory fails you, Rùnach my lad, but I didn't go with you half a year ago when you wanted company. Now you know why."

"Ah, but the king has since made a special request that you come for a visit," Rùnach said. "Who am I to deny him his whims? Either go, or be without magic for a century."

Acair could scarce believe he was having his current conversation. "Have you lost all your wits?" he said incredulously. "I'm not going to give up magic for a fortnight, much less . . . well, I'm not even going to dignify that suggestion by repeating it." He looked at Soilléir narrowly. "I suppose that leaves you with only one choice, which is to take it from me."

"I wouldn't dream of it."

Acair grunted, not believing that for a moment, then considered the pair thoughtfully. There was something else afoot, something he didn't care for. Those two there had dragged him with them all over the Nine Kingdoms for months, showing him off like a prized monkey, humiliating him at every turn. Surely they'd had enough of that sort of entertainment to suit even their unwholesome need for the same.

Nay, there was something else going on.

But simply asking certainly wouldn't provide him with answers. He would have to play the fool for a bit longer. Unpleasant, but he obviously had no choice. The things he had been forced to do . . .

He made a production of nodding knowingly. "I see where this is headed. You do indeed fear my mighty power and despite your fine words you want it for yourselves."

Rùnach only lifted his eyebrows briefly. "An interesting thought, but nay. I have enough magic of my own, thank you just the same. I would suspect my lord Soilléir feels the same way."

Acair couldn't believe Rùnach would be satisfied with anything that wasn't *more*, but what did he know? Soilléir likely had too much of it, but what decent mage wasn't interested in adding to his cache of spells?

Nay, mischief was being made right there in front of him and he didn't care for it when he wasn't the one at the helm, as it were. But if he'd learned anything over the past several months, it was that his companions were tight-lipped about their plans. He was going to have to pretend to go along with their plans until they made a misstep and he could see what they were truly about. Patience wasn't anything that came easily to him, but if having it at present would win him freedom from the meddling ways of the two alewives sitting across from him, he would use any last bits of it he might still possess.

He would pay the price, but not gladly and he would certainly take note of every pesky moment of it for use later. He didn't like to admit any sort of defeat, but he knew when to pause and retrench. The inability to do that was his sire's fatal flaw, a flaw he had no intention of allowing to take root in himself.

"Very well," he said heavily, "let's have this over with. To spare myself an endless existence on the front stoop of some mindless faery, as well as secure the guarantee that I'll never have to encounter either of you again unless there are spells of death involved, I will agree to a month without magic."

"A century, Acair," Soilléir said mildly.

"Absurd," Acair said. "Two months and no more."

Soilléir only looked at him. Acair managed to keep himself from rubbing his arms against the sudden chill that blew over him but damn it if he couldn't keep himself from shifting.

"Very well, a year," he snarled. "And not a heartbeat longer."

Soilléir and Rùnach exchanged a look. Acair sensed a softening of the resolve of the pair, something he didn't dare disturb with even a mild epitaph.

Soilléir looked at him. "Very well, then," he said. "A year. Upon your honor."

Acair refused to respond to that. "I assume you are leaving me free to roam where I choose to," he said. Considering the number of souls he had been less-than-friendly with in the past, the list of places where he might find sanctuary was very short indeed. There was, of course, no use in pointing that out. The two fools across from him knew that very well.

"Oh, nay," Rùnach said, with a feeble attempt at solemnity, "we wouldn't dream of leaving you so—how shall I put it, my lord Soilléir?"

"Exposed," Soilléir said.

"Exposed," Rùnach agreed. He smiled. "We wouldn't want you to be vulnerable, of course, which is why we've selected an appropriate destination for you. Lots of opportunities there to do good. You've become so adept at that sort of thing, we thought you might want to keep on with it for a bit longer."

Acair thought many things but decided it would be best if he didn't voice any of them. He would have attempted a smile but found it was simply beyond him. He settled for something just short of a grimace. "Where?"

"Sàraichte," Rùnach said, looking terribly pleased with himself. "A stroke of genius, if I do admit as much myself."

Acair was past surprise. "Indeed."

"I suggest a labor of some kind," Soilléir said thoughtfully. "With your hands."

Besides wrapping them around your neck? was what came first to mind, but Acair decided that was perhaps something also better left unsaid. If he didn't get away from the pair of imbeciles in front of him, he was never going to be able to speak again.

"I don't need a labor when I can . . ." He paused and frowned. It was going to be a bit difficult to feed himself if he couldn't pluck the odd piece of Nerochian gold out of thin air now and again. "I'll need magic to conjure up funds from time to time."

"Use it and become a conversation piece for a faery," Rùnach said. "Isn't that right, my lord Soilléir?"

"That did seem to be our bargain."

Acair wriggled his jaw to loosen it. There had been no bargain; there had simply been a chess game that he'd played very badly.

But Sàraichte? Could there be a place in the whole of the Nine Kingdoms less appealing?

Well, he supposed there could be and he could name several of them without effort, so perhaps he would be better off to simply keep his mouth shut and carry on as if he were bested yet again. He looked at his companions coolly.

"Very well, I'll go," he said with as much politeness as he could muster. "I don't suppose that as a courtesy you two would spot me a sovereign or two to help me on my way, would you?"

Meager funds were produced and pushed across the table. Acair collected them—he was a pragmatist, after all—and pocketed them. Obviously, he would be sleeping under the stars more than he cared to, but he couldn't see how anything could be done about that at present. But later? Aye, there would be retribution. He stood up and pulled his cloak around his shoulders.

"Don't make this any worse for yourselves," he warned. "And you know exactly what I mean by that."

Rùnach lifted his cup up in salute. "Wouldn't dream of it."

"Oh," Soilléir said, holding up his hand, "one more thing. You are forbidden to reveal your identity to anyone who doesn't already know you."

Of course. Acair glared at Soilléir. "Anything else?"

"If I think of anything, I'll let you know."

Acair snarled a curse at him, sent his half-brother a look of promise, then stomped out of the pub and into the twilight. He might have enjoyed the rustic view, but he had the feeling he was going to be seeing far too much of that kind of thing in the future, more particularly from his vantage point on the ground. The pleasures of flying along as a terrible wind were obviously lost to him for the moment.

But damnation, what choice had he had? The past half year had truly been an unsettling one, full of unpleasant experiences he would have preferred to forget, and all because of a rather innocent piece of magic he'd decided to attempt after a rather tedious and uninteresting decade. The idea had come to him as he'd been wandering about a library in a locale he didn't care to visit again and he'd stumbled upon a book of—

Well, perhaps it didn't matter what the book had contained given that it was now safely tucked behind an impenetrable wall of his own spells, spells apparently he couldn't unlock for at least a year. He would have pointed out that fact to Rùnach—it was Rùnach's book, after all—but he'd been too damn distracted to.

A year without magic. Absolutely preposterous.

And all because he'd simply attempted a rather substantial theft of the world's magic and failed spectacularly. If that hadn't been enough, he'd taken a blade to the chest and almost lost his life. Rùnach had been the one to heal him with some damned elvish rot that Acair was convinced had left something untoward behind where the wound had been. He'd been suffering ever since from foul dreams and the like. Add that to the sad truth that Soilléir had been stalking him for the past several months, threatening him— still—with life as an inanimate object if he didn't grovel before a lengthy list of offended busybodies . . . well, as he'd reluctantly admitted before, those lads from Cothromaiche gave him pause. He didn't know their spells, but he knew what they could do.

He didn't fancy life as a rock.

Given that was the case, he would trot off loudly into the Deepening Gloom, looking appropriately contrite no matter what it cost him, then duck off the road when he could and slip off to some exotic locale where he would lie low until his year's sentence was up—

Or, perhaps not.

He walked for another half-league before he finally turned around and stared at what had been following him.

A spell.

He wasn't unfamiliar with spells, as it happened, having a truly staggering collection of them at his fingertips. He created his own spells, of course, though he generally thought it a better use of his time to simply appropriate what he needed. But never in his long life of encountering magic had he ever seen a spell that simply stood there and watched him, as if it had legs. It was an odd spell, though, one that didn't seem to want to reveal its purpose. For all he knew, it was designed to watch to make sure he followed Soilléir's instructions to the letter.

He made a rude gesture at that nasty piece of magic, ignored the snort that answered him, then turned and started off toward a destination he absolutely didn't want to visit.

Sàraichte. Ye gads, what a hellhole. If he'd had so little to do that he would have needed to amuse himself by making a list of places to visit, he suspected that port town in the middle of nowhere would have had very few other locales competing with it for last on the list.

Damnation, it was going to be a very long year indeed.

One

The port town of Sàraichte was a locale with absolutely no redeeming features.

The list of its flaws was long and well-examined. It wasn't as large as Tòsan, nor as elegant as Taohb na Mara; it was a city of unremarkable size that one tended to forget as quickly as possible in order to erase the unfortunate memory of having passed through it. Its harbor was endlessly needing a good dredging whilst its inhabitants seemed to be perpetually needing a good bath. The food was terrible, the accommodations disgusting, and the scenery flat and uninspiring. There was only one thing about the place that spared it from the need for a good razing.

The stables of Briàghde.

Léirsinn of Sàraichte leaned against an outer wall of Briàghde's labyrinth of stalls and considered the truth of that. She wasn't one to be effusive with praise or stingy with censure, which left her looking at the bare facts to judge them on merit alone. And the simple fact was, the horses that came from the stables in which she stood were absolutely beyond compare.

She knew this because she was responsible for it.

It wasn't something she thought about very often, actually, for a variety of reasons that left her feeling rather uncomfortable if she gave too much thought to them. But the weather was brisk, the barn cats feisty, and the horses very full of themselves. If that had infected her with a bit more spirit than she usually dared allow herself, so be it. Besides, she was the only one inside her head, so perhaps she could be permitted a bracing bit of truth to enjoy privately.

And the truth was, she was damned good at working horses. It was in her blood, or so she understood, which she supposed helped quite a bit. The rest of it was simply years of seeing horse after horse come through Fuadain of Sàraichte's stables and watching how they matured. She'd had the good sense to know which horsemen to listen to in her youth and perhaps even better sense to keep her mouth shut when it would have been easier to call other men who thought they knew horses idiots.

She was growing rather tired of that last bit, actually.

But biting her tongue allowed her to continue to watch what came and went in Lord Fuadain's stables and, better still, quietly have charge of their training. Of course she never spoke her opinions aloud, but she and the stable master, Slaidear, had come to an understanding a decade ago. He would stroke his chin and consider the beast on display before him, glance her way to see if she raised a single eyebrow or not, then take her opinion as his own and offer an aye or nay as necessary.

Many fine animals were turned away as a result, left with no choice but to find homes with lesser masters. Only the most spectacular beasts were invited to stay to either be bred or trained, sometimes both. The fees charged for either privilege were so high, Léirsinn was frankly amazed anyone managed to pay them. But they seemed to, and gladly.

Of course, she saw no share of that gold, but she couldn't have realistically expected anything else. Fuadain was her uncle, as it happened, but she was one of his much lesser relations by marriage. She was fortunate to have a roof over her head and enough to eat. She had incomparable horses to train, though, which made up for quite a bit.

As did the sea, which was perhaps the one redeeming feature of Sàraichte. She could see the faint sparkle of it from where she stood. If she'd had money enough, she would have built a house near it, with an enormous barn and a path that led to the shore where she could have ridden a different horse each day along the edge of the water. She would have had peace and quiet and the freedom to think whatever thoughts she cared to without having to guard her expressions.

With any luck she would have that, though perhaps not as quickly as she would have liked. She looked down at the coins she held in her hand. It was her se'nnight's pay, those three coins that would scarce buy her a decent meal at the worst pub in town. But she would add them to the rest of what she had, as usual, and continue on as she always did.

She pushed away from the wall and walked into the stables, noting the condition of the floors between rows of stalls—one might eat off them if one were so inclined—and the condition of the horses housed inside those stalls—one might ride them to the ends of the earth if one were so inclined. She tried not to think about that possibility very often, lest the temptation prove to be more than she could bear.

The stables were less populated by lads than usual, but perhaps they'd snuck off for a bit of rest. She couldn't blame them. The work was endless and they didn't have the privilege of riding any of the horses they tended. The work was endless for her as well, but she was at least allowed to ride what she tended. If she generally limited herself to riding the finest horses in the barn, who could blame her?

She made her way without undue haste to her private tack room. In truth, the damned place was no larger than her uncle's smallest wardrobe, but it was hers alone and there was a lock on her door. She was fortunate to have that much and she knew it.

She entered, then closed the door behind her purposefully, as if she indeed had many important things to do. She lit a lantern, then kept herself busy doing absolutely nothing for another few minutes until she was as certain as she could be that she wouldn't be interrupted.

She carefully removed a stack of dusty, ancient saddle pads to reveal a very worn box full of half-used bottles of horse liniment. She looked at the nastiest of the lot but didn't disturb it until she had made certain it hadn't been moved by someone else. Finding everything to be as it should have been, she lifted the bottle and looked at what lay underneath it.

A key.

That key opened a lock that was found on a box that wasn't found on her uncle's property, a scheme that had been casually suggested to her a handful of years earlier by someone in town. She'd agreed just as casually that such seemed like a fine idea. The box in question, tended by that same trustworthy soul in town, was full of more silver than gold, but the modest collection of coins was hers, ruthlessly saved against a time when she might find it useful. She didn't want to admit that she couldn't imagine when such a day might come, but it had seemed a bit like having a loft stacked with a winter's worth of hay. Security was nothing to be sneered at.

She deposited her trio of coins next to the key, then replaced everything in a way that left no indication that it had been moved. She sat down on a stool that still rocked despite the attempts she'd made over the years to file the legs to the same length. Her pay would be safe enough until she was able to get to town and put the coins where they needed to go. She took a deep breath, then let herself think thoughts that seemed so dangerous, she rarely entertained them. But since it had been that sort of day so far, she continued on with the anarchy.

She was going to get herself and her grandfather out of Sàraichte.

The truth was, she didn't need a house by the sea. She wasn't even sure she needed a house. All she needed was enough money to collect her grandfather from her uncle's manor and spirit them both away to somewhere safe. Her grandfather's frail condition demanded a place where she could find work and he could be cared for, but that was done easily enough. A town with a decent barn and a fair supply of women skilled in the arts of physicking would serve. Perhaps in time she might even find someone willing to try to heal him, for enough gold. She seriously doubted she would find anyone to do it out of the goodness of his heart—

A knock startled her so badly, she almost fell off her stool. She took a deep, steadying breath, then rose and opened the door. "Aye?"

Her head groomsman, Doghail, stood there. "Thought you should know that Fuadain's in a temper," he said in a low voice.

"When is he not?" she asked lightly.

"Aye, well, he seems to be in a particularly difficult mood today. You might want to keep that in mind."

Léirsinn didn't even consider arguing with that assessment. Doghail was a short, thin man who had spent the bulk of his life racing horses for this lord or that. He was wiry, malnourished, and canny as hell. The horses did his bidding without hesitation. She understood that. When he pulled her up with a pinky finger on her reins, she never hesitated to pause. If he said her uncle was in a temper, she was going to keep her ears forward—

She shook her head. Perhaps she had spent too much time in the company of horses. She was starting to think like one.

"I sense something afoot," Doghail added. "He's sacked half the lads for imagined slights." He paused. "I just wanted you to know what was blowing your way so you'd be prepared."

She stepped outside her closet and pulled the door shut behind her. "Where is he now?"

"Entertaining up at the house, but one of the kitchen lads scampered down to tell me that they're almost finished with their port."

"But 'tis barely noon," she said in surprise. "Into their cups so early?"

"Aye," he said grimly, "and if that doesn't give you pause, I don't know what will."

She shook her head less in surprise than resignation. Her uncle was very fond of his drink. If he'd already been in a temper that morning, she almost hesitated to think what he would be in by the time he and his luncheon companion stumbled through her doors. She looked at Doghail.

"Where's Slaidear?"

"At Himself's elbow," Doghail said in disgust. "Where else?"

Where, indeed? Why Fuadain had ever made Slaidear his stable master—nay, there was no point in revisiting that piece of stupidity because she knew exactly why her uncle had done the like. Master Slaidear might have known next to nothing about horses, but the man knew how to flatter a lord with mercurial moods.

She had complained about Slaidear's lack of knowledge to a stable hand when she'd first arrived in Sàraichte—once. That lad, who had long since laid himself down in a mouldering grave, had put her some deep knowledge, as he would have said, and told her to keep her bloody mouth shut and her eyes and ears open. And she, a poor shivering, sniveling child of eleven summers, had had the wit to listen.

That had been almost a score of years ago and she had never once regretted forming that habit.

As it happened, in time she had managed to gain Slaidear's trust. If he used her taste in ponies to secure his own place, so much the better. She was free to train what she liked whilst someone else was paying for it. There was a certain beauty in that, which likely said something about her that she didn't want to examine too closely.

She looked at Doghail. "Any ideas what he'll want to see?"

"His companion is a genteel gentleman," Doghail said knowingly.

She laughed a little in spite of herself. "No money but quite a title, is that what you're getting at?"

"Exactly." He squinted back down the way. "I imagine we'll have word from Slaidear at any moment on which horses to prepare. Somehow, I suspect they might be the same ones you would think of."

"Funny thing, that," she said. "Very well, let's settle on a simple beast who wouldn't mind a life in modest surroundings. If we flank him with a less desirable pair of nags, he'll shine well enough."

"Tell me which ones and I'll ready them."

She considered, named a trio of horses she thought might suit, then watched Doghail walk off to do what he did best. Unfortunately that left her with nothing to do but linger in the passageway and wait.

She wandered down toward the entry to the barn, leaned back against a handy wall, and contented herself with yet another recalculating of her funds.

Would that it took more time than it did.

She straightened immediately at the sight of her uncle marching purposely toward the barn, his guest in tow. She waited without shifting until he arrived, then strove not to flinch as he stopped in front of her.

"What are you doing lazing about?" he demanded.

She made him a small bow. "I was simply waiting here to attend your pleasure, as always, and await Master Slaidear's instructions."

"I should think so," Fuadain huffed. He looked at his companion. "Come, Lord Aidan, and we'll endure a bit of dust to see what Slaidear has produced."

Léirsinn held back as her uncle and his obviously inebriated companion walked rather unsteadily into the barn. Slaidear looked at her quickly as he hung back behind the pair. She nodded ever so slightly and he continued on, obviously reassured.

She suppressed the urge to sigh. Her uncle was at least a bit lordly looking, his unsavory self aside. He was tall, with silver hair and a noble brow. Slaidear, on the other hand, was a short, round little fellow who looked as if he belonged on the edges of a tale about hard-working dwarves, not up to his ears in the demanding labor of overseeing a large barn full of extremely valuable horses.

Then again, he knew what to say and when to say it. Perhaps that made up for his lack of wit.

She realized with a start that there were no stable hands rushing to go hold the horses Doghail had surely selected. There was only Doghail, standing at the gate to the arena, waiting for her with only one horse in tow. She cursed under her breath and walked swiftly down the aisle to meet him.

"No lads?" she asked, feeling a little breathless.

"Later," he said, handing her the reins. "I'll go tack up the other two. Save the best for last, aye?"

She nodded, put her questions aside, then led a perfectly serviceable but hardly spectacular gelding into the arena. A lad came skidding through the dirt to hand her the pair of gloves she'd apparently dropped in her haste, then backed away at a curse from Slaidear. If that one avoided a right proper sacking, she would be surprised. She consigned him to whatever fate awaited him without hesitation and turned her attentions to her own business.

It was obvious from the first turn she took about the arena that Fuadain's luncheon companion wasn't interested in a horse. He knew nothing about them and likely wouldn't have been able to afford what he was looking at even if he had.

That wasn't her affair, though, so she showed the first two ponies to their best advantage, because she couldn't in good conscience do anything else. She swung up onto the back of the finest of the lot, knowing it was pointless to ride him, but it would at least save her the time of working him later—

"Doghail, you'll ride the last one. Girl, get off him and let the man show us what he can do."

Léirsinn didn't move at first, but that was only because she'd spent the better part of her life never allowing herself to show any reaction to anything her uncle said. She took her time dismounting but didn't dare exchange even a quick glance with Doghail as she fussed with the stirrups.

"Make haste, you stupid girl!"

Léirsinn bobbed her head toward her uncle. "Of course, my lord." She handed Doghail the reins, then gave him a leg up. She put her hand on the gelding's neck and bid him silently to be gentle. She was well hidden by the horse's head, so she took a chance and looked up at Doghail.

He was white with what she never would have suggested might be called fear. His morning ale likely hadn't agreed with him. The man had a reputation for having ridden horses that no one else would dare come close to; the pony he was on at present hardly qualified as uncontrollable. If he had, several years earlier, tempted fate one too many times and found himself fair trampled to death as a result, well, that sort of thing occasionally happened, didn't it? It was understandable that he hadn't been up on a horse since he'd managed to relearn to walk, something her uncle knew damned well—

"Put him through his paces, Doghail," Fuadain boomed. "Surely you can manage that."

Léirsinn didn't contemplate murder often—very well, she thought about it every time she saw her uncle, but it seemed counterproductive to slay him only to find herself in a dungeon as a result. Better to let him live out his miserable life in peace. Perhaps one day he would face himself and realize what he'd done to those around him.

She put her hand on Doghail's boot briefly, ignored the trembling she could feel there, then stepped away. There was nothing else to be done.

The gelding behaved perfectly in spite of the lump of man who simply sat on his back, no doubt concentrating only on not falling off. The horse showed his gaits because she clicked at him discreetly as he passed her. That, and he was a brilliant, reliable pony who likely could have even kept a fool like her uncle on his back.

Fuadain tired of his sport after a bit and suggested a return to his solar. He passed her and looked down his nose as he did so.

"Spend your afternoon shoveling," he commanded. "'Tis all you're good for, isn't it?"

"Of course, my lord," she said, keeping her eyes lowered. She felt the breeze from his hand as he attempted to cuff her and missed.

She supposed it might have gone badly for her if his guest hadn't laughed and pulled him along out of the arena. She remained exactly where she was until they had gone, then she ran over to where Doghail was still sitting atop his gallant steed.

He managed to get his feet out of the stirrups, dismount without falling on his face, then stumble over to the railing before he started heaving his guts out. Léirsinn pretended not to notice, biding her time by stroking a painfully soft horse's nose and finally wrapping her arms around that sweet gelding's neck in gratitude.

Doghail cursed his way back to her, then kept himself upright by means of a hold on the gelding's saddle. He patted the horse, then looked at her.

"Don't know how you put up with him," he croaked.

"Fuadain?" she asked. "I suppose I manage, don't I?"

"I would never tolerate what you do."

She pursed her lips. "Of course not, but you have more courage than I."

Doghail dragged his sleeve across his mouth. "Today, lass, I'm not sure what I have." He shook his head, then squinted at her. "Thank you."

"No need."

"You have a way with beasts."

She smiled. It was a conversation they'd had scores of times as she'd tried to hold on to the faint memories she had of her parents. "I understand my mother was fond of horses."

"Her blood runs through your veins, obviously."

"I believe it just might."

He took the reins from her. "I'll see to this one," he said, his color starting to return a bit. "He deserves a few more oats than usual for not leaving me to make a fool of myself."

"He had a care for you," she conceded, "but what else could he have done? Your reputation precedes you."

"Of course it does." He shook his head. "Heaven knows what these ponies will be saying after this one here tells them what he's seen of me this morning." He paused, then nodded toward the arena opening. "I have the feeling Himself will be back after his guest is snoozing comfortably before the fire. Why don't you take yourself off toward town and fetch me some liniment from the apothecary?"

She looked at him evenly. "You don't have to protect me, you know."

"You did me," he said with a shrug. "Turn about, and all that. Get on with ye, gel. I'll see to your chores."

She considered refusing but couldn't deny that a bit of freedom might be a good thing. She patted the gelding, thanked Doghail again, and left the barn with less regret than usual.

Her uncle was growing increasingly unreasonable, even she had to admit that. He had never managed to strike her save once or twice, a handful of years earlier, when he had caught her on the shoulder. She half suspected those times had been accidents, but he had seemingly taken a liking to how they had made him feel. Her respect for him, which had never been very great, had completely disappeared after that.

She had, out of necessity, grown very adept at staying out of his reach. She supposed she wouldn't manage that forever, which was perhaps why she needed to find more coins than she was going to be able to earn on her own. She had to leave Sàraichte soon, and she couldn't go without her grandfather.

She was sorely tempted to take one of those coins she'd hidden under filthy blankets, chuck it into the fountain in the midst of the village green, and wish with all her might for a Hero to come striding out of the gloom and rescue her from the unrelenting reality of her life—

And that would be exactly as far as any of it went because Heroes didn't exist, her reality was what it was, and if she used one of her coins in such a stupid fashion, she would be unrescued, red in the face, and holding on to one less coin.

Truly, she had to get hold of herself.

She concentrated on where she was going only because she was desperate for some sort of distraction. She walked on the outside of the wall that surrounded the manor and its gardens—on the outside because only servants employed up at the house and family were permitted to walk on the inside and she was definitely not considered either of those. She had walked that path so many times she hardly thought about it any longer and she only looked at the house out of idle curiosity, not desperate longing.

The manor wasn't an ugly place, but there wasn't anything truly lovely to recommend it. Everything about it was designed to attract attention and lead anyone looking at it to believe that the lord who lived there was very important indeed. She thought it overdone and garish, but what did she know? In truth, she preferred a clean stable and a fast horse. She hardly cared where she laid her head and she had no desire to impress anyone who might be examining her flow-erbeds for weeds.

She considered that for as long as it took her to leave the manor behind. She turned the corner toward town, then paused in mid-step. It wasn't a lad with less-than-chivalrous thoughts on his mind, or a dog eyeing her leg purposefully, or even a clutch of nettles that left her frozen in place.

There was something there on the ground.

She took a step backward, made a fruitless grasp for her good sense, then surrendered and simply stared at what lay there before it. It was a hint of shadow where there should have been none.

That might not have seemed so strange save that it was barely past noon, there were no clouds in the sky, and there was nothing around her to cast any hint of darkness on the ground.

She frowned thoughtfully. She realized with a start that it wasn't the first time she had seen something odd in the vicinity of her uncle's house. When had it been—oh, aye. A pair of fortnights past. She'd seen something similar on the ground but dismissed it as her having had not enough sleep, because shadows cast on the ground by nothing at all, in broad daylight no less, were impossible.

She was tempted to step on it and see what happened but

something stopped her. Good sense, perhaps. A finely honed sense of self-preservation, assuredly. She took a deep breath and walked around the patch of nothing, giving it a very wide berth.

She decided that perhaps the best use of that rather long walk into town would be to spend the time chiding herself for being a fool. Her imagination was getting the best of her. She might as well revisit her thought of wishing for a decently executed rescue as to give any credence to what she thought she had seen.

She would go to town, procure what Doghail wanted, then spend the rest of her day mucking out stalls.

It was obviously her only hope of having any of her good sense return.

Two

If penance was best done in Hell, Acair thought he might have arrived at the right locale for it.

Sàraichte was without a doubt the ugliest place he had ever seen. He stood on a small bluff on the edge of town and examined what was to be his prison for the next year. It was a typical port town, only it didn't seem to have the usual niceties most port towns boasted such as a decent pub, a bustling market, and a stiff breeze to wash away the lingering odor of fish.

He wasn't sure how any of the ships in the harbor managed to escape its clutches once they were in them, but perhaps magic was needed to save the day. Why he couldn't have been saddled with that sort of work for the duration of his sentence, he surely didn't know. He could have stood on a hill and directed the ships in and out, offering a helping hand occasionally, collecting exorbitant fees always. It would have been altruistic from stem to stern, as it were, aiding those who couldn't aid themselves and pocketing a bit of coin in the bargain. Yet with all his magic simply begging to be used, where was he going?

A barn.

Somewhere, Rùnach of Tòrr Dòrainn and Soilléir of Cothro-maiche were having themselves a right proper chuckle over the thought.

He could only muster up a lackluster amount of enthusiasm over the thought of murdering them both, which would have alarmed him if he'd had the wherewithal to examine his own appalling condition. He wasn't sure he could state it often enough: do-gooding had done him a terrible disservice. Gone, at least temporarily, were the days when he'd looked forward with glee to a well-planned and flawlessly executed piece of mischief. But a fond memory were the long afternoons when he had sat in this exclusive salon or that high-brow inn, ignored his hosts, and made with a languid hand lists of vulnerable mages and monarchs. All that was left was the shell of a man who couldn't put up a decent argument as to why he shouldn't spend the next year shoveling horse manure.

Damnation, he was a ruthless, remorseless seeker of power and a damned good conversationalist at dinner. That he'd had to remind himself of that more than once on his journey south was simply beyond the pale.

He rubbed his chest absently. That damned Fadairian spell of healing Rùnach had used on him the year before had somehow taken root inside him. He wasn't sure quite how to remove it short of either cutting his own chest open or making a polite social call to his half-brother and threatening him with something dire if he didn't undo what he'd done. There was the question of whether or not either would kill him, so perhaps that was something that could be put off for a bit longer.

The truth was, he was doomed to endure that damned spell for at least another year until he could remedy the situation himself. All that was left for him to do at present was soldier on as best he could and make note of slights that would need to be repaid.

Breakfast. He latched onto that idea with a fair bit of enthusiasm and in spite of his doubts about the quality of victuals he would find in a place that smelled so strongly of rotting fish. Food was food and he hadn't had anything to eat since the disgusting fare he'd choked down the night before.

He shook his head wearily. Ah, for the days when he had enjoyed

fine meals wrapped in elegant evenings spent in exquisite surroundings. He had enjoyed many of the same and, better still, he wasn't
too stupid to understand why. Eligible—and not-so-eligible—
maidens wanted him within reach because he was dangerous, their
mothers wanted him in their salons because he knew which fork to
use when, and husbands and fathers wanted him contained in their
halls where they could keep an eye on him.

He had never bothered to inform those fathers and husbands
that they would have been completely unable to stop him if he
decided to do something vile. If they couldn't have seen that for
themselves, he hadn't had the patience to enlighten them.

The women, though, now there was something he would miss.
Sweet perfume, witty repartee, lovely gowns, decent entertainments . . . in short, he'd had all the benefits of being Gair's bastard
son without any of the true dirty work of being black mage.

He paused, wrestled briefly with his damnable and quite inescapable propensity to always tell the truth, then relented. The truth
was, he had walked in places that would have given his father
nightmares, all in search of the elusive and unattainable. Those
places had been very dark indeed.

Of course, he had balanced that out quite nicely by poaching
spells and vexing other mages as often as his social schedule permitted, always taking time out to make life as much a hell on earth
as possible for Sarait's children and those other bastards his father
has sired, including his own brothers, but what else could he have
done? A man needed things to do.

There was something to be said for settling down, he supposed,
but his father had been much older than he when he'd had his first
serious liaison, something that had resulted in Acair's eldest bastard
half-brother, a dashing if not completely stupid man named Gla-
moach. The others, a motley collection of perhaps a dozen lads—it
was impossible to get an accurate count—who seemed to have managed to escape their mothers' wombs without having had anything

heavy fall on them immediately afterward, were of varying ages but sharing the same unpleasant personalities and bitter feelings toward their sire.

Acair didn't share those feelings. He had learned over the years to be simply indifferent to Gair. He had watched his own brothers angst over winning their father's approbation, watched his other half-brothers spend their very long lives trying to match him, and watched his half-brothers by that elven princess do everything they could to stop him from doing what he damned well pleased. He had determined that, for himself, he would stay out of the fray, use his father's reputation to gain entrance where useful, and distance himself from the man everywhere else.

He had envisioned his life stretching out in front of him in a long series of glittering parties, his post endlessly containing large stacks of invitations to other things, and perhaps even another stab at draining the world of all its magic. His quiver, as it were, was full of useful skills and he had a code of honor that even one of those lads from Neroche might envy.

Added to all that magnificence had been the poaching of many terrible spells, the humiliating of many annoying mages, and an endless amount of the good-natured ribbing that went on amongst gentlemen of his class. If his peers had been less-than-pleased about his nicking their art, priceless treasures, and the occasional wife or daughter, what could he say? Some people just didn't have a sense of sport.

It had been a very good life indeed.

But it was obviously a life that was out of his reach for the foreseeable future. He glanced over his shoulder to find that damned spell standing a handful of paces behind him, peering at Sàraichte just as he was. If he hadn't known better, he would have suspected it shared his thoughts about the truly dismal appearance of the place.

"You could go away, you know," Acair said pointedly.

The spell only tilted its head and regarded him. Acair rolled his eyes, cursed a bit to make himself feel less like a fool than he already did for talking to nothing, then tugged on his cloak and marched off into the fray.

He knew exactly where he was going, where he was *intended* to go rather, because a breathless lad had caught him up at a derelict pub a pair of nights ago and told him as much. He had refrained from telling the lad where Soilléir could take himself off to and what he could do with himself once there simply because he hadn't wanted to cause the lad to forgo paying for their supper. It had been painful to watch that envoy eventually scamper off toward the road, then change himself into something with wings without so much as a sigh of exertion.

Acair sighed presently because he'd forced himself not to then. Truly, it was going to be a very long year.

He continued on his way with another sigh, asked the first soul he encountered where he might find the stables of Briàghde, and was somehow unsurprised to find that not only were they on the far side of town, they were a great distance past the far side of town. The only way it could have been more inconvenient would have been if he'd had to march through a wall of irritated mages with terrible spells to hand to get there.

It might behoove him, he decided reluctantly, not to alert anyone in the area as to his arrival. He refused to think about the fact that if someone he'd encountered before encountered him, things might become a bit dodgy. He had survived more dire situations than that and come away unscathed. Still, no sense in putting his foot in a pile of trouble if he didn't have to.

He purchased food on his way through town, trying not to shudder at the potential for untoward substances having found their way inside what he'd eaten, then found himself all too soon on the far side of town, looking at a manor he never would have lowered himself to frequent in the past without formidable inducement. He was halfway to the front door before he realized that he wasn't heading toward the right place.

He sighed, then turned away and followed his nose to the stables. They were, when smelled from the outside, rather less fragrant than other stables he'd been to, though he supposed he might not be the best one to judge. He looked for a likely opening for humans, took a deep breath, then walked in with what he hoped was an appropriately servile mien.

He stopped short and stared at his surroundings in shock. Good lord, horses. He could easily see a dozen of them and that was just from where he was standing.

They were looking at him as if he might make a tasty morsel to enjoy over the course of the afternoon, that much he could see right off. He didn't like horses as a rule, though he supposed the quality of steeds his father had kept had been very low. His only other experience with them had been hiding in their stalls whilst about some piece of mischief or another. He had discovered rather quickly that they didn't like that sort of thing.

"Help you?"

Acair looked at a small, wiry man who had simply appeared out of thin air. He would have suspected the other of magic, but could sense none of it in him. Perhaps he was just canny.

"I'm looking for—" He had to take a deep breath before he could carry on. "Work."

"What can you do?"

That was a list worthy of lengthy examination, to be sure, but Acair wasn't sure the ability to pick any lock he faced, a deft hand at fleecing any card player he encountered, or the possession of magic that gave even the most powerful pause would be of any interest to the man standing in front of him.

"Whatever you need," Acair said. He wasn't exactly sure how much confidence to display, so he settled for what he thought Rùnach might look like when faced with one of those damned dreamspinners his wife kept company with. "If it isn't too difficult."

The man looked him over for a minute, then held out his hand. "Doghail."

Acair assumed that was his name, not what he did for a living, so he shook the man's hand and nodded. "Acair."

Doghail nodded. "Had a missive from one of your former employers this morning."

Acair could only imagine. He gathered from Doghail's expression that it hadn't been anything too damning, so perhaps 'twas best to simply not ask too many questions.

"From whence do you hail?" Doghail asked.

"I've traveled so much, 'tis hard to say."

Doghail studied him more closely than Acair was comfortable with. "Any experience working with horses?"

"I've ridden a pair of them," Acair conceded.

"That doesn't sound too promising."

Perhaps that recommendation had been less flattering than he'd supposed. He could hardly believe he was having to peddle himself to a man he would have walked past without noticing in any other situation, but perhaps that was simply part of the bargain. He had done worse.

"I am honest," he said, latching onto his one virtue. "If that's worth anything to you."

Doghail lifted his eyebrows briefly. "You might be surprised. And aye, 'tis enough. Fortunately for you, the master came through in a temper recently and sacked half the lads because they dared meet his eyes. You might keep that in mind for the future."

Acair had no idea who the master was, but he didn't like him already. What sort of pompous blowhard walked through a place and terrorized those who dared look at—

Well, he was that sort of pompous blowhard, but perhaps that wasn't a useful thing to admit at the moment. And if he were more apt to meet many of pairs of eyes and reward them accordingly than insist they avert their gazes when he passed, who could blame him? The only thing he loved more than a well-stocked, inaccessible solar full of priceless treasures was a rollicking good skirmish with a mage who didn't make him yawn.

He was, in truth, a simple man.

"You'll earn ten coppers a week," Doghail said. "Can't do more or I won't eat."

"Coppers," Acair repeated. "*Coppers*?"

Doghail made a noise that could have passed for a laugh. "Coppers," he repeated. "You know, those wee coins worth nothing?"

"Ah," Acair said, feeling somewhat at a loss. He wasn't sure he'd ever seen a coin of so little value. He tended to operate in piles of gold sovereigns, but that was obviously not going to be his lot at present. As he'd said before, he was in Hell for the duration.

"Generous, I know," Doghail said dryly. He nodded toward the barn's innards. "I'll show you where you'll bunk, then you can be about your business."

"Delightful," Acair said. He followed Master Doghail through what seemed to be an endless maze of stalls containing an equal number of what looked to him to be rather disagreeable-looking equine . . . things. He caught sight of a lad or two apparently doing what he was going to be required to do and was powerfully tempted to take his chances with that damned spell and bolt for civilization.

Doghail stopped in front of what could have only been termed a minor passageway in a very poorly funded butler's pantry. Indeed, *passageway* was too grand a term for it and *closet* didn't describe the painful smallness of the place. He was half tempted to call it a *stationary dumbwaiter*, but he couldn't find his tongue to speak.

"Luxurious, isn't it?" Doghail said, without a shred of irony in his tone. "Fortunately for you, all the lads with seniority were sacked, leaving this place free. You look, if you don't mind my saying so, like you're accustomed to only the finest."

Acair gave up trying to express his thoughts. They weren't pleasant ones anyway.

"You'll want to change, no doubt," Doghail continued mercilessly. "Wouldn't want to get anything on those very fine boots of yours, I'm thinking."

"Change into what?" Acair asked.

"I'll find you something."

Acair would have put his foot down at wearing another man's boots and cloak, but he supposed he wouldn't need a cloak for long and he wasn't keen for anything to land on his own footwear, so he exchanged his handmade Diarmailtian leather boots for something that felt a bit like a cobbler's experiment gone terribly wrong.

Doghail smiled, then handed him a pitchfork. "The tool of your trade, my lad."

Acair promised himself many, *many* hours of thinking on a proper repayment for a certain Cothromaichian prince who possessed spells just waiting to be appropriated, then took the pitchfork and followed his employer to a stall containing a horse that looked as if it were none-too-pleased to see him. He looked at Doghail. "You want me to go in there?"

"Unless you've some other way to remove their droppings that I'm not familiar with."

Acair considered. This was a place where a bit of magic certainly would have come in handy, but there was nothing to be done about it. He eyed the horse inside that stall and had a rather unfriendly look in return.

"Or you could present yourself at the manor and see if Himself might need someone to clean his privies."

"Ah, I think not," Acair said without hesitation. There were some things that even he wouldn't do, no matter the consequence.

He nodded to Doghail, took a firmer grasp on the handle, and hoped he would survive the day.

By the time the sun had set, he was sore, out-of-sorts, and so filled with a desire to wrap his blistered fingers around a certain mage's neck, he was almost tempted to tell that spell of death to go to hell so he could chance a bit of shapechanging and be off to do what needed to be done.

And if that weren't enough to add insult to injury, someone had stolen his good boots.

He accepted Doghail's invitation to see what all his labor assisted, though he couldn't imagine it could possibly be anything he would be interested in. What he wanted to do was take himself off to that pitiful scrap of floor, cast himself down on it, and sleep like the dead. If he were overrun by mice and other vermin, he honestly didn't care. It might send him off more speedily to that place in the East where he could rest from his labors. At the moment, nothing sounded better.

But unfortunately his form was frighteningly resilient and his will to live apparently too strong to be overcome. He suppressed the urge to sigh and simply followed Doghail without comment.

They stopped at the end of a very large expanse of dirt that lay adjacent to the stalls. It must have been quite valuable dirt considering the entire bloody thing had a high roof, no doubt to protect the ground against the weather. All Acair knew was it was a place he hadn't wanted to become familiar with earlier because he'd suspected it would take him half the night to muck it out and if he were found too close to it, that was exactly what he would be doing. Fortunately for his hands, it was being used at the moment for what he could only surmise was horsey exercise.

There was a tall, slender figure out in the middle of it, running a horse in circles around himself. It looked like foolishness to him, but what did he know? Obviously there were things he didn't understand about the whole endeavor, things he certainly didn't want to learn.

He looked about for a distraction and found it in the persons of the two men standing to one side. He looked them over ruthlessly and decided that one of them had to be the lord of the place, Fuadain. The man's clothing was likely the best Sàraichte could produce, his boots certainly better than what Acair was currently wearing, and his mien one of a man who was accustomed to having his way. If he had magic, it was of a very common, vulgar sort. Acair saw nothing that gave him pause, even in his current state of not having anything but threats with which to defend himself.

The man standing next to the assumed Fuadain of Sàraichte was a shorter, rotund sort. Acair dismissed him immediately, mostly because he found that his attentions were relentlessly drawn back to the lad working the horses.

He realized with a start that *he* was a *she* and he wondered how he had missed that the first time around. That it was a girl and not a man handling what he could see was an irascible stallion left him wondering quite seriously about her state of mind.

"You stupid girl, run him harder!"

Acair looked at Fuadain and decided that whatever else he might ever come to think about the man, he most definitely was never going to be fond of him. There were ways a man comported himself with the fairer sex and there were ways he didn't. Acair was very clear in his own mind about which was which.

The truth was, he loved women. He loved their small-talk, the way they smelled, how they moved. He had spent a great deal of time winding yarn, judging stitchery, refilling cups of coffee and tea. And that was just for the genteel ones who weren't coming at him with spells to rival his own or plotting behind their fans to take over thrones. He had never met a horse gel before, but he wasn't opposed to the idea, especially after he beat some manners into the lord of the hall—

"I wouldn't."

He glanced at Doghail. "I beg your pardon?"

Doghail looked pointedly at Acair's hands.

Acair realized they were balled into fists and he was halfway to stirring himself to go do something about what he was seeing out there in that dusty space—

"Arena."

He looked at Doghail with a fair bit of alarm. "Am I speaking my thoughts aloud or are you reading them?"

"You're muttering."

"I do that."

"You might want to not."

"Mutter or go kick sense into those two whoresons out there?"

"The latter," Doghail said seriously. "I would leave Lord Fuadain alone because he could have you slain as easily as to look at you and no one would ever find your body."

"Could he indeed?" Acair drawled before he could check himself. He took a deep breath and reminded himself of what he was supposed to be pretending to be. "I meant, *I'll remember that.*"

Doghail looked unimpressed. "The other is Slaidear, the stable master. I wouldn't cross him either or he'll sack you. I'm sure you wouldn't want to miss out on any of those coppers, now would you?"

"Absolutely not."

"Why don't you take a walk around the grounds, go see the big house, then come back and shovel a bit more. Do you a world of good, that."

"And it will accustom me to boots which are not mine."

"Now that you mention it," Doghail said with a faint smile, "that too."

A year? He wasn't going to last a fortnight. But he decided that if he were offered a few minutes of liberty, he wasn't going to sneer at them. He doffed a non-existent hat Doghail's way, then left the stables before he had to listen to any more of what was being shouted at that girl.

He was half tempted to begin a diary of his adventures. If nothing else, his mother would have been interested in his adventures. The first entry would surely have been a detailed examination of his surprise over what bothered him the most about not having magic and that would have been the lack of ability to repay arrogant men for things they deserved to be repaid for.

He had absolutely no desire to consider how that might apply to himself.

He left the barn and walked out into the twilight. A year. How

the hell was he going to keep his mouth shut and his hands in his
pockets for an entire bloody *year*?

Well, he would spend a great deal of it considering several pieces
of mischief he hadn't had time to see to properly in the past and
deciding which one he would be about all of a quarter hour after
he was released from the scrutiny of the spell that still followed
him. That might take up a good bit of the all the mindless time to
think he was finding his days becoming filled with.

He would go mad else.

Three

"He knows nothing."

Léirsinn looked up from the tack she was polishing. It wasn't something she generally did, but the work was mindless and she needed a bit of that at the moment. Besides, they were definitely short-handed and the work wasn't going to do itself.

At least it was work she didn't mind. The day before had been endless and full of things she hadn't enjoyed doing, such as biting her tongue. Better to be about something that kept her out of sight and earshot.

"Léirsinn?"

She looked up at Doghail and blinked. "What?"

"I was telling you about the lad we hired yesterday."

It was a testament to how preoccupied she was with other things that she didn't remember having hired anyone. "Yesterday?"

"You're distracted."

"Trying to be," she agreed.

"I'd ask from what, but I imagine I don't need to."

She imagined he was right. Her uncle's treatment of her the day before was nothing out of the ordinary, but she feared she was reaching the point where she had almost had enough of it. Much more of that sort of belittling and she would do something she shouldn't.

If he had perhaps struck her, she would have felt justified in retaliating. As it was, he generally just looked at her with the same sort of annoyance a great lord generally displayed after having gotten something on the bottom of his boot whilst having absolutely no idea what to use in scraping it off. She knew that look because she'd seen it worn by many great lords over the years. She'd had boot scrapers installed in strategic locations several years ago, something that had seemed like a reasonable thing to do. Her uncle had pulled the expense of it out of her meager pay, of course, but she had expected nothing less.

"Léirsinn?"

She dragged herself back to the matter at hand. "A new stable hand," she said, reminding herself of the current topic. "How much nothing does he know?"

"I had to show him which end of a manure fork went into the straw."

That was indeed nothing. "And just what do you want me to do about that?"

He looked at her pointedly.

She sighed. It wasn't as if Slaidear would lower himself to train the lad and Doghail had obviously reached the end of any patience he might have had. "Very well," she said, crawling to her feet. "Show me the damage and I'll sack him straightway."

"You may want to reconsider that after you think about what you've been doing all morning and why." He paused. "Besides, this one . . ." He shook his head. "There's something different about him."

"Apart from the fact that he knows nothing?"

Doghail lifted his eyebrows briefly. "You should have seen his boots."

Léirsinn considered. "Worn?"

"Pristine."

She felt her mouth fall open before she could stop it, then she looked at him narrowly. "I cannot believe you hired a lad who knows nothing simply because his boots were pretty."

"It wasn't just his boots," he said dryly. "Besides, it'll take me a solid fortnight to poach as many lads as I need from other places. Another pair of hands is another pair, no matter how useless."

"That depends on how useless," she said grimly. Damn her uncle for his stupidity in ridding them of most of their help. "I wonder what set Fuadain off yesterday?"

"Hell if I know," Doghail said, "and damned if I care. Just keep out of his sights for the next pair of days. He'll blow himself out eventually."

And that was generally where Doghail's advice ended. He didn't care for her uncle, but since she didn't either, they generally left their final opinions of the man himself unsaid. As for what the irritation had been, it could have been anything from a poorly fried egg to perhaps turning over in his sleep once too often. With Fuadain, one just never knew.

"One keeps an ear to the ground and a hand on his horse to survive in this world," Doghail said philosophically. "If you want my opinion—"

"Which I always do," Léirsinn said absently.

"I think what set him off might have been news from Up North."

Up North was Doghail's term for the schools of wizardry. She had her own thoughts on Beinn òrain and the wildly improbable nature of the university there—she was certain lads went there not to learn magical spells but to waste their parents' gold at cards and dice—but she supposed those thoughts had been shaped rather strongly by Doghail's own opinions.

"Any ideas on what that news might have been?" she asked.

"Wizards and noblemen are fickle," Doghail said wisely. "Perhaps Himself lost a sale."

"That would be sufficient, I imagine."

"*Stupid* might be a better thing to call it," Doghail muttered, only half under his breath. "He sacked one lad yesterday morning for not moving quickly enough out of his path, another two for meeting his eyes, and another pair for simply breathing."

"Excessive," she said. Her uncle tended to fire stable lads only in pairs, so perhaps he'd lost not only a sale but the final hand at cards.

"Short five hands," Doghail continued, "and there I was wondering what the hell I was going to do to replace them when up saunters this lad who looks as if he should be sitting at Himself's card table instead of begging for work."

"A gambler down on his luck, do you think?"

"Who knows? He's there around the corner, no doubt still grappling with the mystery of the pitchfork. You won't have trouble identifying him."

"You aren't coming with me?"

He paused and looked at her. "Do you *need* me to come with you?" he asked, obviously amused.

She glared at him. "I will remember this sport at my expense, you know."

His smile deepened the lines on his face already made by years out in the sun and wind. "Then perhaps I will come along after all. If I'm going to pay a price for my cheek, might as well earn it, eh?"

Léirsinn scowled at him, then walked without dawdling to where he had indicated. She supposed she wouldn't have needed those directions given that she could have found the lad in question by the volume of his salty language alone.

She would have said she had skidded to a stop because of the view—and she had to agree that it was very fine—but it had no doubt been a stray handful of straw scattered where it hadn't been meant to go that had left her with her feet suddenly unsteady beneath her. Obviously, she would be having strong words with the man who, as Doghail had said, clearly knew nothing about mucking out a stall.

She started forward, fully intending to strip a layer of hide from the man for thinking he could come into her stables and pretend to know what he was doing whilst throwing the whole place into disarray, then found herself coming to another ungainly halt. It took her a moment or two before she realized what was so odd about the scene in front of her.

The best stallion in the barn was standing there in an open stall, regarding the man as if he might find him interesting enough not to stomp into oblivion. That was a first. Falaire was without a doubt the most majestic horse she had ever seen. He had in his short ten years covered a dozen mares who had produced exceptionally valuable foals, but none to equal him. If she had believed in things she couldn't see—which she most assuredly did not—she would have suspected he had something magical running through his veins. Perhaps there was Angesand blood somewhere in his line, or something unusual from some stable in the East where horses were more valuable than men, or . . .

She lost her train of thought when the man obviously trying to decide how best to get into Falaire's stall paused and looked at her. She wasn't one to be overcome by the looks of anything not trotting about on four legs, but if that one there had been a horse, she would have beggared herself to buy him.

The unavoidable truth was, he was stunning. Tall, dark-haired, pale-eyed, with a face that stopped just short of being pretty. She found that once she started looking at him, she simply couldn't stop. It was as if she had just seen her first priceless treasure, sparkling, stunning, and impossibly out of reach. If there had been glass between them, she felt quite certain that she, even with all her years on her shoulders, would have been standing there like a ten-year-old with her nose pressed against it.

She heard Doghail laugh and walk away. She would have cursed him but she didn't want to waste the energy for that when it could be so much better used admiring—

"Finished?" the man asked, dragging a dusty sleeve across his forehead and leaving a trail of dirt there.

She blinked. "Finished with what?"

"Watching me at this fine labor?"

She felt her face grow hot. She wasn't sure if that counted as blushing or not, but she couldn't say she cared for the embarrassment that went with it. She pulled herself back from her gaping and struggled to reach for her good sense before it scampered completely away.

"Finished?" she echoed. "Aye, I am and so should you be." She shook off the spell she had obviously been under—if she believed in spells, which she didn't—and walked over to take the pitchfork away from him. Unfortunately, that put her far closer to him than she was comfortable with, but there was nothing to be done about it. "Who the hell are you and whatever left you thinking you could muck out a stall?"

He shot her a look she might have been offended by if she hadn't had the same sort of disdain tossed her way more than once from the horse on her right.

"I am Acair of—" He stopped suddenly, then pursed his lips. "Just Acair."

"Have you ever mucked out a stall, Acair?"

"Absolutely not."

"If I weren't so desperate for help, I would throw you out right now."

His mouth worked for a moment or two, as if he simply couldn't bring the right collection of words to the fore.

"I'm not interested in what you have to say," she added. "I'm only interested in your apparent inability to shovel manure."

He pursed his lips. "I am more familiar with that than you might suspect."

She highly doubted it, but there was no point in arguing over it and nothing to be done about it at least for the day. "You've been hired, I'm desperate, and so we'll proceed."

"I've already been told how to use this damned thing."

"Did you listen?" she asked pointedly.

He looked horribly offended, which led her to believe he had never set foot in a barn unless it was to accept a leg up onto the back of a very expensive horse.

"I listened very well," he said. "This work is simply more dangerous than I was expecting." He pointed at Falaire. "That damned nag tried to bite me."

"That damned nag is the most valuable horse in the barn," she said evenly, "and if he bit you, you got your hand too close to his mouth."

"He didn't bite my hand," Acair shot back, "he tried to nibble my arse!"

Only years of hiding her emotions—ah, hell, there was no hope for it. She stared at that ridiculously handsome man standing there covered in dust and straw, looking as if he'd just endured affronts he simply couldn't tolerate, and laughed. She didn't laugh often, but she couldn't stop herself at the moment.

"I beg your pardon," he said stiffly.

She shook her head. The situation was beyond hope. She exchanged a look with a smirking Falaire, then handed Acair the pitchfork.

"Don't turn your back on him," she suggested. "I will give you a simple lesson in the management of powerful beasts—nay, do not speak—and then you can be about your work."

"I know a great deal about managing powerful beasts," he muttered.

She was going to have to stop looking at him very soon or she wouldn't get a decent day's labor out of herself again. "Horses?"

He seemed to be chewing on his words. "Are horses' arses close enough, do you suppose?"

It had been a very long day already. That was the only reason she didn't take the pitchfork he was holding and stab him with it. She forced herself to look at him sternly when all she truly wanted to do was continue to laugh. She got hold of herself, then turned a stern look on him. Once she'd made sure he was paying her heed, she drew an imaginary box in front of and including Falaire's head.

"This is his domain." She paused and looked at him. "Do you understand?"

Acair glared at her. "I am not such a simpleton."

"And I'm not the one with horse slobber on my arse, so swallow your pride and learn. Just as he has his domain, I have mine. I don't enter his; he doesn't enter mine."

"Then how do you get a bloody rope around his neck?" Acair asked in exasperation.

"Halter," she said. "It's a halter and you put it over his head. He tolerates it from me because I've told him that is what he will do."

"Bossy, aren't you?"

"I am First Horse," she said simply. "I will admit I am forced to remind him of that every time we have tea. I would say his memory is poor, but the truth is, he's a stallion. He would run over me as soon as look at me if I allowed it."

Acair frowned. "I daresay he doesn't have that same respect for me."

"He can tell you don't know the first thing about his noble kind, pitchforks, or the amount of manure the prince of beasts produces. I doubt he'll let you anywhere near him until you remedy all three."

He snorted. "Not a prince, surely. Something far more lofty."

"Nay, kings generally sit upon their sorry arses and issue edicts. Princes do all the real labor."

Acair turned and looked at her. "A useful thought issues forth."

"I have many more of those," she said smoothly, "and at the moment most concern where you might take yourself off to and what you might do there once you've arrived."

He looked briefly startled, then he smiled. "Do tell."

"I imagine you would enjoy it overmuch," she said. "Besides, the horses might hear. Wouldn't want to ruin their innocence."

He pointed at Falaire. "That one there is not an innocent."

"And how would you know that?"

"He has that look about him." He stared suspiciously at the stallion. "He knows things I think I don't care for him knowing."

Odd, but Falaire was studying Acair with a fair bit of interest himself. He generally took no notice of who came to tend him save her and, on occasion, Doghail. He didn't care for Slaidear or her uncle, but she supposed that shouldn't have surprised her. That he was willing to even favor Acair with a look instead of a hoof in the gut was something indeed.

"I do believe he knows what I'm thinking," Acair said finally.

"I wouldn't be surprised."

Acair frowned. "I hadn't considered such a thing possible, but . . . well, it has been that sort of year so far."

She suppressed the urge to ask him what a man of his obvious breeding found himself doing in a barn, mostly because she was tired and cross and there was a substantial number of stalls still to be tended. She took a halter off the stall door, then walked back to Falaire and looked at him briefly before she slipped the halter over his head.

"Ah," Acair said, "you're intimidating him."

"As I said, he and I have an understanding."

"I don't think he'll care for that sort of thing with me."

"Do a decent job of his stall and I'm sure he'll reconsider." She led Falaire out into the passageway, then stood with him while Acair did the worst job of mucking she'd ever seen.

It took him at least half an hour and she suspected by the time she'd corrected him for the sixth time that he was close to losing his temper. But he did the work just the same, then moved the wagon away from the stall door.

"Satisfactory?"

"Your work? Barely. Your attitude? Definitely not."

"Would you prefer it if I were to whistle a cheerful tune or dance a jig as I'm about these fine labors?"

Falaire snorted. Léirsinn reminded herself of all the reasons why she couldn't sack the man standing in front of her, then held out the lead rope she was holding.

"See if you can come to an understanding with him. He'll talk to the rest of the ponies about you, you know. I'd be worried about what he'd say."

Acair looked at Falaire warily, then approached him hesitantly.

"He'll bite you again if you do it that way."

"Damn it, woman, then what am I to do? Tell him I will do a half-arsed job on his stall if he refrains from biting me?"

Léirsinn would have suggested that he might want to be mostly concerned that Falaire would kick the life from him, but she decided that was likely something she didn't need to say. Besides, she was suddenly distracted by the sight of Acair facing off with her favorite horse. He drew himself up and sent Falaire a look that . . .

Well, it almost had her backing up a pace. She wouldn't have said she was frightened, but she realized immediately that whatever else Acair from nowhere understood, he understood how to intimidate. Falaire, however, merely snorted at him, leaving him a small gift of drool on the shoulder of his tunic, then he stretched his neck and snuffled Acair's hair.

Acair cursed, but didn't move.

"First Horse," Léirsinn said pointedly, "which you are most definitely not."

"He's trying to win me over."

"Believe that if you like," she said. She leaned against the wall as Acair led Falaire back into his quarters. Falaire had a look at his surroundings, then expressed his opinion on the work done in the form of a deposit upon fresh straw.

Acair looked at her in surprise. "Damn him to hell. Why'd he do that?"

"Why don't you ask him?"

"I think I won't," he said. He looked at the lead rope in his hand, then handed it to her. "He's all yours."

She would have happily made that so, but even if she could have afforded him, her uncle would have kept her from buying him out of spite. She'd watched him do it to souls he was far fonder of than he was of her. She took off Falaire's bridle, promised him his supper in an hour, then shut him into the stall. She looked at Acair.

"Only twenty more to see to. Perhaps more. I lose count easily."

"I imagine you don't lose count of anything," he said. He walked off, muttering something she didn't understand.

Well, as long as he did what he was being paid to do with any success at all, she didn't care what language he cursed her in.

She leaned against the wall and watched him work on the next stall. Falaire was hanging his head out his window, watching as well. Even horses needed their amusements, she supposed.

'Twas blindingly obvious that the man hadn't a clue how to properly do barn work, which left her wondering why he'd sought work in a stable. She had to admit Doghail had judged his appearance aright at least. He was terribly beautiful in a rakish sort of way that she was certain had left more than one woman in a state of incapacitation. Fortunately, she was not swayed by a pretty face and there were still two dozen stalls left to see to before the day was over.

"Mistress Léirsinn?"

She turned to find one of the housemaids standing there. The girl looked so out of place in her starched uniform, Léirsinn had a hard time believing she wasn't a specter of some kind.

"Aye?" she said carefully. "Is there something wrong?"

The girl looked around as if she expected someone to leap out of the shadows and fall upon her. Léirsinn nodded toward an empty passageway. The girl trailed after her, but Léirsinn could tell it wasn't willingly done. She looked to make sure they were alone, then turned to the servant.

"What is it?"

"Your grandfather," the girl whispered. "He looks poorly."

The man is completely incapacitated, was almost out of her mouth before she realized the girl wasn't a child fresh from her mother's hearthfire. She obviously had the wit and age to judge things for herself.

"What do you mean, poorly?"

The girl shook her head sharply. "I don't know and I daren't speculate. I tend him, you see, and—" She looked around herself again. "Something's amiss. More than the usual something." She shifted uneasily. "There is danger in the house."

Léirsinn was grateful for years of not reacting to even the worst piece of gossip. It was all that saved her from panicking at present. She nodded, because that made her feel in control.

"Thank you," she said. "I'll see to it."

The girl looked at her, then bolted. Léirsinn took a moment or two to compose herself, then left the passageway. She could hear Acair cursing and Doghail laughing at him, so she supposed those two would keep themselves busy enough.

She walked through the aisles between stalls as casually as she could, though in reality she was so panicked she could hardly breathe. Her grandfather wasn't well, that was true, but for someone from the house to actually venture into the barn to find her spoke volumes about the possible worsening of his condition.

She found herself starting for her uncle's grand house before she knew that was where she intended to go. She wasn't supposed to show her face there until the end of the month, but this was an emergency. She forced herself to walk when she would have preferred to run, then presented herself at the back kitchen door. She knocked and waited for what seemed to be an excessive amount of time before one of the under butlers opened the door. He looked down his long nose at her.

"Yes?" he asked crisply.

"I need to see my grandfather."

"Your appointment with His Lordship is in a se'nnight, Mistress Léirsinn, not today."

"I need to see my grandfather—"

"Not today."

"But—"

The door shut in her face. She would have knocked again, but she had done that before and been escorted back to the barn by a pair of rather hefty guardsmen with no sense of fair play. She turned, leaned back against the door, and forced herself to remain calm. For all she knew, the maidservant had been imagining things, or someone had sent the wench off to stir up trouble as a lark, or she herself hadn't listened closely enough when the girl had been speaking. The possibilities were many, truly, and varied. Her grandfather was likely just fine and she would see that for herself when she was allowed inside the manor.

She pushed away from the door and walked down the stairs into the garden. She was distracted enough that she almost stepped into a patch of . . .

She stepped back casually, then let out her breath slowly. She was losing what few wits were left her. That was the only reason she continued to see those patches of shadow where they shouldn't have been.

She looked about her to make certain no one would see her at the piece of madness she contemplated and was satisfied that she wasn't interesting enough for anyone to watch. She glanced at the spot in front of her as casually as possible. It was perhaps a foot across and surely no longer than that. Roundish, yet not quite a circle.

She found herself again terribly tempted to touch it, but decided rather abruptly that that would be a very bad idea indeed for the simple reason that she sensed she was being watched.

She rolled her eyes. Of course she was being watched. The entire bloody manor staff was probably watching her, laughing their arses off at her stupidity. She looked over her shoulder, fully prepared to give as good as she was no doubt getting, only to realize that there was only one person staring at her.

Her uncle.

He was standing at an upstairs window, looking down at her. He was perfectly motionless for a moment, then he dropped the curtain.

Léirsinn wished she hadn't seen that.

She made a production of looking at something on the other side of the path, some rubbish bit of fauna she was sure she couldn't have identified even if death had loomed, then took herself back to where she belonged as quickly as possible. She spoke to no one, ignored a pair of new lads Doghail had unearthed from heaven only knew where, then fetched a pitchfork and set to work on stalls that Acair had already done.

She fully intended that the work should drive that feeling of something she refused to call terror out of her, but it only seemed to magnify it. Something foul was afoot and she absolutely didn't want to be in the midst of it. The sooner she got herself and her grandfather out of Sàraichte, the better, no matter what she had to do. She could only hope she would manage it before it was too late.

A se'nnight. Surely nothing terrible would happen in that time. She had no idea what she would do if it did.

Four

Acair prayed for death.

He didn't pray, as a general rule, though he'd surely listened to his share of prayers being blurted out by those he had plied his usual trade on.

Then again, those lads had been fearing for their lives from things they should have been afraid of. He was simply suffering from an abundance of sore muscles. He wondered why anyone would choose laboring in a barn for his life's work. If the flies weren't biting, the horses were, and that didn't begin to address all the things on his boots—boots that weren't his lovely, handmade, buttery-soft, black leather boots—he wasn't accustomed to.

He was now fully convinced the only reason Soilléir and Rùnach had sent him to his current locale was to torture him. Keep him safe? What an enormous pile of horse manure.

He had to admit it was possible that he deserved a bit of it. He didn't have very many redeeming qualities, but he was at least honest about his failings. He was a bastard and he knew it. That complete lack of kindness and mercy served him well, but it tended to earn him powerful enemies. It had never occurred to him that he might someday count a stableful of annoying horses in that number of souls who didn't care for him, but it had just been that sort of year so far.

He shifted on a rickety stool that was absolutely not equal to the task of providing him with any secure place to rest and wondered what insult would come his way next.

He watched in less astonishment than resignation as a very plump pigeon flapped into the barn and came to perch on his knee. Unoriginal, but he was generally the only one in any given locale with any imagination. He was accustomed to lesser offerings.

The bird proffered its leg as if it knew what its business was, which it no doubt did. He untied the message attached there, then unrolled it.

Do one good deed a day. I'm counting.

It wasn't signed, but it didn't need to be. Rùnach wouldn't have cared what the bloody hell Acair did with his days; Soilléir, on the other hand, was enjoying the entire fiasco far too much. This was exactly the sort of thing he would have done to pour salt in the wound.

The bird plucked the message out of his hands, tossed it up in the air, then managed to swallow the damned thing whole. Well, at least it hadn't left a mess—

He looked down at his boots, then back at the bird. Damn him if the beast didn't laugh at him and flap away. Acair stared at his boots and supposed pigeon leavings were no worse than horse droppings. Since at least one of the two seemed to be his lot in life for the foreseeable future, no sense in getting himself in a snit over it.

He listened to the thoughts running through what was left of his mind and could only shake his head over them. He who had never once appeared in a salon with a hair out of place, reduced to a stable lad with droppings on his boots. A sorry state of affairs, truly.

He attempted to work out an unfortunately large collection of knots in his neck only to realize that the collection extended down the middle of his back where he couldn't reach. No wonder those horses rolled about in the dirt, scratching things they couldn't reach either. He understood.

He shifted so he could lean back against a wall—something that took absolutely no effort given the straitness of the space he occupied—and decided to take a moment or two to re-examine how he had come to be wallowing in the misery that had become his life. He knew he would soon be called upon to once again take up his sword, as it were, and see to the evening's dirty business so 'twas best to seize the peace for thinking when he found it.

There he had been a few years earlier, going about his daily affairs as usual, spending his energies plotting and scheming in his accustomed fashion, when things had begun to go slightly awry. Just little things: a missed opportunity to do someone an ill turn; a scheme foiled by the slightest hesitation before dropping a well-deserved spell of death; a heartbeat too many spent looking at a potential victim and wondering how it might feel to be stalked by someone as evil as he himself was. Little things, true, but unsettling nonetheless.

It had been almost enough to leave him wondering if perhaps he hadn't been at the business of black magery just a bit too long.

Knowing that that couldn't possibly be the case, he had pulled himself up by his bootstraps and set to his most brilliant piece of business to date with renewed purpose and enthusiasm. A theft of the world's magic had seemed like a fitting way to spend the previous fall, though he'd certainly been laying the spells necessary for such a feat for far longer than that. Indeed, if he were to be entirely honest, the thought had occurred to him several years earlier when he'd decided that draining his sire of all his magic just wasn't going to be enough to repay the stingy old bastard for an endless list of abuses. What he'd wanted was to hold the world's magic in his hand and mock his father for not having had the imagination to do the same.

The notion had been rendered substantially more appealing by his half-brother Ruithneadh's having done him the favor of leaving Gair trapped in the most uninspired and magickless country in all the Nine Kingdoms. No magic, no traveling about from glittering salon to gilded audience chamber, no cellar of fine wines to accompany sumptuous suppers. That had been a fair punishment, true, but to have done what his sire had never thought to do?

The idea had been irresistible.

He would have managed it if it hadn't been for that damned Rùnach and his dreamspinning bride, which was a tale better told after a substantial amount of ale. All he knew was that he'd been left with merely dreams of the world's magic, a spot in his chest that ached from time to time with a truly alarming sort of tingling, and the prospect of a year without a single spell at his fingertips stretching in front of him as if it had been a long, dusty, straight road through country that, unsurprisingly, resembled exactly where he found himself currently loitering.

It could have been worse, he had to concede. He could have been fleeing all over Durial at present in an effort to dodge the spells of that cranky bastard who knew far more dark magic than he ever let on in polite company. Then again, Uachdaran of Léige spent his time digging deep into the mountains. Who knew what he found there?

Well, Acair had a fairly good idea, having done his own bit of digging in an effort to use Durial as a means of siphoning off magic from other places, but he would be the first to admit that dwarvish magic was very odd. He supposed he could spend a century trying to unravel it and still not have all its secrets. Not that he intended to spend any time at it anytime soon.

That Cothromaichian twinkling was something else entirely. Now that he was being shadowed by something created by that damned Soilléir of Cothromaiche, he thought it might be not unthinkable to give as good as he got. The moment he had his power back to hand—not that it wasn't at present, of course; he was just not stupid enough to use it—he would turn his sights back to that very enticing prize.

"You're free to take the afternoon off, if you like."

Acair could scarce believe he was allowing someone else, a stable hand of all people, to enter his chamber without permission, much less tell him when he could move about freely.

Well, again, *chamber* was too lofty a term for his bit of passageway strewn with what he hardly dared hope was decently clean straw, but he supposed he couldn't ask for anything more. Perhaps not complaining loudly and at length about the conditions to anyone who would listen could be counted as his good deed for the day.

Doghail tossed him a handful of copper coins. "Your pay. Thought you might want it early."

Acair looked at the coins he'd caught. "For an entire se'nnight," he managed.

"You agreed."

"I must have been mad."

Doghail only grinned at him and walked away. Acair considered what he was holding in his hand and shook his head in disbelief. He was well-versed in all the different coinages of the world at large and he preferred Nerochian strike simply because those lads were congenitally incapable of deceit and could be counted on to always mix the full complement of whatever metal the coins boasted. He used other coins when discretion called for it, but he had to admit he had never imagined that the mint at Tosan could produce coins that had so little value. Hardly worth the trouble of pounding some random lord's visage into them.

Well, if there were a decent pub in town, it would be the beneficiary of his largesse. Anything to get away from the swill he'd been imbibing for the previous several days.

His father would have been absolutely appalled by what he'd been reduced to, which was reason enough not to enlighten the old whoreson. He also would never divulge the same to any of his brothers. They would never recover from their laughter at his expense.

He heaved himself to his feet, groaned because he couldn't stop himself from it, then stretched his abused back until he thought he might manage to walk with any success. He pulled his cloak from off the nail it had been using as a resting place, half surprised

someone hadn't filched that as well, and left his piece of
passageway.

He supposed it was less thought than habit that had him pulling
himself back into the shadows before he walked out in full view of
those standing by the edge of the enormous arena, as Doghail had
called it. He had called it many things as he'd finally been pressed
into the service of walking over every foot of it, looking for horse
droppings to scoop up.

"She doesn't ruin the horses, but perhaps that is just dumb luck."

Acair recognized Fuadain, that unimportant lord of whatever
they called his derelict manor that found itself on the less-desirable
side of Sàraichte. He didn't recognize the guest, but the man obviously believed himself to be exceptionally important. Whether it
was due to money or title, Acair couldn't have said and he didn't
care to investigate. His interest only extended to wondering when
they would shut up and move on.

"Fetch one of the mares," Fuadain commanded. "One commen-
surate with Lord Cuirteil's stature. But your stature in the world,
not at table, eh, Cuirteil?"

Acair watched Fuadain elbow his guest in his ample belly, listened to the two of them guffaw as if they actually found themselves
amusing, then considered the unusual position he found himself in.
Normally, he would have been keeping his ears open for insults
and preparing a proper retribution. It was, he had to admit, somewhat freeing to just not give a damn.

Was that how normal men lived?

It was an astonishing thought, actually. He wasn't sure he was
comfortable even entertaining it, so he let it continue on past him
where it could trouble someone else.

Doghail brought out a fine-looking though feisty mare that
Acair had already become acquainted with thanks to it almost
taking a decent bit of flesh off his upper arm. Would that that one
would take a bite out of Cuirteil's ample backside.

The mare was handed off to that gel who had been so rude to

him about his stall mucking however many days ago it had been. He wasn't sure he had even heard her name, which saved him the trouble of remembering it. What he could plainly see, though, was that she knew what she was doing. There was no nipping, balking, or sneering coming from that mare, something Acair felt now qualified to judge. And once she directed the mare to run about her in a circle, albeit attached to a long length of rope, the mare did so without question.

"Corr," a voice said breathlessly from beside him, "she's powerful good at it, ain't she?"

Acair looked to his left and found one of the new stable lads standing there, his mouth agape, his eyes bright with admiration.

"Corr," Acair agreed, trying not to shudder at the absolutely revolting nature of the local vernacular, "she is, ain't she?"

Good lord, his father would have cuffed him into the adjacent county if he'd heard such a thing come out of his mouth.

"I forget her name," Acair said casually. "Too much drinking and wenching drove it right out of my head."

The lad looked at him with wonder. "Truthful?"

"I never lie." And that was, he could say truthfully, the absolute truth. His father had mocked him for it, but one lived with one's failings as best one could. And he had spent a goodly amount of time *thinking* about drinking and wenching whilst he'd been about his most recent labors, which perhaps made it truthful enough for the present circumstances.

"Léirsinn," the lad said. "Don't suppose she's a lady, even if she is Lord Fuadain's niece."

Acair could scarce believe his ears. "Errr," he said, scrambling for the right words, "you ain't in earnest—ah, tellin' the truth. Rather." He gave up. There was no hope for it, but perhaps his companion wouldn't notice.

"She is," the lad said, "and I hears he done treats her awful."

Indeed he did. "Why does she endure it, do you suppose?"

"Her grandfather lives up at the big house," the lad whispered.

"'Tis said he can't move or speak. She works for his keep, so they say."

Ah, altruism. Acair would have pointed out to anyone who would listen that this was where that sort of thing led, but he supposed the present moment wasn't the proper one for that sort of instruction.

Interesting, though, the twistings and turnings of Mistress Léirsinn's family tree. If she was Fuadain's niece, why was she in the barn? If her grandfather was up at the house, why wasn't Fuadain seeing to his care? Unless the man was not a father but a father-in-law and Fuadain was absolutely without any sort of conscience.

"Oh, you are useless," Fuadain snapped suddenly. "Slaidear, take this horse away from her!"

Acair watched as who he had come to learn was the stable master walked out onto the field and took the rope away from Léirsinn.

"'E gives me cold chills and no mistake."

Acair had to agree with his rustic companion that that was indeed the case, but he did so silently. There was something about Slaidear that was . . . unusual. It was obvious he wasn't in his position because of any affinity with horses—something Acair could understand rather well at present—which begged the question of just why he was there.

It didn't take a Cothromaichian lad's powers of observation to see that there were foul things afoot—and that wasn't just the pile of manure Acair realized he was standing in. He rolled his eyes. Would the indignities never end?

Slaidear continued to make a great hash of working that mare and Fuadain continued to berate Léirsinn for things she wasn't doing. A first-rate bastard, that one, far beyond the behavior a petty lord in an insignificant port town might allow himself. Léirsinn was good at swallowing all manner of insults, perhaps either because she was too stupid to know she'd been insulted or perhaps she was simply too accustomed to being treated like a slave.

In time, Fuadain seemed to grow bored with his sport, Lord

Cuirteil announced the need for sustenance, and Slaidear apparently realized he was about to be trampled if he didn't find someone else to see to that horse. Léirsinn led the mare out of sight until the men had left the arena, then she brought the horse back into the arena to work it herself.

Acair remained in the shadows for quite some time, listening with half an ear to the whispered babbling of his new friend and mulling over what he'd seen.

Intrigue and the possibility of mayhem. He had a nose for that kind of thing and what he was smelling at present was rank indeed.

"We're headed to the pub up the way," the lad said suddenly. "Comin' along, are ye?"

"Wouldn't miss it," Acair said. "You go ahead and I'll catch up."

That seemed to be answer enough. The lad departed for more promising locales, leaving Acair to his thoughts. He folded his arms across his chest and leaned back against the wall, settling in for a proper rumination.

Doghail took the mare away and soon brought Léirsinn that damned stallion she seemed to think was so marvelous. Acair thought the beast was a demon, and he'd had experience enough with the latter that he thought he might not be overestimating his ability to recognize the same.

There was a bit of a battle of wills, it seemed, before Léirsinn reasserted her authority and the stallion did as he was told. He was, Acair had to admit, a handsome beast as far as horses went. He trotted, he pranced, he raced about as if he would have preferred to be flying. And all the while, Léirsinn stood in the center of his world, turning with an almost imperceptible motion, demanding the horse change gaits with a whistle or a click.

Corr, indeed.

He continued to watch until he grew tired and thought he might like to sit down somewhere. Unfortunately, the only ones who seemed to get any rest in the place were the horses. He wasn't sure if he envied them for it or loathed them for the same. He didn't particularly like horses, which he imagined Soilléir and Rùnach were still giggling over, but he had to admit the past se'nnight had given him a different view of them.

Fortunately for them all, Doghail came to lead the horse away. Léirsinn waved him off, but Acair supposed he should have expected that. She seemed like the sort of lass who liked to do things herself. He followed her at a safe distance—*safe* meaning, of course, too far away to be called on to do any labor—then found himself a bale of hay to sit on. Congratulating whatever enterprising soul had determined hay was best used as a seat by gathering it together in a cube, he then sat, leaned back, and promptly fell asleep.

He woke only because he had spent decades honing the ability to know when his quarry had escaped. He pushed himself to his feet, suppressing the urge to groan, then looked for his missing horse gel.

"She went that way."

He shot Doghail a look. "Never know what sorts of lads might mimic their master's ways, would you agree?"

"Protective."

"Looking for better ale than you serve, actually."

Doghail smiled briefly. "She won't appreciate it, but I've done it as well. Off you go. And as repayment, I'll see to your stalls for you."

Acair blinked, not exactly sure what he should say. "Well," he managed finally.

Doghail shook his head and walked off.

Now he was certain Soilléir and Rùnach were sipping sour wine from Penrhyn and laughing their arses off at him, no doubt having scryed the entire scene in whatever bloody glass ball Soilléir was using these days for the conjuring up of his visions.

He shrugged off the vague feeling that he should have said something polite, then set about his normal work of poking his nose where it absolutely shouldn't go.

It took him far more time to catch Léirsinn up than it would have normally, leading him to believe he hadn't had nearly as much rest as he should have. He followed her without thinking until he realized she was headed toward the manor house. She kept to lesser paths that skirted substantial gardens, obviously something she did regularly because she seemed to know where she was going. He did spare the energy to wonder if she hadn't had perhaps a cup too many of Doghail's brew given the way she would walk in a perfectly straight line, then suddenly stop, step around something, then continue on. It only happened a pair of times, but he wondered what in the hell she was doing. Practicing dance steps?

Had she been enspelled?

He considered, then decided against that latter idea. He couldn't use his magic, of course, but he damned well had all of it to hand and along with that power came the ability to recognize magic in all its forms so he didn't walk straight into a web of spells without realizing it. Nay, she wasn't enspelled.

But she was turning to look behind her, giving him hardly the time to leap off the path and duck behind a shrubbery before he should be discovered. Something poked him—as usual—in the arse so painfully he almost yelped. He was made of sterner stuff than that, however, so he bit back a very vile curse and peeked over the greenery.

'Twas a pity, to be sure, that a woman that beautiful should be wasted in a barn. Worse still that she should have lost her wits at such a young age. To look at her, one would have thought she was a fair-faced, mild-mannered wench with money and pedigree enough to secure a fairly well-heeled husband to take care of her properly for the rest of her days.

He considered. *Mild-mannered* was likely not the right thing to call her. He'd watched her manage that stallion and he'd listened to her call him a fool for not knowing how to tend a horse. Acid-tongued and daft as a duck was likely closer to the mark. But she was indeed lovely in a way that was mesmerizing enough to leave him crouching stupidly behind a bush that he realized with a start contained a hive full of angry bees, one of whom had obviously decided the horses were right in their choice of locations on his poor person to abuse.

He jumped back out onto the path and trotted off after his quarry, hoping he was moving quickly enough to allow his former winged companions to find something else to torment. His handful of coppers were clinking in his purse along with what remained of the meager funds he'd extorted from Soilléir and Rùnach, damn them both to hell. If things continued on the way they seemed to be going, he was going to arrive back home in a year much thinner than he was at present because he would never manage to afford a decent pub meal.

The only positive thing he could see was that he was so far out of any sort of decent civilization that no one would recognize him. Considering that he had absolutely no way to protect himself save his fists, that wasn't something to be taken lightly. He wondered how Léirsinn kept herself safe and what it would be like to know that the only thing you had standing between you and death was some sort of barn implement.

He had the feeling he was going to become much more familiar with that than he cared to.

He was tempted to stop, turn himself back toward the barn, and go find a horse trough in which to soak his head. He couldn't protect himself in his usual fashion, he had a very light purse, and there were some very unusual things going on in Sàraichte. If he'd had the modicum of good sense the gods had given a slug, as his father would have said, he would have abandoned his current path and trotted back to his closet.

But that lass there in front of him was walking into the gloom without anyone to guard her back, her uncle seemed perfectly content to treat her very poorly, and Acair was beginning to wonder if she might have red hair. He didn't know any flame-haired wenches, but he'd heard tales of their tempers. If there was anything he found hard to resist, it was a feisty woman in a temper.

Perhaps he would buy her supper and count that as yet another good deed for the day.

He shoved aside memories of a certain dwarvish princess of uncommon feistiness who hadn't been all that receptive to his offer of a fine meal, reminded himself that there were quite a few women who had accepted his invitations to supper, and strode off into the twilight. Nothing ventured, nothing gained.

Even with a stable lass who controlled horses he hardly dared come close to.

Five

Léirsinn walked quickly toward town, knowing she would likely arrive too late for what business she wanted to accomplish but unable to do anything else. She needed advice and the one reliable place to get that was from Cailleach the fishwife.

There were numerous sellers of fish in town, that was true, but there was something about Mistress Cailleach that hinted of her knowing things that others might not. Unusual things. Just the sorts of things Léirsinn thought she might need to know, such as how the hell she was going to take two decades of the meanest of wages and turn that into enough money to spirit her grandfather away from a man she feared she could no longer call benign.

Trolls. Léirsinn nodded to herself over that idea. Her store of knowledge about things that lurked in forests and assaulted unwary travelers was extensive thanks to the tales her parents had told her during her childhood. In spite of whatever other sorts of mischief they combined, trolls were famous for having hoards of gold—

Nay, that was dwarves. She stopped and looked up at the darkening sky. Trolls hoarded all sorts of things, or so she thought, but dwarves collected gold. She considered that for a moment or two, then conceded she wasn't entirely sure of that either. Perhaps dwarves collected mountains of gems.

Well, whoever collected what, she thought she might have to

make a visit to one group or another, her grandfather in tow, and offer to trade her services as stable master in return for a safe haven. Barring that, she would have to stifle her doubts, take a barge to Beinn òrain, and indulge in the always reliable activity of stealing a wizard's purse. And if she couldn't manage that, she would simply help herself to the loose coins of the next rich man who walked into her barn.

She ignored the fact that she'd never stolen anything in her life and wasn't sure she could begin at the ripe old age of almost a score and ten, but dire circumstances called for desperate measures. She would do what she had to in order to keep her grandfather safe. She was beginning to wonder if she might have to be about that sooner rather than later and with fewer coins than she might need.

Why had her uncle been watching her from his window?

She shivered in spite of herself. There was something afoot inside the manor, something not right. She continued on, walking briskly. Even if she couldn't find the answers to her problems in some mythical forest, she could ask Mistress Cailleach for her thoughts on an inexpensive haven within running distance and where she could possibly find someone willing to transport her grandfather there for only a handful of poor coins.

Perhaps she might even be able to get away from those spots of shadow she had encountered not once but three times in the previous se'nnight. It was enough to make her wonder if she might be losing her mind.

She didn't entertain that thought very often, if ever. Her life was made up of very sensible things: horses, leather, and sweet-smelling hay. Those were things that made perfect sense, never changed, never did what was unexpected or untoward. Those shadows, though, were things she didn't understand at all—

Nor did she understand how she had walked for so long without realizing she was being followed.

Unfortunately she was on the outskirts of town, so there was no shop window to aid her in determining who was on her heels.

She supposed the only thing to be done was stop at a pub and hope
her potential attacker would find himself distracted by the thought
of food.

She bypassed the first place she came to because it was disgusting even by Sàraichte's very low standards. She continued on her
way, realizing she had acquired not just one but a handful of shadows. Fortunately, she was no more than a quarter mile from *The
Preening Pelican*. Indeed, she thought she might gain the doors if she
bolted, but before she could make up her mind exactly what she
should do, she felt a hand on her arm.

"Blimey, mates, look at what we 'ave 'ere."

Léirsinn peeled his fingers from her arm and turned to face him.
"What? My boot in your arse, *mate*?"

The trio of lads there seemed to find that amusing enough,
though the fourth, obviously their leader, did not. His smile left his
face as if it had been struck from it and he stepped closer.

"You stupid—"

That was the last thing he said unless she was to count curses
that were quickly reduced to a single groan that accompanied his
journey into senselessness. A cloak was thrown in her face, which
was more alarming than a hand on her arm. She pulled it off from
half over her head, fully prepared to throw it back, only to realize
it was Acair's and he was busy doing what could have been considered defending her honor. He might not have known how to use a
pitchfork, but he apparently knew how to use his fists.

He was outnumbered, but that didn't seem to bother him. In
fact, he paused at one point to ask one of the three remaining lads
if he had any companions who might want to come join the fray to
make things more interesting. Léirsinn would have smiled at that,
but she was too busy being surprised that anyone would make the
effort to rescue her.

It took but a few minutes before only the burliest lad was left
standing. Acair pulled him close and said something she didn't quite
catch. The lad looked at Acair as if he had just peered into the pit of

Hell and seen himself at the bottom of it, then turned tail and fled. Acair smoothed his hair back from his face, then turned to face her.

She thought she might understand what had frightened that last bloke.

There was something in Acair's eye, something that wasn't at all pleasant. She didn't know how to name it, but she thought she wouldn't care for having that look turned on her. It wasn't the same look he had given Falaire. That look had been a warning. His current look was something else entirely.

She held out his cloak. "Thank you," she said simply. "And don't say to me what you said to that last lad."

He took his cloak back and snorted. "I simply suggested that he find his sport elsewhere. He was a coward."

She didn't doubt that. "What are you doing here?"

"I was hoping you would buy me a drink."

"There's a horse trough over there," she said because she was suddenly quite chilled, "and I wasn't talking about that. Why are you following me? And what of your stalls?"

"Already done."

"Did you do them well?"

"I didn't hear any horses complaining." He paused. "If you must know the truth, Doghail promised to finish my stalls for me so I could follow you." He looked at her seriously. "As for the reason why, you might call it chivalry if you like."

"I usually don't attract much attention."

"I find that very difficult to believe." He tossed his cloak over one shoulder, then looked at her. "You should have a dagger. It isn't safe for a woman to go about without one."

"I wouldn't know what to do with one if I had one," she said frankly.

"The general idea is to bury it to the hilt into the gut of whoever is threatening you," he said. "I'll show you how later. For now, let's go find something to eat, unless you're off to do nefarious deeds. I wouldn't want to get in the way of that."

She looked at the sky, then sighed. "I had hoped to be to town before dark, but I don't think I'll manage it. I suppose all I can do is turn for home and look for supper."

"Not if you value the condition of your tum, you won't," he said. He nodded up the way. "What of that place there?"

"The food isn't terrible and the ale is better than what Doghail serves, but I haven't enough coin for myself, much less the two of us."

He shot her a look. "As if I would allow a woman to pay for a meal for me."

"Wouldn't you?"

He paused. "Well, I would actually, but not recently. I've turned over some sort of new leaf."

"And found vermin under it?"

He smiled. "Exactly that." He nodded toward the pub. "Let's go, woman. I'll see if I can't parlay my excessive earnings into at least a mug or two of ale and some crusts of bread."

"And just how do you intend to do that?"

"Cards," he said easily. He glanced at her. "Ever seen any?"

"Ever had a boot up your—"

He tsk-tsked her. "You shouldn't use that sort of inflammatory rhetoric unless you have the ability to follow it up with physical damage. I see no dagger in your hand nor sword strapped to your back which leads me to believe that you are merely bluffing with your threats."

She didn't bother to respond, mostly because he was right. She generally relied on the fact that she had a stallion in tow to keep herself safe. That didn't help her all that much in town, but since she went there only during the daytime, she had never truly considered her lack of protection to be a problem. That looked to have changed recently.

She didn't like change.

"Let's be off before this refuse awakes," he said, nodding toward the road. "Also, I fear the stench of that pub behind us is making me queasy."

She had to agree with that, so she nodded and walked away

from the lads Acair had left in a tidy heap. She looked at him out of the corner of her eye as they walked because it was difficult not to look at him. His hair was mussed, but other than that, there was no sign that he had just been in a brawl with four men who hadn't been shy about throwing their fists.

"Do you have brothers?" she asked.

"Several," he said, "and each more vile and reprehensible than the last."

She smiled in spite of herself. "How many?"

He shot her a brief look. "Let's just say my father was not unwilling to sire the occasional bastard. My mother bore him seven sons, of which I am the youngest. After gazing for quite some time on my admittedly superior self, he decided he had done all he could with my dam and cast his eye elsewhere. I am also unhappily aware that my mother was not his first encounter with the fairer sex given that I seem to never be able to turn a corner at home without running into yet another of his early forays into fatherhood."

"A busy man, your father."

"Extremely."

"Do you have large suppers together with the extended relations?"

He lifted an eyebrow. "You're very cheeky."

"And you're a terrible stable lad."

"Which is obviously what makes you curious about my true skills," he said. "A pity I am unable at the moment to enlighten you. Rest assured, the list is very long."

She could only imagine and she suspected that *stable hand* was definitely not on that list. She wasn't sure she wanted to know what *was* on that list. She'd had watched too many things over the past few days turn out to be something other than what she'd expected them to be.

That thought was unsettling enough that she decided perhaps a change of plans was in order. She would indulge in a quick, cheap mug of ale only because she'd come too far to refuse it without looking like a fool, then she would turn around and go back to where she belonged before she found herself embroiled in things she had the feeling she wouldn't like at all.

"Do you have brothers?"

She looked at him in surprise. No one ever asked her about her family, as a rule. Doghail had, when they'd first met, but she hadn't cared to talk about them so he'd never brought it up again. Of course Acair couldn't have known the particulars of her past, so she supposed that was reason enough not to give him the look she generally reserved for lads too stupid to know when to keep their mouths shut.

"One," she said. "And a younger sister. Both gone now."

He studied her casually for longer than she liked, but he was apparently wise enough to know when not to pursue forbidden topics of conversation.

"I'm sorry," he said simply.

She nodded briskly, then continued on with him toward *The Preening Pelican*, congratulating him silently on his good sense. That task accomplished—and far too quickly—she turned to wondering just who he was and why it was he found himself in Sàraichte. It was truly the last place she would have chosen to live if she'd had a choice.

Perhaps she did have a choice. If there were any way to increase her funds, surely Mistress Cailleach would know. If all else failed, perhaps Acair, if he proved adept with cards, could teach her how to make a decent living at it. She could imagine worse occupations. Well, perhaps not very many, but a few—

She pulled up short, putting her hand out to stop Acair before he walked into a patch of shadow. He stopped, then looked at her.

"I beg your pardon?"

"Nothing," she said quickly. "Let's, ah, go over there. Better to admire the signage from a different angle, wouldn't you agree?"

She didn't dare look at him. It was enough to think herself daft. Seeing irrefutable proof that someone else thought the same might be more than she could take at the moment. She stood well away from the spot she had seen and looked at it without trying to appear as if she were looking at it. Unfortunately, she couldn't deny that she was seeing what she *couldn't* be seeing because there was simply no possible way that shadows that weren't shadows could be lingering on the ground in odd, random places—

A lad came around the corner of the pub and walked right over the patch of ground before Léirsinn could stop him. He froze, as if something were holding him there. She felt a cold chill settle over herself that had nothing to do with the twilight. What in the hell were those things?

The lad suddenly came back to himself from wherever he'd been. He shook himself like a dog, then continued on his way as if nothing untoward had just befallen him.

Léirsinn couldn't look at Acair. If he looked at her as if she were mad—

"Let us be about seeing to our supper," Acair said, taking her by the arm and tugging her toward the door to the pub. "I'm starved."

"Again, what is it you expect me to do about that?" she asked, her mouth utterly dry. She looked up at him to find that he was watching her far more closely than she was comfortable with. "Shall I whistle a cheerful tune or dance a jig?"

"You're throwing my words back at me, which means you were paying enough attention to me to remember them." He nodded knowingly. "Promising, that. As for your task, it is to merely sit quietly whilst I see to the necessary funds."

"I'm not accustomed to sitting quietly," she managed.

"Consider this a challenge, then," he said. "You can intimidate stallions again on the morrow, hopefully much better fed than by the slop your man Doghail prepares."

"He's not the cook," she said, trying not to shudder. "You wouldn't want to meet the man who prepares our meals."

Acair made a noise of disgust, which she had to admit was entirely justified. If he steered them both past that shadow that shouldn't have been there, he made no note of it and neither did she.

She simply walked with him and was happy to reach somewhere at least marginally safe, even if she only had enough coin for a small mug of ale.

Unfortunately, now that the moment was upon her, she found it was coin she couldn't bring herself to spend. She stood at the threshold of the pub, frozen as surely as a pony might have been when faced with a locale he simply couldn't enter.

"I promised you supper," Acair said easily. "Allow me to see to it."

"But—"

"'Tis as simple as that, if that concerns you."

She couldn't begin to describe what concerned her, so she took a deep breath and settled for a nod before she walked on. He found a darkened corner near the fire, saw her seated, then went to the bar to order. She had no idea how he paid for their ale, but he seemed to have funds enough for that at least. He set a mug down in front of her, sat down next to her, then looked around the gathering room.

"This will do nicely," he said pleasantly.

"Are you a gambler by profession?" she asked, realizing how prim she sounded only after she'd said the words.

He raised his eyebrows briefly. "Not in the sense you intend it, certainly. I'm not above attempting the impossible, but I generally don't do so unless I know I'll win." He looked at her. "Do you play cards?"

"Only children's games."

"Collecting animals of a certain color?"

"Something like that." She sipped her ale and tried not to sigh in pleasure. "You?"

"I don't think anyone here is going to ask for purple dragons anytime soon, so to answer your question, nay. Not in years." He had a large drink of his ale, then draped his cloak over the back of his chair. "Wait here. I'll be back soon enough."

She didn't suppose waiting was going to be much of a hardship given that she was sitting next to the enormous hearth, the fire was crackling nicely, and she had a very drinkable mug of ale in her hands. As long as Acair didn't behave badly and get them thrown out, she thought she might be able to allow herself the pleasure of simply being warm and doing nothing for a bit.

She watched Acair introduce himself to a group of men sitting at a table, already hard at their evening's labors. She had to admit that for as brutal as he'd been to those men who had wished her ill, he was utterly charming to those gamblers he was soon sitting down to join. If she'd been at that table and he'd asked her to hand over all her green ducks, she would have done so just to have him flash that smile of his at her—

She put her hand to her forehead and suppressed the urge to place it there repeatedly and with vigor. Obviously too much intrigue at the barn had left her considering things she never would have if she'd been in her right mind. She had a hefty swig of ale and hoped it would not only settle her stomach but clear her head.

It took three generous sips before she began to feel any more like herself. She kept hold of that cold pewter mug and watched Acair with a newfound detachment. He labored in her uncle's barn and he was spotting her coin for supper. He was no more interesting than that.

He waited until the game had ended and a new one was in the offing before he showed his companions a coin they seemed to find to their liking—a Nerochian half-sovereign, whatever that was. He joked affably with them as they set to their labors. She shook her head. He looked harmless enough, but she couldn't let go of the thought that he just wasn't at all what he seemed.

Why would a man that handsome find himself mucking out stalls to feed himself? If his sire had so many sons, then why—

She stopped herself before she wasted the effort to finish that thought. If his sire had so many sons, perhaps he hadn't been able to provide for them all properly. For all she knew, Acair, being the youngest, had been at the tail-end of the line when it came to an inheritance and found himself with absolutely nothing to his name but a handsome face and some skill with cards.

Or perhaps no skill with cards. She watched him and felt a bit of alarm sweep though her over the way he was frowning, as if he hadn't a clue what he was doing. The truth was, he was losing badly. He scratched his head, made a few noises of dismay, and looked at his cards as if he'd never seen anything like them before. One of the men at the table made a rather vile jest at Acair's expense. Acair only laughed in a good-natured fashion, then set to another bit of looking at his cards with an expression of utter bafflement.

And then, quite suddenly, he wasn't losing any longer.

He won several hands in a row, gathering to himself a respectable pile of coins. The others fought valiantly, but in the end, the rest of the table threw in their hands in disgust.

"You cheat," a man said, rising and pointing a finger at Acair. His face was mottled red. "You're a bloody cheat!"

Acair looked up at him coolly. "If you're going to call a man a cheat, friend, you'd best have damned good proof of it, don't you think?"

"Ralf, he bested you fairly," one of the other men said with a sigh. He looked at Acair. "He does this to everyone. Can't say I'm happy about losing my gold for supper, but I watched you closely enough. I saw nothing foul."

Acair rose. "And with that, my good man, supper and ale for the three of you is yours. Your friend can go drink out of the horse trough."

The man seemed to find that a reasonably acceptable outcome and gathered up his companions to go find the innkeeper. Léirsinn glanced at them, then looked back at the possessor of many more coins than he'd started the evening with. He sat down at the table, apparently not needing to go stand at the bar and wait for someone to take his supper order. A barmaid was immediately at his side, breathlessly inquiring about his desires. Unsurprising, but Léirsinn wasn't about to argue. Acair might have been a rogue and a gambler, but he was generous with his funds. He ordered food to feed them, paid for meals for his newly fleeced friends, then looked at her.

"I hope that will suit."

"I can't repay you."

"Don't think I asked you to."

She studied him because she liked to know what she was facing. "You didn't, which bothers me."

"You might just be grateful." He stopped, then frowned. "What a notion."

"Being grateful?"

"Well, the very idea of doing something pleasant for another soul is appalling enough, but doing it without expecting something very dear in return is another thing entirely." He looked at her. "I think I've been in your barn too long."

She almost smiled. "Not accustomed to that sort of altruism, is that it?"

"That is it," he agreed. He had another substantial drink of ale. "I believe I might be losing what few wits remain me."

"Where did you lose the first batch?"

He opened his mouth to speak, then pursed his lips. "I'm not at liberty to say specifically, but I believe I may have lost most of them at a table just like this."

"Playing at cards?"

"Nay, talking to my half-brother and one of his do-gooding companions."

"Horrors."

"If you only knew," he said with a fair amount of feeling, "and look you here is supper, come at just the proper time to prevent me from answering any more questions I'm not free to answer."

She had never in her life seen food appear so quickly. Then again, if she'd been that barmaid, she would have served Acair just that quickly and returned often simply for the chance to have another look at him. "Are you on a mission of secrecy?"

He glanced around himself as if he feared someone might be listening, then looked at her. "As it happens, aye, I am. And unfortunately, giving you any details at all will be detrimental to my health, so I will forbear."

"Then what shall we discuss?" she asked. "Your skill with cards?"

"As interesting a topic as that is, perhaps we should save that for later." He had another sip of ale. "Instead, why don't we talk about what you keep avoiding on the ground?"

She would have spewed out what she was eating, but she hadn't managed to yet get a spoonful of stew to her lips. She did drop that spoon into her bowl which had the same effect given that she was now wearing a decent amount of broth. Acair sighed lightly and signaled for the barmaid. Léirsinn would have protested, but she didn't have a chance before she was presented with a towel and a new supper.

She honestly couldn't remember when she had seen so much food in front of her at one time.

"I'm not avoiding anything," she said, holding on to her spoon and keeping it well away from anything spillable.

"I believe there are those who consider lying to be a sin."

"I'm not lying."

He leaned forward with his elbows on the table. "I am not a good man," he said seriously, "and my failings are legion. But I will tell you that the one gift I have from my mother is the ability to tell the absolute truth at all times. As a tasteful accompaniment to that unfortunate shortcoming, she gave me the ability to spot a lie from a hundred paces. And you, mistress, are lying."

"I don't want to tell you the truth," she said.

He grunted. "Well, now there is a piece of truth." He studied her for a moment or two, then nodded slowly. "Very well, keep your secrets. I understand that well enough. Let's speak of supper instead. Is yours edible?"

"Surprisingly."

"Considering what you've likely been eating, I understand. How long have you been at the barn?"

"Since I was scarce ten-and-two," she said, because she supposed there was no harm in saying as much.

"Did your parents send you off to work for your uncle or was that your choice?"

She wasn't surprised that he knew her connection to Fuadain; it was common gossip amongst the lads. She couldn't say she was interested in knowing what else they said about her, though. She was even less interested in giving anyone details that would likely be spread about just as quickly.

"My parents are dead," she said, because that was also common knowledge. "And so I've been at the barn for several years now." She looked at him to find him looking at her not so much with calculation as pity. "My uncle thought I might find a happy distraction amongst the horses."

"How generous of him."

She looked at him sharply. "It could have been worse."

"Aye," he agreed, "it could have been."

"I don't want to talk about this anymore."

"I understand. Let's talk about this fine meal and how we might lure the innkeeper's cook out to your uncle's stables."

She supposed that might have been a fine distraction, but it proved not to be necessary. The lads Acair had bought supper for asked if they could join them at their table and the rest of the evening passed very pleasantly in a discussion of local politics. If Acair said absolutely nothing of substance, Léirsinn supposed she could only credit him with an impressive display of mining for a great deal of information without giving any up. He might never have set foot in a barn before, but she had the feeling this wasn't his first pub.

She was starting to wonder with far too much enthusiasm just who he was.

The lads left eventually, well fed and properly watered, with praises to Acair's name on their lips. Léirsinn toyed with her mug, feeling rather decently fêted herself, then looked at her benefactor.

"You made a trio of friends there."

He shrugged. "Idle conversation and edible food. That doesn't seem very memorable, but perhaps for them it was."

"Where are you from?" she asked, because she had been fighting the question all evening and found she couldn't resist it any longer.

He was leaning back in his chair, looking like nothing more than an average, if not painfully handsome, man with no remarkable past. "I can't answer that."

"Why not?"

"You wouldn't believe me if I told you and the telling of that particularly useless piece of trivia would hardly pass my lips before I was dead."

She would have laughed at him, but she could see he was serious. "But you aren't a stable hand."

"I am for the foreseeable future."

"That doesn't reassure me about your character, you know."

"I didn't imagine it would." He set his mug on the table. "You are a wise woman, Léirsinn of Sàraichte, and you should follow your instincts and stay very far away from me."

"Unless I'm off to a pub at dusk."

"Well, I might come in handy then." He smiled briefly. "Shall we turn for our luxurious accommodations?"

She nodded, though she had to admit that for the first time in as long as she could remember, she wasn't particularly keen to return to the barn. It wasn't that she didn't love the horses there.

It was that she loathed her uncle.

There, she had said it. Not said it, but actually thought the words with a clarity that she had never dared use before. She looked at Acair to find him studying her closely.

"He's a bastard," he said mildly.

"Who?"

"The one you're thinking of."

"Cards *and* the reading of thoughts?" she said lightly. "What next?"

"The heavens weep over the thought, I'm sure." He rose and picked up his cloak, but said nothing else.

She understood. There was nothing to say.

She walked out into the night, flinched a bit at the chill, then took a deep breath and put her foot to—

Nothing, actually, because Acair pulled her aside. He did it so casually, she might not have noticed if she hadn't been the one being pulled. She looked at him in surprise, then watched him point to a spot where she had almost put her foot.

A shadow was there.

She looked at him quickly, but he only lifted one eyebrow briefly, then walked with her away from the pub. It took her several minutes to be able to speak and even then she suspected that nothing useful would come out of her mouth.

"I think I'm losing my wits," she said finally.

"I would suspect that comes from all the time you have no doubt spent over the years sneaking whiffs of very strong horse liniment, nothing more."

She would have agreed with him, but she found she couldn't say anything else. All she could do was put one foot in front of the other and continue on to a place where she wasn't sure she could live much longer. She had to get her grandfather out of the manor house and herself out of Sàraichte before something dire happened to them both.

Acair fell silent, which she appreciated. Her head was spinning not only thanks to a decent meal, but also from plans she could only dream of putting into motion. It was a testament to how fixated she was on the thought that she didn't realize how close they were to the barn until she was standing inside it.

She looked up at Acair. "We're here."

He nodded. "And so we are," he said quietly. "Keep a weather eye out."

She had to take a careful breath. "You too. Thank you for supper."

"My pleasure." He smiled briefly. "Got work to do."

"Me too."

She watched him go, then took hold of herself and walked off to see to her own work. She was fortunate, she supposed, that she had been doing it for so long that she didn't need to remind herself of what to do next. That was the only thing, she was sure, that saved her from standing there, wringing her hands.

She put her hand over a charm she wore constantly under her shirt, something she'd been given by someone who firmly believed there were unseen forces at work in the world, forces that could be counted on for aid. Léirsinn could only hope that was the case because if anyone needed help beyond the norm, it was her. There was mischief afoot in Sàraichte and she wanted no part of it.

Unfortunately, she had the distinct feeling she wasn't going to escape it.

Six

Acair stood outside the stables, leaning against a bit of stone fence, and wondered just what in the hell he was thinking. He could hardly believe he'd been up before the sun so many days in a row without having spent entirety of the night before making mischief, but that seemed to be his lot in life of late.

Do-gooding was, he had to admit, exhausting.

But so was mucking out stalls, which was why he had greeted with such joy the tidings he'd had not a quarter hour ago that he had a day of liberty to look forward to. If he used that day of liberty to skulk about satisfying his curiosity, who could blame him? He was less than a fortnight into his sentence and already he was desperate for something interesting to do.

Ah, and there went something interesting, just as he'd suspected.

He pushed off from the wall and followed the lady of the barn at a respectable distance. Now, that one there was a mystery. He could scarce believe she could control the sorts of equine brutes she faced, yet she'd been completely bested by the thought of his buying her supper. She wasn't afraid to give a lad a right proper ticking off, but she had no weapon to encourage the same lad to take her seriously.

And she saw shadows where there were none.

That was the strangest thing of all. He had honestly thought her daft as a duck when he'd followed her on his last foray to the local pub, but when she'd pulled him aside, he'd seen what she had been avoiding and couldn't deny that there was something quite untoward about it. There were shadows, of course, and then there were *shadows*. What he had seen had been a less of a shadow than a hint of magic. Watching a lad step into its embrace, pause as if he'd had his will to move briefly stolen from him, then carry on as if nothing had happened to him . . . 'twas passing odd, that.

He paused, but that was only because he'd just realized that Léirsinn had stopped, turned, and was currently glaring at him. He examined her for implements of death, then shook his head. As he'd told her a few nights ago, she was going to have to learn to protect herself. He was frankly quite surprised she had reached her current age without having had something dire happen to her.

He might have suggested a thing or two she could do to make herself a bit more terrifying, but he wasn't entirely sure how one went about teaching a mere mortal how to defend herself. The women he knew saw to that sort of thing thanks to garrisons with sharp swords or their own sweet selves with complements of terrible spells. Léirsinn only had a glare and it wasn't even a very good glare.

He caught her up, then stopped a pace or two away and inclined his head. "Mistress Léirsinn."

"What are you doing?" she asked shortly.

"I understand I've been released from the delights of shoveling horse leavings for the day."

"And you thought to follow me?"

He shrugged. "I was going your way."

"Which is why you were waiting for me earlier?"

She had a point there, but he wasn't sure how to admit to that without admitting to more than he wanted to. The truth was, he'd had a fairly pointed conversation with Doghail the night before during which they'd discussed a few things about the lady in question, namely her propensity to simply trot off into the fray without thinking about her safety. He suspected that was why he'd been set free for the day.

The other problem, though, was that he was terrible at small talk. He usually conducted his business with a rakish smile and a quick and dirty spell. Also, he wasn't sure how one went about talking to a horse miss. Stable lass. He hardly knew what to call her and he suspected that referring to her as Fuadain's niece wasn't going to get him anywhere—not that he wanted to get anywhere with her. The woman needed a keeper and that keeper was not going to be him.

He supposed that begged the question of why he was following her, but that wasn't a question he wanted to answer at the moment.

"I was resting," he said, nodding back toward the barn. "Very comfortable wall there."

She snorted. "Resting is generally best done in a bed and, without being too blunt, let me say that I don't require company at present."

"But I'm such good company," he said. "Plus, I'll buy you luncheon."

"Do you have coin left over from the other night?"

"Enough for one meal. We'll share."

She frowned at him, then walked away. He caught up to her easily and walked with her. He couldn't deny that there were strange things afoot in Sàraichte, but given that the place found itself in the most tedious country he'd ever seen save Shettlestoune, perhaps the inhabitants were desperate enough for something to do that they had to invent trouble.

Léirsinn stopped suddenly and put out her hand. He would have protested, but he had also caught sight of that thing lying there so innocently on the ground. He started to lean over to study it a bit more closely, but was interrupted by an angry shout.

"Oy, out of the way!"

Acair would have told the man to go to hell, but he supposed Léirsinn would pay for that in some way. He instead simply moved with her off the path as a groom came toward them, leading a horse

that Acair could see was not terribly fine. The man stepped on the
spot, paused, then shook himself and moved on.

The horse, however, looked down at the spot, hesitated, then
stepped over it without touching it. Acair watched the groom and
the horse continue on their way, then glanced at his companion.

"That was interesting," he said carefully.

She looked at him. "You see them too."

"Aye."

"What are they, I wonder?" she asked, looking profoundly
uncomfortable. "They seem . . . evil."

He studied the pool of nothing that lay there in front of them
but found it surprisingly difficult to identify anything about it that
might have pointed to its creator.

That was odd in itself.

"Not that you would know anything about evil," she added.

He made a non-committal noise. If there was one thing he knew
very well, it was evil.

"And it isn't as if it could be something, you know, *magical*." She
laughed, but she didn't sound at all amused. She sounded completely
unnerved.

Acair smiled brightly. "Why would it be?" Indeed, for all he
knew, the local wizardling had more time than good taste and had
decided that he would have a bit of sport at the local populace's
expense.

It was odd, though, how when a man stepped in that little patch
of nothing, he seemed unable to move, even for the briefest of
moments.

"I have to go," Léirsinn said suddenly, walking away. "Important
things to do."

Acair caught up and continued on with her, watching her whilst
trying to look as if he weren't staring at her to determine just how
unnerved she truly was. "What sorts of things?"

"I need to talk to someone in town."

"Your local wizard?" he asked politely. "A little witch keeping a shop down a side street in a tattier part of town? A less visible purveyor of charms and potions?"

She shot him a look. "I don't believe in any of that sort of rot. I will allow that the woman I'm off to see looks a bit more, ah, *supernatural* than most in the market, but I think she's been selling fish for quite some time. I'm sure the two are connected somehow."

He wasn't going to argue with her. In his vast experience with things of a nasty bent, he had learned it was better not to poke a hornet's nest unless one was prepared to have it vomit out its contents all over the lad with the stick. Besides, if he had any sort of virtue besides honesty, it was the ability to be patient. He would do a bit of snooping about untoward things, keep his eyes and ears open, and with any luck at all he might have a mystery to keep himself awake for a fortnight or two.

The journey to town seemed rather less tedious than it had when he'd made it by himself going the other direction and they arrived at the market just as things were beginning to look lively. One thing he could say for the inhabitants of the port of Sàraichte, they were early risers. He walked across cobblestones that were slick partly from the dew but mostly from the ubiquitous wooden boxes full of freshly caught fish that were being carried to at least two dozen fishmongers.

"Wait here a minute," Léirsinn said, looking at him seriously. "I have business to conduct privately, then you may come."

He would have told her that he never wriggled his nose into places where it didn't belong, but that was his stock in trade. Then again, he was turning over a new leaf. That he was giving her privacy might be counted as a good deed if one looked at it in the right way.

So he clasped his hands behind his back and remained where he was as Léirsinn approached an ample, white-haired woman with a voice like a ship's captain, pulled coins of her purse, and handed them over.

He considered, then shrugged. Perhaps Léirsinn trusted that

woman to keep her funds safe. He generally kept his treasures far away from where he slept, so he understood the compulsion. Léirsinn then had a brief but obviously earnest conversation with the woman. Whatever was said didn't seem to satisfy her, which was no doubt why she was frowning when she beckoned to him.

He approached, then stopped behind Léirsinn's choice of someone who looked a bit more supernatural than most—

And he suddenly understood why.

"What are *you* doing here?" the woman asked, sounding thoroughly annoyed.

Well, that was his damned aunt and he was wishing he had somewhere at present to hide from her, that's what he was doing there. Actually, she wasn't his aunt, she was his great-aunt on his mother's side and there was a very good reason Léirsinn had considered her to have a bit of a supernatural sheen to her. Whilst his mother's sisters were off doing good, something for which they were endlessly mocked, that one there was knee-deep in the family business.

Damn. What to do now?

"Léirsinn, my love, take these coins and run off to fetch me a pint of ale, would you? I can tell already it's going to be a *very* trying morning. I'll put your lad there to work. It looks as if he could stand to do a bit of laboring with his hands."

Léirsinn nodded, then looked at him pointedly. "Don't discuss anything important while I'm away."

"I'm sure I'll spend the time shoveling fish guts," Acair said. "A nice change, actually."

Léirsinn nodded then walked off, looking a time or two over her shoulder. Acair smiled encouragingly until she was gone, then he turned and looked at Léirsinn's, for lack of a better word, banker.

"Auntie."

"Don't you *Auntie* me, you miserable little wretch," Cailleach of Ceal said with a snort. "I know you and your ways. You've likely come to try to appropriate a bit of my magic."

"Wouldn't think of it," Acair said, "and that isn't simply because of my recent quite dire and terrible straits."

Cailleach looked behind him, then made a sound of satisfaction. "Ah, what a lovely little spell you have following you there. What's its purpose?"

"I believe its task is to slay me if I use any magic."

Cailleach looked at him for a moment or two in silence, then she threw back her head and guffawed loudly enough to send a flock of something feathered flapping off in terror.

"Oh," she gasped, reaching out and grasping his forearm in a grip that brought tears to his eyes, "that is rich. Let me see if I can guess who is behind it. Not Nicholas of Diarmailt—"

"I think he might be dead," Acair hedged.

"You know he isn't." She wiped her eyes with her apron and chuckled a bit more. "He was at your half-sister Mhorghain's wedding not a pair of years ago. I understand you didn't get an invitation, which I suspect wasn't an oversight." She was momentarily distracted by tossing a fish at a woman and expertly catching a coin in return. She pocketed it smoothly, then looked at him. "Your father, I understand, is indisposed at the moment, which leaves me with a substantially reduced list of souls who would either care enough or have the power to send such a thing off to vex you." She considered, then looked at him from shrewd bluish-green eyes that were mirrors of his own. "That little prince from Cothromaiche is responsible, isn't he?"

Acair was utterly unsurprised that Soilléir would be the one she would settle upon. Would that she would settle something a bit more substantial on the man, say perhaps a man-sized boulder. "Aye," he admitted crossly, "damn him to hell."

She laughed again, then sat herself down on a stool. "Have a seat on the shorter, less comfortable stool, little one, and tell Auntie all your troubles. But first, why are you keeping company with that lovely piece of goodness I just sent off?"

Acair sat down next to his great-aunt and accepted a sip of
something from a flask she produced from under her table of wares.
He gasped, then blinked until his eyes stopped watering.

"You wee babe," his great-aunt said, clucking her tongue. "Never
had strong drink, eh?"

"I'm afraid 'tis true," he managed, wishing he'd sent Léirsinn
off with enough coin for something for him that wouldn't feel as if
it had just peeled a layer of flesh from off the inside of his throat.
"And whilst I'm accustoming myself to this delicious brew, might
I ask why you find yourself here?"

"Because it was the most interesting place available."

Acair didn't like to argue with age—very well, he relished arguing with anyone older than he so he might put his mighty wit and
magic on display. At least he had until he'd acquired a damned
shadow in the person of that spell that seemed to be ever watching
him for the slightest misstep. It was a novel sensation, that not
wanting to draw attention to himself. He could only hope that was
an aberration that would eventually pass.

"I don't know, Auntie," he said, dredging up what he hoped would
pass for a respectful tone. "It seems a bit on the dull side to me."

"I despair for the future of the race," she said, shaking her head.
She reached out and cuffed him on the ear. "Everything flows through
here, whelp. Tales, magic, mages. Everything. And don't think a
decent amount of all three doesn't come through this market."

"But," he said gingerly, "why do you care?"

"I like to be in the know." She patted her hair carefully. "Keeps
me attractive, you see, to the lads. Don't know that I won't find one
I fancy one of these days and have myself a bit of an amorous
adventure."

The thought made him want to go have a little lie-down. The
woman was twelve hundred years old if she was a day.

"And don't think I haven't had several very important and handsome lads pursuing me of late," Cailleach added.

"Of course," he said quickly, fearing she might cuff him again

if he didn't express his agreement with the proper amount of enthusiasm. She had reached for her walking stick and was fingering it
purposefully. "I wouldn't think anything else. I also wouldn't presume to ask for their identities lest it ruin the surprise when one
comes calling very soon and you choose to announce the name of
that fortunate lad."

"I'm surprised at your discretion, but perhaps you're growing
up. You didn't answer my question, though. Why are you trailing
after Léirsinn like a lovesick pup?"

He didn't bother to take issue with her term. The woman was
nothing if not a hopeless romantic. He also supposed he wouldn't
be rubbishing any terms of his sentence if he told her as much truth
as he could stomach. He sighed heavily. "The tale begins with the
fact that I am on a penance tour."

Cailleach blinked, then a corner of her mouth twitched. "Trying
to make up for a bit of that magic-stealing you did last year, eh?"

"Among other things," he said grimly. "'Tis a ridiculously useless
exercise given that I didn't achieve my nefarious designs thanks to
that damned elf-spawn I must unfortunately admit is a brother."

"Rùnach paid a heavy price for your sire's evil," Cailleach said
seriously. "He deserves every happiness. You, though? I'm not sure
what you deserve."

"A hot fire, cold ale, and a handsome wench or two," Acair said
distinctly, "and in that order." He looked at his aunt. "That my needs
are so few makes me feel old."

"And that spell following you will age you further very rapidly
if you tangle with it. But I've interrupted you. You were on a penance tour, and . . ." She looked at him expectantly.

He suppressed the urge to swear. "To finish off my miserable
year of do-gooding, I was given two choices: apologize to Uachdaran of Léige for I haven't a clue what or be without magic for a
century." He wasn't about to tell her just what he'd been up to in
that accursed country of Durial on the off chance that he managed
to return and finish that glorious piece of business. Better to leave

that undisturbed. "I bargained it down to a year," he continued. "I was sent here, if you can believe it, for my own safety, and that bloody thing there watches me to make certain I don't stray off the path."

"And if you do, its task is to slay you?"

He pursed his lips. "As I said. I suppose that's preferable to Soilléir's alternative which was to turn me into a birdbath and set me in some garden full of elves or faeries." He shuddered. "I don't like to think about it, actually."

"I'm surprised he didn't promise to send you to live with your sire in that magic sink he occupies."

"I would prefer death."

"I imagine Soilléir knows that." She tilted her head and studied him for a moment or two. "And so you wound up at Fuadain's stables at Briàghde, took one look at that red-haired angel, and lost your heart."

"My mind, rather," Acair said. "My heart, black as it is, remains untouched."

Cailleach laughed. "Ah, Acair my lad, you are a sorry thing, aren't you? You should be so fortunate to have someone like that gel look at you twice." She took the flask from him, had a healthy swig, then looked at him knowingly. "I can't imagine you aren't about some piece of mischief or other, never mind what Prince Soilléir might have intended for you."

"Now that you mention it," Acair said, "I am curious about a few things. One thing, actually."

"Of course you are. What thing?"

"This will sound daft."

"Acair, I would call you many things—and have, believe me—but daft is not amongst them." She reached out and patted his hand with surprising gentleness. "Tell Auntie what you've seen."

He looked about him for eager ears, but saw nothing but the usual rabble that loitered about in such a locale. He turned back to his great-aunt. "I've seen shadows."

"Those are the souls of those you've slain, love."

He considered, then leaned closer to her. "I refuse to admit to actually having slain anyone," he said, "but don't spread that about."

She gave him what for her was an affectionate shove. "You've had more than your share of souls die of fright on your watch, which you must admit."

"I won't say that I haven't helped a few continue on the path they'd already chosen to that peaceful rest in the East," he conceded, "and perhaps with more gusto than necessary, but that seemed the least I could do."

"Altruistic."

"I know," he said with a sigh. "One of my greatest failings, and one that has caused me no small amount of grief over the past year." He glanced about himself once more, unwilling to provide fodder for any eavesdroppers, then looked at his aunt seriously. "About those shadows: I don't like the feel of them."

"Know who created them?"

"I haven't had a chance to investigate properly yet."

"Leaving me to do your dirty work for you," she said with a sigh. She heaved herself to her feet. "Let's go for a little stroll and see what's there to be seen."

"You might be robbed whilst we're gone."

She only smiled in a way that left him doubting that such a thing would ever happen. She nodded to a small, sharp-nosed lad who took over her spot and her walking stick. Acair had the feeling he would use both to their best advantage.

Léirsinn was nowhere to be found, which he supposed should have alarmed him a bit, but he counted on daylight to at least be of some aid to her and continued on with his aunt. They didn't have to go far.

"There," he said, nodding to a spot ten paces in front of them. "By the wall."

Cailleach watched as someone stepped into that shadow, paused, then stepped out of it.

Acair looked at her closely, but her expression gave nothing away. He waited, though, because whatever she lacked in manners she more than made up for in experience and canniness.

She finally shook her head, then looked at him. "I don't think you should get involved in that business there," she said very quietly. "*I* certainly wouldn't."

"But, Auntie, your magic gives even me pause."

"I should hope so, Acair. What flows through your veins is half ours, you know. Gair is nothing but flash and theatrics. The real power, the power that will come to you when his is blown off like chaff? *That* is what you should have been chasing after all these years."

He didn't believe that for a second—

He paused, then studied his aunt for a moment, seeing her with a clarity he'd certainly never taken the time for before. The woman who stood before him, as demure as her booming fishwife voice would allow her to be . . . aye, he'd underestimated her. Badly.

She gave him a knowing look. "Arrogance was your sire's downfall."

"I'm working on humility," he promised.

She blinked, then threw back her head and laughed. Again. He would have been offended—indeed, he was, rather—but perhaps a string of endless days shoveling horse manure had done a goodly work on him somehow because his first instinct was to protest his innocence, not drop a spell of death on her head. She looked at him as if she knew exactly what he was thinking, reached out and pulled him into a fragrant embrace, then patted him rather gently on the back.

"You're a horrible little piece of refuse," she said, shoving him away and smiling, "but perhaps there is a hope of your improving at some point. Not enough to merit that one coming our way, but perhaps someone more shrewish and unpleasant."

Acair knew he should have protested that he wasn't looking for a woman and wouldn't have wanted a horse girl if he had been, but there was no point. He saw Léirsinn standing twenty paces away, staring at the patch he could almost see there to the side of the thoroughfare, tucked discreetly near a barrel of—what else?—fish.

"You know where curiosity lands you," Cailleach said lightly.

"My mother is curious," he reminded her.

"Aye, but she would have the good sense to exercise some self-control here." She shot him a look. "Leave this alone, Acair. You won't like where it leads."

He was tempted to argue with her, but decided that perhaps there was no point in it. He had to wonder, though, just what she had seen to leave her feeling so strongly about something that looked so unremarkable.

He speculated until Léirsinn had joined them, then continued on with that same activity whilst he escorted those two demure flowers back to Cailleach's stand where her lad seemed to be doing an extremely brisk bit of business. He then loitered about uselessly, mulling over what he'd heard until Léirsinn and his aunt had apparently discussed their business to their satisfaction.

He bid his aunt a good day, collected his horse miss, and left before Cailleach could say anything else untoward.

"Chummy, weren't you?" Léirsinn asked. "One would think you knew her."

"One shouldn't ask questions I can't answer."

Léirsinn stopped and looked at him in surprise. "You *do* know her."

"I can't say."

"You know I'm going to ask her about it the next time we meet."

"You do that." He could only imagine what his auntie would decide to reveal about him, so perhaps he would be offering to run errands in town for the foreseeable future to spare Léirsinn any details she didn't need to know.

He supposed he could think of worse things than to be doing something—anything—besides the backbreaking labor of endlessly moving horse droppings from small piles to much larger piles. If one more horsefly landed on his arse . . . well, he couldn't bring to mind exactly what he would do because the choices were so dire—

"Watch out!"

She hadn't shouted, but she'd come close. He waited until an appropriate number of locals had looked at him as if they pitied him for his companion's obviously damaged sanity, then he looked at the shadow in front of him. It was smaller than the others, but even he could see its edges.

He didn't pause to think; he simply ignored the warning bells going off inside his head and stepped into the middle of it.

He lost his breath. Nay, he hadn't lost his breath, it had been ripped from him by claws. The spell continued to tear at him in a way he honestly couldn't describe. His mind, his memories, his very essence was being pulled from him with a ruthlessness that astonished him. It took an effort that was impossible to even begin to calculate to wrench himself out of its terrible embrace—

He stepped back and leaned over, struggling to simply draw in breath, until he could put his finger on what had happened to him.

He had lost a piece of his soul.

It was excruciating.

He was vaguely aware of Léirsinn pulling his arm over her shoulders and taking a good deal of his weight onto herself, but he couldn't find the strength to protest. It was all he could do to breathe in and out.

"What happened—"

"Find a quiet place," he begged hoarsely. "I'll be fine in a moment."

"I don't think—"

"*Please.*"

She looked at him in surprise. He imagined he was wearing the same expression. He had never in his life uttered that word—

Well, that was a lie, but he would be damned if he would revisit when he'd last begged for anything.

The next thing he knew he was sitting in a darkened corner of a gathering room, there was a fire within reach, and Léirsinn was fumbling with the purse at his belt.

"I should be enjoying this," he wheezed.

"First a gambler and now a lecher," she said sternly. "What else have I yet to discover about you that's worse?"

"Don't ask." He closed his eyes because the chamber was spinning so wildly, he thought he might lose what breakfast he'd forced himself to ingest that morning.

He suspected he might have slept, for the next thing he knew, Léirsinn was shaking him awake. He pried his eyes open, then accepted something that someone might have termed ale if they'd never tasted the same before. He drank, though, because feeling nauseated from bad ale was better than feeling half dead from what he'd just had done to him. He looked at Léirsinn but could scarce see her. She leaned closer to him.

Her eyes were green. Not greenish-blue like the sea, but green like spring leaves in the most beautiful parts of the elven gardens of Seanagarra where he had only dared venture once during a year when Sìle had been abed with exhaustion from some piece of elvish rot . . .

He could honestly hardly bear to look at her, she was so haunting lovely.

"What do you think?" she whispered.

He let out a very ragged breath. "I think you're beautiful."

She rolled her eyes. "Nay, about . . . well, about those things. There's something untoward about them, isn't there?"

He closed his eyes. "Considering I couldn't possibly know anything of magic and that sort of rubbish," he managed, "perhaps I'm not the best one to judge."

"You know, you look like you're going to puke."

"Aye, well, I *can* judge that," he agreed. He opened his eyes and looked at her. "I'll think I'll forgo the pleasure for the moment."

"I ordered food."

"Or something resembling it," he said with a groan.

She smiled, but it was a very strained smile indeed. "I think I might be afraid."

"I think you might be a very wise gel," he said. He looked around the pub blearily for anyone who might want him dead, saw no one, then leaned his head back against the wall and closed his eyes. "Wake me if someone wants to kill us."

"If you like."

He wasn't sure he dared express what he would have liked. The list began with wishing that damned spell following him had at least warned him before he lost part of his soul to some spot a crotchety old village warlock had likely laid on the cobblestones for his own amusement. His list ended with renewed determination to give his constant companion the slip the first chance he had, even if that meant he had to clout it over the head with a pitchfork. Given his newfound abilities with the same, he thought the bloody thing might never see that coming.

All he knew was that the last place he wanted to be was in the middle of mayhem without any way to protect himself—er, protect Léirsinn, rather. His good deed for the day, surely. It had better count for something, because he suspected he was the only one attempting the like.

He didn't want to think about what the mage who had created those shadows was attempting.

He wanted even less to be forced to wonder just what in the blazes he was going to do about it without a single spell to hand.

Damn it anyway.

Seven

Léirsinn stood at the door to the kitchens and took several deep, even breaths before she lifted her hand to rap smartly on the door. That knocking was, of course, absolutely pointless. She knew she'd been marked long before she'd managed to force herself up the trio of steps to the kitchen's meanest entrance. Those inside made her knock because it made them feel important and relegated her to something less than a servant.

She could have told anyone who would listen that she already knew her place very well, but that last thing she wanted was to find herself barred from the house. She had to see how her grandfather fared, then get through her interview with her uncle without killing him. Truly, she had a full night of delights yet in front of her.

Those were delights, though, that she was anxious to be seeing to without delay. It had been a se'nnight since she'd heard the tidings of her grandfather's condition from that housemaid. She had no idea if he lived still or not, though she supposed Fuadain would have trotted out his best black suit of clothing if there had been a death in the family. Anything to focus attention to himself.

She put her hand on the door to try to draw some sense of calm from the wood. Mistress Cailleach had sent her word that morning about the state of her funds. She had more than she'd thought thanks to the fishwife's shrewd investing in various things, but it was far less than she knew she would need to have to escape. If she'd had the strength, she would have taken on employment as a barmaid. It was the only thing she could think of to do after evening stables that seemed reasonable.

But not even the addition of a barmaid's wages would give her what she needed.

What she needed was a miracle.

Trust.

That was the last thing Cailleach's note had said. It had been underlined and circled a pair of times, as if the woman had been afraid Léirsinn either wouldn't see it or wouldn't understand it.

Trust. Trust what? Trust that she would wake up and find a pile of gold at her feet? Trust that someone would come to help her when she was the only one who cared what happened to her or her grandfather?

Trust she could do the impossible when every single thing pointed to her not being able to accomplish the same?

What she needed wasn't trust, it was something far beyond the usual business she engaged in, say . . . magic. She could hardly believe she was entertaining a thought so ridiculous, but after her last journey into town, she was prepared to think quite a few things. Most of them, she had to admit, had to do with those spots she was starting to see with alarming regularity in more places than she was comfortable with. It made her wonder if perhaps they had been there for far longer than she had realized. For all she knew, she'd been stepping in them for months without knowing it—

Nay, she couldn't bring herself to believe that. Not after what had happened to Acair. She could still see the agony on his face as he'd pulled himself away from that shadow and almost collapsed at her feet. If she hadn't spent so many years hauling bales of hay and endless buckets of grain, she likely wouldn't have been able to get him across the road, never mind to a pub where she thought they might hide.

She shook her head at that thought. Hiding. When in her life had she ever considered that to be necessary?

Acair had recovered, seemingly, and been busily shoveling manure ever since, but she'd found him more often than not shadowing her, especially after dark. She would have—and likely should have—told him that it wasn't necessary, but she'd never been able to get the words out. Whether or not those spots were evil, she couldn't say. She just knew she wanted to be very far away from them as soon as possible.

She glanced around herself, but saw nothing out of the ordinary. Acair wasn't leaning negligently against some topiary in the garden, watching over her. Then again, she'd left him listening to a very long list of things Doghail wanted him to do, so perhaps she would have her interview with her uncle and be back to the barn before he finished. Not that she cared what he did, of course.

She closed her eyes briefly and got hold of herself. Truly, she needed a change of scenery. The sooner she was able to manage it, the better.

All of which would start by finding out exactly how dire her grandfather's straits were and managing to endure her uncle's company without losing more than just her entire month's pay because she couldn't keep her mouth shut. The man didn't like to be argued with, to be sure.

She put her shoulders back, took a deep breath, then reached out and rapped smartly on the door. It wasn't opened right away, which gave her ample time to look at the façade of the damned place and wonder why she spent so much time looking at the outside of it instead of sitting comfortably on the inside of it.

The manor in which her uncle lived was so grand she never dared enter it without spending at least an hour cleaning up her boots. She had no clothes except what she wore for barn chores, but she at least attempted to make certain those were clean. In truth, it wouldn't have mattered what she did, her uncle would have still found her lacking. If there were one thing that could be counted on to remain steady, it was that Fuadain of Sàraichte would never be satisfied with anything that went on around him. 'Twas little wonder he had buried three wives and was well on his way to sending a fourth off into the ether.

The door opened slowly and doubtfully, if such a thing were possible, and she was left facing Fuadain's chief butler. He looked through her for a moment or two, then deigned to acknowledge her. He was little better than any of the rest of them, but at least he was more inclined to ignore her than sneer at her.

"Clean your boots," he commanded.

She suppressed the urge to take one of her boots and plant it firmly against his backside. The whole situation was ridiculous. They had been doing the same thing for so many years, she wondered why he even bothered to speak. She cleaned her boots of any remaining, imaginary dirt as instructed, then followed the butler into the house. Not by the usual way, of course, because that would have elevated her to a status she certainly wasn't entitled to. They went through the servants' quarters and up the back stairs. She couldn't remember the last time she'd been up the regular stairs. It might have been once during the first fortnight she'd been in Sàraichte. Certainly not since then.

There was a chamber just off the turn of the stairs where she paused. The butler paused as well, though he didn't look at her. She put a coin into his gloved hand, then waited as he moved on down the passageway. He stopped in an alcove where she was quite certain he'd hidden a bottle of His Lordship's finest port—for emergency's sake, of course—and proceeded to ignore her, as usual.

She made certain the passageway was empty, then opened the door and slipped inside the room.

It was a rather shabby chamber, all things considered. There was nothing to be done about that, though, so she didn't let it bother her. She walked over to the fire where her grandfather reclined, propped up in a chaise that was at least comfortable and solid. She pulled up a stool next to him and sat down.

"Good e'en, Grandfather," she said pleasantly. "How are you?"

He didn't look at her, his breathing didn't change, his limbs didn't move, but she didn't expect anything else. Why he lived still, she didn't know, but perhaps there was a purpose in it.

She took his hand and looked at him critically. He didn't look any different than he usually did, which left her wondering just what that serving maid had been thinking. Unfortunately, it wasn't as if she could linger by his side and see if she noticed anything too subtle for a quick, cursory glance.

She thought, not for the first time, that it was a damned shame that there was only magic in faery tales. Well, in those and perhaps a few less civilized parts of the Nine Kingdoms where she would never wish to go. What she needed, if she could have had anything, was a mage. The sort of man who, if he existed, could be prevailed upon to visit her grandfather and simply heal him with a mighty spell. She had no idea what that sort of business might cost, but perhaps an attempt could be made, for the right price.

It was, after all, why she saved her coins, ate the pot scrapings after the stable lads had taken their share, and wore the same clothes she'd been wearing for at least a decade. Everything she had, as meager as it might have been, she put toward her only goal, which was escape. They would escape and her grandfather would be whole. She would accept nothing else.

She took a minute or two to tell him of her most recent adventures, not because the conversation was anything but one-sided, but because she thought that somehow, he might be hearing what she was saying.

It hadn't always been that way. She had very vivid memories of her first encounter with Tosdach of Sàraichte. She had been brought inside the manor house, out of the rain, bedraggled, hungry, and exhausted. She honestly had little memory of the journey there save an endless, terrifying flight in the care of people she couldn't have identified at present if her life had depended on it. Her parents had been slain, her siblings gone, and she alone had been spirited off for reasons no one would tell her. She'd been a child, so she had learned to think of it as a rescue.

Her grandfather had met her in the garden, scooped her up into his arms, and carried her off to a spot in front of a hearth in a far nicer chamber than he enjoyed at present. He had sung her to sleep with a lullaby her own father had sung her countless times. She remembered nothing more of that day save that he'd promised he would take care of her.

The next morning, she'd woken to find him in his current state and her uncle looming over her with a frown of disapproval on his face. She had been told to dress herself, then she'd been taken to her accommodations in the stables and given a pitchfork.

She didn't like to think about that next pair of years.

She heard a footstep outside the door and realized she had stayed too long. She squeezed her grandfather's hand, then rose and hurried to the door. She cast one last look behind her but nothing had changed. Her grandfather still sat there, reclining, unmoving. He didn't look worse, though, which she supposed was the best she could hope for.

She wondered what that housemaid had seen.

She slipped out into the passageway, then followed the butler through increasingly opulent surroundings until he stopped in front of a heavy wooden door. He knocked and waited until he received a reply in the affirmative. He opened the door and stood back. Léirsinn took a deep breath, put on an appropriately submissive expression, then walked inside her uncle's study.

She ignored the richness of the surroundings. She'd been ignoring it for years because the thought of how much money he spent on his own comfort while ignoring the needs of those around him made her so angry she could scarce control herself. Better to simply keep her head down and be about the evening's business, silently.

Slaidear was there as well, looking grave. She nodded respectfully to him, because she had to, but it was almost all she could do not to point out to him what an idiot he was. Again, why he was in charge of her uncle's stables was something she had never understood. He spent most of his time trailing after her uncle, licking his boots. It earned him a very fine little house near the stables and definitely better food than the rest of them enjoyed, but she wasn't sure it could possibly be worth the price he had to be paying in pride.

She looked at her uncle and made him a low bow. "I have come at your pleasure, Uncle."

He was sitting behind a desk, the stable's ledger open in front of him. He didn't look angry, but Fuadain rarely looked angry. He simply wore a look of faint disapproval, as if everything around him just wasn't quite right.

"I see there is an accounting of less grain in the buckets than I should have expected to see," he said thoughtfully, trailing his finger along the page. He glanced at her. "Less."

"I apologize, Uncle."

"I'm not blaming you, of course," he said, "but the grain is gone and I didn't take it. You are the only other one with a key."

That wasn't true—Slaidear, for one, had a key to that tack room—but there was no point in arguing. She'd tried that for years but found it absolutely useless. There were times she wondered just what her uncle had been like as a child. Too coddled, perhaps, with everyone around him rushing forward to make certain he never had to suffer the consequences of his actions. The fault for anything was never his.

Slaidear remained silent, but that wasn't unusual. She was the target, always.

"I will take the discrepancy out of your pay," Fuadain stated slowly. "I have no choice."

"Of course," Léirsinn said.

"Do you have an issue with that, Léirsinn?" He closed the book with a snap that echoed off the paneled walls. "I provide you with food, a place to sleep, and a little occupation to keep you out of trouble. And now you're arguing with me over a few *coins*?"

"I wasn't arguing," she said quickly.

"Perhaps you forget that I am housing your grandfather."

"Your father," she said before she thought better of it.

He lifted a single eyebrow. "And so he is, though I keep him here for you, my dear, that you might visit him from time to time. It would be a shame if something dire befell him."

Worse than what has already? was almost out of her mouth before she could stop it. She bit the words back and forced herself to set aside all the things about the situation that didn't make sense to her. Tosdach was Fuadain's father and the rightful lord of Briàghde, or at least he would have been if he'd been able to move and speak. It made her wonder, also not for the first time, if her uncle might have had something to do with his father's condition.

"I understand you were in town a pair of days ago," Fuadain said, looking at her from under heavy eyelids. "An interesting place to go for your day of liberty."

"I go to see if there are tidings of new horses that might be interesting to you, Uncle."

Fuadain laughed shortly. "As if you would have any idea what a decent horse looks like. You're dismissed. Slaidear, see her out."

She nodded and waited for Slaidear to open the door for her. She nodded to him, because it didn't serve her to be impolite, then hastened down the passageway. She managed to get herself around a corner before she had to stop, lean against a wall, and force herself to breathe slowly and evenly.

So her uncle had indeed been watching her, but obviously more extensively than she'd suspected. For all she knew, he'd also seen her acting daft by avoiding those damnable spots on the ground. Perhaps he was making a list of all her offenses, a list he would then use to have her taken away and locked up somewhere.

She suppressed the urge to run and continue to run until she felt safe. She had to at least pretend that nothing had changed. The last thing she could afford was to have fewer coins to hand off to Mistress Cailleach at the end of every week or find herself in a place where she couldn't aid her grandfather.

She let out a shaking breath. She wasn't sure what she had expected, but she had gotten nothing more than she'd known in her heart she would get. She couldn't afford to take her grandfather from Fuadain's house and she couldn't doom him to whatever fate he would suffer if she went to look for work elsewhere. Leaving him in Fuadain's care was tantamount to turning him over to a madman. She was, as always, trapped. It was a pity those spots of shadow weren't gates to some other world . . .

She waited for another quarter hour to make certain her uncle and his lackey would have forgotten about her before she pushed away from the wall and made her way from the manor through the kitchens, as usual. She didn't breathe easily until she had left the house through a generally unused and very darkened doorway.

She supposed, looking back on that moment after she'd realized how close she'd come to walking into something foul in the shadowed garden, that it was a very good thing indeed that she had spent so much of her life avoiding notice. Notice was hard to avoid when one was in the middle of an arena, working a staggeringly valuable horse, but surprisingly easy in other places.

She froze and pulled back into the shadow of a column. She didn't recognize any of the voices murmuring not ten paces away from her, but she supposed that didn't matter. All she knew was that she most definitely didn't want them to know she was within earshot. Unfortunately, there was nowhere for her to go. She would have to stay where she was until they left first.

That was, she decided after another moment or two, going to be much harder than she'd suspected it would be. If those spots on the ground made her uneasy, that trio of men there left her terrified. Whoever they were and whatever they were doing, they were evil. There was nothing else to call them.

"He will need to die, of course."

"As you will, master. When?"

"As soon as is convenient. Before dawn, if it can be arranged."

Léirsinn felt a chill slide down her throat and settle in her belly. She could hardly believe her ears, but they were certainly working as they should have been. The men continued to discuss the death of that unknown man as casually if they argued companionably about where they might have supper later. But she knew, in a way she couldn't describe, that they weren't simply chatting for the sake of listening to themselves talk.

She wasn't afraid of anything, as a rule, and had faced down both men and beasts who should have sent her running the other way. But this was something else entirely. The first voice was so utterly devoid of emotion, so seemingly callous to a discussion of when it might be most convenient to end a man's life—

She froze. Her grandfather. They were talking about her grandfather.

"There is the matter of his magic, master," a third voice said.

"I have sensed no spells about him. He is unprotected."

Léirsinn suppressed the urge to rub her ears. Magic? How absolutely ridiculous. Perhaps the trio there was drunk, not evil. That wouldn't have surprised her—

"But if he wakes before the deed is done . . ."

"Then slay him in his sleep," the first voice said with a hint of irritation. "Acair of Ceangail is a mischief-maker and I don't want him nosing about. He's already seen more than I would have wanted him to."

Léirsinn shook her head. When that didn't clear it, she shook it again. Acair? They were planning to murder *Acair*?

Ceangail. So that was where he was from. She wondered why he'd been reluctant to tell her as much, but she was more curious still as to why the men in front of her would know not only his name but have an opinion about him. That place, Ceangail, sounded familiar, though she was the first to admit she never paid attention to anything outside the barn, only listening to talk of Sàraichtian politics when she had no choice. She'd known Acair was not a local lad, but apparently she had given him too little credit for an ability to pull up stakes and land somewhere else.

"But his magic, master," the third voice protested hesitantly. "And with his being who he is—"

There was the sound of a slap, but not one made by a hand across a face. Léirsinn had never heard anything like it before, but she heard the resulting gasping for breath at least one of the three was engaging in.

"Rein in your companion," the first voice said coldly, "lest he find himself in the same condition as Gair's son. Do not trouble me again until the deed is done."

The three shadows then simply vanished into thin air as if they had never been there. She realized quite abruptly that she was no longer standing. The ground was dependable, though, and she had no complaints about it under her backside.

It was the only thing that seemed solid, however. First her eyes had deceived her, then her body had deserted her. She didn't want to think what might be coming next.

Magic? Murder? Good hell, what next?

She clutched the gravel that had already cut into her hands. It should have been comforting but it wasn't, most likely because it couldn't erase the memory of the previous few minutes. She had heard voices, seen human forms, then watched three men disappear into nothing. She would have suspected that she was losing her mind, but she knew herself too well to believe that. She had seen what she'd seen—or not seen, as it were—and it frightened the bloody hell out of her.

At least they weren't coming for her grandfather.

The moment the thought crossed her mind, she thought she should have at least felt some sense of remorse for having thought it. Her grandfather was safe, but Acair was apparently not.

She sat in the same spot for perhaps half an hour before she thought she might be able to stand with any success. She pushed herself to her feet against the stone of the hall, scraping her back but unable to care. She was numb with something. Terror, perhaps. The terrible knowledge that she had grossly underestimated what the world contained, definitely.

She waited until she was absolutely certain she was alone, then she walked quickly but soundlessly back to the barn. She nodded

to lads as she passed them, ducked out of the way when she saw
Slaidear, then snuck into the graining room only to find Doghail
occupying her preferred spot.

"Hiding?" she asked breathlessly.

"Beat you to it, I'd say."

She rubbed her arms. "I believe autumn has arrived."

"It arrived last week," he said. He looked at her. "What are you
running from?"

She opened her mouth to reply, then realized she couldn't force
the words out of her mouth. She wasn't sure she trusted even
Doghail, a man she had known for the whole of her life in Sàraichte.
She attempted a smile. "Just work, as usual."

He didn't look convinced, but he was rarely convinced by anything he hadn't thought up himself. He only shrugged and rose.

"Have my spot."

"Oh, nay," she said, moving back toward the door. "I have things
to do."

He looked at her and pulled the pipe he was smoking out of his
mouth. "As you will, Léirsinn."

She nodded, then left him to his business. She slipped along in
the shadows, then got herself inside her own private little spot
without any fuss. She lit a lantern, hung it on a hook, then leaned
back against the door.

Her life had changed.

She didn't like change.

She suspected, though, she would like cleaning up the aftermath
of murder even less. She gave that a bit of thought, then considered
things she hadn't in years. Seventeen years, to be exact. She turned
an idea over in her mind for several minutes before she made a
decision. She hung up her cloak, then started digging.

She didn't have very many personal possessions. Indeed, she supposed if someone were to come and try to dig through her closet,
they would find only tack, cleaning rags, and, if they were exceptionally diligent, the key to her box. She, however, was past exceptionally

diligent and there was something she owned that not another soul alive would have found.

It cost her a good hour, several bruised and bloodied knuckles and fingers, and finally a hoof pick wielded with great vigor to dislodge the wall boards near the floor. She pulled them aside, then sat back on her heels and looked at the space she'd uncovered. She hesitated, only because what was wrapped in that cloth hadn't been disturbed in years. It didn't appear to be covered with venomous spiders or shadows, so she removed what she'd hidden there. Her hands were shaking as she unwrapped what she'd hidden, but she supposed that couldn't be helped. Once she was finished, she set everything down on the floor in front of her and looked at it all.

A crossbow lay there, along with two lethal-looking bolts.

The arrows were covered with something unusual, not unlike the shadows she'd seen, but this something was not evil. It was . . . perilous. At the moment, she wasn't sure there was a difference, but perhaps she would have a different opinion if she managed to use those bolts to fend off murderers.

She could hardly believe she was contemplating such a thing.

She had no idea who had given her what she currently held in her hands. The bow and bolts had simply been inside her wee chamber one day, as if she had taken them out to examine them and not had the time to put them away. Perhaps there was no use in speculating on their origin. She had a weapon and obviously a great need for—

She stopped herself in mid-thought and wondered if she had gone mad.

What she'd heard in the garden had been nothing more than three men who'd obviously had too much to drink. For all she knew *slay* was just another way of saying *I think I know a lad we can rob for the sport of it.* Those men were probably the same ones Acair had played cards with several nights ago. Or perhaps he had since been to a different tavern where he had encountered a few gamblers who had been less-than-pleased with his skills. Perhaps the men she'd just heard had had retribution on their minds and were expressing it with ale-inspired enthusiasm. *Slay* didn't mean actually do Acair in, it likely meant *lighten his purse.*

She didn't allow herself to think too hard about the fact that she was using the same excuse more than once, rephrasing it to make it sound more reasonable.

She gave herself a good shake and forced herself to address the rest of the recent madness she'd encountered. She hadn't seen those lads disappear, of course. She had simply been overcome by worry for her grandfather and taken by surprise by what she'd heard. Indeed, 'twas possible that she had blacked out for a moment or two. Hadn't she found herself rather suddenly on the ground? All that talk of Acair and magic and things that couldn't possibly find home in her safe, sensible world had been too much for her and she'd been overcome. All she needed for everything to return to normal was a good night's sleep.

Surely.

She propped bow and bolts up in the corner, replaced the missing board, then sat down on her stool and decided that she could perhaps take a few minutes and wait for the barn to settle down before she turned in. Sitting there with a cross-bow nearby was . . . well, it was daft, but for all she knew, those men had known she was there and they'd been talking about murdering Acair to keep her from learning of their real purpose which was to steal a horse. Being prepared for that sort of thing was prudent.

She considered, then moved the bow and bolts so they were right next to her. She pulled a horse blanket over herself and her weapons and supposed that was enough secrecy for the night. If anyone came inside her closet, they would only think her chilled, not daft.

She closed her eyes and leaned her head back against the wall, but knew she wouldn't sleep.

Eight

❧

I t was a dance, that slipping inside a place to do a bit of burgling. Unfortunately, Acair found himself inside the great house of Briàghde not for such a lofty activity, but rather a pedestrian bit of eavesdropping. Less challenging, true, but the sort of thing that proved rather valuable from time to time.

He stood in the shadows of an alcove and studied the passageway he'd watched Léirsinn walk down earlier. He had, in the past, done more than his share of both listening to conversations not meant for him and nicking things that didn't belong to him, so his present activity was nothing out of the ordinary. What was different, however, was why he was about his goodly work.

He was following her because he was—and he could hardly believe he was admitting it—worried about her.

But what else could he have done? Doghail had filled his ears full of all manner of tales about Fuadain's treatment of her, told him in even more detail of Léirsinn's interviews with her uncle at the end of every month, and then left him to consider what he could do about it. Short of turning the lord of the manor into a mushroom— he was seriously revisiting his need for a Cothromaichian spell of essence changing to make that sort of change permanent—he feared he was unfortunately quite powerless to aid her. That didn't set well with him at all.

Concern. He shuddered delicately. Even his mother might have approved of the sentiment, which he knew should have made him very nervous indeed.

He rolled his shoulders as carefully as possible to ease the stiffness there. Whatever else that damned spot on the ground had done to him, it had left a lasting impression on his form. He didn't dare hope that protecting Léirsinn and doing a robust bit of snooping would provide him with any answers as to what those shadows were, but stranger things had happened. He knew, because he had been the instigator of stranger things happening to others. That the like was coming back to bite him in the arse was rather unpleasant.

A year. He could hardly believe he'd agreed to a year in his current locale, a year without the basic necessities of life his magic could provide him. 'Twas utter madness, but there was a spell slinking along behind him doing its own impression of a burglar that told him the madness was going to be his to enjoy for quite some time to come.

Oh, the retribution he would exact . . .

He forced his attentions back to the mischief at hand. No one ventured forth from any of the chambers he knew were occupied, which was something of a frustration. His disembodied companion didn't offer any suggestions, which left him, as usual, the only one in the area with any decent ideas. He leaned back against the wall and suppressed a sigh. Reduced to putting his ear against a door. He couldn't remember the last time he'd stooped so low.

He paused. Very well, he could remember with perfect clarity the last time he'd donned black, slid tools for the picking of locks into his pocket, and scaled the outer walls of an impenetrable fortress in an utterly magickless fashion in order not to set off any alarms put in place for just such a lad as he, but perhaps that was a memory better left unexamined at present. In the end, he'd managed to get himself inside the place, had an unfortunate encounter with the lord of the hall in that lord's private study, then barely

escaped—eventually—with his life. Again, a rumination better left
for a more comfortable locale.

At present, he was safely inside another man's domain and that
man was nothing more than an annoying gnat compared to what
he'd faced in the past. There was mischief afoot and the pretentions
of a minor lord in a backwater hellhole weren't going to keep him
from finding out what he wanted to know.

He glanced at the butler he'd left sitting, quite senseless, in a
comfortable-looking window seat. He'd appropriated the man's
jacket without compunction, a jacket which of course didn't fit his
fine form as it would have if he'd been able to do a bit of altering
on the fly, as it were. At least he'd done the old fellow the courtesy
of clipping him under the chin before he pilfered his coat instead
of simply ripping it off him and daring him to do anything about
it. Acair suspected the man would wake with something of a headache, which was likely less than he deserved. Perhaps he would
think twice before he was rude again to a stable lass who didn't
deserve that sort of treatment.

He sighed at his seemingly uncontrollable instinct to display
chivalry where Léirsinn was concerned, then took up a tray topped
by a decanter of port and a trio of crystal glasses. He considered
the possibilities, then turned and headed down the passageway as
if he knew where he was going.

His first stop was the room Léirsinn had first exited. He
knocked, waited, then decided perhaps the libations were more
desperately needed than he might have thought. He opened the
door, then peeked inside the chamber.

He almost dropped his tray in surprise.

Very well, so the very quiet conversation he'd utterly failed at
making out between Léirsinn and the chamber's occupant had been
rather one-sided. He was sure he'd distinctly heard her call the man
grandfather. It wasn't possible that man lying there before the fire
was the man she'd been talking to, was it?

He moved inside the chamber, set his tray down on a handy side table, then closed the door behind him. He found himself quite at a loss for words, which was alarming in and of itself. What he was seeing was the last thing he'd expected.

Léirsinn's grandsire, if that's who that was, was completely incapacitated.

Acair glanced about the chamber and was genuinely surprised by how shabby it was. These were servants' quarters, surely not worthy of use by the lord of the hall's father. He frowned thoughtfully as he walked across the threadbare carpet to have a closer look at the lone occupant.

The old man was lying on a chaise in front of the fire, wrapped in blankets, scarce breathing. He seemingly couldn't even move his eyes, though he did occasionally blink. Acair thought it best to offer some sort of assurance.

"I mean you no harm—"

Ah, hell and damnation. He leapt back across the chamber and had his tray back up in his hands before the door finished opening. It was Léirsinn's uncle, Lord Fuadain. The man looked at him with a surprise that wasn't of a pleased sort.

"What are you doing in here?" he demanded.

"Wrong chamber, milord," Acair said, ducking his head.

Fuadain backhanded him. Acair couldn't remember the last time he'd been struck. A spell of death was halfway out of his mouth before he realized what he was doing. He kept his head down, congratulated himself on not dropping his burden, then made Fuadain a small bow.

"Thank ye for the correction, milord," he said in his best working man's accent.

"See that I don't find the need for the like again. Now, get out."

Acair got out, but he would be damned if there wouldn't be some repayment for that. He stood outside the door, shaking, silently cursing everyone he could think of until he settled finally on a certain Cothromaichian prince and his elven companion.

He walked a bit farther down the passageway, just to give himself time to cool his temper. He turned the corner the first chance he had and found himself facing what appeared to be Fuadain's suite of rooms. He looked about himself to make certain he was alone, then poured the port into a pair of boots that had been left out for a polishing, shoved the decanter and glasses into a planter, then suppressed the urge to take the silver tray and fling it at someone.

Truly, it had been a trying few days.

He got hold of himself, then went back to the corner near where he'd come from and listened again. He could hear only the faintest murmur of voices, but 'twas obvious Fuadain hadn't left the grandfather's chamber. He slipped back down the way, stopped in front of that worn door, and put his ear to the wood.

"And so you see, Tosdach . . . why . . . die."

Acair cursed the builder of the manor for having seen to the privacy of any given chamber's occupants so well, then gave up when he heard voices coming closer to the door. He headed off down the passageway as if he had business elsewhere, but he was considering things he didn't particularly want to.

Who needed to die? Whilst he wasn't opposed to sending a ruffian or rogue elf speedily off into the next life, he liked for there to be some reason for it. That had to have been Fuadain speaking. The man was a bastard of the first water, brutal to his servants, and unkind to his relatives.

He suppressed the urge to find a polished glass and have a good look in it. 'Twas possible he might have recognized those traits because they were his own, but that was something he could think about later. That list of items was growing very long, but he would simply put *think about the list* on the bottom of it and it would endlessly rotate, leaving him too busy watching that rotation to give the items it contained any thought.

He waited a moment or two longer, then left down the same passageway he'd walked up. The whole evening had been a completely useless exercise, but the truth was, he was not at his best. That encounter with the shadow had left him far more drained than he wanted to admit. All he truly wanted to do was find his pile of straw and cast himself down upon it.

There was something going on inside that manor house, though, a plot that he could smell the rankness of from fifty paces. And if there was anything he knew the stench of, it was a vile plot. Fuadain was obviously in the thick of it, which was worrisome. Unfortunately, he could do nothing else that night.

He trudged back to the barn and sought out his scrap of floor, hoping rather uneasily that he hadn't given in too soon.

He woke to darkness. He didn't awaken during the night usually, a gift no doubt reserved for those with either a clear conscience or none at all. The one thing he could say for certain was that he could see in the dark as well as any feline, a rather useful gift he had from his father, the old rapscallion. It usually served him quite well.

At the moment, it only served to let him know he was a heartbeat away from death.

There were two mages there, hovering over him like specters, very thorough and businesslike spells of death on their lips. He hardly had the chance to remind himself that he couldn't unleash the same without that damned spell that followed him falling on him, much less weigh the certainty of that against the possibility that the two trying to slay him might not be able to manage it.

And then, quite suddenly, they seemed to be doing less floating and more falling. He watched with a good deal of surprise as each mage in turn flinched as if he'd been struck, flapped around a bit, then landed in a heap, one atop the other. Acair sat up, knowing he was gaping and wishing he could look a little less astonished.

A match sparked in the darkness, a terribly pedestrian way to call fire, but he wasn't going to argue. The light the subsequently-lit lamp gave wasn't at all steady, but he suspected that might have been thanks to the trembling of the hand holding that lamp. He looked to find Léirsinn there, looking as if she were the one who had just narrowly escaped death.

She was also holding an empty crossbow.

Acair scrambled to his feet with no grace whatsoever, took the lamp from her and hung it on a hook, then caught the crossbow as she dropped it.

"Are they—" She looked to be attempting to swallow. "I mean, are they—"

"Dead?" he supplied. "I certainly hope so."

She looked horrified. "I didn't mean—"

"I should damn well hope you meant to," he said. He shivered. "A fortunate thing you came along when you did."

She was silent for so long, he began to wonder if there were things going on that he might be interested in knowing. He looked at her in surprise.

"Did you know that they intended?" he asked. "Do you know *them?*"

"Must we discuss this now?"

He glanced at the heap of dead mage, then back at her. "I'm not sure there would be a better time, but I've been known to be wrong about that sort of thing before. What do you think?"

"I think I might be ill."

Well, she certainly looked as if that might be the case. He didn't suppose she would do any more damage to his poor floor than had already been done, though, so he mentally gave her permission to vomit if she needed to and turned his mind back to the matter at hand.

"I wonder who those lads were," he mused.

"I overheard someone talking in the garden," she managed. "About you. I didn't see who it was, but it might have been those two." She wrapped her arms around herself. "I couldn't believe my ears, if you want the whole truth."

So he wasn't as anonymous as he'd hoped he would be. He
frowned. "Did they name me by name, or was it just general mayhem they were about?"

"I'm not sure," she said miserably. "They said much I didn't hear
and more I heard but didn't understand, but there was definitely quite a bit about murder and magic and . . . aye, they used
your name."

Perfect. He sent a silent curse wafting heavenward in the direction of a certain pair of busybodies, then looked at his savior. "You
didn't see them?"

She shook her head. "I just heard them." She looked at him then.
"They were here for you, weren't they?"

"'Tis possible," he said, because it was the best he could manage
on short notice. Aye, those two were obviously there for him, but
the question was why?

His list of enemies was extremely long, something he'd been
quite proud of in the past, but he couldn't bring to mind anyone
who would know where he was at present save Rùnach and Soilléir
and they wanted him alive to enjoy his current straits. His Aunt
Cailleach knew where he was, but it wasn't possible she would have
sent mages to kill him. He was family. Possibly undesirable family,
but she had little room for criticism there. If she'd wanted to off
him, as she was wont to say, she would have gotten her hands dirty
herself. Nay, those lads weren't from her.

He hadn't seen anyone else he knew, he hadn't spread his presence about, and he hadn't dropped pieces of mischief along behind
him like bread crumbs.

He had, however, touched a patch of darkness.

And he was looking at a woman who perhaps hadn't been as
discreet about being able to see them as perhaps she should have
been.

"Did you tell anyone?" he asked.

"Tell anyone what?"

"What you can see."

She looked at him as if he'd just announced he was, well, who he was. "Are you daft? Of course not."

"Why did you tell me then?"

She started to speak, then shut her mouth. She seemed to be casting about for something say, then finally shrugged helplessly. "I don't know. I thought you might understand, though I've no idea why."

"You're wise beyond your years," he muttered. He studied the mages on the floor at his feet, still as death, then looked at her. "You're certain you didn't tell anyone else about those spots? Servants? Stable boys? Potted plants?"

"Nay, none of the three, though I can't imagine what a potted plant would reveal."

"It could be a mage disguising himself as a plant."

"You are mad," she said without hesitation. "How could a man turn himself into a plant?"

There was no point in even starting down that road. "I have an overactive imagination."

"I'll say."

He watched as the mages in front of him began to steam. Interesting. He realized, as they began to simply vaporize, that the woman beside him was about to faint. He caught her before she fell, sat down rather heavily on his stool, then landed on his arse as the stool collapsed under their collective weight. He clapped his hand over Léirsinn's mouth as a courtesy.

She put her hand over his hand, then clutched his arm with her other hand. She was strong, he would give her that, but he'd be damned if he squeaked. She pulled his hand away slowly.

"Holy hell," she breathed.

"Hmmm," he agreed as the vapors swirled up into the faint light from the lantern. They made a keening sound that was almost too faint to hear, then vanished. He nodded abruptly. "Well, that takes you out of the running for lass-least-likely-to-kill-a-mage. Nicely done."

"I don't believe in mages," she wheezed.

He nodded toward the spot where the bodies had lain. "What would you call that, then?"

"Part of my nightmare?"

"Believe that, if you can." He patted her back. "Time to go."

She looked at him. He noticed that she had freckles sprinkled across her nose. The quintessential country miss, to be sure. The quintessential country miss who had apparently just encountered things she had likely never dreamed about even in her nightmares.

"I thought mages were just make-believe characters in those tales told down at the pub," she said very faintly. "Or in faery tales. If they existed in truth, I assumed they lived in nasty places up north where I never want to go."

He had no comfort to offer her on that score so he sighed lightly and attempted a shrug. "Apparently not."

"I thought magic was limited to charms and love potions and silly things that old women invented to keep food in their pantries," she continued, as if she hadn't heard him. She looked absolutely shattered. "You know. Lies told to give people comfort."

He met her eyes. "I'm afraid not."

She looked at him as if she'd never seen him before. "They said you had magic."

"Lads say many things," he said dismissively, "most they don't mean."

She pulled away from him and scrambled to her feet. She looked at him in alarm. "Who *are* you?"

"I can't say."

"Why would those—" She pointed at the spot where the pile of mage had most recently resided. "Why would those things want you?"

He heaved himself to his feet, not entirely happy with how drained he still felt. "I can't say that either."

The lump of cloaks shifted suddenly—one last farewell, he supposed—and he found himself with his arms full of horse girl. He wasn't sure he had ever over the course of his very long, very

selfish life ever offered another soul comfort unless it was to wish
them a good journey as he sent them off to hell with a well-crafted
piece of magic. He wasn't quite sure what to do with the woman in
his arms, partly because he wasn't at all good at that sort of thing
and partly because he was mightily distracted by a piece of stool
that was still poking him in the arse.

He reached around and removed the splinter. He was half
tempted to save it so he could use it to drive home a fitting piece of
retribution somehow, but he wasn't sure it was worth holding on
to for as long as he feared he would need to.

So, lacking anything else better to do, he put his arms around
Léirsinn and rocked her just a bit. He wasn't sure how to do it
properly—and suspected he was doing it poorly—but what else
could he do? His mother rocked herself, but she did that whilst
muttering incantations over a bubbling pot, so perhaps she wasn't
one to emulate.

He soon felt very silly indeed, so he patted Léirsinn again and
set her away from him.

"Time to go."

She blinked. "Go? What in the hell are you talking about?"

"We must leave and the sooner, the better."

She looked at him as if he'd lost his mind. "I'm not going
anywhere."

"I suggest you rethink that," he said seriously. "I am guessing—
and only guessing, mind you—that those two were sent after me
because I disturbed those spots you don't want to talk about. And
I'm not the one who saw them first, if you see what I'm getting at."

"But I'm no one," she protested. "Just a stable hand."

"If I were you, I wouldn't want to remain here to see if I might
be mistaken about that."

"I'm not going anywhere," she said desperately. "I have respon-
sibilities."

He studied her for a moment or two in silence, glanced at the
pile of cloaks still lying near where he'd almost died, and wondered

just how he was going to talk sense into the woman standing in front of him.

"If you stay, things could go very badly for you," he said finally.

"I'll take that chance. You go ahead and scamper away, though, if you like."

Her words stung, mostly because he was fairly sure she'd muttered *coward* under her breath. He reached down, picked up her crossbow, and handed it to her. "Interesting weapon, that. Best fetch the bolts before someone else does."

She clutched the bow to her. "I will, thank you. Enjoy your life."

"I'll think of you fondly whenever I breathe."

"You do that." She moved past him to collect the crossbow bolts, then paused before she touched them. She took a deep breath, gathered them up, then turned to look at him. "Why are you still here?"

He refrained from comment, partly because his offended feelings—and there weren't many of those, truthfully—never stayed pricked for more than a moment or two and partly because he knew she was speaking from a place of fear. He couldn't blame her for that, but the truth was, he had to leave—and quickly. It was one thing to hide in a barn and try to be a regular sort of bloke. It was another thing entirely to have a pair of mages know who he was and want to kill him.

He was starting to have a bit of sympathy for those he had stalked over the course of his long and illustrious career of making hay. That feeling unsettled him almost more than knowing how close he had come to dying a handful of moments ago. Things had to change. The next thing he knew, he was going to be offering to hoist a sword in the defense of a horse miss.

"Don't let me keep you."

He shot her a look. "You go first."

"Nay, you. I'll follow right behind."

He blew his hair out of his eyes, then turned and left what had served as a bedchamber of sorts for far too long. He realized after a handful of steps that he'd forgotten his cloak, which he supposed, in hindsight, was what kept him from walking them both into something that might have gone badly for them.

Three men were entering the far end of the passageway, obviously coming inside to see to something. Acair backed up a pace or two into deeper shadows. He felt Léirsinn's crossbow in his back and hoped she would have a moment of altruism and refrain from using it on him. He held his breath as the men came their way. Fortunately the trio of whoresons continued on past them as if they'd noted nothing amiss, which Acair supposed had been the case.

"Move," Léirsinn whispered. "I want to see what they're planning."

"A quick return to bed after they scrape the manure from their boots would be my guess," he murmured.

"They're in a barn," she said pointedly. "Unless the world has changed a great deal in the past hour, they're here for a horse. I have to see which one they're looking at."

Acair sighed. Horses. Women. Intrigue. Soilléir couldn't have given him three things more bothersome if he'd planned it, which Acair wasn't at all sure he hadn't.

He stepped aside. "Best of luck to you."

She hardly glanced at him as she pushed past him, which he supposed shouldn't have offended him. She was a horse miss, he was a powerful mage with plans to rule the world when his sentence of having to be pleasant had ended. He couldn't have cared less if she looked at him or not. There were princesses and noblewomen and even the occasional wizardess who found him quite to their liking—

He rolled his eyes. He was losing his wits, that was it. Too much do-gooding was, as he had noted on more than one occasion, very bad for a man.

He took a moment to consider what he might do next. Perhaps he could find a wooded area and live off the land, robbing the occasional unwary nobleman, and refraining from killing the ones who annoyed him. That would surely satisfy that annoying finger-waggler from Cothromaiche and then he would have some peace and quiet.

That might also mean that he would no longer be troubled by manure, minor noblemen with delusions of grandeur, and red-haired stable lassies who had somehow found their way under his skin and troubled him even in his dreams. The sooner he was away from all three, the better.

He swung his cloak around his shoulders and strode off toward the nearest exit. His future awaited and it would no doubt be one full of deeds worthy of song.

Nine

Léirsinn wondered when her life was going to return to normal. First it had been the shadows that weren't quite shadows but apparently existed with enough substance to affect those who came near them. Then it had been eavesdropping on men she couldn't and didn't want to identify, men who had been instructed to kill Acair because he had—she had to take a deep breath to even dredge up the word—magic. That right there should have been enough to send her off either into gales of laughter or straight to her bed. What a daft idea. Men were men, horses were horses, and things were as she had come to count on them being.

But Acair? Magic?

She pushed aside the thought, though it was difficult to push it far enough away from her to make her comfortable, mostly because she had actually seen two men hovering in the air over Acair like a pair of vultures. She hadn't imagined it, she had seen them there. And if she hadn't taken that bloody crossbow and put arrows into both those monsters, they would have slain Acair.

She would be long in forgetting that sight.

She was fast coming to the realization that she would have to concede that there were things afoot in Briàghde, things she didn't want to get close to. And if murder and mayhem were the order of the day on her uncle's land, who knew what sorts of things were going on in greater Sàraichte? Given the fact that Mistress Cail-leach and Acair seemed to know each other, perhaps there were things in town that might make her uneasy as well. Who knew how far the madness extended?

At least Acair was gone. One less distraction for her. He would be safely off doing whatever he did with whatever supernatural abilities he might or might not have had and she would return to her sensible, normal life. Perhaps even those odd shadows would disappear, then no one would even give her another thought. It wasn't as if she intended to say a damned thing about them. Perhaps with a bit of luck, she would find a way to earn more and do that more quickly, then she could also be away from Sàraichte and at peace.

She slipped in and out of the shadows, a task made much easier by the utter lack of light in the barn save for where her uncle stood with Slaidear. Their companion had obviously been sent on ahead in the company of Doghail, who had obviously been roused from his bed for that purpose.

She stopped far enough away from her uncle that she was fairly sure he wouldn't see or hear her, but she could certainly see and hear him.

"My lord," Slaidear said slowly, "I don't see—"

"Slaidear, your task isn't to see, your task is to do," Fuadain said. "If you won't kill her yourself, find a man in the village willing to see to it. A rough sort. You know the type."

Léirsinn could hardly stop herself from making a noise of hor-ror. What was he planning now, to start slaying horses? She quickly ran through the list of mares and wondered which one Fuadain could possibly be talking about—

"But Léirsinn is your niece."

Léirsinn froze. She would have rubbed her ears to make sure they were functioning properly, but she found she simply couldn't lift her hands. It was all she could do to allow them to remain by her sides and shake.

"My *niece* sees too much," Fuadain said sharply.

"She sees too much of what, my lord?"

"Things you don't need to know about," Fuadain said shortly. "If you want to make it as clean as possible, slay her, then blame it on that new lad. Kill him afterward." He paused. "Odd, isn't it, that name? Acair?"

"Very odd," Slaidear agreed.

"I wonder . . . nay, the one I'm thinking of would never find himself laboring in a barn. Now, if you haven't the stomach to see to this yourself, trot off to the village and find someone to do it for you. I'm off to sell a horse."

Léirsinn started forward to protest only to find there was a hand suddenly on her arm, pulling her back into the shadows. She went, because apparently she had lost all ability to do anything but stand about stupidly, stunned by what she was hearing. The only thing she could say for herself at present was at least she hadn't fainted. She thought that might be due to Acair's holding her up.

She somehow wasn't surprised to find that he had returned and rescued her. It was becoming something of a bad habit for him.

She didn't argue when he pulled her behind him. She would have told him she had no intention of forgoing the opportunity to use him as a shield, but she couldn't form words at the moment. She leaned her head back against the wall and fought the urge to indulge in some sort of display that wouldn't have done her credit. Histrionics, or a swoon, or perhaps simply bursting into loud, messy tears.

Acair was very still and his stillness rapidly became hers. His hand on her arm was warm, all things considered, and gave her an unexpected measure of comfort. The beating of her heart was so loud in her ears, though, she feared that everyone in the barn might be able to hear it. She forced herself to ignore it and see if she could hear any more details from the men conversing about her death, but they had obviously finished and were both off to see to their tasks. Acair fumbled for her hand.

"Let's go," he whispered.

"But—"

"Come *now*. You don't want to have anything to do with any of this."

She would have argued a bit longer, but it wasn't every day that she listened to someone plot her demise. She slipped through the shadows with Acair, remaining on her feet only because he kept her moving as surely as she would have a recalcitrant colt. Terror was apparently a very good means of inspiring all sorts of things, mostly flight. She was fairly sure she didn't take a decent breath until they were outside the barn and out of sight behind a pile of lumber intended for future fencing. She looked at Acair.

"Well, I'm here," she said, taking hold of the first thing that came to mind. "What do you want?"

He looked at her in disbelief. "I want you not to be dead."

"Very kind of you."

"Trust me, I'm not usually this altruistic."

"Then I've caught you on a good night," she said. "But you needn't worry. I'm not going to die."

He turned to face her. "Weren't you listening?" he asked in astonishment. "In truth? Léirsinn, they weren't making a jest at your expense. Your uncle wants you dead!"

"He wants everyone dead," she began, then a thought occurred to her that she likely should have had long before then and that was that perhaps Acair and her uncle knew each other far more intimately than she suspected. She looked at Acair and felt as though she'd never seen him before.

"Oh, nay," he began. "Don't start with that."

She backed away. "He said you were going to kill me—"

"Nay, he said someone *else* was going to kill you," he said, reaching for her, "and make it look as if I'd done it."

She held him off. "You could be lying."

"I don't lie. 'Tis my one and only virtue." He took a step closer to her. "Think it through, Léirsinn," he said urgently. "If I were going to kill you, why would we be here right now?"

"So I won't bleed on the barn and leave Doghail to cleaning it up on the morrow?"

He didn't smile. "If I wanted to do you in, I wouldn't have brought you outside where you could run. I would have pinned you in a stall where you couldn't escape."

"You sound far too familiar with that sort of strategy for my peace of mind," she said, her teeth beginning to chatter.

"I'm familiar with many things that would make you uncomfortable, but let's discuss those later. For now, believe me when I say that I don't want you dead. Unfortunately, others apparently don't share that sentiment, which is why we need to go *now*."

She wished she could stop shivering. She couldn't believe she was having a conversation that involved death, more particularly *her* death. It felt as if she'd stumbled into a play where she'd been drawn up onto the stage and forced into a role she'd never wanted and didn't know how to escape.

"Let's go."

She realized Acair was still talking to her and she'd missed what he'd been saying. She started to walk, then what he'd said actually made sense to her. She pulled up short.

"Go?" she echoed. "Go where?"

"Out of Sàraichte, obviously," he said. "I don't think either of us is safe here any longer. I didn't intend on bringing company along with me, but 'tis obvious you can't remain behind."

"But I'm not going anywhere with you," she said in surprise. "I can't leave my grandfather."

"Don't worry about him," Acair said dismissively. "He'll be fine."

She could scarce believe her ears. "You're daft," she managed. "They'll kill him as well!"

"Killing your grandfather is the last thing Fuadain will do," he said seriously.

"But why would they keep him alive if they were willing to kill me?"

"Leverage," he said. "They believe you know too much about

things you apparently shouldn't, which is why they want you dead. If you flee, they'll want you to come back here so they can, again, see you dead." He shrugged. "Leverage."

She felt something slide down her spine. "How would you possibly know that? Are you in league—"

He shook his head sharply. "I don't know your uncle, but I know his type very well."

"But I can't leave my grandfather," she said firmly. "I have a responsibility to keep him safe."

"At this point, neither of us can keep him safe here," he said. "We definitely cannot bring him with us."

She looked at him in surprise. "I didn't ask you to."

He looked around him, as if he feared something might be listening, then he took her by the arms. "I *can* save him, but not at the moment. I definitely can't save him if I'm dead. You can't save him if you're dead either. Hence our need for saving our own sweet necks first."

"You're speaking in riddles."

"I know," he said grimly, "and it's giving me pains in my head." He blew out his breath. "I am almost an entire bloody year away from being free of a charge laid on me. Once that sentence is served, I can return and see to your grandfather."

"Sentence?" She looked at him narrowly. "You've escaped from some sort of gaol, haven't you?"

"I would say I'd walked right into one, but you can think of it however you care to. As for your grandfather, if you can trust me, I can help you. But I can't help either of us if we're dead, which is why we need to escape Briàghde before your uncle realizes we've left."

"Who *are* you?" she asked. "More to the point, why do I keep asking?"

He smiled. She had to admit that he was terribly handsome when he frowned, but when he smiled . . .

She shook her head to clear it. Perhaps there was magic after all and she'd been put under some horrible spell that was attempting to lead her away from her very sensible existence where the only sort of males she had to encounter had four feet instead of two. The current one walking on two looked around him, then leaned closer as if he had some terrible secret to share.

"I shouldn't tell you this," he whispered, "but I think I might be allowed this much." He paused. "The truth is, I am a mage."

She blinked, then smiled. "Of course you are."

"You don't believe me?" he asked in surprise.

"Of course I don't believe you," she said with a snort. "Magic? Are you utterly mad? I think what you're suffering from is an enormous ego and delusions of grandeur, but perhaps that's too blunt."

"I deserve this," he muttered. "And somewhere, someone is having himself a jolly good laugh over it all." He looked at her. "Believe me or don't, at this point it doesn't matter. All that matters is that we get away from this place as quickly as possible."

She stopped just short of wringing her hands. "But how do I leave him behind?" she whispered. "He's helpless."

Acair chewed on his words until he seemingly found ones he could spew out. "How long had his illness been coming on?"

"I can't say with certainty," she said slowly. "He took care of me the night I arrived and seemed perfectly sound. The next night he was in his current state."

"And what happened to you when he had this sudden decline?"

"I was sent to the stables."

He closed his eyes briefly, then put his arm around her shoulders and turned her away from the pile of timbers. "I didn't have a very good look at him, but I'm guessing the cause of his illness wasn't natural, if you know what I mean."

"I'm ignoring that because it's ridiculous."

"All the more reason to have a bit of faith in it," he said firmly. "And if this makes you feel any better, I think the more notice you take off him and put on to yourself, the better off he will be. Fleeing Sàraichte is a fine way to do it."

She didn't want to agree that might be true, but she could see the sense in it. She considered, then looked at him. "Where are we going to run *to*?"

"I haven't decided yet. I don't have very many safe harbors."

The poor man. "Because you're a mage," she said slowly.

"A bad one."

"As in, you don't mage very well or you do it too well and people don't like you for it?"

He shot her a dark look. "You aren't taking me at all seriously, are you?"

"Of course not."

"What of those lads you slew in the barn?"

"Oh, those," she said. She took a deep breath. "I don't know what to think. I could have been imagining them."

"Believe that as long as you can." He looked to his right, swore, then pulled her back behind the fencing. "At least one of our friends is off into the night. Your uncle, by the looks of him."

"That's Falaire he's taking," she began.

"Get back down," he whispered fiercely. He peered over the top of the planks of wood, then ducked back down himself. "Damnation, this is a new wrinkle I didn't see coming."

"What new wrinkle—and believe me, I don't want to be interested in your answer."

"That man with Fuadain? He's the servant of one of the masters at the schools of wizardry."

She had to clap her hand over her mouth to stifle her noise of disbelief. She settled for a silent rolling of her eyes. "Again, men in pointy hats with delusions of grandeur. I'm sure they think they have magic as well—wait." She looked at him in surprise. "Someone from Beinn òrain is taking my horse?"

"I believe *has taken* is closer to the mark."

She cursed quietly. "What will I do now? I know I don't own him, but I've known him since he was a foal. Any bad manners he has, I taught to him!"

"I knew it," Acair said, smiling at her briefly. "As far as horses go, I think he's a good one."

"He's peerless," she said. She stood up. "We must stop that man from taking him."

Acair caught her by the arm. "What if we could escape Sàraichte and fetch your horse with one perilous, dangerous journey?"

She glanced at him. "Perilous and dangerous?"

"Two different things, but equally thrilling when viewed in the right sort of light."

"I think you're daft." She watched Falaire until she could see him no longer. "Even if I could follow him," she managed, "how would I rescue him?"

"Why don't we worry about that when we get to Beinn òrain?"

"Get to Beinn òrain? I can't even get myself to a decent pub!"

"I'll see to it."

She turned away from a horse she loved like her own soul and looked at Acair. "I don't have the money to repay you and I don't like not making my own way."

"I understand that," he said, "for I live by the same code. When I'm free, I'll stock a fine stable with a score of peerless horses and you can train them all. That will be repayment enough. Until then, we have more dire things to worry about."

She hesitated. "But the rest of the horses—"

"Someone will continue to feed and water them." He looked at her seriously. "Trust me, Léirsinn."

She felt Acair take her hand and found no small measure of comfort in the fact that his hand was warm. If he were unnerved, he certainly didn't show it.

Trust.

She supposed she had no choice. If she left, she would have to leave her grandfather behind. If she stayed, she would lose her horse and no doubt her life. There seemed to be only one clear path, as draped in shadow as it was.

She nodded, then followed Acair into the darkness.

. . .

The port itself was not a pleasant place. It was farther east than the market itself and definitely in a nastier part of town than even she was accustomed to. It looked less dangerous when she found herself accompanied by someone who didn't mind throwing the occasional fist to keep drunkards and fools at bay, but not by much.

She paused in the shadows with Acair and watched as Falaire was led toward a relatively large boat. Her uncle was nowhere to be seen.

"That boat there looks as if it intends to go out to sea, not up the way to Beinn òrain," she ventured.

"I would agree with you, but I know who bought your horse. It's heading upstream." He nodded up the quay. "We'll take that boat there that looks to be casting off soon."

"I have no coin."

"Not to worry," he said. "We'll have gold soon enough."

She wasn't sure how he intended to see to that given that she doubted anyone would be interested in playing cards that early in the morning—or late at night, depending upon one's point of view—but Mistress Cailleach's suggestion continued to sound in her head like an annoyingly loud supper gong.

Trust.

It looked like she wasn't going to have much choice.

She walked with Acair through a press that consisted mostly of sailor types, though she supposed there were passengers enough among the lot. Passengers and loudmouthed rich men, as it happened, which she discovered were not necessarily the same thing. She watched a portly, angry man shouting at his serving lad and wondered what the poor boy had done to displease his lord so thoroughly. Acair seemed to be so distracted by the shouting that he lost his footing and tripped into the man.

"Oh, desperately sorry," he said, straightening the man's clothes and smiling. "Obviously the riff-raff haven't been at their work of sweeping the streets, have they? Bloody lazy whelps."

Léirsinn tried not to gape. Acair sounded as if he'd just exited some king's audience chamber. Where he'd learned that posh accent, she couldn't have said, but he was definitely using it to its full capacity.

The gentleman so bumped looked at Acair and his scowl lessened a bit. "This entire place smells strongly of fish," he announced.

Acair smiled. "Doesn't it though? I prefer the good, clean smell of Durialian dark ale myself, but that's just me."

The man gave Acair a suddenly friendly look. "I compliment you on your taste, good sir. I have a glass of dwarvish brew as often as possible, but I must say I would travel quite a pretty league for a robust apple beer from Gairn."

And with that, they were off comparing drink until she thought she might like them to stop. She could hardly believe that the man she was watching charm and amuse a soon-smiling landholder was the same man who had been shoveling horse manure the day before, but obviously he had hidden talents.

She stood to the side and waited until Acair had apparently chatted himself out, listened to him express his sincerest regrets that nay, unfortunately he didn't have time for even a brief mug of whatever could be found locally, then followed after him as he started off toward the other boat.

"And what did that accomplish?" she whispered, catching up and walking next to him.

He dangled a small leather bag in front of her. She felt her mouth fall open.

"You *robbed* him?"

"I offered him an unthought-of opportunity to do a good deed," he corrected. "It is his, as they say, pocket money. That bloody satchel he has strapped over his ample middle is where the true cache of coin resides."

"How do you know?"

He shot her a look. "I'm not sure you want to know that."

"I believe you have a very checkered past."

"And I believe you have a finely honed ability to sniff out a scoundrel at fifty paces. Sniff later in this case. We'll have to hurry to make that boat."

"You didn't save the lad."

He stopped and frowned. "What lad?"

"That man's serving lad," she said. "That lord will beat him to death when he finds his coin missing, you know."

Acair studied her for a moment or two with a look she wasn't sure she cared for.

"Did he," he said very slowly, "ever lay a hand on you?"

"My uncle?" she said, her mouth rather dry. "Once or twice, before I learned to duck."

"Then he will pay, once or twice," Acair said calmly. He took a careful breath. "I'll remember that, trust me. As for the lad, I'll go see to him if you insist."

"I insist."

He shot her another look, shook his head, then turned and started back through the crowd. She propped herself up against a handy building and watched him until she couldn't see him any longer. She felt suddenly quite cold, as if she were being watched. She wished for a cloak, or less lamplight, or someone to stand behind, but there was none of those to be had easily or quickly. She shook her head. It was terrible how quickly one could accustom oneself to things one shouldn't, like safety or protection or a man who made a very handy shield.

She had to admit she was rather glad to see Acair coming back her way. He caught her hand and continued walking, leaving her trotting to keep up with him.

"Well?"

He blew out his breath. "I saved enough for our passage and a meal, handed the lad the rest, and sent him on his way whilst his master was off relieving himself. Satisfied?"

She smiled. "Thoroughly."

"The things I do for you, woman . . ."

"Good deeds are never wasted."

"Ha," he said. "That one counts at least for today, then." He glanced at her. "I hesitate to think about what I'll find myself doing tomorrow."

She couldn't answer, mostly because they were now facing what she supposed might be charitably called a boat and the reality of her situation was staring her in the face.

She was leaving the only home she could remember, she was leaving behind the one person she'd sworn to protect at any cost, and she was heading off into the dawn with a man who was currently paying for their passage with stolen coins.

What in the hell was she thinking?

Acair took her by the elbow and looked at her. "Walk on, gel," he said quietly. "You know what lies behind."

Unfortunately, she did. She nodded, then forced herself to put one foot in front of the other until her feet had carried her where she had never thought to go.

Trust.

It was more difficult than she'd suspected it would be.

Ten

There was truly no other place in the whole of the Nine King-doms so full of reprobates, layabouts, and villainous characters of all stripes.

And that was just the schools of wizardry.

Beinn òrain as a whole wasn't any better. Acair walked up from the quayside through a maze of streets he wouldn't have batted an eye at a fortnight ago but now found less to his taste than he might have otherwise. He was quickly coming to the realization that his fists were not as mighty as his spells. He should have insisted that Soilléir allow him to conjure up a sword before sending him off into the fray.

Swords were not his weapon of choice, of course, but he did know which end to hold one by and could generally do a bit of damage with one under the right circumstances. At the moment all he had to hand was a dagger he had pinched from a sobbing and profoundly annoying black mage he'd stepped all over several months earlier as he'd been taking a bit of a breather from all that apologizing. He'd left the lad the rest of his gear, which he had supposed at the time could be construed as a moment of charity. And what had it gotten him? A relatively dull dagger down the side of a boot that was definitely not his. Unsurprising.

He glanced at Léirsinn, but she was doing nothing past watch-ing their surroundings with wide eyes. Then again, it wasn't as if she'd said all that much on the journey north, a horrific, interminable amount of time spent upon a barge that only spared itself from being called a raft by the fact that it had two-foot-high sides all around. It had been powered by magic, but that magic had been so feeble, he'd been tempted to volunteer to take up a set of oars. As it was, he'd sat with Léirsinn at the back of that damned raft and counted the hours until the torment would end.

The only good thing to emerge from the journey had been knowing that they had arrived before Droch's man, which meant they wouldn't be encountering the master of Olc anytime soon. If there was one thing Acair was sure of, it was that Droch of Saothair never would have lowered himself to meet anyone at the dock.

That was just as well given that he didn't particularly care for an encounter with him whilst he was in his current state. Any other time? Droch wouldn't have elicited more than a yawn. But now, when he had no magic he could use and Droch had a very long list of insults to repay him for, aye, he would be happy to get in and out of Beinn òrain as quickly as possible.

He had every intention of doing just that. He needed to find Soilléir, inform the man curtly that the current situation was absolutely unacceptable, then demand that that bloody spell of death be sent speedily on its way to the nearest rubbish heap. It was one thing to be shuffled off to arguably the most tedious spot in the whole of the Nine Kingdoms and be required to labor with his hands, it was another thing entirely to be leaving bits of his soul behind whilst being stalked by lesser mages he couldn't fight off with even the mildest display of annoyance.

He was finished with the ridiculous business he was embroiled in. Soilléir had best agree or he would be finished too. There was still a country full of Cothromaichian magic just ripe for the poaching and Acair had far more experience with how to fail at that sort of thing than he'd had a pair of years before. If there was anything he thought he could do better with practice, it was the acquisition of unlimited power.

But until that happy moment arrived, he would find a decent place to sleep, eat something that hopefully wasn't infested with vermin, then present himself at Buidseachd's gates at first light. He was finished.

He stopped at the first reasonable-looking place he could find— *The Uneasy Dragon*—and took a chamber under the first innocuous name that came to mind. He shepherded Léirsinn up the stairs to a decently clean if not sparsely furnished chamber that at least had no spots of shadows. It was full of the echoes of centuries of magic made within its confines, but he wasn't unaccustomed to that sort of thing. It was safe enough for the moment.

"I can't do this."

He let the curtain drop—no sense in not having a look at the garden below to make certain there weren't mages with evil intentions lurking there—and looked at his companion.

She was wringing her hands. He'd never seen anyone do it— well, that wasn't entirely true. He'd watched a few grown men wring their hands when faced with his mighty magic. He wanted to feel guilty about that, but—well, he likely should have felt terrible about the terror he had inflicted, but there was nothing to be done to change the past. Yet another thing to add to the list.

"You can't do what?" he asked, dredging up as much patience as possible. He hadn't eaten and he hadn't slept. Both tended to make him short-tempered, but he supposed that was nothing he should apologize for.

Apologize? He shook his head. Truly he was beginning to feel like his underpinnings were eroding. What next? Voluntarily traipsing all over the Nine Kingdoms, looking for things to do to better the lives of those he encountered?

"This," she said, waving her hand about. Her hand was trembling badly. "I can't do this. I want to go home."

He sat down on a chest near the window and looked at her. She was standing in the middle of the chamber with her arms wrapped around herself. He suspected she was as weary as he was, for she certainly hadn't slept on the boat. She looked like a country miss who had just seen her first sight of a large city and hadn't liked it one bit.

"Have you ever been away from Sàraichte?" he asked.

"Not since I arrived," she said, then she turned and walked to the door.

He leapt up, reached it first, and put his hand on the wood. He had business to see to and no time to be chasing women who could apparently scarce bear the sight of their own village square, never mind anywhere more sophisticated. He paused and frowned. Of all the things he could call Beinn òrain, *sophisticated* was the very last.

Truly, he needed to be back to his accustomed way of living.

He looked at the woman standing not a pace away from him, shaking, and thought she looked like nothing more than a poor, terrified filly, being asked to do more than her heart could bear. Something welled up in him that left him profoundly uncomfortable. Pity, perhaps. A strong desire for even stronger drink, no doubt.

"Why don't we have supper first?" he offered, latching onto the first reasonable thing that came to mind. "I find things always look better after a decent meal."

She didn't release the door latch. "Let me go. I'm going home."

He tried another tack. "I won't stop you if you truly want to go," he said—and he could scarce believe he was being so conciliatory—"but I will remind you of what you left behind."

"Everything that was familiar," she said, glaring at him, "thanks to you."

"Me?" he echoed in surprise. "Why me?"

She swore and turned away from the door. He watched her cross the chamber to stand in front of the fire and thought he might understand why none of his brothers had wed. Women were . . . well, he didn't care to repeat what his father called them. His mother referred to the fairer sex as mysteries that only few men were clever enough to solve. That was his mother, though, and what she said about men was likely nothing useful to repeat at the moment, either. 'Twas a wonder he managed to converse with anyone at all with any success given his parental examples.

He leaned back against the door and watched Léirsinn of Sàraichte wring her hands a bit longer. As he watched her, it occurred to him what was wrong, something he hadn't considered before.

She was truly afraid.

He felt something in him shift. To be honest, he didn't like the place where that shifting had occurred—in the vicinity of his heart—and he knew exactly whom he would eventually repay for that, but there was no denying that something in him was moving about in an untoward way and affecting his good sense. For the worse, no doubt, but there you had it. He was being blown about by the winds of events he couldn't control and now he was having feelings of . . . compassion? Sympathy?

Indigestion?

Hard on the heels of that unsettling development was the realization that he had never suspected the woman in front of him might be afraid of anything. She handled enormous, biting beasts without even pausing. She bit her tongue and took speech from her uncle he wouldn't have listened to more than once without retaliating, all to save her grandfather who would likely never speak again.

She was, he had to admit, rather spectacular.

He took a deep breath and walked across the chamber. He pulled up a chair for Léirsinn and invited her to sit. He, the youngest natural son of the worst mage in recent memory and the beloved youngest brat of a woman who he was certain gave Soilléir of Cothromaiche nightmares, perched on a stool and attempted a soothing noise.

"Are you choking?" she asked.

Damnation, he was so much better at terrifying those he met. "Something like that," he said quickly. He cleared his throat and tried another tack. "Léirsinn, you can't go home."

"Why not?"

Well, because they would slay her the moment she set foot inside that damned barn, that was why not. She knew as much, so why she was refusing to let that desire to stay alive be her guide, he couldn't fathom. He hardly dared follow where his thoughts were now leading him, but he found he had little choice. Either she missed her grandfather, she missed her horses, or she couldn't stand the sight of him.

He could understand any of the three—well, perhaps not the last, but the woman was obviously not thinking clearly—but the truth was, they had to press on. He had business in Beinn òrain that needed to be seen to as quickly as possible and she needed to get as far away from her uncle as she could manage.

Once he had his magic back, he would rid the world of the lad who was putting those damned shadows on the ground, instruct her uncle in proper comportment when it came to nieces and servants, then see Léirsinn and her grandsire comfortably settled in a place far less tedious than Sàraichte. Then he could take up the reins of his own vile life again and turn his mind to things that horse gel there would laugh off whilst tossing that glorious red mane—

He drew his hand over his eyes. He had to find Soilléir and soon. He couldn't take much more of looking at the woman in front of him.

"You're afraid too."

He blinked, realizing only then that she was studying him and he was likely babbling his idiotic thoughts aloud. "Ah," he said, scrambling for anything to say that sounded reasonable. Of course he wasn't afraid. He was never afraid. "I am afraid for you," he said finally, because that was the truth. "I want to keep you safe."

"Do you?" she whispered.

"Of course I do. Besides, if you leave, who will see to rescuing your little horse? He'll just bite me if I try."

"You were in earnest about that?" she asked, looking as if hope might just bloom in her with enough encouragement.

Bloody hell, his life was intolerable. He rubbed his chest in annoyance. That damned Fadairian spell of healing was like a worm, eating away at his flesh and his good sense.

"Well, no sense in not making the attempt at least," he said. "He's obviously very valuable, which might be of some use to you in the future. If the man who's purchased him—Droch of Saothair—wants him, there must be a good reason. Perhaps he's a magical pony."

She looked at him in silence for a moment or two, then she smiled. "Thank you. A bit of humor was helpful."

Good hell. He stole a look or two about the chamber, wondering where that shapechanging Cothromaichian whoreson had to be hiding, no doubt in a form that wouldn't be readily spotted. Perhaps Soilléir and Rùnach both were lingering, as the saying went, as flies on the walls. Acair vowed that if he saw anything with wings, he would use the bottom of his boot to its best advantage.

He put on a smile and didn't bother to set Léirsinn straight on matters of magic. She looked as if she might bolt at the slightest misstep as it was.

"Well," Acair conceded, "he is a very fine horse, as I said and as far as I know. Indeed, I'm sure there are many who might call those fine qualities *magical*." He saw no point in telling her that Droch never would have purchased a horse that couldn't—

He felt himself go very still. Well, save his stomach, which was rumbling, but that couldn't be helped.

Droch had sent his most valuable man all the way to Sàraichte to purchase a horse when he likely had scores of horses being brought to Beinn òrain by all sorts of noblemen and mages, horses that most assuredly would have had a few extra talents perhaps not visible to the ordinary eye.

Why would Droch have looked in Sàraichte for something to add to his collection?

There was something foul afoot. He could smell it from a hundred paces.

"Acair?"

He pulled back on his rampaging speculations with a skill

perhaps even Doghail might have commented on, then looked at Léirsinn.

"Was I muttering?"

"Looking horrified, actually."

"I'm hungry," he said, "and I made the mistake of revisiting the memory of that rubbish we ate on the boat." He shuddered. "Awful."

"Hard to ruin apples and cheese," she offered, "but possible, apparently."

"Don't remind me," he said. "You know, I think supper might be what we need at the moment. Then, whilst we're lingering in this lovely city by the river, I thought I might pay a polite social call to someone I know."

"You know someone here? Is this where you're from—nay, one of those men—" She had to take a deep breath. "They said you were from Ceangail."

"A little nondescript, nasty place in the mountains," Acair said dismissively. "I wouldn't suggest a visit. I do have acquaintances here, though. The man I need to see is a friend of one of my half-brothers."

"What does he do?"

She was obviously trying to distract herself. Acair watched her smooth her hands over her leggings and rest them on her knees as if it were something she had to think very carefully about in order to manage.

"Ah, what does he do?" he said, wondering just what he was going to have to do not to be distracted by her. "He meddles, for the most part. He's also a master at the schools of wizardry."

She blinked. "A master? A master of what?"

"Do-gooding," Acair said distinctly. There was no point in attempting to describe whatever other rot Soilléir dabbled in. He highly doubted Soilléir could describe it himself with any success. "I think we could pay him a small visit in the morning, nip over to the stables afterward and make certain your horse is being well cared for, then we'll do what you want to."

"In truth?"

Why did she have to look so damned grateful? He supposed she was very near to the end of whatever tether she held on to, which was something he couldn't blame her for. He had been at that place once or twice in his life as well, though he had at least had magic to help him cling to his sanity. She had only her will.

"In truth," he said. "We'll see to it all on the morrow."

Her fingers that had been clutching her knees relaxed a bit. "So, how do you know all these people?"

The spell in the corner cleared its throat pointedly. Acair didn't bother to offer a rude gesture in return. More alarming than that piece of unconcern was the fact that he hardly noticed that vile spell any longer unless it announced itself. In truth, he hardly recognized himself any longer.

He shrugged and dragged himself back to sifting through what he could and couldn't say. "My father travelled a great deal and I carried his bags for him."

"Is that the truth?" she asked.

"Almost."

She sat back in her chair, which he thought might be a good sign. "So, I suppose we find this friend of your brother's—"

"Half-brother's," he interrupted.

"Half-brother's," she said. "Then we find my horse, then I go back home."

There was no point in arguing with her over that at the moment. Perhaps later, after she'd had something to eat, a decent night's sleep, and a gentle reminder about why they'd fled Sàraichte in the first place.

"I need to learn how to play cards," she said thoughtfully.

He realized he'd missed something. "Cards?"

"So I can earn enough gold to rescue my grandfather."

He could think of worse ways to earn the odd coin. "I think you might be very good at it," he conceded. "You have an honest face, which would serve you well."

"Will I need to learn how to cheat?"

He started to tell her nay, then realized what she was implying. He scowled. "I don't need to cheat."

"You're that skilled?"

"Six brothers," he reminded her, "and an indeterminate number of half-brothers. I learned early on to read faces. And count what had been played, if you must know the truth of it."

"No sleight of hand?"

"As tempting it might have been, nay," he said. His brothers would have abused him mightily for that sort of thing and he had wound up on the bottom of the pile often enough without that provocation. That had only lasted until he had taken them one by one and helped them realize that he had become the sort of man who didn't put up with abuse.

"You're cursing."

He blinked, then sighed. "A terrible habit." He rose. "I'll find food and drink. Do not leave."

She looked up at him. "I've exchanged one gaol for another it seems."

"You've forgotten what you heard in the barn in the middle of the night, obviously."

She nodded. "And so I had. Thank you."

He suppressed the urge to curse again, wondering why in the hell he bothered with manners given who he was, then left the chamber before he suffered from any more altruistic impulses.

He didn't need to bother with cards given that he had, on the way to the inn earlier, lifted the fairly substantial purse of a lesser master he'd bumped into—ill-gotten gains on that man's part if ever there had been any. He ordered a meal to be sent upstairs, ordered one for himself, then bought a round for a group of students who looked as if they needed it. He'd been inside Buidseachd himself on more than one occasion and sympathized with them.

He sat down before he did anything else utterly out of character.

He watched Léirsinn's supper be carried upstairs, then attended to his own. The food was better than he had expected, but his expectations had been very low indeed.

It was profoundly odd, he decided as he lingered over a mug of reasonably tasty ale, to be in a city where he'd been so many times before yet have everything be different. He was not sweeping in on the wings of an evil intention, fully prepared to do whatever was necessary to achieve his dastardly ends, he was . . . well, he was fully prepared to do something dastardly and admittedly he was there to save his own sweet neck, but he had taken a chamber for a rustic miss and he wasn't going to force her to sleep on the floor. If that wasn't altruism in action, he didn't know what was.

He studied without excessive interest the souls gathered about the tables in the gathering room. Most he could tell were from Buidseachd, given their dress and conversation. He supposed a single day of liberty was the best they could hope for in such a place. At least the food was better at the pub than what they were eating up the way. He'd filched more than one meal at the castle and regretted it each time. He'd half suspected there was someone there who purposely ruined as many suppers as possible, just to give the lads something proper to complain about.

There was a table more sparsely populated than the rest, but he understood that. It looked to be a few older, perhaps lesser men associated with Buidseachd. Servants or minor magelings hoping to better their lot, no doubt. Acair wished them well and left them to it.

Until he realized his name was being bandied about.

He normally would have been satisfied with being spoken of as the creator of all kinds of trouble, but he was appalled to realize how annoying it was being credited where credit was definitely not due. He was being blamed for mischief he never would have bothered with. It was insulting, truly.

He had to put an end to the farce before he lost all claim to his former character. He was a black mage, damn it to hell, and one that gave other black mages pause. His father might have been terrifying and his mother unnerving, but he was all that and definitely more when it came to instilling fear and a desire to immediately do whatever he asked.

He downed his ale, set his cup down, then left the gathering chamber. He would find Soilléir, get him to take that damned spell back, check on Léirsinn's horse for her—that was the very *last* pleasantry he would engage in—then he would be back to his usual way of carrying on.

Murder, mischief, and mayhem. He would embrace all three with renewed affection and commitment.

He had to, before he completely lost himself.

Eleven

Léirsinn stood near the chamber door and watched Acair look out the window. It was almost exactly what they'd been doing the day before. The only difference now was she'd had a pair of remarkably tasty meals and a good night's sleep. She wasn't sure what Acair had had. He'd returned from the gathering chamber the night before in a foul mood. If he'd been a horse, she would have put him in his stall and left him to sort himself on his own. Since that had seemed a rather useful idea, she'd put herself to bed and left Acair to work through whatever was troubling him.

His mood hadn't improved much after breakfast, but she supposed she couldn't blame him. He was obviously concerned about something and she suspected she knew what it was. As much as she tried, she couldn't forget the sight of those two things hovering over him . . . how long had it been? Two nights ago? She thought it might have been no longer than that, but that night plus the journey to Beinn òrain, then a very uneasy sleep the night before—it was all a bit of a blur. If Acair wanted to look out the window and make certain he wasn't being stalked by more of those things, he was welcome to his looking.

"Let's go," he said, dropping the very worn curtain.

She said nothing, mostly because she was afraid if she started talking, she would never stop. It had been the most unsettling pair of days she could ever remember having had. Perhaps she was more a creature of habit than she'd ever dared suspect.

The discomfort had started the moment she'd hidden behind that pile of fencing and watched someone walk off with a horse that wasn't hers by right but definitely was by affection. Her unease had only increased as she'd boarded a boat that could hardly have been seriously considered the same, spent the entire trip wishing she'd had the courage to turn and heave her guts over the side, then disembarked in a city that made Sàraichte look like a pristine habitation for elegant faeries from one of the tales she remembered her parents having told her as a child.

"Are you unwell?"

She realized that she had simply come to a stop on the stairs. She wondered if she had been babbling aloud. She looked at Acair.

"I'm not sure."

He held out his hand. She looked at it, then at his face.

Magic? Him?

He reached for her hand and pulled. "Don't start with those looks. If we can gain this man's chambers, I promise you a very stiff drink. Do you a world of good, I'm sure."

She walked because he gave her no choice. She supposed she didn't want to remain behind, especially when she realized that a pair of men standing at the bar, nursing mugs of ale, were looking at her.

"Keep walking," Acair said under his breath. "Don't look at them."

She was happy to comply. She left the inn with him, then kept her head down as he traded places with her and put her farthest away from the street. She would have thanked him for the courtesy, but the truth was, speech was simply beyond her. She was so far out of her normal routine, the routine she'd been engaging in on a daily basis for the past eighteen years, she hardly knew what to do with herself. She was absolutely adrift in a sea full of creatures she fully expected to drag her under at any moment.

The cobblestones were slick and treacherous under her boots, something that only added to her discomfort. She watched them for most of the journey up the hill, desperately latching onto something that looked familiar. She stopped Acair before he walked into a pool of shadow with a casualness that should have alarmed her. That she was only tempted to yawn should have alarmed her more.

Acair caught himself in mid-step, then blew out his breath. "Thank you. The last brush with one of these was rather unpleasant."

And it had led to those two creatures trying to kill you, was what she thought to say but didn't. She simply walked around the shadow, then continued up the way.

At one point, she hazarded a glance at where they were headed, then realized that she hadn't paid any heed to the castle as they'd been on the boat and she definitely hadn't seen anything of it from their chamber. She stopped still and gaped. She had never in her life seen anything so large.

"Tatty old thing, isn't it?" Acair remarked. "Don't know how anyone manages to live here."

Tatty was not the word she would have chosen, but what did she know? She nodded because speech was beyond her, then continued on with him right up to the front gates. She wasn't sure how he expected that anyone should let either of them inside, more particularly she herself, but he seemed to have no fear of being rebuffed.

He glanced her way. "My welcome here may not be warm."

She opened her mouth to speak, then shut it. She was so far out of her depth, all she could do was look at him and hope he wasn't walking her into some sort of terrible trap from which she would never emerge. He smiled briefly, then turned and knocked on the gates.

She was accustomed to barn doors, not castle entrances, but she had to concede that those gates didn't look particularly intimidating and there was no portcullis that she could see. Perhaps the garrison was very fierce and the lords who sent their sons there had no fear for their safety. In truth, what did she know of great men and their progeny save Fuadain? He had a handful of sons, but they obviously didn't care to pass any time with their sire for she hadn't seen them in years.

A guardsman appeared suddenly, simply bristling with weapons and surliness. "Who are you?" he demanded.

"Er, Buck," Acair said.

"Buck," the man repeated. He looked over his shoulder. "Another of 'em. He looks to be kin of the one we let in last year."

"'Tis a family name," Acair said quickly. "There are many of us."

Léirsinn would have asked him what the hell he was doing, giving a name that wasn't his, but what did she know of these sorts of things either? 'Twas obvious that Acair moved in a level of society she didn't understand. At the moment, she thought she might be rather happy about that.

Another guardsman came eventually to take the first's place. He looked equally surly yet far less prone to surprise. He sized Acair up, then pursed his lips.

"Family name?" he asked skeptically.

"I fear it might be," Acair said, "amongst some of my kin."

"I believe I know the kin that name might find itself amongst," the man said, "and I'm not sure I haven't seen you here before a time or two as well." He considered Acair a bit longer, then shrugged negligently. "Him you're looking for isn't here."

Acair looked at him in frank surprise. "How can you possibly know who I'm looking for?"

"Because I am far less stupid than my fellows, which is why I'm captain of the guard and not one of the regular lads," the man said. "If you don't mind my saying so."

"Oh, please, say on," Acair said in exasperation. "Where the hell is he, then, if not here where he's supposed to be?"

"Off on holiday."

Acair's mouth moved but no sound came out. Léirsinn thought he might be the one who needed a stiff drink sooner rather than later. He finally shook his head enough that apparently he shook sense back into it.

"On holiday where?" he demanded.

"Tor Neroche," the guard captain said with a bit of a smirk.

"Of course," Acair said bitterly, "where else?"

"Seanagarra?"

Acair shot the man a look that should have had him backing up a pace or two. Léirsinn was very impressed that he didn't so much as twitch. There was a fellow who obviously dealt with his share of feisty stallions. She had no idea why Acair found that name so offensive, but what did she know of anywhere outside her barn? She was moving in a world she wasn't accustomed to.

She wasn't sure she liked it, truth be told.

"Your humor is misplaced," Acair said coldly.

"And I'm safely tucked inside the gates, which offers me the safety to exercise my tongue even at the expense of someone like you."

Léirsinn wanted to hold up her hand and ask exactly what the man meant by that but before she could, Acair was distracting her with some extremely vile language.

"That coward," he said finally, apparently having exhausted a rather long list of slurs. "What gives him leave to take a bloody *holiday*?"

"Are you going to be the one to tell him he cannot?" the guard captain asked politely.

"Aye, the first chance I have!"

"Feel free to do so, my—"

"Buck," Acair interrupted. "Just Buck."

"Buck," the man repeated slowly. He shook his head. "Not very original, but I don't suppose you care about my opinion. Since you've made the trip here, would you care to see anyone else, Master Buck?"

"Thank you, but nay."

Léirsinn wasn't sure what she expected, but to have the conversation end without any further niceties was definitely not it. Acair nodded briskly to the guard, nodded at her, then walked away. She didn't bother with the guard. She ran after Acair because she wasn't about to be left behind in a strange city where she knew absolutely no one, had absolutely no money, and didn't have a bloody clue how to get herself back to where she'd come from.

Acair paused, waited for her to catch up to him, then cursed and strode furiously down the street.

"Who is Soilléir?" she managed, running to keep up with him.

"No one of import," Acair snarled. "Just a bloody—ah, damn it all, what next?"

Kitchen refuse, apparently. Léirsinn couldn't say she was growing accustomed to hiding behind heaps of things with him, but she could say it was becoming something of a bad habit. She was, however, growing unfortunately quite adept at leaping over things to use them as shields. She forced herself to breathe evenly until she caught that breath, then she looked at Acair.

"The things we're using as barriers seem to be growing increasingly fragrant," she noted.

"I'm happy to see your sense of humor is returning."

"I'm numb."

"That works as well."

She hazarded a glance between piles of rotting vegetation. "Who is that we're hiding from?"

"Droch of Saothair," he murmured. "Not a nice man."

She couldn't even nod. She wasn't one to exaggerate or fall into needless faints, but if she had been that sort of woman, that man standing there a dozen paces from them would have inspired both. The evil simply poured off him, as if it were a foul sort of perfume. It was all she could do to breathe without screaming.

She distracted herself by trying to decide which feeling was most loudly clamoring for her attention. Revulsion was near the top of her list, but fear was there as well, but perhaps that fear was quickly morphing into terror. Acair reached for her hand and held it, hard. She nodded and clapped her other hand over her mouth. It seemed prudent.

Acair didn't seem to need to watch the man they were hiding from. He simply bowed his head and breathed lightly—

His fingers were suddenly **wrapped** around her wrist. She understood why only after she realized she was halfway to her feet. She crouched back down next to him, but he didn't release her. He looked as if he fully expected that man to leap over the rotting vegetables and half-broken crates and strangle them both. Given how unpleasant Droch seemed, she thought she might understand. She caught sight of him thanks to a hole in a pile of molding greens and studied him with as much objectivity as she could manage.

The truth was, he was very handsome in a distinguished, aloof sort of way. He reminded her a bit of some of the men who came to look at her uncle's horses, only there was something about his aura that made him seem so far above any of those other men, she was a little surprised Fuadain sold any of his ponies to anyone else.

Droch frowned, then walked on. Acair waited a few more endless moments, then let out his breath slowly and looked at her.

"He is the master of Olc, if you're curious."

"I wasn't," she managed, "but what is Olc?"

"Magic," he said.

"Rubbish."

"Do you think so?" he asked. "Even now?"

She shivered. "He could just be the sort of man to beat his horses and his servants. That's evil enough for me."

"I imagine he does that too," Acair said, "but along with that, he is the keeper of a very dark magic. Useful, of course, but not all that welcome in polite salons."

She looked at him then. "And you've spent enough time in polite salons to know?"

He lifted an eyebrow. "You continue to think of me as a country mouse."

"I don't know any city rats. You're the best I can do."

He smiled. When he smiled, she had to admit, she wanted to sit down. The truth was, she could see him in any number of very polite salons, surrounded by very polite misses who had likewise decided they could admire him more easily if they were sitting down instead of falling at his feet in an artful swoon.

"Let's just say that that man is one you don't want to encounter in a darkened alleyway. If you ever do meet him, feign death."

She had the feeling she wouldn't have wanted to meet that man anywhere, which led her to thinking that she would be far better off going back to Sàraichte. Perhaps her uncle could be placated so he didn't want to murder her any longer. In time, she might even learn not to feel pain when she walked past Falaire's empty stall . . .

Acair straightened. "He's gone and so should we be, and quickly."

"I don't like scurrying from place to place," she said.

"I agree, actually, but things are what they are at the moment." He pulled her up to her feet. "I need a place to think."

"The inn?"

"We can't go back there."

"But our gear—"

"What we had will be gone. Remember those lads we saw in the gathering room?"

"Aye, unfortunately."

"Droch's spies," Acair said shortly. "They'll have ransacked our chamber by now, looking for anything useful to identify us."

"Why do they care?" she asked, then she realized quite suddenly what the lay of the land was in truth. She looked at Acair. "That man, Droch. He wants you, doesn't he?"

He shrugged. "He's not fond of me. If he had the chance to do me an ill turn, he would take it simply out of spite, but he wouldn't go out of his way to hunt me down. But if he can harm you in the bargain, he would do it because he's that sort of man."

"I don't think I like this place," she managed.

"Very wise," he said. "Let's go see about your horse, then we'll find a place to hole up for a bit. I think I'm finished with crouching behind piles of rubbish."

She had to agree that a bit of fresh air would be very welcome and she quite happily left that pile of rotting veg behind and walked quickly with Acair, trusting he would be able to find her horse.

The truth was, whilst she would happily look at Falaire, she had no idea what she would do about him when she saw him. The thought of him going to a man like that Master Droch was almost more than she could take.

She turned away from the thought because there was nothing she could do about it short of stealing her horse and then what would she do? She couldn't feed herself, much less a stallion. And it wasn't as if she could steal him, then ride him back to Sàraichte. She didn't want to admit it, but the place was a hellhole and she had a relative there who apparently wanted her dead. She could only imagine his fury if she arrived at the barn with a horse he'd sold and she had subsequently filched. The whole situation was untenable—

She realized quite suddenly that she had run into Acair's arm and he had jerked her behind him. She almost went stumbling into the side of a very derelict building as a result, but when she looked over his shoulder, she decided abruptly that that might have been preferable to what she was facing—or not facing—at the moment.

Master Droch stood there. He had simply materialized out of thin air, which she knew was impossible. It should have been impossible, yet there he was.

Impossible, but undeniable.

"I heard that you were in town," Droch said in a voice that was so polite as to leave ice hanging in the air as an accompaniment. "I am surprised you haven't yet come to pay a call on me."

"Oh, so many things to do, my lord," Acair said in much the same tone. "One has regrets, of course, but circumstances ofttimes override social niceties."

Droch stepped closer. "You little whoreson," he hissed. "If you think I'll overlook your last visit to my private apartments, you're as foolish as your sire."

"I vow I have no idea what you're talking about."

Léirsinn realized Droch had moved to where he could see her and she hadn't been paying enough attention to avoid it.

"Ah, who is this?" Droch purred.

"No one," Acair said briskly. "A whore. You don't want her."

Léirsinn would have protested, but she had the distinct feeling that the less she said, the better off she would be. She slid behind Acair, which she knew was becoming a bad habit, but he was tall and unafraid and made an extremely handy shield.

"That one is far too pretty to be a whore," Droch said. "I wonder what she is to you?"

"Again, nothing," Acair said. "Now, if you'll excuse us, my lord, we'll be on our way. Wouldn't want to keep you from your important business of making the world a better place."

"Scamper off now, if you like," Droch said dismissively. "I won't lower myself to brawl in the street with someone of your ilk. But you will pay, Acair, and dearly for your cheek. And if you think I don't have the stomach or the power to see you repaid properly, think again."

"I wouldn't think either, my lord," Acair said politely. "If you'll excuse us?"

Léirsinn found herself pulled to Acair's right as he brushed past Droch, which left her quite happily with Acair between her and someone even she could sense was, well, evil.

She honestly didn't care for how often she'd used that word of late.

Acair continued on at a brisk walk until they turned the first corner they came to, then he pulled her into something just short of a run. She was grateful, all things considered, that he'd kept her to his right side then pushed her in front of him, which had the benefit of keeping her out of Droch's view. She found she couldn't speak. She scarce managed to breathe. All she wanted to do was find somewhere to hide.

"Don't," he said quickly.

"Don't what?"

"Don't look back."

"I wanted to see if he was following us."

"He doesn't need to follow us."

She felt her mouth become very dry. "Why not?"

"Again, not something you want to know right now. Just keep going."

She didn't want to know why that was. She had no idea who Droch was in truth; she just knew that when she was within ten paces of him, she wished she could lie down and pull a building over herself.

"Think about something else."

She looked up at Acair. "Am I saying things aloud?"

"Nay, I just know him and know that what he'll try to do is lay a spell on you to convince you to give up and give in. Then he'll slay you. After that, he'll attempt the same with me."

She would have pulled her hand away from his, but he seemed like the only solid thing she had to cling to. "How in the hell do you know that?" she asked faintly.

He glanced at her. "I already told you."

"You're a mage. You said that yesterday."

"I said too much." He steered them abruptly around yet another corner, then leaned back against the side of a building and caught his breath. "I forget from time to time just how much I loathe that man."

She would have smiled, but she was too unnerved to. "What did he ever do to you?"

"Nothing particular comes to mind. He's just an annoying, arrogant git who loves nothing more than to draw hapless souls into his web and terrify the bloody hell out of them. Standard fare for any decent black mage." He paused. "It sounds fairly vile when put that way, doesn't it?"

She had no idea how to respond to that and she supposed there was no point in arguing about mages and magic and other things that couldn't possibly be true. If he wanted to believe in faery tales and mythical beasts invented by bards who'd had far too much strong ale, he was welcome to it. She would continue on with horses, because horses were always just what they were, never changing, never suddenly sitting back on their haunches and demanding tea with their grain.

She liked things that were predictable.

"Let's keep going," Acair said, taking a deep breath. "The sooner we're out of here, the better."

She considered, then frowned. She had been dragged out of her home, such as it was, brought to a city she most certainly did not like, assailed by rumors of mages and magic and other things that just couldn't possibly, shouldn't possibly, find home in any reasonable woman's life, and she was finished. She folded her arms over her chest.

"I'm not going anywhere else until I know what we're doing," she announced.

He looked at her seriously. "We're going to steal a horse, then ride him out of this damned place."

She blinked. "Steal?"

"If the word *steal* troubles you, think of it as a rescue instead. We are going to liberate your pony from where he's no doubt currently decorating freshly laid straw with unmentionable substances. The alternative is your favorite horse going off with that man you just saw."

He had a point there, she had to admit.

"I also need to find Soilléir of Cothromaiche and with what's following us, I'm not going to manage that on my own two feet. We need help and I think your horse might just be the lad to provide that timely bit of aid. Let's be off."

She had to trot to keep up with him, but, again, it seemed better than the alternative of being left behind. She knew she should have been surprised he seemed to know where he was going, but obviously he had been in the city before. She just didn't want to think about why.

What continued to surprise her more than it perhaps should have was how adept he was at slipping into places that should have remained closed to him. Perhaps a stable wasn't exactly that sort of place but the stables he let them into without a key were exceptionally fine, which meant they housed extremely expensive horses.

Horses that were apparently guarded by a burly stable hand posted at the front door for obvious reasons. He leapt to his feet when Acair pulled the door open.

"Oy, what are you about—"

Léirsinn watched in astonishment as Acair plunged that poor man into unconsciousness.

"Wha—" She reached for him. "What are you doing?"

"Saving his life."

She eased past the unconscious man only because she didn't want to be blamed for having rendered him senseless. At least she hoped he was merely senseless.

"Is he dead?" she whispered in horror.

"He'll wish he were with the headache he wakes up with. Here's your horse."

She felt a chill start at the back of her head and slide down her spine. She reached out and held on to the very fine wooden door of the stall simply to keep herself on her feet. "I don't think I want to come with you," she managed. "I don't like how you're doing this."

He picked the lock on Falaire's stall with tools she realized he'd used on the front door, then slid the door open.

"I told you I was not a good man. I'm saving my life, your life, and this damned horse's life. I can't help how 'tis done."

She tried to shut the stall door. "The means don't necessarily justify the end—"

He turned and faced her. "Listen to me," he said in a low voice, "and trust me that I know of what I speak. We are dealing with people—" He blew out his breath in obvious frustration. "These men here would slay you with the lifting of a single finger without so much as a flicker of remorse. They would kill me not quickly but over as long a period of time as they could manage. I can guarantee you that neither of us would find the experience pleasant. I cannot fight them in my current state. You might try but in the end you would pay a steep price before your life was snuffed out, again without a second's thought."

She didn't have very many skills, she supposed, but she knew when someone was lying. Perhaps it came from so many years of living with horses. They were mirrors, she supposed, of men's hearts. If she had learned anything over the past almost two score years, it was a good deal of horse sense. Acair, whatever and whoever he was, was not lying.

She looked over Acair's shoulder to find Falaire sticking his beautiful nose out into the free air.

He seemed to consider, then he snuffled Acair's hair. Acair froze.

"He's going to bite my ear off, isn't he?"

"Wouldn't surprise me."

Acair reached up hesitantly and stroked Falaire's nose.

The stallion tried to eat his fingers.

Acair winced and pulled his hand away. He wiped his fingers on his cloak, then looked at her. "Come or not, as you like. I can't force you."

"But you'll steal my horse."

He pulled Falaire's halter off its hook and handed it to her. "I can't keep either of us safe—and I'm speaking of you and me—or solve the mystery of those spots, or save your grandfather, unless I have a very pointed conversation with one particular man. To get to him, I need your horse."

"Then you're not offering me the choice to stay or go," she said slowly, taking the halter and clutching it so she didn't drop it. "Not truly."

"I can't force you," he repeated, "and I'm not quite sure how to persuade you except to lay the facts out in their unpleasant starkness as I've already tried to do." He considered then shrugged. "If you want my honest opinion, you would be mad not to leap at the chance to be off on an adventure with a lad such as myself, but that is, again, just my opinion."

She would have smiled but she was too cold to. "You're daft."

"Pragmatic," he corrected, "and very fond of my life. Your endlessly hungry horse here is obviously begging to be involved in a fine piece of mischief. I imagine if he could say as much, he would advise you to come along." He nodded. "Not to be missed, truly."

Falaire ducked his head, obviously to make it easier for her to slip his halter over his ears. She clutched at the leather in her hands, taking comfort from the familiar feel of it there. She looked at Acair, but he was only standing there, waiting patiently. She looked at her horse, but he was simply standing there with his head still bowed, sliding her a sideways look. If he could have spoken, she supposed he would have been telling her to get on with things.

She put his halter on, then buckled it. She had hooked on a lead rope before she realized what she was doing. Years of habit apparently. She stroked his nose, then looked at Acair.

"I don't see how we're going to get him out of the city in the middle of the day."

Acair smiled. "'Tis still early yet. Anyone important is still lingering over his coffee. We'll just march about as if we're supposed to be here. You know what to do. Look as though someone is paying you to do it." He stepped back. "You lead."

"I imagine that isn't something you say often."

"I imagine it's something I say never," he said with a snort. "You see me in reduced and very unusual circumstances. Trust me, they won't last. Off we go."

She took a deep breath, then led Falaire out of his stall. Fortunately, she'd had enough experience in barns that finding her way out the back door wasn't a problem. She led them past several turnouts and continued on to the furthermost one as if she knew what she was doing, all the while looking for a gate.

It was found with less trouble than she'd feared, a poor stable lad was invited to turn around and forget having seen them—Acair handed him a pair of gold coins for his trouble at least—and they were outside almost before she realized just what she'd done.

She'd stolen a horse.

Whether by design or sheer good fortune, they managed to catch up with a group of travelers who were heading over a bridge to the far side of the river. Falaire was obviously not a cart horse, but no one said anything. Acair didn't look approachable and she shrugged off the first two questions she was asked.

She was fairly sure she hadn't taken a normal breath until they were out of the city, they had left their companions behind, and she was standing with Acair well off the road in a clearing. He left her there and took a little stroll through the surroundings, presumably to make sure they hadn't been followed. He returned and stood in front of her.

"Let's lay out our journey," he said briskly. He picked up a stick and drew in the dirt. "Here we are. Neroche is there. The place we need to reach is in the northwestern corner of that country."

"That far?"

"Aye, 'tis several hundred leagues, even as the crow flies."

"You're going to ride all the way—" She pointed to the far corner of his map. "—there."

"Nay, I'm going to fly all the way there."

She wondered if too much skulduggery had done a foul work on his wits. "On what?" she asked skeptically. "A bird?"

"A horse, actually."

She could hardly bring herself to spare the energy to snort at him. "You're mad," she said. "Horses can't fly."

"Droch wouldn't want this horse without very good reason, so I suspect he can do quite a few things your average fellow can't do." He looked at Falaire uneasily. "I need to ask him a question or two, but I'm not sure he'll answer me." He looked at her. "You ask."

"Ask him what?"

"Ask him if he can shapechange."

She blinked. "Do what?"

"Shapechange," he said. "You know, change his shape."

She suppressed the urge to stick her fingers into her ears. The man was daft. "He could change his shape into a barrel with legs," she said, starting to feel a little irritated, "but only with enough sweet spring grass."

He made a sound of impatience. "What I want to see is if he has magic in him. Most horses don't, but there are some who do. I can't believe Droch would want a horse that couldn't at least do something besides take hay in one end and expel it out the other."

She blew out her breath. Perhaps 'twas best to humor him before she clunked him over the head with the heaviest branch she could find so she could get herself back home. "And you want me to tell him all that?" she said as patiently as she could.

"I think he's already heard it and he looks like he would like to repay me for it with a bit of a nibble." He moved closer to her. "Show him an idea in your head of a pegasus or some prancing, frilly thing with wings on his hooves. Something that flaps . . . off . . ."

Léirsinn let go of the lead rope quite suddenly. She did that because not only had Falaire pulled it out of her hands, surprise had left her unable to clutch it any longer. Actually, surprise hadn't just left her without a rope in her hands, it had left her with a numbness that had started at the top of her head and seemed to be working its way downward.

Falaire had trotted around in a circle, come to a stop several paces away from them, then reared. When he came back to ground, he was wearing wings. Er, he'd sprouted wings. Ah, there were things protruding from his back that looked like wings.

He was whinnying. Acair was purring.

She was fainting.

She felt arms go around her as she started to fall.

"Ah, not this, I beg you!"

She looked into sea-green eyes, nay, blue-green eyes, with flecks of gold—

"Léirsinn!"

"I can't take anymore," she murmured.

Then she closed her eyes and let darkness descend.

Twelve

Acair stood in a clearing not nearly as far away from Beinn òrain as he would have liked to have been and was, frankly, rather relieved to be standing on the ground having gotten there of his own volition instead of being dropped there. During their recent and rather unpleasant journey, he hadn't been all that certain that Léirsinn hadn't been about to elbow him off the back of her horse. Given the way she'd shrieked for him to get them back on the ground after she'd regained her senses, he hadn't been at all certain that damned Falaire wouldn't have happily aided her in that endeavor.

It wasn't that he hadn't ridden things with wings before, but he tended to prefer dragons. They were arrogant, showy creatures who always seemed to be more concerned with keeping their riders on their backs than scraping them off at the first opportunity. Pride of the guild, no doubt, and all that.

Horses, though. He shook his head. He wasn't terribly fond of them—various parts of his form agreed—and he wasn't at all sure that damned Falaire wasn't snickering at him every time he whinnied, but he supposed that was the least of his worries.

He had a horse miss standing ten paces away from him, looking as if she might come undone entirely if he didn't do something very soon.

He had no experience with women on the verge of losing their sanity. The women he knew were cold, calculating shrews who thought nothing of incurring their collective fathers' ire to be seen dancing with him or sitting next to him at table. He was accustomed to mages in skirts who had ambition to match his own and were willing to meet him head-on.

This was something else entirely.

"Léirsinn," he began, dredging up his most reasonable tone, "we've come too far to turn—"

"You should have given me the choice!"

"I tried—"

"You did not!"

He shut his mouth and scowled. Aye, this was what the rescuing of a damsel in distress got a man. A prickly, unpleasant—ah, nay, not tears. He shifted uncomfortably. "Um, the weeping—"

"I'm not upset," she spat, "I'm furious!"

He considered that. "So you're weeping instead of reaching for a blade—oh, you don't have a blade—"

"Weeping seemed a more reasonable thing to do than kill you, which was my first choice!"

Well, the woman was terribly proficient with a pitchfork, but he suspected she didn't have the heart to inflict any serious sort of damage on anyone. At the moment, though, she looked as if she might be capable of quite a few things. It was likely best to simply humor her and see if they couldn't get that pony back up in the air and be on their way.

"I appreciate the concession," he said. There, that ought to do it. "Very kind," he added, on the off chance the former hadn't been enough.

Er, it hadn't been enough.

She was looking around for a weapon. At least they'd left her crossbow and bolts somewhere behind them, likely back in Sàraichte. Well, there was no time to go back to get them, which he hoped wouldn't come back to haunt him in the future.

"You cannot go back," he said with another attempt at sounding reasonable. "Remember what lies in wait."

"My uncle making a bad jest," she said dismissively.

"And those mages who tried to slay me?"

"Lads with the right idea," she said shortly. "I should have let them have at you."

"We can argue that point later if you like," he said carefully, "but let's look at the bigger picture—"

"Aye, the one in which I push you off the back of my horse and ride back home!"

He looked at her standing in the last rays of sunlight that streamed over the plains of Ailean and had to pause to wonder at her hair. Whilst he was wondering, he wondered how it was he'd missed the true nature of its color for so long. He realized that for the most part, she had worn it tucked up under a knitted cap, no doubt to keep it out of her way, or perhaps so all the lads in the barn didn't stare at her as stupidly as he was doing at present, trying to decide what to call her hair.

He settled on red.

It wasn't a deep red, like fine port viewed by firelight in perfect crystal. It wasn't a pale red that could have charitably been called blonde. Her hair was red, simply red, like the depths of a fire on a bitterly cold night when a man could appreciate that sort of thing whilst warming his hands against it.

Apparently with that red came a temper.

"What in the blazes are you doing?" she demanded.

"Trying to decide what to call your hair. What are you doing?"

"Looking for a rock to use—nay, let's do this." She looked at him purposefully. "Show me what you did to that lad in Falaire's barn, the thing where you rendered him senseless but not dead."

"Why?"

"So I can do it to you!"

He found himself, surprisingly enough, rather glad that she had no magic. If she had, he suspected she would have turned him into something small, then squished him under her boot.

He cast about for something useful to say. He was accustomed to foul-tempered mages, angry monarchs, and outraged wizards with spells and finely honed senses of justice. A flame-haired barn gel in a towering temper?

He hadn't a clue.

"And look," she said, pointing to Falaire with a shaking hand. "What is *that*?"

"That," he began carefully, "is a horse."

"He has wings!"

"He's masquerading as a pegasus," he offered. "They generally have those sorts of appendages."

He suspected wings weren't all that pony could conjure up given the right incentive, but he supposed that might not be anything to put on a list of useful things to say at present. 'Twas no wonder Droch had wanted him.

The question that had nagged at him over the past several hours was how Droch had known what he could do and where to find him. Very curious, that.

"Wings!" Léirsinn repeated. "Wings that aren't merely for decoration!"

"So it would seem," Acair ventured. "Would it ease you any and perhaps leave things seeming a bit more familiar if I bent over and let him take a generous bite from my arse?"

She looked at him for a moment or two, then she went very still. To his horror, she started to weep in truth. It wasn't the loud, boisterous sort of thing most women he knew indulged in order to garner the maximum attention possible. It wasn't the sort of weeping he was accustomed to from mages who generally found themselves on their knees in front of him, begging him for mercy.

He sighed. He was not a pleasant sort.

Nay, this was a different sort of weeping entirely. Léirsinn stood there as still as stone with tears simply rolling down her cheeks.

There weren't very many tears, but he suspected each one cost her a great deal.

He took a deep breath—and his life in his hands, no doubt—and walked over to her slowly. She didn't move; she simply watched him with those bright green eyes that were seemingly dry except for the tears they continued to produce. He stopped in front of her, then considered. She didn't have a dagger, so he thought he could safely assume his gut would remain unpierced. Her hands were down by her side and clenched, which he supposed boded well for her not having a rock to bean him with. That didn't address all the other things she might try, which gave him pause.

"You look like *I* might bite you."

He smiled. "The thought had crossed my mind."

"I don't need comfort," she whispered. "I need a sharp something so I can be rid of you and your schemes. I don't like either of you."

He could only hope she wasn't entirely serious. He took a deep breath, then reached out and put his arms around her.

It was badly done, he would be the first to admit it. His experience with women, which included the aforementioned terrifying creatures, was limited to courtly activities, dancing, and battles with spells. He wasn't sure that he had ever, in his long and illustrious career as black mage extraordinaire, offered one of those women comfort. Wine, a coveted seat at table, and perhaps an elegantly wrapped spell, but comfort?

Never.

He patted Léirsinn's back. He patted her hair, once, then ceased immediately when she growled. Or at least he thought she had growled. The truth was, he had no idea what she was doing until she let out a shuddering breath, then leaned her forehead against his shoulder.

Well, he was going to catch his death from the damp, obviously, but perhaps it would count as his good deed for the day.

He patted a bit more, avoiding commenting on the color of her hair, then waited until she had stopped weeping, if that's what it could have been called. And once she was simply standing there, breathing raggedly, he thought he might attempt a bit of speech.

"Here is the most of the truth I can give you," he said finally. "Would you prefer to sit as you listen?"

"I'd rather stand," she said, her words muffled against his cloak. "Easier to run that way."

"Very well," he said. He looked around briefly to make certain they were still alone, then considered what he could say without causing that spell of death that had seemingly come along with them, no doubt clinging to Falaire's tail, to fall upon him and slay him. "The truth is," he said gingerly, "I fear that somehow my stepping in that spot of darkness alerted someone to my presence."

"You being an important mage and all."

He didn't miss the mockery in her tone and wondered that she managed it whilst still sniffling into his shoulder. "Aye, that. You saw the results, which left me feeling less than comfortable in Sàraichte. Hence our journey to Beinn òrain."

"And since you didn't find your friend, you want to continue on looking for him." She pulled away and looked at him. "Is that it?"

"I must," Acair said. "I can't believe these words are leaving my lips, but he is the only one who can save me."

"In Tor Neroche."

"Aye, in Tor Neroche. 'Tis a bit of a slog on the best of days, which is why I need your horse."

"I don't want to go with you."

He understood that. He didn't particularly want to go with himself either. The last time he had been in that corner of the Nine Kingdoms, he'd been the guest of one Lothar of Wychweald—an unwilling guest, it had to be said—and he'd barely escaped with his life. He had most definitely left his dignity behind in the haste and unpleasant nature of his leave-taking. But that was a tale better left for a different day and then only after a substantial amount of very strong drink. At the moment, necessity left him little choice in his selection of places to visit and his current straits dictated how quickly he needed to travel there.

He put his hands on Léirsinn's shoulders, which she didn't seem to care for, so he fussed instead with her cloak that was completely inadequate to the chill that he could already feel settling into the air. If he'd had magic to hand, he would have conjured up something very luxurious and wrapped it around her. As it was, all he could do was hope to eventually beg a cloak from someone else.

He paused, then an idea struck him. "I could leave you somewhere safe, with people who have sterling reputations. That way, you could remain in comfort whilst I see to my business."

"*If* I loan you my horse so you can go off to find this Master Soilléir."

"Aye."

She walked a few paces away from him, then turned to look at him. "I don't think I believe in magic."

"You just rode a pegasus partway across the Nine Kingdoms."

She shivered. "I'm not sure I didn't dream that."

"Well, you were in a bit of a faint for most of the journey."

"I'm tempted to indulge again."

"The rest of the journey might pass more comfortably that way," he offered, "though I think you would miss a delightful view. One way or another, the sooner we're gone, the better."

She wrapped her arms around herself and looked thoroughly miserable. "I don't know what to do. I don't think I can go back to Sàraichte."

"I don't think so, either," he said as gently as he could manage. "But that doesn't mean we won't pop in and out to liberate your grandfather when the time comes for it. But there are things we—I, rather—must do first."

She took a deep breath. "I feel like I'm trapped in a nightmare. Or a very bad faery tale." She looked at him. "It seems very foolish at my age to wish for a Hero to come rescue me."

"Not foolish," he said, though he knew several of the lads those tales had been patterned after and had always found them to be far more priggish than the tales told. "A rescue might be perhaps a bit out of reach at the moment. You are, poor gel, left with just me and your flying horse."

She looked as if she couldn't decide which was worse, but he thought it might be best to not press her for a decision on that. He was more relieved than he likely should have been when she nodded, then walked with him over to Falaire. A few days of travel, a few games of cards to win them supper, then a very pointed conversation with the man he needed to see. Things would then return to normal. He would see her off to somewhere safe, then he would be back to the business of magic and mischief.

He could hardly wait to begin his list of whom he would ply his usual trade on first.

Several hours later, he suspected he knew exactly who would claim the coveted first spot on that list.

He wasn't a complete failure with maps and he'd had the wit to choose an excellent rider to manage their steed, yet as the sun was rising, he realized he had misjudged the lower corner of a country he definitely hadn't wanted to visit and he and Léirsinn had just been shot out of the sky.

Falaire was the most great-hearted animal he had ever encountered, the pony's propensity to gnaw on things he shouldn't have aside. The noble steed managed to get them to the ground before he went down on his knees, folded his wings, and didn't move again save for very labored breathing. Acair fell out the saddle, rolled up to his feet, and was marshalling his worst spell of death with the most painful accompaniments possible when he realized he was facing the captain of Ehrne of Ainneamh's guard on the wrong side of the border.

He remembered his half-brother Rùnach having described a

fairly recent, choice encounter with the elves of that realm, something he'd dismissed at the time as the babblings of another elf with
hurt feelings. Now, given the sight of half a dozen elves with arrows
pointing directly at his own black heart, he knew better.

He drew himself up and pointed a finger at the guard captain.
"Heal him."

"I beg your pardon?" the elf asked mildly. "Heal who?"

"Heal that horse, Surdail, damn you to hell," Acair snarled. "The
innocent beast you just shot out of the sky. Heal him!"

"A rather pedestrian looking animal," Surdail of Ainneamh said,
looking down his long nose in Falaire's direction. "I think perhaps
we should just put him out of his misery."

Acair supposed the only reason he managed to take a step back
from a place of fury such as he'd never before experienced was that
he felt the arm of Soilléir's damned spell go round his shoulders. He
wasn't entirely sure the thing hadn't blown in his ear as well. He
shook it off in annoyance, then took a deep breath.

"Please," he said through gritted teeth. "Please heal him."

Surdail looked at him in astonishment. "Did I hear a polite word
in there, little one?"

Acair let slip a few suggestions about what Surdail could do
with his condescending attitude, then he bit back the rest of what
he wished desperately he could say. He indulged in a brief moment
where he honestly couldn't decide if he should or shouldn't take his
chances with trying to destroy the spell standing beside him so he
could slay the elf standing in front of him, then he took hold of his
good sense and attempted a bit more polite speech.

"Please," he repeated, making a great effort not to snarl. "Not
for my sake, but for my companion's."

Surdail looked at Léirsinn and his eyes widened. Acair suspected that might be the reaction she got everywhere she went. The
woman was truly more beautiful than she had any right to be. And
that hair . . .

"And what sort of mischief do we find here on my humble soil?"

Acair closed his eyes briefly at the sound of that voice, dripping as it was with monarchial self-importance. If Surdail of Ainneamh was intolerable, his lord and master King Ehrne left everyone in his vicinity wanting to kill themselves quickly to avoid having to listen to him talk any longer than necessary. The sad truth was, if there was one thing Ehrne of Ainneamh loved, it was the sound of his own voice.

He looked at the king and forced himself to incline his head in as much of a bow as he could manage. "Your Majesty. A pleasure, as always."

Ehrne looked at him coldly. "Give me a single reason why I shouldn't slay you on the spot."

"You wouldn't manage it," was out of his mouth before he could stop himself.

"You are within my borders, whelp, and I am able to manage quite a few things you wouldn't care for," Ehrne said sharply.

"Acair, he's dying."

He looked behind him to find Léirsinn sitting at Falaire's head, stroking his face. Her cheeks were dry, which concerned him more than what he'd seen before. He met her eyes, winced, then turned back to Ehrne.

"Heal the horse your men tried to slay," he said in a low voice, "and I will stand here and take whatever abuse you care to heap upon me."

"Anything?"

"Anything," Acair agreed. He had to swallow not only his pride but his gorge. "Please."

Ehrne looked at him for so long in silence, Acair wondered if the man had died from surprise or merely from the memories of all the misery he had inflicted on those around him. Acair honestly wouldn't have been surprised by either.

Then Ehrne walked over to Falaire. If nothing else, the elf had a soft spot for horses. He knelt down and put his hand on Falaire's forehead. He stroked the horse gently, then looked at Léirsinn.

"Yours?"

"My uncle sold him to Droch of Saothair," she said bluntly, "and we stole him. So, not mine by exchange of funds, but mine by affection."

Ehrne looked over his shoulder. "Who shot this beast?"

One of the guardsmen suddenly found himself standing in front of his fellows who had immediately taken a pair of steps back.

"Surdail, strip him of his privileges and set him outside the border." He turned back to Falaire, put his hand on the beast's neck, then closed his eyes.

Acair didn't hear the words spoken, but since the result was all that concerned him, he was happy enough when Falaire leapt to his feet and whinnied at the king of their current and quite unfortunate locale.

"Well," Ehrne said huffily, heaving himself to his own feet, "*I'm* not the one who shot you and I disciplined that lad well enough. You may leave off with your snorts. Surdail, have him fed and tended. Now, tell me again who you are, girl?"

Acair watched Léirsinn scramble up to stand next to her horse, gaping at the king as she did so. He wondered if he dared intervene or if that would simply make matters worse.

"I'm no one," Léirsinn said, sounding stunned, "but thank you for, ah . . . whatever it was you just did."

"What we call it here, you rustic miss, is *magic*. Have you learned nothing from that reprobate you're obviously keeping company with? You also, if it hasn't escaped your notice, own a shapechanging horse."

"I didn't know he could do that," she said. "And if you'd told me a fortnight ago that he could, I would have called you a liar. I don't believe in magic."

"You know Acair of Ceangail well enough to travel with him yet you don't believe in—" He stopped suddenly, then frowned. "There's something here I'm missing."

"And here we go," Acair muttered under his breath. If he allowed the king to put even a single foot to that path, they would be standing there for a fortnight, listening to him blather on.

He wasn't above using whatever connection he had with the elves in question in order to get himself and Léirsinn out of Ainneamh before Ehrne heard more than he needed to, so he turned his best smile on the king.

"Cousin," he said pleasantly.

Ehrne wasn't one for family, something Acair knew but had hoped he might successfully ignore. The king pointed a finger at him.

"Do not call me that," he said haughtily, "you piece of filth. How dare you imply that we have any connection."

"My father is your uncle's son—"

"And you are your father's bastard son," Ehrne thundered. "Which makes that woman there—" He paused and looked at Léirsinn. "Who are you again?"

"No one," Léirsinn said. "No one at all." She took a step closer to Falaire. "Just a stable hand."

Ehrne frowned at her, then went to stand next to his captain. "Surdail, there is something going on here that escapes me and, as you know, nothing escapes me. I must give this more thought."

"Wise, Your Majesty."

"Your Majesty?" Léirsinn echoed. "Are you a king?"

Ehrne started to splutter. Acair would have enjoyed that, but he was in too much of a hurry for it. That, and he'd traded his pride for Falaire's life. That payment had yet to be exacted, but he thought it might be a bit more bearable if Ehrne didn't have too many details beforehand. Too much chit-chat and the king would find out all sorts of things he didn't need to know.

"She means nothing by it," Acair said quickly. "She's been sheltered the whole of her life in the country. Elves are nothing more than marvelous creatures from myth to her. You can safely assume you're in your rightful place in the heavens in her eyes."

"But she knows who you are," Ehrne said, "and therefore what you are . . . or does she? And whilst we're about these mysteries, why didn't you heal that horse yourself?"

Acair would have given much to have had any sort of tale to tell other than the truth. The laughter at his expense would be unpleasant, but he had the feeling things would go further south very rapidly once Ehrne realized just how powerless he was to repay that laughter—or anything else, for that matter.

He didn't hear Léirsinn come up to him, but he felt her suddenly standing next to him. He looked at her.

"You may not want to stand too close."

"Heal Falaire?" she asked. "What does he mean you should have healed him yourself?"

Acair didn't have the chance to begin to explain before Ehrne was interrupting him.

"Hold your tongue, you wee mortal," the king said, "and leave me in peace to find the beginning of this tangle and start there." He folded his arms over his chest and studied Acair for a moment or two. "You didn't heal the horse, your little miss there doesn't believe in magic, and here you are in my land without making mischief or tossing about your mighty spells."

"So it would seem—" Acair began.

Ehrne cut him off with a look, then turned to his captain. "Surdail, I believe we have a situation on our hands."

"There does seem to be something unusual going on, Your Majesty," Surdail agreed. "Perhaps Prince Gair's son would care to enlighten us."

"Prince Gair?" Léirsinn echoed. "Who is that?"

Acair looked at her quickly. "Don't ask." He turned to the king of the accursed soil under his boots and attempted an appropriately contrite expression. "I am under a curse, if that would describe it adequately, and cannot use my magic."

Ehrne blinked. "A curse? Explain further."

"I'd rather not."

"And I'd rather see you full of arrows, but I am nothing if not

magnanimous and generous to all those around me. Now, spew out
the details, you little bastard, before I forget all my better qualities
and wield a bow myself."

Acair knew he had no choice. "Very well," he said, as politely
as he could manage under the circumstances, "I agreed to spend a
year not using any spells."

Ehrne's mouth had fallen open. "And what," he managed, "will
befall you if you do?"

Acair pointed over his shoulder without looking. "A Cothromaichian spell of death will fall upon me and do its worst."

"Do they have spells of death there, Your Majesty?" Surdail
asked. "I suspect Prince Gair's wee one there would know, wouldn't
you imagine?"

Ehrne likely couldn't imagine anything past his next meal, but
Acair thought it wise to keep that thought to himself. He watched
the king scratch his head, as if he were truly puzzled by the whole
thing.

"I feel as though I'm still missing something," Ehrne said slowly.
"Why would Soilléir waste time to send one of his spells trotting
after you . . . unless there is something else involved."

"Soilléir," Léirsinn said. "Isn't that—"

"Aye," Acair said quickly. "That's the one." He looked at the king.
"I think it might be enough to—"

"Wait," Ehrne said holding up his hand. "I heard some ridiculous
tale that you'd been on a sort of penance tour for the past several
months, cozying up to rulers and magistrates and everyone else
you'd made miserable." He began to smile. "Soilléir's making you
do more of that, isn't he?"

Acair looked down his nose at his cousin. "I think I'm finished
with this conversation."

"And look you there, Surdail," Ehrne said, nodding toward
Léirsinn. "She hasn't any idea what we're discussing. He hasn't
told her."

"I wonder, Your Majesty, if perhaps he's not allowed to say

anything about himself. It seems that might be an added insult, wouldn't you agree? For a black mage of his reputation to be forced to crawl about as a mere mortal?" Surdail looked at Acair. "Is that the case, Master Acair?"

Acair glared at him. "I cannot enlighten anyone new as to my identity, aye. Those who already know me are, of course, free to bring to mind my past deeds and tremble in fear."

Ehrne began to smile. "No magic and no ability to intimidate with your reputation alone. I do believe Soilléir has hit upon the perfect combination. What a pity that you must take the barbs and insults reserved for lesser men."

"Perhaps, Your Majesty," Surdail said thoughtfully, "we should discuss a few things for which he might deserve those barbs." He looked at Acair blandly. "So his little miss knows exactly whom she's keeping company with, since I suspect he hasn't seen fit to tell her yet."

"Oh, there's no need for that," Acair said, then he shut his mouth around whatever other protestations he might have offered. The look Ehrne was giving him left him thinking that might be a very prudent thing to do.

"That is the price for the horse," Ehrne said coldly.

If the ancient elf wanted to put it that way, Acair realized he had no choice but to watch as the pair set off, as the saying went, to the races.

There wasn't a damned piece of mischief they didn't examine at great length, tripping over themselves to top the other with things Acair had to admit he had definitely said and done. He did his best to ignore the endless list of his misdeeds that the king, his captain, and his steward, who had apparently dropped in to add a few things to the conversation, seemed determined to spew out.

It was a very long list.

It was a collection of things he was very familiar with, though, so he had little trouble ignoring it. Unfortunately, they didn't limit themselves to simply that. They soon moved to a great whacking list of people he had done dirty, as his mother would have said. Mages, monarchs, maidens, mavens: there wasn't a damned one of them they didn't identify and have a wee chuckle over.

"Is it possible that there is anyone left for him to ply his black magic on, do you think, Surdail?"

"I daresay there might be, Your Majesty. The world is a very large place."

"Large and uninteresting when it doesn't find itself within our borders."

"True, my liege. Very true."

Acair wondered if breakfast might be forthcoming if he looked hungry enough. He had begun shifting a good half hour before, but he decided the time had come to perhaps make his position a bit more obvious. He yawned, stretched, then looked about himself purposefully for what he hoped might be a servant bearing a tray laden with fine edibles.

Ehrne glared at him. "Are you listening?"

"I grew bored," he said, before he could stop himself. "In truth, I don't believe I've heard anything but a great, bloviating bit of hot wind. Odd for this time of year, but there you have it."

Ehrne spluttered, gestured when words seemed to fail him, then glared at his captain. "Throw that little whoreson in the dungeon."

Acair looked at him in surprise. "I beg your pardon?"

"Aye, you'll do that and more before I send you to your death. Surdail, put the woman there with him. Who knows who she truly is."

"Not her," Acair said immediately. "She knows nothing." Good lord, elves. Such mercurial blowhards with absolutely no sense of humor. There was a reason he avoided Ainneamh so religiously. He would never make the mistake of misjudging that border again.

"She might be a black witch," Ehrne said darkly.

Acair suppressed the urge to roll his eyes. "There are no such things," he said, "and I would know, wouldn't you think?"

Ehrne ignored him and looked pointedly at Surdail.

Acair held out his hands. "Not her," he said quickly, trying not to sound as unnerved as he suddenly was. "Put her across the border and content yourself with just me. In truth, she knows nothing of me or my business—"

Ehrne shot him a look that Acair had to admit he would have admired in different circumstances. He shut his mouth because he wasn't a fool. Saying anything else would get him nowhere. He could scarce believe how things had unraveled so quickly, but he had little trouble recognizing the feel of hands on his arms as he and Léirsinn were escorted away.

"My horse," Léirsinn protested.

"He'll be fine," Acair managed. He didn't dare hope as much for either of them, but Falaire at least would be well cared-for.

Damn that Soilléir of Cothromaiche. If he survived the next few hours, he would find him and repay him. It wasn't possible that the man would be peering into the gloom, as it were, and see their rather dire straits, then come to rescue them, was it? Nay, he would have to see to things himself, as usual. He turned his attentions to memorizing the path to the dungeons. He would need it so he might retrace his steps when he managed to liberate himself and his companion.

A year with no magic. What had he been thinking?

If things didn't change very soon, he wasn't going to be thinking any longer because he was going to be dead.

He put that thought aside as something to think about later, then concentrated on making certain he could get them back out of where he most certainly didn't want to go.

Thirteen

Of all the places she had ever thought she would find herself, Léirsinn had to admit a dungeon was the very last.

They had been escorted there politely, all things considered, though with a fair amount of suspicion. She thought that might have had to do with Acair. She couldn't imagine it had had anything to do with her.

She currently sat on a stone bench that was as cold as she would have expected it to be and looked at the man sitting under the window who was not at all what she expected *him* to be.

She wasn't sure what to think at the moment. She had listened to him plead for the life of her horse, volunteering to suffer what had sounded rather like the word *anything* if the king would heal Falaire, then listened further to a rather thorough and robust recounting of his past misdeeds. It had been a list that had made her hair stand on end.

Was it possible to drain the world of its magic?

Magic. She could hardly believe she was allowing the word to take up any sort of residence in her head. It was just too ridiculous a notion to take seriously. She supposed that if she repeated that often enough, she might be able to ignore all the things she had seen over the past pair of days, things that had left her wondering about the world in a way she never would have otherwise.

She started with the thing she had closest to hand, namely the man sitting across the dungeon from her. She studied him and tried to reconcile what she was seeing with what she'd heard about him. If she'd met him at a grand ball, she likely would have thought him terribly handsome but too important for someone as simple as herself. If she had encountered him first in a barn, she would have thought him impossibly easy on the eye but absolutely useless with a pitchfork.

She paused and considered that. Perhaps he'd never had to use a pitchfork before. If he possessed unusual means to see to his business, then he certainly wouldn't have had to do any sort of manual labor. Indeed, it was possible he didn't know *how* to do any manual labor.

She realized with a start that he was watching her. She wondered briefly if she should be afraid of him, but hard on the heels of that came the memory of how far he'd been willing to go to save her horse.

Evil men didn't do that, she didn't think.

"This was not in my plans," he said. "On the off chance you were wondering if this was part of our grand tour of the Nine Kingdoms."

"Oh, I don't know," she said, squinting up at the weeping ceiling. "I imagine there are worse places."

"There are."

She looked at him then. "And you would know?"

"I would know."

She nodded, because she wasn't quite sure what to say. She was in a dungeon, which was unusual, and she was there with a man who had reputedly made so much mischief over the years that kings and guard captains had an apparently inexhaustible supply of items to discuss, which was also unusual. Her life had become, she had to admit, very strange.

She thought it might have all started when her horse had sprouted wings.

Nay, it had been before that. It might have been the first time she'd seen Acair attempting to muck out a stall while Falaire had been eyeing him as a potential morsel to enjoy before supper. In truth, she wasn't entirely sure she hadn't at some point before that occasion wished for a new direction in her life.

She would have to remind herself to avoid that sort of wishing in the future.

She returned to her study of the man sitting several paces away from her. He didn't look evil. He looked rather tired, actually, and as if he would rather have been sitting in a sunny spot, having a bit of breakfast and offering to pour her some tea. Him, a black mage? Even if she'd believed in magic, which she most assuredly did not, she wouldn't have believed that of him.

Perhaps King Ehrne and his cohorts were simply having a bit of sport at his expense. What did she know of great men and their ways save how rude they could be to those they thought were their inferiors?

She looked about herself, desperate for a distraction. She'd had faery tales read to her as a child, of course, a cherished memory from her time with her parents. Either her mother or her father had read to her every night, then she'd listened to them continue the tradition with her younger sister, even past the point where she'd been too old for the same. She had never argued and they had seemingly taken great pleasure in handling one of the trio of books they had owned.

Dungeons had of course tended to figure prominently in Heroic tales and she had spent many an hour in delicious terror over the thought of just how awful they must be. The dungeons, not the Heroes. She thought the reality was less horrifying and more musty-smelling, but that was just her opinion.

"Where are we?" she asked absently.

"The Kingdom of Ainneamh."

She looked back at him. "And what do they do here?"

"They talk a great deal," he said, then he shrugged. "They're elves. They go about sparkling and glittering and generally leaving everyone who encounters them wishing they were very far away."

"Elves," she repeated with a smile. "Of course."

He leaned his elbows on his knees and folded his hands together. "Don't believe in them either?"

"Of course not," she said, but she couldn't manage it with her customary snort of derision.

Her world was shifting underneath her and she didn't like it at all. Things she had fully believed to be a certain way had become things she was being forced to consider might be another way entirely. And it was becoming increasingly hard to deny what she was seeing.

The king of the, er, *elves* had put his hands on her horse, spoken a few words under his breath, and Falaire had leapt to his feet, completely whole and sound. That had been odd in itself, but there was more. Those men, the king and his men, didn't look like average blokes. The more she thought about it, the more she realized they had been frighteningly beautiful, as if they had stepped out of a dream that she thought she might be able to remember with enough effort.

She looked at Acair and wondered if what they had said about him was true as well. He didn't look evil, but he didn't look harmless either. In truth, he had a bit of that elvish look about him, though perhaps not so unearthly as the men who had escorted them rather politely into the dungeon.

She was accustomed to the powerful men who came to Fuadain's stables to purchase the best horses in the barn, so she didn't find herself particularly intimidated by Acair's mien or his looks. But if he had magic . . .

He had told her he was a mage, hadn't he? He'd also told her that he never lied. If he were telling the truth, then that meant that there were things in the world that existed beyond her imagination.

Magic.

Power.

Mischief of a dangerous and unwholesome sort.

"Léirsinn?"

She took a deep breath. "I'm thinking about things I haven't thought about before."

He smiled gravely. "The world is very large and full of unusual things."

"And you would know."

"I would."

She rubbed her arms. "Why didn't you tell me?"

"Because I am—unwillingly, I might add—silenced about my identity by the threat of a spell of death. Not that you would have believed me anyway."

"I wouldn't have," she agreed. "I didn't, if you'll remember, when you tried to slip that sort of ridiculousness into polite conversation. But a spell of death?" She tried to smile, but she feared she was less successful at it than she might have liked. "Really."

He pointed to a shadow in the corner.

There was certainly something there, but it didn't look terribly intimidating. She rose and started toward it. Acair held out his hand to stop her.

"Don't," he warned. "The man who fashioned it is not one you would want to tangle with and his spells are a reflection of that, to be sure."

"Soilléir?"

"The very same."

"Is he so powerful then?" She looked down at him. "You realize that deep down I still think this is all rubbish, don't you?"

"I know."

She looked at him and tried not to be dazzled by the fairness of his face. She couldn't help but wonder how many of his victims—alleged victims, rather—had simply agreed to whatever he wanted so he would favor them with one of those smiles.

She frowned, then avoided his hand and walked over to where there was definitely a shadow of something slouching in the corner. It did shift a little as she approached, which startled her. She gave it a stern look, which seemed to intimidate it into shrinking back from her. It folded itself into itself, then slid down to land in a tidy heap on the floor.

She almost joined it there.

"Ah," she managed, "I think I'll resume my seat."

"Very wise," Acair said.

She walked back to where she'd come from, then turned and sat down heavily. When had the damned place become so terribly cold?

"Who are you?" Her voice broke on the last word, but she didn't imagine Acair would care. She felt cold and frightened and very, very lost. "In truth."

He rose, took off his cloak, then walked across the dungeon and draped that cloak around her. He hesitated.

"I could sit next to you," he offered. "Warmer that way, if the thought isn't utterly repulsive."

She studied him for a moment or two. "Not very good at the chivalry thing, are you?"

He sighed. "My manners are generally much better than this, no thanks to my mother. Blame her for their occasional lack and my father for my terrible arrogance and evil intentions. But given that I'm not completely without the odd, redeeming moment of pleasantness, I'll sit next to you and keep you warm."

"Fair enough." She patted the spot next to her and found that she wasn't unhappy for a bit of company. She considered for a moment or two, then looked at him. "Will they hurt my horse? You know, after they put us to death."

"They won't put us to death," he said with a snort. "Ehrne will bluster about it, but he won't actually do anything. At the very least I'll see that you are set safely across the border. Once you're there, go east to Lake Cladach. Seek out Prince Sgath and tell him what madness Ehrne is about. He'll fetch your horse for you." He looked at her. "He is my father's father, but I'm not sure you should give him my name as a character, if you know what I mean. He is a good man, though."

She felt her mouth become suddenly quite dry. "And you?" she asked. "What will they do with you?"

He pursed his lips. "Absolutely nothing." He nodded toward the spell in the corner. "I am examining that beast there for flaws even as we speak. When Ehrne sends men to come fetch me, he will find them returning empty-handed . . . or not at all." He looked at her seriously. "I don't fancy ending my life here."

She considered what troubled her most for rather a long time before she managed to look at him. "Is what the king said about you true?"

"Well—"

"Don't you think that since I already heard a lifetime's worth of your achievements upstairs, that thing over there won't mind if you fill in the bits the lads upstairs missed?"

Acair looked at the spell folded neatly in the corner, then looked at her. He shifted a little on the stone, but not farther away, which surprised her. She didn't argue. She was freezing and miserable and even rusty chivalry was very welcome.

"What the king said about me was true," he said with a sigh.

"And those other two, er—"

"Elves," he supplied.

She shook her head. "I refuse to believe it, but go on. Don't forget what those other two said."

He slid her a sideways look. "You don't have anything approaching the proper respect for my terrible reputation."

"You saved my horse, not once but twice. How bad can you be?"

"I'm worse," he said, "something of which I was extremely proud in the past."

"I don't think you sound any worse than your average rich man's spoiled son," she said. "Ever lusting after power and gold."

He sighed. "You weren't listening very carefully, something for which I find myself surprisingly grateful."

Actually, she had listened quite carefully, openmouthed and absolutely stunned at what she was hearing. If the king of the, ah, *elves* was to be believed, Acair had been cutting a swath across the Nine Kingdoms for decades, leaving behind in his wake destruction, the thefts of priceless treasures, and an ever-growing collection of important people who wanted him dead.

"How old are you?"

He looked at her in surprise. "After all you've heard, *that's* what you want to know?"

"You don't look any older than I am, but I'm rather old at almost score and ten. I was going to be impressed that you had squeezed so much bad behavior into so few years."

"I'm a pair of years shy of a century," he said grimly. "Very old indeed."

She blinked, then she smiled. "You said you always told the truth."

"It *is* the truth and today I feel every one of those years, believe me."

She couldn't help a bit of a laugh. She looked at him and shook her head. "I'm not sure how many more fanciful imaginings I can stomach today, but continue if you like. If you think that—" she could hardly call that thing in the corner a *spell* but she had nothing else to name it "that spell won't slay you for it."

He smiled wearily. "We'll see, I suppose." He rubbed his hands together. "I suppose we should start at the beginning."

She pulled his cloak closer around her and smiled. "And thus have always begun my favorite bedtime tales."

He shot her a dark look. "To begin at the *beginning*," he said pointedly, "we must discuss magic."

"Am I going to fall asleep soon?"

He made a sound of exasperation. "Woman, you . . . you have a very bad habit of making light of very serious things."

"And you don't, which is why my perspective is so valuable to you. Say on, lad. I'll try to stay awake."

"I will elbow you if you nod off," he said. "Now, as I was saying, there is magic and then there is *magic*. Even a village alewife is familiar with the former, for every time she seeks out a potion or a charm or a harmless little spell from the local witchwoman, she is using the first."

"Like Mistress Cailleach?"

"Mistress Cailleach isn't exactly a harmless village alewife," he said. He shifted. "She's my great-aunt."

She looked at him in surprise. "She isn't."

"She is, and believe me when I say I was no more surprised to find her in Sàraichte than you are to hear of my connection to her, a connection I'm not entirely sure she's pleased about. She cuffed me so hard when I saw her, I think she may have permanently damaged the hearing in my left ear."

She felt a little faint. "And she is a . . ."

"Witch," he said.

"Which means your mother is a witch."

"My mother is most definitely a witch."

She hoped she would soon be able to stop shaking her head. "I think this just might be a bridge too far for me. Mistress Cailleach sells fish and keeps my box of coins, nothing more."

"I'm surprised she hasn't tried to trade you a spell or a charm for some of your coins," he said, "but she likes you so perhaps she wouldn't. I would hazard a guess she's collected plenty of gold from others in Sàraichte."

Léirsinn put her hand over her heart, then realized what she was doing. She coughed discreetly and patted her chest, lest she have given anything away. A charm lay there, a tiny figure of a mythical beast. Mistress Cailleach had given it to her almost five years ago.

'Tis time you had this, dearie, she had said. *Remember what it does.*

Léirsinn had tried to pay for it, but Mistress Cailleach had refused to hear of it. It had seemed a pleasant gift, something to keep her courage up. Now, she wondered if it might be something more—

Nay 'twas impossible.

She put her hands back in her lap, then decided they were too cold for that, so she tucked them under her arms. It hid their trembling a bit better that way.

"So, what sort of magic does your great-aunt dabble in?"

"The dangerous kind," he said, "but perhaps not as of late. Who knows? I wasn't about to ask her. The woman is terrifying."

"Must be why I like her."

He smiled briefly. "I daresay." He glanced at the corner, then continued. "We'll leave those little magics alone, for they're unimportant. The bigger magics are what we'll concern ourselves with now."

"Oh, please, let's."

He pursed his lips. "I'll ignore that, because I'm that sort of lad." He paused, then seemed to be looking for the right words. "Most magic, well, all magic actually, is blood magic."

"Blood magic," she echoed, trying not to sound as skeptical as she felt.

He nodded. "It runs through your veins by virtue of your parents, or occasionally the country of your birth, or now and again because of something untoward hiding in the unexamined lives of your progenitors. Taken Ehrne, for instance. He is the king of Ainneamh, of course, but the magic he uses, the magic that is slathered over this place like a vile fog, comes to him through his father and his father's father and so on."

"Where did it start?"

"I have no idea. Perhaps in the beginning, a group of the first souls to inhabit the Nine Kingdoms sat about a table playing cards and the winner took the best stuff available whilst leaving the rest for the others."

"I don't think I would be surprised." If she were going to allow for things of a supernatural nature, why not allow for a ridiculous beginning to them? "So, all this magic has come down through the ages, then what?"

"Mages use it to do what they do," he said. He looked at her and frowned. "It seems rather commonplace when you think of it that way, doesn't it?"

"Isn't it commonplace?"

He shifted to look at her. "What did you think when your horse
sprouted wings?"

She started to toss off a careless reply but found she couldn't.
"I don't know," she hedged.

"I don't know what you thought either, but whatever it was, it
was apparently enough to leave you in a faint." He smiled briefly.
"Some magic is good, some is bad, and some simply is. Your horse's
magic simply is. Ehrne's . . . well, I suppose we can argue the merits
of what he has at another time. I wouldn't call him a black mage."

"A black mage?"

"Someone who uses evil magic."

"You?"

"Not of late, if you must have the truth, but previously? Aye."

"Did you enjoy it?"

He looked at her as if he'd never seen her before. "What a
question."

"Are you going to answer it?"

"I'm not sure I want to," he muttered. He took a deep breath. "At
the moment, I'm not sure I'm enjoying much at all. I suppose there is
a fair amount of satisfaction that comes from dealing out just deserts,
though I fear I must admit I've done more than my share of dealing
out deserts that weren't so just simply because I could." He shrugged.
"As for other magics, in the end, one can generally only use the magic
one is entitled to by birth. I suppose, though, that with enough power,
one can use whatever one has the stomach for."

"And you have a very strong stomach, is that it?"

"I draw the line at prissy elven rot," he said firmly. "But anything
else? Aye." He shrugged again. "As I said, when one has enough
power, there isn't much out of reach. I'll describe a few of those things
for you—"

She could scarce believe she was listening to what he was now
going on about, much less taking any of it as anything but a very large
pile of horse manure. He seemed to believe it, which she supposed
said something. He also seemed convinced that that thing in the corner

was watching him, which she supposed she could understand as well. Whatever it was, it seemed to want to keep Acair in its sights. She was half tempted to ask him to trot out one of his spells to show her, but she thought she might have seen enough over the past few days. What she thought she wanted to do was have a bit of a rest.

"That's all very interesting," she said with a yawn.

"You haven't been listening to anything I've been saying, have you?"

"I've reached my limit of unbelievable things for the day. I heard something about history and books, and then I lost interest." She smiled. "Sorry."

He shut his mouth, which had been hanging open. "You are the damndest woman."

"Thank you. Now, why don't you leave off with all that other rot and tell me just about you. What was the first naughty thing you ever did? That will hold my interest, I'm sure."

He smiled. "Very well, if you insist. I think the first spell I ever used was one that set my oldest brother's trousers on fire." He looked at her knowingly. "A spell of just five words. Quite a feat for a lad just starting out."

She smiled. "I don't believe it."

"Would you believe three words?"

"Aye, *that* I would believe," she said dryly. "I'm talking about something besides familial pranks. Some glorious thing you did that you shouldn't have done."

He studied her. "I believe you're having a bit of sport at my expense."

"Again, you need someone who isn't intimidated by your terrible reputation or your vast amounts of mythical power to help you not take yourself so seriously." She pulled his cloak more closely around her. "Impress me."

"If I haven't managed to impress you without having to sing my own praises, there is no hope for it. But if I'm able to stretch my memory back so far into my innocence—"

She snorted before she could help herself.

"My *innocence*," he said pointedly, "I would have to say the first bit of true trouble I got myself into—and out of brilliantly, I must admit—was a rather pedestrian excursion into the back garden of a neighbor who I will admit intrigued me simply because of the things he was growing where nothing should have grown. And once I'd helped myself to several of his peaches, I couldn't resist a wee peek into his solar."

"Where you found him snoozing in his chair before the fire?"

"Nay, I found a spell sitting on his mantel."

She looked at him with a frown. "How does a spell sit?"

He pointed to the corner. She had to admit that thing wasn't so much sitting as it was slouching, but perhaps mages didn't make distinctions about that sort of thing.

"It was wrapped in other spells," Acair continued, "which to a lad of eight summers was an irresistible temptation. I unwrapped, examined, then panicked and fled past the man out through his garden." He paused. "I fear I might have knocked him off a ladder on my way by."

"On purpose?"

"I refuse to answer that," he said promptly. "I escaped home as a nasty little crow and didn't say a word to anyone, mostly my sire, when the man came calling to see if we had seen a short, highly skilled thief in the area."

"He never caught you?"

"Never."

"What did the spell do?"

Acair shook his head slowly. "Honestly, I don't remember. It was so terribly disappointing after all the things it had been wrapped in that I believe I tossed it into the fire and it went up in smoke. I'm not sure I could begin to remember what its original purpose had been."

"So you began to look for better spells."

"Aye," he agreed. "Lesson learned. No green peaches and no boring spells. Others have done much worse with lesser codes of conduct."

She supposed they had. "So," she asked, because she was chilled and frightened and talking about ridiculous things was rather soothing, all things considered, "what's the difference between a witch and a mage?"

"Levels of snobbery."

She smiled. "Is that so?"

"It is so." He shrugged. "A witch will have a fair amount of power or not, depending on her position in life, but neither a witch nor a warlock will have the sort of power a mage can boast. Then you have your garden variety wizards, who are generally nothing but pompous blowhards, endlessly trumpeting their complicated spells which are absolute rot."

"What does that leave?"

"Oh, a never-ending list of other practitioners of magic of various kinds including elves, dwarves, dreamspinners, and others who do things in places you wouldn't want to go."

She watched him in silence for a moment or two. "And did you do all those terrible things they say you did?" she asked finally.

He took a deep breath. "Aye."

"Should I be afraid of you?"

"I've never done worse to a woman than insult her gown, if that eases you."

"You called my hair red."

"Your hair *is* red."

"Did you truly try to take all the world's magic?"

"*Try* is the word you should concentrate on there."

She shook her head, then laughed because she simply couldn't believe any of it. Elves, dwarves, dragons, magic, it was all absolute fantasy created no doubt at one point by a pair of very desperate parents with overactive imaginations who couldn't get their children to sleep. The shadows she had seen on the ground were nothing but *her* imagination, Ehrne upstairs was a pompous ass, and the man sitting next to her . . . well, he looked capable of several things. She just wasn't sure she was ready to believe any of those things.

His hand was on her arm suddenly. "Don't move."

"Why not?

"I hear something."

She felt her heart stop briefly. "At the door?" she managed. "Have they come for us?"

He shook his head, then pointed at the window where there seemed to be a bit of a shimmer. He put his finger to his lips and rose, pulling her up with him. She found herself backed up against the wall with Acair standing in front of her. He might have been a black mage of the first water, but he did display a decent amount of chivalry when it was called for.

She held her breath as she listened to . . . absolutely nothing. Acair didn't move, though, which she wondered about. She finally looked around his shoulder to see a slender shape slither into the dungeon through the window where bars had been before. The slight figure landed in a crouch on the stone under it, straightened, then hopped off the bench as if he did that sort of thing every day.

"A rescue?" Acair asked carefully.

The man pushed the hood of his cloak back and Léirsinn realized she had seriously misjudged what she'd been seeing. That wasn't a man there, it was a silver-haired woman of advanced years. She didn't move like an old woman, though. Perhaps magic was involved.

"I heard a rumor there were two souls lingering in a dungeon where they didn't belong," the granny said. "I thought a little rescue was in order. Acair, how are you, love?"

Léirsinn eased past him and looked up at him. "Do you know her?"

"I'm surprised to find I do," he managed.

"Who is she? Witch, wizardess, mage in skirts?"

He took a deep breath. "She is Eulasaid of Camanaë."

Of course she was. Léirsinn smiled briefly at the woman, then looked up at Acair, who she had to admit was rather pale. She took hold of his arm because he looked as if he might need that sort of thing. "And you know her, how?" she ventured.

Acair took a deep breath, then let it out slowly. "She is my grandmother."

Léirsinn knew she shouldn't have been surprised. She smiled at Acair's grandmother when what she really wanted to do was find somewhere to sit down. When would things return to the way they had been so she could carry on with her normal, uninteresting life?

She wasn't sure she dared ask that question seriously.

Fourteen

Acair had honestly believed he'd seen it all. He had enjoyed spectacular sunsets and the occasional lovely sunrise—he was not an early riser by nature—priceless treasures, gilded halls with thrones he'd lounged on whenever possible, and magic that was nothing short of breathtaking. He had reveled in everything the world had had to offer and then quite a bit more that he'd taken without invitation.

He had never in his long life thought he would ever see the granddaughter of the wizardess Nimheil standing in a dungeon dressed all in black, come to rescue him.

"Um," he managed.

Eulasaid only laughed softly. "And so the journey is repaid tenfold." She put her hand briefly on his arm, then turned to Léirsinn. "And you are Léirsinn of Sàraichte."

Léirsinn looked at her in astonishment. "How did you know?"

"Your pony told me." She smiled. "He's a lovely little fellow. Very chatty."

Acair glanced at Léirsinn to see how she was taking that. She looked past surprise, which he supposed was understandable. For a gel who had fainted at the sight of wings on her horse, she had shown a remarkably strong stomach over the course of the past several hours, facing all sorts of things he was certain she hadn't wanted to believe.

"Of course," Léirsinn said faintly. "I don't suppose that if you're rescuing us, you could point me toward the barn so I can liberate that chatty pony, could you? I can't leave without him."

"Oh, not to worry, love." Eulasaid patted her pocket. "I have him right here. You might want to take him to Hearn to investigate his genealogy properly, but in my brief conversation with him, we identified at least one of his noble dams who had magic. I suggested a pair of shapes he might try and he took to the smallest without any trouble."

"Shapes," Léirsinn echoed, but the word was more of a choked whisper than anything.

"You might be surprised by what lies inside those you love." Eulasaid smiled. "You see, I'm a gardener by trade and I like to see the possibilities in things. Seeds, horses, grandsons."

Acair was still trying to find his tongue, but if he'd had a better grasp on his traitorous form, he would have disabused Léirsinn of the notion she might be getting from that diminutive granny standing there that said granny had never done anything more serious than turn a spade of soft earth. That one . . . he shook his head. The tales of Eulasaid's exploits were the stuff of legends. She had faced off with black mages, renegade wizards, and all types of other nasty things without so much as a light sigh of exertion. She was older than Soilléir, canny as hell, and had likely forgotten more spells than Acair had ever known.

And she was, as he had said before, his grandmother.

He had never presented himself at her table, of course, because he was who he was and she was who she was and he hadn't wanted to interrupt any of her dinner parties. He could hardly believe she would even acknowledge him, much less rescue him.

Truly, his life had become very strange.

"You came to rescue us," he said, because he still couldn't quite believe what he was seeing.

"Aye, *both* of you, Acair," Eulasaid said with a small smile. "We heard tell that you were unwilling guests here, so your grandfather

and I thought you might be pleased to see a friendly face or two."
She rubbed her hands together. "I'm not as spry as I used to be, of
course, but I think we'll manage well enough."

"I don't want to be rude," Acair said gingerly, "but we are on
the wrong side of Ainneamh's borders and the king is not without
power—"

"Ehrne is an ass," Eulasaid said. "I have no fear of him. I happily
amuse myself by unraveling his border spell when it creeps into my
garden, so I'm familiar enough with what he creates. This thing
guarding his dungeon was, I daresay, created by one of his lesser
grandchildren several centuries ago. It hasn't been tended very well,
but even so I suggest we don't linger. We still have a bit of a walk
in front of us."

Acair nodded. "Too far for a dead run," he agreed, "even for me.
You should go ahead with Léirsinn. I'll distract the guards and
follow as I can."

"Not to worry, love," Eulasaid said cheerfully. "The guards are
sleeping soundly and Sgath is making a nuisance of himself upstairs
to give us a chance to be away. You know Ehrne. He'll be arguing
with Sgath for hours over past imagined slights. We'll have time
enough for a leisurely stroll, though I think we'd best be about it.
I believe I might have left the kettle on."

Acair wasn't about to argue. He boosted his grandmother, then
his, er, whatever that red-headed gel was, then hauled himself
through the window without delay. He looked over his shoulder in
time to watch that damned spell of death reach out with long,
spindly fingers and pull itself up and out of the window as well.

"You have a friend," Eulasaid remarked, brushing off her hands
and settling her cloak.

"My constant companion," Acair said sourly. "Don't suppose
you could destroy it for me, could you?"

"Oh, I don't like to interfere," she demurred.

"Ha," he said with a snort, then he clamped his lips shut. "Forgive me, my lady."

She laughed, a delightful sound full of good humor. "Absolutely nothing to forgive, love, of course." She glanced at the spell again. "An interesting little thing there. Perhaps I'll have a wee conversation with it later, just to see if it has anything interesting to say. But I think it has a purpose in your life that I don't dare disturb." She smiled at him. "Let's go home, shall we?"

Acair didn't want to acknowledge the small . . . something . . . those words gave him in his chest. A feeling of fondness toward a woman who could have flattened him with the smallest lifting of her pinky finger, perhaps. He shook his head in resignation. 'Twas that damned spell of healing Rùnach had used on him the year before, rearing its ugly head yet again. He was never going to be free of its vile effects.

"Why don't you children go on ahead," Eulasaid suggested. "I find that I suddenly have business behind us. I'll be along shortly, I promise."

Acair considered protesting, but Eulasaid was who she was, after all. Whilst she might enjoy a proffered arm on the way into supper, she didn't need a lad with spells to aid her if she had a bit of business to see to. Given that he was unable to use any of his magic, he supposed there was no use in tagging along after her. That and he suspected nothing he could say would dissuade her, so he made her a brief bow, then took Léirsinn's hand and continued on with her as quickly as he thought they dared.

"That was interesting," she remarked.

He shot her a look, then shivered. "Wasn't it, though? And there I'd been, racking my wee head for ways to get us out of that damned place with as little fuss as possible. I can't believe I'm saying this, but it helps to have powerful friends."

"I'll say. Did I also hear her say my horse was in her pocket?"

"I believe you did."

She was quiet for a goodly while as they walked swiftly through the forest, draped as it was in pre-dawn light. He didn't dare speculate on what she was thinking; he was too busy trying to keep pace with her. He wasn't unaccustomed to making hasty exits, but he had to admit he was hard-pressed to keep up with Léirsinn when she was in a hurry.

He found himself unaccountably relieved, a fair bit of time later, to see the thin blue line marking Ehrne's western border. He made certain Léirsinn was beside him, then crossed it without delay. He hunched over with his hands on his thighs and simply breathed in air that he didn't have to share with monarchs who wanted him dead.

He supposed that was going to be something of a rarity.

He heaved himself upright eventually and found his companion simply standing there, watching him. He was tempted to reach for a spell of protection, then caught himself halfway to doing the like. It gave him pause, honestly more than anything that he'd faced over the past year.

Perhaps he needed a change.

"Who was that again?" she asked.

He latched onto the distraction without delay. "That," he said, "was Eulasaid of Camanaë."

"Is that a place or a magic?"

He reached for her hand and tucked it under his elbow. He started down the path with her, happy to discuss anything that didn't have to do with his own sorry self.

"It is both, as it happens," he said. "Not far from here, as fate would have it, is that lovely little country, full of all sorts of magical things and beings. Unfortunately, I doubt we'll have a chance to make a visit."

"And she's your grandmother," Léirsinn said slowly. "This Eulasaid of Camanaë."

"To her continued surprise, no doubt," he said. "She's my father's mother and the granddaughter of the Wizardess Nimheil."

"One of those women who only dabble in lesser magics?" she asked politely.

Where to begin with that? He decided 'twas best not to begin at all. "Nimheil is definitely an exception to that rule," he said. "Her granddaughter is as well. A very powerful gaggle of hens, that lot from Camanaë."

"Do you honestly think they would appreciate being called a gaggle?" she asked, sounding amused.

"I think any of them would attempt to slay me on the spot just for the sport of it, leaving me to scamper behind my father's mother's skirts," he said with a snort, "so what I call them is likely the least of what they'd be interested in."

She looked up at him seriously. "I would ask you if you dine with your grandparents often, but I'm guessing not."

He shook his head, but couldn't bring himself to make light of it. He had spent more than his share of time in exclusive and very luxurious places, which he had always told himself made up for the rest of his life. Now, though, he was starting to wonder if there might have been things he'd missed out on, things he should have made more of an effort to be a part of.

He rubbed his chest in annoyance. That damned spell. If he ever managed to get Rùnach of Tòrr Dòrainn properly cornered and cowed, he would be insisting on a few changes.

"Where are we going?"

He was grateful for not only the change of subject but the necessity of thinking about his next move.

"My list of safe harbors is very small," he said slowly, "and the ones where I'm welcome is even smaller, I fear. I believe we should accept the lady Eulasaid's kind offer and make for Lake Cladach. You'll be safe there whilst I turn for Neroche."

"Where a warm welcome also awaits?"

He looked at her narrowly. "Throwing a man's past in his face is hardly the way to give him room to carve out a new, less murderous, future."

She smiled faintly. "I don't think you're nearly as evil as you would like everyone to believe."

"I'm worse, trust me," he muttered. "You would be wise to keep as far from me as possible."

"Too late now, I imagine. Besides, you hold the key to my grandfather's salvation."

He shook his head. "Heaven help you if I'm what you're relying on, which you are, poor girl."

"I'm a score and ten, Acair. I can think for myself."

"I'm two years shy of a century, and I'm not sure I do much thinking at all."

She laughed at him. He didn't bother to assure her that her laughter was misplaced.

"I still think you're inventing most of this as you go," she said, "but I will admit that I've seen things that give me pause. Your grandmother, for instance, is rather spry for what I'm assuming is a rather substantial tally of years."

"A tally I won't reveal, because I am discreet like that," he said archly.

She smiled. "And so you are, to your credit. Now, tell me again how you're related to her? She's your father's mother?"

"Aye," he said, looking briefly over his shoulder to make sure Soilléir's spell wasn't going to object to that small bit of truth. After all, it wasn't as if Léirsinn didn't now know who he was. Given that he hadn't been the one to tell her, perhaps adding a few more details past what he'd given her in Ehrne's dungeon wouldn't upset the damned thing overmuch.

"And she's a safe harbor for us?"

"I can't imagine she would rescue us only to toss us in her dungeon," he said, "not that I imagine they have one."

"Generous."

"Aye, they are, so it seems." He paused. "I think perhaps we shouldn't roam about their little kingdom, though."

"Why not?"

"Because my half-brother Ruithneadh and his lady wife live across the lake from them, or so I understand."

"And they wouldn't be happy to see you?"

"No," Acair said without hesitation. "We share a father,

Ruithneadh and I, but that is exactly all we share." He looked at her, then sighed. "The situation is a bit complicated. I'm not sure if I was entirely clear about this before, but my father was a bit of a rogue. He carried on with my mother for quite some time yet never found the opportunity to wed her."

"How long is quite some time?"

"Several centuries, at least. What he was combining before that, I couldn't say." He looked at their surroundings for a moment or two to make sure they were still safe, then continued on. "After my father and my mother had parted ways, I understand he managed an invitation to Toirmisgeach of Dùinte's salon and there he saw Sarait, the youngest of the five daughters of the king of the elves."

"Isn't his dungeon where we just were?" she asked.

"Nay, Sarait is the daughter of Sìle, king of the elves of Tòrr Dòrainn. Much more exclusive, that lot. Their land is to the east of Ehrne's. The elves of Tòrr Dòrainn do not wed with any who aren't their sort of people, if you know what I mean. But my father fell madly in love with Sarait and would not be gainsaid, or so I understand. How he managed to win her, I don't know."

"Wait," she said slowly. "If King Ehrne is your cousin, that would make you an elf. Part, at least."

"To my continued surprise, aye, it does."

"And part witch."

"Wizard," he said, "through my mother and the lady Eulasaid, whom you've met. Aye to that as well."

She stopped and looked at him. "But if your cousin is the king of Ainneamh, does that make you a prince?"

He had to admit he rarely thought of it that way, but there was truth to it, he supposed. "If it earns me entrance to a dining hall that sets a decent table, absolutely."

She smiled. "Your needs are fairly simple, aren't they?"

If she only knew. He supposed he would have been far better off in the past if he'd limited himself to what he'd intended to eat each night and left other things alone. "You're a wise lass for noticing that," he said. "Supper, cards, the odd, irreplaceable knick-knack. I'm honestly not at all sure why I have so many enemies."

"I can't imagine either," she said solemnly, "but King Ehrne certainly seems to fall in with that lot."

"The feeling is quite mutual, I assure you," he said. He paused, then looked at her. "He may have more reason for that than I'm allowing. 'Tis possible that I may have vexed him overmuch in the past."

"Pinch something or just insult him?"

"I removed his crown from where it had fallen half off his head whilst he was napping in his great chair, hefted it, then tossed it back at him as not worth the effort." He shrugged. "I may have also insulted his wife."

She laughed a little. "I should be appalled."

"Likely so, for you have to know I'm leaving out the more unsavory bits in deference to your finer sensibilities," he admitted. "He is an ass, as anyone will tell you, and deserves everything I've taken the time to do to him over the years. Sarait's father, Sìle, though is a different sort. I'm honestly not sure why he gave my father permission to wed his daughter, but Gair is nothing if not charming."

"It must have been difficult to have him start over with someone else," she said quietly.

"Especially given what brats he sired on her," Acair said with a shudder. "Awful souls, every last one of them."

She nodded and walked on with him. She was silent for so long, he finally looked at her. She was watching him out of the corner of her eye.

"You don't have to tell me more," she said.

"I'm honestly not sure I can," he said. "And stop looking at me with those eyes of yours that see too much. 'Tis no wonder no stallion in your barn manages to be about a decent bit of mischief with you watching."

"I am a good judge of hearts."

"Don't judge mine."

She only smiled briefly, then turned back to watching the path in front of them. He wasn't entirely sure she hadn't murmured *too late* under her breath, but he wasn't about to ask her to repeat it so he could be certain.

He said nothing more, for there was nothing more to say. She could peer inside his black heart all she liked, but she wouldn't find anything good. He had burned it all out decades earlier. No matter what horrors that Fadairian spell of healing had done to him, in the end, there was nothing left of his heart but the ashes from too many evil deeds.

More the fool was he for indulging in even the slightest wish that things could be different.

He gathered up a few thoughts of mayhem and wrapped them about him like a cloak. They were comforting and left him feeling much more at ease. He nodded briskly to himself and marched on with purpose. He would stash Léirsinn comfortably at Sgath and Eulasaid's lovely palace, then be off on the hunt for that lazy meddler from Cothromaiche so he could have that damned spell of death properly disposed of. Once that was done, he would solve Léirsinn's mystery of those annoying spots of shadow, rescue her grandsire, and see her settled somewhere safe. He would then be back to his normal way of doing things.

He hadn't the heart for anything else.

A pair of hours later, he supposed it might take him a bit longer to be on his way than he'd feared. He was sitting in the very cozy nook of a welcoming kitchen, enjoying a glass of excellent wine and watching the three other souls there discuss—what else?—horses.

Sgath was a keen horseman, Acair knew from rumor alone. Angesand foals occasionally found their way into Sgath's stables, something Acair knew was so rare as to be relegated to the stuff of legends. Eulasaid was just as enthusiastic and Acair imagined she was the one who managed, on those rare occasions when managing was accomplished, to talk Hearn of Angesand out of his beasts.

He watched his father's parents chat with Léirsinn, interrupting each other with affection, finishing each other's sentences with smiles of good humor. He had to use a great deal of energy to ignore a pang of something that might have been called envy. He had no memories of his father ever having had anything to do with his mother and, if he were to be completely honest, he thought it might have been better that way. If ever two were not meant to live together in bliss, it had been those two.

He couldn't help but wish that he'd attempted a visit to his current location much sooner.

He set his glass down, smiled, then pushed his chair back. Too much sentiment was obviously detrimental to his health. "I'd best go see to . . . er, the out of doors. Rather."

"Wouldn't want it scampering off," Eulasaid said with a smile. "Go ahead, darling. Walk all you like."

He was ninety-bloody-eight years old, yet he left his pride behind at that damned table and bolted. It took him a dozen turns about the garden before he thought he might have gotten control over his traitorous heart. Damned thing. He should have told Rùnach to rip it from his chest, not heal it—

He ran bodily into his father's sire before he realized what he'd done. "My apologies," he said, reaching out to steady Sgath.

His grandfather only laughed. "I'm not so far into my dotage as all that, lad, but I thank you for your pains just the same." He nodded toward the path. "A decent moon tonight, as well as your grandmother's spells of lamplight tucked artistically into the trees, which I'm sure you've already noticed. Another few turns about the old place, aye?"

"Ah, I'm sure I have something to do elsewhere—"

"And I'm fairly certain that whatever that thing might be, it will wait. Don't you think?"

Acair looked at Sgath evenly. "Are you taking me out to the proverbial woodshed, Your Highness?"

Sgath only grinned at him. "Too late for that, young one, so I suppose we'll just have to take a walk and see if that keg of ale I stashed behind one of your grandmother's prized rosebushes has survived the fall prunings. Interested?"

Acair couldn't deny that he was, so he nodded and walked with the man who had watched his own son turn away from everything he'd taught him and choose a far different, more unpleasant path.

"You could have come sooner," Sgath said mildly, at one point.

Acair looked at him quickly. "Would you have allowed me inside the gates?"

"After a trip to the woodshed, most likely."

Acair almost smiled. "Just as I thought."

Sgath clasped his hands behind his back. "I hear you've been making a few social calls over the past several months."

"Unfortunately."

Sgath laughed softly. "I won't rub your nose in it, son."

"No need," Acair said. "Soilléir's done enough of that for the both of you."

"I imagine he has. And look you there; our destination comes into view." He nodded up the path. "Tiptoe if you can. Eulasaid isn't particularly keen on the places I store my creations."

"Eulasaid wishes only that you would stop crushing her rose-bushes with them," Eulasaid said, stepping out of nothing onto the path. "Let me take a turn with my grandson while you find a pair of mugs and an equal number of stools, then I'll leave you to your ruminations." Eulasaid linked arms with him. "Come along, dar-ling, and we'll leave your grandfather to his preparations. You know, Acair, you could have come to visit sooner."

Ah, not more of that. He looked for aid but Sgath was pointedly ignoring him. Sgath did send a quick wink his way, then ambled off to apparently find the appropriate *accoutrements* for the night's activities. Acair supposed he was doomed, but his father's mother had rescued him from a dungeon earlier, so perhaps he owed her a bit of conversation.

"Thank you for the rescue and a delightful meal," he said politely.

Eulasaid lifted her eyebrow briefly. "You have lovely manners."

"I didn't learn them at my mother's table."

"Ah, Fionne," Eulasaid said with a smile. "She is a force unto herself."

"With absolutely no sense of right and wrong."

"Well, I suppose that could be debated endlessly without any useful conclusion being reached," Eulasaid said. "She has very strong opinions, to be sure, and those opinions are her own. But you must admit she is loyal to a fault."

"I think I disappoint her."

"I think she senses that you're conflicted in your heart." Eulasaid looked up at him. "Good and evil are powerful forces, Acair. I suspect that no matter how much you want to choose the later, the former tugs at you."

"Good?" he said, trying to put just the right amount of dismissiveness in his tone. He didn't want to think about how soundly he'd failed. "Boring stuff, that. I choose evil every time."

Eulasaid squeezed his arm. "You try, I'm sure," she said easily. "I suspect you think about the consequences of each too much. If you could just press on without thought, you might manage to embrace darkness more fully."

"Like my father?" He regretted the words the moment they left his lips, then realized what he was regretting and cursed himself for it. What did it matter to him if his father's mother suffered grief over her son's choices or was reminded of the same?

"See?" Eulasaid said with a faint smile.

He frowned fiercely. "I vow I don't know where these annoying thoughts come from. I believe I'm not sleeping enough at present. It leaves me unable to embrace my true self."

"I believe, love, that you're just finding out who your true self might be."

"With all due respect, Mistress Eulasaid—"

"Granny. You could call me Granny, if you liked. Or Grand-mother." She smiled at him. "What do you call your mother's mother?"

"Nothing. We're always too busy blurting out spells to ward off whatever evil minions she's sent after us to manage any polite greet-ings. When we attempt to visit, that is." He shrugged. "She isn't much for family, I daresay."

Eulasaid laughed. "I'm not at all surprised. I believe I've met those same minions myself. That and her trollish neighbors do give one pause." She stopped and looked at him. "And here we are by the infamous and well-hidden keg of ale." She leaned up and kissed him on the cheek. "I'm happy you are here, Acair. Come more often."

And with that, she started away.

"Mistress—er, Grandmother?"

She turned and smiled. "Aye, love?"

"Thank you again for the rescue this morning."

"It was most definitely my pleasure, darling. Sleep well."

He watched her go, completely bemused. He would have rubbed his cheek to see if she'd left a mark, but he simply couldn't bring himself to. He walked over to where Sgath was pouring two sub-stantial mugs of ale, sat down where instructed to, and looked at his father's father in consternation.

"She does that," Sgath said.

Acair blinked. "Who? What?"

"Eulasaid. She throws people off balance."

"Is that what she did with me?"

Sgath handed him a mug. "I think with you she was just telling you that she loves you. She always has, truth be told, even when you were off combining terrible mischief. But she doesn't like to interfere overmuch."

"I can think of several people, one black mage in particular, who would say she did."

"Ah, well, Lothar of Wychweald needed to be stopped and she was at hand." He smiled. "She doesn't like to take credit for it, even though the masters at Buidseachd do send her gifts each year on the anniversary of her having tossed Lothar out their front gates."

Acair imagined they did. He sipped his ale, then looked at his grandfather in astonishment. "This is delicious."

"As your grandmother said, you should have come earlier."

"If I'd known this was what you were brewing, I would have."

Sgath laughed easily, then continued to smile. "You would be most welcome. Your brothers? Perhaps not so much."

"They are a sorry lot," Acair agreed, "and I the worst of them, I'm afraid."

"The youngest," Sgath said, "but not the worst."

"I should be offended," Acair said, enjoying another pull. "I've worked very hard to earn all my accolades and the terror they inspire."

Sgath smiled briefly, then he sobered. Acair was tempted to shift, or suggest that perhaps a visit to the woodshed would be less painful than what he suspected was coming his way, but he found that all he could do was sit there and brace himself for what he was certain would be a terrible dressing down.

"I have watched you over the years."

Acair nodded grimly. "I wouldn't be surprised."

"I will tell you this, not because you asked but because I'm well-seasoned and my opinion is always of great interest to those around me." His expression was very serious. "I don't think you have it in you."

Acair frowned. "Have what in me?"

"That which my son has in him, that hard edge that makes him what he is."

"But of course I do," Acair protested. "Murder, mayhem, mischief. I live for that sort of rot."

Sgath shook his head. "I am not young, Acair, and I have seen the comings and goings of all sorts of elves and wizards and mage kings. I will tell you this, not to flatter you, but because you need to hear it. Gair was my son and I loved him. I still do, because he is my son. But there is a cruelty to him that has not found home in you. Your brothers, aye, and Doílain is the worst of that lot, but not you. Oh, you might try to wallow in foul deeds and I will concede that you richly deserve everything Rùnach and Soilléir have put you through, but I think you give yourself too much credit for wanting evil."

"I don't want evil," Acair protested, "I want the world at my feet."

"Try charm," Sgath said dryly. "You have enough of that and to spare."

"You mean as in be polite, flatter, ingratiate myself with those I intend to rob of their magic?"

"Aye, something like that." He chuckled a bit, then shook his head. "Why you want power from anyone else, I don't know. You have a vast amount of it all on your own."

"Is it ever enough?"

"I think so, but perhaps I have a different perspective," Sgath said. "I'm not one for glittering salons."

Acair wouldn't have admitted it under pain of death, but he wasn't sure he cared for it all that much any longer himself.

"By the way, I think you won't have much anonymity going forward," Sgath remarked. "Ehrne wasn't shy about letting anyone who would listen know that he had you in his dungeon. He'll invent some rot about having been magnanimous enough to have let you go, of course."

"I wouldn't doubt it," Acair said. He took a deep breath. "Thank you for the rescue. I'm not too proud to say I couldn't have managed it on my own."

Sgath smiled. "You're welcome, grandson."

"I've never thought of you that way," Acair said slowly. "As a relative."

"You were too busy wreaking havoc to have time for social niceties."

"Probably," Acair agreed. "Black magery is time consuming."

Sgath laughed. "I imagine it is, my boy." He gestured to Acair's mug. "Drink up. There's more where that came from and we have a pleasant stretch of peaceful evening ahead of us. You can worry about the rest on the morrow."

Acair wished all his troubles could be dismissed so easily, but perhaps he could think on them later. Sgath brewed a very fine ale and, as he said, there was a pleasant stretch of peaceful evening there in front of him.

He suspected it might be one of the last he would enjoy for quite some time to come.

Fifteen

Léirsinn wondered how anyone at Lake Cladach accomplished anything with so much beauty to look at every day.

She walked along the shore and looked out over the sparkling water. She could hardly believe that less than a se'nnight ago, she had been doing her usual chores in her uncle's barn, never imagining that another sort of life might ever exist for her.

The other thing she hadn't expected was to have Falaire walking along behind her, nibbling greenery, and looking completely at his ease. While she understood the usefulness of a barn, she couldn't deny that horses looked happiest when wandering about on grass.

It was cool out, but she'd been provided that morning with a bath, clean clothes, and a cloak that was softer than anything she'd ever felt save Falaire's nose. She'd enjoyed a delicious breakfast, then accepted the invitation to make herself at home and perhaps take her pony for a bit of a walk. She had turned him loose on the greensward, then taken herself for a wander near the water.

She had finally sat down on the edge of a dock that stretched out into the lake. It was the stuff of dreams, truly. The sound of the water lapping against the shore, the warmth of the sun on her back, the sight of her horse . . . ah . . .

Shapechanging.

He stood on the grass twenty paces from her, looked at her for a moment, then tossed his head and disappeared. Or, rather, he sprouted wings, snorted, then leapt up into the air.

And so began a display of, ah, shapechanging that left her gaping. Animals with four feet, things with wings, things with large, terrifying teeth, other creatures that she was perfectly confident came from myth. She climbed up onto the pier because she had to move. She thought better that way. She didn't want to follow where her thoughts were leading, but she realized she simply couldn't deny any longer what she was seeing.

Magic existed.

Perhaps she should have begun to think something was unusual about the fact that Falaire had sprouted wings just outside Beinn òrain. It might have made sense to admit that there were things beyond her ken when she'd come face-to-face with an elvish king. She could have set aside the last of her doubts when she'd listened to a very long list of Acair's accomplishments.

But now, she was faced with unmistakable proof that things were just not as she'd believed them to be—

"You can blame Eulasaid for all that business," a voice said.

She jumped a little, then realized it was simply Acair's grandfather who had joined her. "Blame your wife?"

"I heard her out here very early this morning, chatting with him." He tapped his forehead. "That way, you know how it's done. My lady wife has an especial fondness for those of an equine persuasion. Given how sheltered your pony has been over the course of his life, she thought it might be interesting for him to consider a few things he might not have before."

"Such as how bumblebees fly."

He laughed. "Exactly that. He seems to have committed himself to a great deal of experimentation."

"As long as he doesn't do that while I'm on his back, I think I'll just let him have his head."

"Wise," Sgath said. He watched Falaire for quite some time, then shook his head in admiration. "He is a magnificent animal."

"He is," she agreed. "Even with what I've seen come through my uncle's stables over the years, I've never seen his equal."

Sgath leaned back against the railing and looked at her. "If you don't mind satisfying my curiosity, you're Fuadain of Sàraichte's niece through what line?"

"My father is his brother," she said, "and we share a grandfather, though I suppose that's obvious."

"You might be surprised," Sgath said with a smile. "The twistings and turnings of some family trees are enough to give pains in the head to even the most strong-stomached of souls. How is it you came to be working in his stables, not lounging in his finest salon?"

"My grandfather requires care," she said, "and since it is so expensive, I . . ." She shrugged. "I was put to work at the stables immediately after I was sent to my uncle, and I never questioned why."

"And you didn't question because you want your grandfather to have the best," Sgath said with a gentle smile. "As is right and proper."

They stood there in companionable silence for a bit longer until she thought the questions burning in her mouth might just light on fire without any help. She turned to look at him.

"Ah, Lord . . . I mean, Prince . . . er—"

"'Tis just Sgath, Léirsinn," he said with a smile. "My claim to any throne is so tenuous, I don't think about it very often."

She studied him. "You were raised in Ainneamh."

"At the palace," he agreed. "Lovely place, that."

"Yet you're here."

"Quite happily. My bride and I aren't much for fancy trappings."

Léirsinn would have pointed out to him that his house was the size of a palace, but perhaps he knew that already. He also looked hardly any older than Acair, which she supposed he also knew.

Things were very odd in the world, she was discovering.

She took her courage in hand. "Might I ask you a question or two?"

"Anything."

She could scarce believe she was going to ask what she intended to ask, but Sgath seemed a friendly, honest sort. Not that Acair wasn't, of course, but her relationship with him was a bit complicated. His grandfather had no reason to tell her anything but the absolute truth, no matter what she might think of it.

"Do *you* believe in magic?" she asked gingerly.

He smiled. "I can't say I've had much choice in that matter, given my parentage. So, aye, I do believe in magic, but likely because it's all I've known in my life."

"And you're an elf," she said. "With elven magic, whatever that is."

"Ah, the magic of Ainneamh," he said with a sigh. "Caoireach is strange, and I say that as one who grew to manhood using it. All magic has its own peculiarities, of course. Fadaire—the magic of Tòrr Dòrainn—is so beautiful, one runs the risk of losing one's place in one's spells simply because the words are so mesmerizing. The magic of my ancestors, though—" He considered. "I would call it hard and glittering, a bit like starlight on a cold winter's night. The magic is powerful and the spells very useful, but I've often thought that my relatives have spent so much time over the centuries wrapped up in the admiration of their own magnificent skill that they've lost the knack of it."

"As out of reach as starlight?"

He smiled. "A good way to put it, though Ehrne will never admit as much. If he were called upon to save the world, he might be able to dredge up a spell or two, but it would be an effort. He fights endlessly with Sìle over a border I suppose he could defend if he had to, but the place is honestly starting to look a bit threadbare. The spells that are there are very old but no one has taken the effort to keep them up. Someday I fear some rogue mage will simply walk across the border and take everything they have."

"But you have that magic?"

"I do."

She had to pause and take a deep breath. "And Acair has that magic."

Sgath nodded. "He does, as it happens. I don't imagine it is the first thing he reaches for, but he has it."

She suppressed the urge to find somewhere to sit, but since she was leaning against the railing of the dock, she supposed that might be enough for the moment. "Why hasn't he walked across King Ehrne's border to take over that throne, do you suppose? If the world's magic is what he's after."

"I don't know if he's considered it or not," Sgath said thoughtfully. "To be honest. I suspect my grandson wouldn't think the crown worth the effort. Ainneamh would be a very expensive prize." He shrugged. "Acair is, above all I daresay, a pragmatist."

"He won't play cards at a table where he won't win?"

Sgath smiled. "Perfectly put."

"He said as much."

"I'm not surprised." He watched Falaire for a moment or two, then looked at her. "Anything else I can answer for you?"

"I think I'm overwhelmed enough for the day."

He laughed a little. "I wouldn't blame you, but you're handling it very well." He paused, then looked at her kindly. "I understand how it is to believe the world to be a certain way, then find it is entirely different and in ways that are too much to be believed. I suppose that sort of thing inspires a return to bed where one might pull the covers over one's head and hope that upon waking, one might find things as they were the day before."

She considered, then looked at him searchingly. "Change makes me uneasy."

"I believe it makes many of us uneasy, my dear," he said with a smile. "There are always things you can rely on to not change, however, and perhaps that will be enough to help you bear the others."

"You mean horses that are always only horses?"

"Perhaps that isn't the best example, given your pony's recently discovered talents, but aye, something like that." He pushed away from the railing. "I'll leave you to your ruminations. If you want a warm place to relax, my study is perilous only because of the piles of books." He smiled. "Make yourself at home."

"I'll put my horse away, then accept that kind offer, if you don't mind. I'd like to look at an atlas."

"I'll help you catch him before he flutters off anywhere else," Sgath said, striding away. "Hoy, wait, you blasted horse!"

Léirsinn watched him run off with the energy of a man—well, she had no idea how old he was, but he looked hardly any older than Acair. Elven blood, apparently.

She watched him lead Falaire off to what she knew were luxurious accommodations, then took herself off to find a hot fire and a decent map. Perhaps if she had some idea where she was in the grander scheme of things, she might find the world less overwhelming.

At the very least, she might know what magical countries to avoid.

An hour later, she was in Sgath's library determining just that. She supposed if she'd thought about it, she might have realized how large the world was, but she'd never had the time to do so. Her days had been full of barn chores, avoiding her uncle, and hurrying into town to give all her money to a woman who was apparently a witch. The things she hadn't known . . .

Perhaps the most shocking thing at present was realizing how far away from Sàraichte she was already. And to travel even farther to Tor Neroche?

What in the hell was she thinking?

She looked out the window and considered her alternatives, of which there seemed to be only one. She could abandon her current path, a path she had definitely not chosen herself, and return to where she had come from. But if she did, she suspected that, as Acair had said, she wouldn't live to see the end of the following fortnight. She wasn't sure where that left her save being committed to going where she wasn't sure she had the courage to go.

She realized suddenly that she wasn't alone. She turned and saw that Acair was standing at the door, watching her.

"You could have announced yourself," she said pointedly.

"I was overcome by the color of your hair."

And she was overcome by the sight of his face, but she thought that might be something she could remain silent about. "You may leave off with the ridiculing of my hair, thank you very much."

"It is actually rather glorious, like fire." He shrugged. "I would wax poetic about it, but then you would be ridiculing me."

She leaned back against a table. "Well, if you're going to make the attempt, it seems that the least I can do is listen."

He started to speak, then shook his head. "I'm not sure I am equal to it at the moment. When I've come up with something appropriately lyrical, I'll let you know." He paused. "Do you mind if I join you?"

"Of course not. This is your grandparents' library, after all."

"And I've never once been in their home, so we're on equal footing."

She supposed he had a point there. She picked up a book she had been thinking to have a look at, found herself a chair by a window, and sat down to read. The only problem was that the words did nothing but swim in front of her, so she finally gave up and shut her book. It wasn't as if she would have been able to concentrate anyway.

The dungeons of the palace of Ainneamh had been perhaps a less-than-comfortable place to think about anything but staying warm, but now that she had a hot fire and a decent seat, she had the time and comfort to consider all the things she hadn't been able to before.

She was, from what a cursory glance at a map had told her, hundreds of leagues from Sàraichte. She had no money, no weapon, and no decent clothing save what she'd been given that morning. She had left behind her a defenseless grandfather, her life's savings, and a nobleman who wanted her dead.

On the other hand, she did have a very valuable horse that she had flapped off with. She had no idea what else to call it, for the truth was she'd stolen the damned beast and would likely hang for that alone. But he was safely trotting about one of Sgath's turnouts, changing his shape apparently for the pleasure of it.

She also had a new vision of the world. She had an even clearer vision of things the world contained that she wouldn't have considered anything but fable not a fortnight earlier. If that hadn't been enough, she now knew that food could be made to taste good, something she had hardly dared hope for previously.

Finally, she was looking at a man who had apparently tried to steal the world's magic. That had seemingly been the culmination of a lifetime of naughtiness he had perpetrated, reputedly simply because he could.

She sat back in her chair and studied him as he prowled restlessly through the library, picking up this book or that, opening it, then closing it and putting it back. That was a point in his favor. He could have just dropped the tomes on the floor.

She moved onto other things. Calling him handsome didn't begin to do him justice. Now that she saw him in the proper setting, she realized just how much like the grandson of a prince he looked. He was dressed all in black, but she supposed that allowed him to engage in nefarious deeds more easily. He was a tall, well-fashioned, extremely handsome man she would have accepted any number of invitations from and counted herself very fortunate indeed.

She realized with another start that he was leaning back against a bookcase, watching her.

"What?" she asked in surprise.

"I didn't want to obscure your view of the books I'm standing in front of."

She realized what he was saying and scowled at him. "I wasn't looking at books."

"Stop," he said, putting his hand over his heart. "I'll blush soon."

"I wasn't looking at you either."

He tsk-tsked her. "That lying," he said, shaking his head. "A terrible habit to start. Besides, you're not very good at it."

"Thank you."

He smiled. "You're welcome."

She set her book on the table and looked at him seriously. "I've been thinking."

He only waited. Her uncle would have made some insulting comment about the effort being too much for her, but apparently in spite of all his flaws, Acair of Ceangail was not that sort of man.

"Let me see if I understand the situation," she said slowly. "I am hundreds of leagues—"

"Perhaps not that far," he interrupted.

"A fair distance from my home, then—"

"Where they were plotting to kill you, remember," he reminded her.

She looked at him in exasperation. "You have a horrible habit of interrupting."

"No patience," he admitted. "There's little point in suffering a lesser mage to go on and on about ridiculous things when you know you're going to destroy him in the end, is there?"

She felt her mouth fall open and couldn't stop herself. "You destroyed mages?"

"Humiliated," he corrected, then he paused. "I may have left a few begging on the streets as well. My memory fails me."

"I imagine your memory doesn't fail you at all. How is it that someone so impossibly handsome and charming can be such an utter ass?"

"You know," he said thoughtfully, "my mother has often said the same thing to me. It is a mystery I have often wished to solve, but alas, no time yet." He smiled. "Impossibly handsome?"

"I misspoke," she said. She suspected the last thing he needed was anything else to feed his enormous ego. "Let's discuss your flaws instead."

He sighed lightly. "I am an evil man, as I said, which has earned me a world full of enemies."

"A whole world?" she asked.

"Are you mocking me?"

"Heaven forbid. But go ahead and make me a list."

"Shall I begin with the kings of nations, their powerful ambassadors, or just the pedestrian landholders? Or shall I go right to the terrible black mages who would happily see me dead?"

She considered. "Are we going to encounter any of them anytime soon?"

"I certainly hope not." He walked across the room and cast himself down in a chair across the table from her. "Since I am seemingly at liberty to say what I care to, I daresay there's no reason we can't speak freely."

"Will you describe for me more vile deeds?" she asked politely.

He sighed. "There are those in abundance, but you've already heard a list of some of the worst. I'm quite certain you'll hear more in the future. Nay, I thought we might discuss our plans whilst we have a bit of peace for that sort of thing. You will stay here, of course, in safety. I need to find that damned Soilléir and convince him to take back his spell so I have magic to hand." He met her eyes. "That rubbish that doesn't exist."

"I've been watching Falaire shapechange all morning," she said wearily. "I believe I've become resigned to a few things I couldn't believe before." She considered. "If you have—" She waved her hand in his direction. "—you know."

"I know."

She took a deep breath. "If you have it, can you not find out what those shadows are?"

"I thought I might try."

"And save my grandfather?"

"That too."

She chewed on what she wanted to say for longer than she liked, but she could hardly bear to ask. "Do you think you could heal him?"

His expression was very grave. "I will try."

"Then do whatever you need to," she said. "I don't matter."

"I think you do."

"I can't imagine why," she said. "I certainly don't have any magic. Not a smidgen of it."

"You know, Léirsinn, neither does Hearn of Angesand—or so 'tis said—and look at what a remarkable legacy he continues to leave trailing along behind him through the centuries."

She looked at him in surprise. He was wearing the same look of astonishment, actually.

"I believe," she managed, "that you should go on to be a philosopher."

"And I believe you should stay here," he said seriously. "I've described those spots of shadow to my, er—"

"Grandmother."

He looked rather uncomfortable. "Aye, my grandmother. She believes they aren't benign, nor are they without some sort of consciousness. We suspect that they aren't simply appearing out of nowhere."

She wished rather desperately for a glass of water. "Meaning someone is creating them?"

He nodded. "Exactly that." He fussed with a pair of books on the table, set them aside with a sigh, then looked at her. "I'll tell you very plainly that you won't want to be anywhere near whoever is creating those spells, nor will you want to see what I'll have to do to stop him."

"Not that I'm terribly enthusiastic about coming with you," she admitted slowly, "but I tend to notice them before you do, wouldn't you agree?"

"I'll pay greater heed to where I step."

"You'll never manage my horse on your own."

He started to speak, frowned, then pushed himself to his feet and began to wander about the library as he'd done before. She watched him pull books from shelves, then put them back almost immediately, as if he couldn't find anything compelling enough to hold his interest. She realized after a few minutes that he was nervous. For some reason, that was the most alarming thing she'd seen yet.

She was accustomed to his wearing irritation like a cloak, wielding haughty words like a sword, and trotting out all sorts of untoward and perhaps slightly dangerous skills in order to save her sorry backside and feed her, but she was seeing a side of him she wasn't sure she cared for.

"Acair?"

He stopped and smiled at her briefly. "Not many people call me by my name."

"What do they usually call you?"

"Do you really want to know?"

She smiled in spite of herself. "I imagine not." She studied him for a moment or two, then folded her hands atop a book on the table in front of her. "There's something wrong."

He took a deep breath, then walked over to her and held out his hand. "There's something you need to see."

She had to admit she was growing increasingly tired of having her heart stop so suddenly, then start up again with a great pounding that was almost painful. "Falaire? Is he injured?"

"Your horse is fine," he said grimly, pulling her to her feet. "The rest of us? I'm not sure." He blew out his breath. "Just come and see for yourself."

She would have run, but she had no idea where she was going and Acair managed to get them lost in a garden so thoroughly that they were forced to find aid. The servant who they pressed into service seemed not to be aware of their desire for haste which only added to her frustration. Acair thanked the man once they reached the stables—more politely than she could have managed—then walked swiftly with her to the stall where she knew Falaire was being housed.

He continued on past that stall, which left her rather short of breath, but he didn't pause. He stopped finally at the gate to a very fine arena and looked at her. Léirsinn was vastly relieved to see

Falaire in that arena, cantering about in his proper shape. Eulasaid was there as well, standing just inside the gate, watching Falaire thoughtfully.

"What—" Léirsinn cleared her throat. "What is it?"

Eulasaid held open the gate for her, then stood next to her after she'd come inside. She nodded toward the stallion.

"Watch."

Léirsinn saw nothing out of the ordinary until she realized there was a pool of shadow not twenty paces away from where she stood. How that accursed thing had found its way there, she didn't know. Falaire trotted over toward her, spotted that shadow, then turned aside to go and have a sniff. She would have started forward to stop him, but Eulasaid put her hand out and caught her gently by the arm.

"Wait," she said calmly.

Falaire regarded the shadow in front of him for a moment or two, then reared. He came down with a snort and stomped the bloody hell out of it.

The shadow splintered into scores of shards that glittered in a way that left her almost dazzled by their beauty. She realized tears were rolling down her cheeks. That something so lovely should have been destroyed—

The shards fluttered suddenly, then gathered themselves back together, forming again that small pool of shadow.

Léirsinn realized Acair's grandmother was surprisingly strong only because the woman saved her from falling straightway upon her arse. She felt behind her for the gate, then leaned back against it. Acair's hand was suddenly very lightly on her shoulder, which she appreciated. She patted his fingers, then nodded briskly.

"I am well."

He made a sound that indicated very clearly that he didn't believe her, but he took his hand away just the same. She looked at Eulasaid.

"What do you think?" she managed.

"I think your pony is obsessed with that shadow," Eulasaid

remarked. "He's destroyed it dozens of times, watched it reform, then destroyed it again. He doesn't seem any worse for the wear, which is reassuring, but he is determined to continue to meddle with it." She looked at Léirsinn. "He saw it before I did, I'm afraid."

Léirsinn nodded, then took the lead rope Acair's grandmother handed her. She walked out to the middle of the arena, had a brief battle of wills with her horse, then led him away. He only hesitated for the first few steps, then he came with her willingly.

It was odd.

It also made her decision for her.

She put Falaire in the stall provided for his use, then leaned on the open window and watched him as he helped himself to a steaming bucket of grain. She didn't so much hear Acair as she felt him come stand next to her. He rested his elbows on the ledge of the window as well and watched her horse.

"I want you to stay here," he said quietly.

"I know."

"I am not ever this altruistic," he continued, "which is what I think should worry you the most."

She looked at him then, reputed son of a black mage, lad with a very disreputable past full of dark deeds himself, and wondered about him. "And yet you're trying to save me."

"I know what lies ahead."

"You're simply trotting off to find a friend," she said with a shrug. "How dangerous can that be?"

He blew out his breath. "Extremely. And I can do nothing to save either of us if trouble presents itself, which I find to be an unacceptable position to be in." He paused. "Also, when I find Soilléir, I might be less than polite."

She smiled in spite of herself. "Harsh language?"

"I may have to resort to that, aye."

She leaned on the wood and shook her head. "How is it you can be so charming yet have such a terrible reputation?"

"I like my victims to feel as if they've had a jolly good time before

I either steal their magic or pilfer their choicest spells," he admitted. "That generosity of spirit is indeed my worst failing."

She stepped back and shut the window. "I'm coming with you."

"Léirsinn . . ."

"Careful, Prince Acair, lest I think you're serious about your concern for me."

"Heaven forbid," he muttered. He shot her a look. "And don't call me that. It might give people the wrong idea about me."

She smiled. "What do people usually call you?"

"I don't use those sorts of words in the presence of ladies."

"I can just imagine." She took his arm. "Let's go, lad, and don't think I'm going to let you scamper off with my horse."

He sighed deeply. "Again, Léirsinn—"

"Don't waste your breath."

He studied her for a moment or two in silence, then shook his head. "Very well," he said, sounding resigned, "we'll leave in the morning. I think Eulasaid and Sgath—"

"Your grandparents," she interrupted.

He looked as unnerved as she felt. "Aye, my, er, grandparents. They would apparently like to see us fed at least one more time in a decent fashion, though I think I'll forgo any walks in the garden with the lord of the house. His ale is delightful, but I think I need a clear head on the morrow."

"Where will we go?"

"I'll consider our route over supper. As I said before, my list of welcoming harbors is quite short."

"I don't suppose announcing you're on a mission of good would change any minds?"

"Change is, I'm finding, difficult," he said. "Allowing someone else to change even more so. Not," he added, "that I want to change. When I have my magic back at my fingertips, the world had best tremble in fear."

"Well, you're certainly dressed for it."

He tucked her hand more securely under his arm. "I don't think you have anything approaching the least amount of respect you should have for my truly appalling ability to make mischief. Ehrne didn't begin to plumb the depths of my foul deeds. I suspect I frighten the hell out of him."

"I hear he's an ass."

"He is, which is why he's never invited to supper here. We, on the other hand, are apparently still in the good graces of the lord and lady of the house, which is fortunate. Better to face death on a full stomach, I always say."

She walked with him out of the barn. "Do you always say that?"

"Always. I find 'tis embarrassing to have an entire keep of mages on their faces in front of me, quivering in fear, and then have my belly betray me by a discreet growl. One must maintain one's reputation, you know."

She looked up at him. "In truth?"

"In truth, I am everything they say I am," he said seriously. "And what I'm finding is no one wants me to be anything else than that."

"I might."

"Ah, a red-haired wench with a shapechanging horse," he said with a faint smile. "'Tis a start, isn't it?"

"I think it might be."

He took a deep breath. "I think we'll make for Angesand. I'll hide behind you as we approach Aherin and you can talk our way inside the gates."

"Aherin?" she echoed. She found herself feeling a little breathless. "Do you think so?"

"I would like Hearn to look at your horse," he said with a shrug, "and 'tis on our road north. If you fold a map in a crumply sort of way and twist it around."

"You're going there for yourself, aren't you?" she said, because she couldn't believe anything else.

"Of course. Why would I go for you?"

Because the man had absolutely no affinity for horses and she couldn't imagine that the thought of frequenting a keep full of them was anything but unpleasant. She looked at him knowingly. "You're taking me along as your shield, obviously."

"As I said."

She walked with him through the garden. "How crumpled?" she asked finally.

"More crumpled than I'm willing to admit—oh, look you here. Someone come to direct us to table."

She had to admit she was rather grateful for the distraction. It had been a difficult few days full of things she hadn't expected and wasn't entirely sure she'd enjoyed. The thought of an unremarkable supper in a beautiful spot was very welcome indeed.

She would face other things later.

A pair of hours later, she sat across from Acair at a worn, farmhouse table and watched him with his grandparents. He was a perfect guest. He seemed genuinely interested in his grandmother's gardening projects, more particularly things that flowered at night and under unusual lunar conditions, and he discussed at length the making of tasty brews with his grandfather as if he truly cared about the man's experiments with various grains and fruits of the vine.

She watched him mostly because he was hard to look away from. She supposed he was capable of all those things he'd been accused of only because she'd seen a look in his eye once or twice that she had been happy had been turned elsewhere. Then again, she'd enjoyed that sort of look from more than one horse, so it didn't trouble her overmuch.

"You're going to see Hearn?" Sgath asked in surprise.

"Thought we would," Acair said, sipping his wine. "Just to put our feet up for a moment or two."

Léirsinn looked at Sgath. "He says it's on the way, if you crumple up a map properly and give it a bit of a twist."

"The twists and turns of my grandson's life are truly something to behold," Sgath said. "I believe he's accustomed to that kind of thing."

He was smiling, though, which she supposed should have left her feeling a bit more at ease. Unfortunately, she hadn't missed the look Sgath had sent Acair or the look Acair had sent back his grandfather's way. There was something else afoot, though she couldn't have said what. If Sgath wanted to have a serious conversation with his grandson, she was absolutely going to get out of his way sooner rather than later.

She pled weariness after a bit and excused herself, and she honestly wasn't surprised to listen to Sgath invite Acair for a stroll in the garden. She was simply happy she didn't have to listen to what they might discuss.

She would go along, because she could see the darkness and because of Falaire. She could only hope that taking care of those two things would be the extent of what she would be called on to do.

But Angesand . . .

The world was truly a magical place.

Sixteen

A cair had always expected that death would catch him up at some point. He had spent the past several decades dodging it, eluding it, ducking under it as it shot its poisoned darts over his head. He had honestly expected it would find him as he was hiding in the shadows of some powerful black mage's personal solar, having poached that mage's favorite spell and perhaps a glass of port to enjoy along with it.

He hadn't anticipated it would come outside the front gates of a horse lord's rather rustic and utilitarian keep whilst he very bravely hid behind a red-headed stable lass.

The hiding wasn't going as well as he might have liked. Léirsinn was tall, but not nearly as tall as he himself was, and she certainly wasn't broad enough to do anything but block the smallest amount of wind that accompanied the curses being spewed their way by the lord of the keep.

Or at least there had been curses at first. Now, there was only a lord surrounded by a dozen burly guardsmen boasting either nocked arrows or well-loved swords.

Acair was beginning to wonder if they'd made a very serious mistake.

Hearn of Angesand was not a small man. Acair wasn't either, though he supposed that whilst he and Hearn shared the same respectably intimidating height, the lord of Aherin had a good two stone advantage. If it came down to a wrestle, Acair felt confident he would lose. Badly.

Hearn was currently having a long look at Léirsinn. "So," he said slowly, stroking his chin, "you're from Sàraichte."

"Aye, my lord," Léirsinn said breathlessly. "And it is an honor to even stand at your gates and imagine what finds home inside."

Hearn grunted. Acair suppressed the urge to roll his eyes. Good heavens, if she complimented the man any more, he would likely roll over and beg her to scratch his belly. If purring ensued, Acair vowed . . . well, he didn't dare vow anything. He was still wondering what in the hell he'd been thinking to come anywhere near his current locale.

Again, a perfect example of what altruism got a man. Bring a horse gel to a horse lord's stronghold? Pay the price in peace of mind and quite possibly the ability to breathe.

"Who is that you have attempting to cower behind you?"

Acair did roll his eyes then. Hearn knew damned well who he was. If the fact that he hadn't looked so much like his sire—admittedly an extremely handsome man, particularly when in his prime—hadn't given him away, the fact that Acair had once slipped over the walls and poked around Hearn's solar on the off chance he might find something useful surely would have.

"This is my escort," Léirsinn said, stepping aside. "You may know him already."

Acair shot her a dark look, then dredged up his most pleasant smile. He knew what it looked like because he had practiced it in a large square of polished glass in his youth. He used it when he wanted to put others at ease. He decided that thinking that he generally put others at ease before he robbed them, terrified them, or generally made a terrible nuisance of himself was likely not useful at the moment.

"You," Hearn said without any inflection in his voice.

"Me," Acair agreed.

"I don't care for your kind," Hearn said.

"My lord Hearn—"

A low rumble started. "I almost lost a horse to a monster Lothar of Wychweald created."

"In my defense, I've never fashioned any marginally sentient beings sent specifically to hunt down certain types of people and slay them as did that particularly vile mage of whom you speak."

The rumble increased to a modest roar. "Nay, you went around to the most powerful people in the world and tried to steal their magic!"

"Well, one does what one must to keep busy," Acair managed.

Hearn didn't smile. "How do you have the cheek to show your face in polite society?" he thundered.

"I'm a brazen bastard," Acair admitted, hoping a little honesty would keep him from whatever painful death Hearn reserved for rustlers of horses and poachers of, well, nothing out of solars.

"You are a bastard in every sense of the word." Hearn scowled fiercely and folded his arms over his chest. "I hear you've recently been trotting off to various locales to apologize for your past misdeeds."

"'Tis true."

"Avoiding places where dwarvish kings might be found, or so I understand."

"I could add *cowardly* to brazen, if you like."

Hearn looked at him narrowly. "Why have you come here? And you had best be speaking the truth."

Acair took a deep breath. "We are on our way north and I thought Léirsinn might want to see your stables since she's so fond of horses and you have so many horses to be fond of." He supposed he could save questions about horses Léirsinn might be in possession of and shadows that seemed to be following her wherever she went for when they actually were inside the gates.

Hearn frowned again, but it seemed to be a frown that reflected less a contemplation of all the ways a black mage without his magic

could be put to death and more a consideration of the usefulness of
that compliment. He looked at Léirsinn.

"Is that true?"

"This is," she said breathlessly, "an honor I never would have
dared dream of. The truth is there was a part of me that thought
you were naught but legend. Your horses? Merely beasts, nay, the
images of beasts someone had pulled from a dream."

Acair struggled to mask his surprise. When had that one turned
into such a flatterer? And damn the woman if she didn't look as if
someone had just told her she could try on each of the crowns of
those on the Council of Kings and decide which one she liked best
before she took it home with her.

Well, that was something that would have had him perking his
ears up as well, even though he'd spent a pair of years slipping into
throne rooms country by country and doing just that.

Hearn chortled a bit in pleasure. Acair suppressed the urge to
throw up his hands. The two of them deserved each other, truly.
He caught the dark look Hearn cast at him and sobered immediately. He attempted a look of contrition, but he wasn't sure he'd
succeeded very well.

Hearn offered Léirsinn his arm and escorted her inside the
gates. Acair darted in behind them the very moment before the
gates banged closed, almost crushing him between themselves, no
doubt on purpose. He bit his tongue, though, because he and
Léirsinn were inside gates guarded by powerful spells and he was
nothing if not practical. That he had to be grateful for someone
else's spells to keep him from dying left him grinding his teeth, but
what else could be done? That damned Soilléir—nay, Rùnach had
no doubt had the idea first. He wasn't sure which of the two to
blame for his current straits, but he thought it might be perhaps
more equitable to simply blame them both. The only trouble he
could see that causing him would be the necessity of trying to
decide whose neck to wring first when he next saw them.

He attempted a pleasant, benign expression as he followed the

lord of the hall and his guest about the keep. He made certain to
nod and make the appropriate noises of appreciation until at a certain point he realized there was no need to feign admiration. There
was a reason Angesand steeds were so coveted and it had everything
to do with the tall man striding about his domain, his eyes missing
nothing, his sharp tongue keeping his lads in line. Fuadain of
Sàraichte couldn't possibly have dreamed of anything like it.

Acair was torn between watching Hearn watch Léirsinn and
watching Léirsinn stare, openmouthed, at the horses that seemed
to be everywhere. He could have sworn he saw her fingers twitch
a time or two as if she were almost unable to suppress the urge to
take reins, swing up onto the back of something, and ride off into
a glorious sunset.

"Don't suppose you ride," Hearn said casually to her at one
point.

Acair supposed that was a reasonable question to ask given that
Falaire had deserted them half a mile from the front gates, flitting
off in some shape Acair hadn't cared to pay much heed to.

"I do," Léirsinn said faintly. "As it happens."

Acair looked at the outdoor arena to his left and suppressed the
urge to cover his backside with whatever he might find. There was
a stallion out there in the middle of that arena who was giving his
handler a towering amount of trouble. The man was obviously well
skilled in his equine sort of business, but that horse out there . . .
Acair wouldn't have come within a hundred paces of the thing. He
looked quickly at Léirsinn to find her assessing the horse with her
usual unforgiving brutality. She considered, then looked at Hearn.

"I can ride that one there, I daresay."

Hearn nodded to one of his lads who ran off, then returned very
quickly with a pair of leather gloves. Hearn took them, then held
them out to Léirsinn.

"Wouldn't want you to lose your grip."

She took the gloves, looked at them for a moment or two, then
looked up at Hearn.

"What's his name?"

"We call him Garg."

"What a horrible name," Acair said before he thought better of it.

"He's a horrible horse," Hearn said, grinning. "He has another name of course, you fool. That's just what we call him. Maybe our little miss here will find out from him what he prefers. Off you go, lass."

Acair leaned against the railing, next to the lord of Aherin, and suppressed the urge to fret. The gate was unlatched and Léirsinn was invited inside. She was fairly tall, true, but so willowy and lovely and . . .

Mad. The woman was absolutely mad.

"He'll kill her," Acair protested.

"Have a little faith, you coward."

"This isn't a matter of faith, my lord," Acair managed, "'tis a matter of maths. He outweighs her and—"

"Shut up, Acair, and let me see what she can do."

Acair would have huffed out an insult in return, but he lost track of that thought for a pair of reasons. One, that damned Falaire had landed on his shoulder and had bitten his ear with a beak that was entirely too sharp for the innocent-looking bird he was carrying on as. Second, Léirsinn had taken that monster's lunge line in one hand, a whip in the other, and was engaging in a battle of wills that Acair wasn't at all sure she would win.

There was rearing and snorting and quite a bit of whinnying coming from that thing that should have been contained in some sort of stall with several locks on the door. Léirsinn ignored it all. Acair had watched her do that sort of thing before, of course, but that horse out there was something else entirely.

"He's a beast," Acair said when he could bear it no more.

"And he's not even the worst I have," Hearn said cheerfully. "She's good."

"I'll tell her you said so."

"Don't bother. I'll nod briskly as she leaves the arena. That'll be enough for her." He shot Acair a look. "Don't you know *anything* about horses and their keepers?"

"I don't like horses."

"I imagine the feeling is mutual."

"I prefer dragons, actually," Acair said, because he thought he should make it clear that he wasn't opposed to everything going about on four feet. "They possess a certain elegance that is unmatched in other things."

"You are a terrible snob."

"Thank you."

"It wasn't a compliment," Hearn said, before he turned back to the display going on in his arena.

Acair understood. He, as Hearn had so rightly pointed out, knew nothing about horses save which end tended to bite, but even he could see that Léirsinn was a master at her craft. He realized that whilst Falaire was magnificent, he was simply a reflection of one facet of what Léirsinn could do.

He wasn't sure how long it took—it felt like hours and left him wishing for a stool of some sort to rest on—but Léirsinn finally convinced Garg that he was not going to push her about. Lead horse and all that, he supposed. He'd thought that sort of business daft at the time, but could see the wisdom of it at present. The horse, a stunning yellowish thing that looked quite a bit like sunlight as he trotted around her, was suddenly utterly obedient to her command. He trotted, he walked, he cantered, and generally behaved himself like a proper gentleman. When she stopped him, handed off the whip, and walked toward him, he merely watched her.

He reared once she was on his back. Once. After that, she kept him so busy, he didn't have time for any mischief.

"I would worry," Hearn mused.

"You would?" Acair managed.

"Nay, *you*. If I were you, I would worry."

Acair looked at him then. "About what?"

"That she'll do to you exactly what she just did to that pony."

Acair had something run down his spine at the sight of Hearn's smile. "I am not a horse."

"You know what I'm getting at."

"I am master of my fate," Acair said, grasping for just the right amount of conviction with which to tinge that statement. He wasn't sure he'd succeeded very well.

"Says the mighty one who can't use any of his equally mighty magic at the moment," Hearn said with a snort.

"And how do you possibly know that?" Acair asked. "I don't remember telling you anything—"

"Soilléir was here a few days ago, of course." Hearn shook his head. "How you've managed to survive for so long whilst being so dense, I just don't know." He sniffed, then chortled. "Ah, how I love the smell of just deserts. Just the thing for a late breakfast, don't you agree?"

Acair would have made a cutting reply, but he suspected that would have earned him nothing but a hasty booting right out the front gates. He hadn't had breakfast, as it happened, and there was no sense in losing a decent meal. "Whatever you say, my lord."

"I say shut up," Hearn said absently, having apparently lost interest in anything but a study of the display going on inside his fence. "I believe we're about to see just what that gel can do."

Acair watched not because he was comfortable watching but because he simply couldn't look away. Léirsinn might not have had magic, but she obviously knew what she was doing with a horse. He hadn't doubted it before, but watching her walk into the keep of Aherin and ride what even Acair wouldn't have gotten close to for the price of a spectacular spell only convinced him further that she shouldn't go back to Sàraichte.

Obviously she couldn't go back to stay, but if she didn't go there, where else would she go? He wondered if she would want to stay in Angesand, but that seemed rather far away from anywhere he might choose to linger.

He wondered with a fair bit of alarm if anyone might have seen that thought cross his face, but a quick look about told him that anyone with sense was watching the woman out there, riding that pony fashioned of sunlight.

He blew out his breath carefully. She was not for him and he was not for her.

Odd how he had to keep reminding himself of that.

Hearn watched her until she walked out of the arena, leading that damned horse who now merely walked docilely behind her, then he turned and leaned against his fence.

"Where are you off to, Master Acair?" he asked. "I'm assuming you have a list of souls you're considering robbing or frightening to death or whatever it is you do—nay, wait." He looked at Acair innocently. "You don't have any magic to hand, do you?"

Acair forced himself to maintain a pleasant expression. "Not at the moment," he agreed.

"Which leaves you incapable of foisting your usual nastiness off on others," Hearn said thoughtfully. "An interesting state of affairs for you, my lad."

"Isn't it though?" Acair asked, trying to be as polite as possible. Breakfast was, as he had noted before, hanging in the balance. "As for where we're going, I thought we would make for Tor Neroche."

"Think little Miach will protect you?"

"Protect Soilléir, rather," Acair said, "for when I find him, I'll kill him."

"I'm sure he trembles at the thought."

"He should," Acair said grimly.

Hearn studied him for far longer than Acair was comfortable with. There was something about those horse people that made him uneasy. They didn't have that Cothromaichian sight, something he was familiar enough with to know how to disparage, but they had something like it. It was perhaps less grand, but rather more ter- rifying. When they looked at him, he feared greatly that they were able to see all kinds of things he didn't want to have revealed.

He didn't like having his heart laid bare.

"What are you here for in truth?" Hearn asked quietly. "And remember, I know more than you think I do."

Acair didn't doubt that. He pointed to the bird still clinging to his shoulder. "I have a question or two about this thing here."

Hearn peered at the bird who wasn't a bird, then let out a low whistle. "Your ear is bleeding."

"He bit me."

"I believe he's rather proud of the fact that it wasn't the first time."

"I imagine he's proud of several things," Acair said. "He is, as I'm sure you realize, Léirsinn's horse. He doesn't like me."

"A wise pony, that one."

"We wanted to ask your opinion about his proclivities," Acair said. "He has become very fond of a certain sort of thing that I find . . . odd."

"I can only imagine."

Acair let that pass. "Then I was thinking that perhaps if you had an older, well-behaved horse in need of a small adventure, I might attempt to come to an understanding with you."

"*That* is why you came?" Hearn asked, looking genuinely startled.

"To be honest, nay. The thought only came to me just now." And that thought had come to him because he was half afraid Hearn would want to trade Léirsinn that demon sunlight horse for the bird sitting currently on his shoulder and he would be damned if he ever got on something that uncontrollable. "What could I give you for one? Any black mages you'd care to have me encourage to give up their chosen trade?"

"Besides yourself?" Hearn asked with a snort. "Don't think so, lad. And given that unavoidable bit of truth, I daresay you'll be using your feet for quite some time to come." He studied Acair for several minutes in silence. "But whilst you're here inside my gates, I think I have something you should see."

Acair hadn't wasted any time hoping for an Angesand steed, which left him not sparing any effort to be sorry he wasn't going to have one. In truth, he would only have been surprised if Hearn had been willing to part with one of his horses, for any price.

He sighed, flicked Falaire off his shoulder—ignoring the subsequent offended chirping—and followed the lord of Aherin across his courtyard.

He saw the spot of darkness before Hearn stopped a fair distance away from it and looked at him pointedly. He felt Léirsinn come to stand next to him, then watched as horses avoided the spot without fail. Most of the men in the keep did the same. Most, that was.

One lad walked right into the darkness. Acair watched with horrified fascination as the boy stood there for a moment or two, perfectly still, seemingly perfectly content. He walked on eventually, but the manner of his leave-taking, if that's what it could have been called, was passing odd. What Acair realized with a start was that the lad hadn't pulled away because he'd chosen to, he'd remained where he was until the darkness had allowed him to go.

Interesting.

"Odd," Hearn said finally. "Isn't it?"

That too. "Is he the only one who's walked through that shadow?" Acair asked.

"One other lad," Hearn said slowly. "Had to send him back to his mother."

"Homesick?"

Hearn looked at him. "He went mad." He nodded toward the young man who had just paused in that spot. "That one, though, not sure what to say about him. Everyone else seems to avoid that patch of ground but him. He walks through it every chance he has."

"He likes it?" Léirsinn asked in surprise.

"He seems to crave it," Hearn said. "If I could use such a term." He shrugged. "Don't know what to make of it, but I imagine someone might find an opinion to offer." He looked at Acair. "You, maybe. Perhaps after a bite to eat and a decent mug of ale."

Acair wasn't sure he wanted to offer any opinions, but he had the feeling he was going to have to. He thought about how Falaire had spent so much time and effort fussing with one of those shadows and felt something settle in the pit of his stomach that couldn't have been termed unease but likely wasn't indigestion.

What sort of mischief was afoot in the world? Worse still, why did it seem to be appearing wherever Léirsinn went?

Perhaps it wasn't just Léirsinn.

"Acair?"

He realized she was still standing with him in Hearn's courtyard and they were alone. Well, as alone as anyone ever got in that hive of equine activity, he supposed. He looked at her.

"I apologize," he said absently. "Lost in thought."

"I understand," she said in a low voice. "I don't like this."

He wasn't sure that began to adequately describe his opinion on the matter. He could hardly believe what he'd gotten himself entangled in so innocently, or how anxious he felt knowing there wasn't a damned thing he could do about what he was seeing. Being a mere mortal was highly annoying. He wasn't sure how so much of the world managed to haul themselves out of bed each day, when that was how they had to carry on their lives.

"Magic is the answer," he said confidently.

"A dodgy answer, wouldn't you say?"

She had no idea, and he thought it best not to enlighten her. However dodgy the business of magic might have been, any business where it wasn't involved was far more perilous. His lack of the same was something he was definitely going to have to remedy without fail and as quickly as possible.

Perhaps if he humored Hearn to a never-before-imagined level, the man might find a nag he was willing to part with. Two horses were better than one, he supposed, when one had a pressing quest before him and a great need of haste.

He would do what he could inside the gates, then be about

solving what looked to be unpleasantness that was affecting more than just him and Léirsinn of Sàraichte.

What a great, whacking piece of do-gooding that would likely count for.

S everal hours later, he was mucking out stalls he was fairly sure had been done at least twice already that day. He hadn't dared protest. If it meant he could sleep somewhere save a pile of manure— he had heard more than one tale of that being the proffered accommodation—and perhaps buy him a bit of goodwill from the lord of the keep, he was willing to shovel all day.

He finished with the last stall, dragged his sleeve across his forehead, then realized Hearn was watching him.

"I've seen worse work," Hearn remarked, peering over the stall door. "Not often, but now and then."

Acair leaned on his pitchfork. "Give me another few months and I'll be an expert."

"I wouldn't dare hope for that, but 'tis a better work than your usual business, I suppose."

"I daresay." He paused and looked at his reluctant host. "I suppose an apology to you might not be welcome."

"Oh, I don't know," Hearn said with a shrug. "Try it and see."

Acair took a deep breath. "I apologize for breaking into your solar. If it makes it any better, I didn't take anything. I'm not sure any practitioner of magic who aspires to true greatness could possibly overlook what comes from your stables and the attached rumors of your own vast, if not unusual and very desirable, magic. The temptation is absolutely irresistible." He paused. "Put simply."

"You talk too much."

Acair, quite wisely to his mind, quickly chose silence.

Hearn shifted slightly. "If we're being completely honest here, I can't say I didn't do my own bit of snooping when I was young."

He leveled a look at Acair. "You, however, have been snooping for far longer than you could possibly be considered young."

"But there are so many secrets in the world," Acair said. "I fear I won't have time to discover them all."

"Considering how old your father is, I'd say you had plenty of time to poke your nose in all manner of places where it shouldn't go," Hearn said. He opened the stall door. "You may live to regret it."

Acair took advantage of the courtesy and didn't curse when Hearn almost shut the door on his arse. The more he'd thought about it, the more convinced he'd become that he needed a horse for himself. He wasn't about to ruin any chances for an Angesand steed with a few extracurricular talents, so to speak, by offending his host.

He handed the pitchfork off to a young lad, thanked him profusely, then put on his most pleasant smile for Angesand's lord. "I appreciate the work."

Hearn pursed his lips. "Flattery will not earn you a pony, so you may as well leave off with it. But you can tell me why you're really here. You've given me a handful of reasons, but I'm still unconvinced. Are you come to sniff out my equine genealogies or something more sinister?"

Acair looked at him seriously. "It is as I said, my lord Hearn. I am on my way north, I have no ability to use my magic, and I genuinely wanted a safe harbor and not just for myself. Léirsinn is horse mad and I thought since she has no memory of any place save that hellhole of Sàraichte, I would at least bring her to your front gates and see if you might allow her to peek inside."

"She does recognize a good horse."

"Do you have any bad horses, my lord?"

Hearn lifted an eyebrow. "You might be surprised, my wee mageling. I don't think your lady would be, though. She's an excellent horsewoman." He glanced at the spell loitering in the corner. "And that?"

"A spell of death that follows me courtesy of Prince Soilléir. I'm surprised it isn't charged with turning me into a lawn ornament, but there you have it. Soilléir has a marked lack of good taste."

"But a dab hand with a powerful spell," Hearn said thoughtfully. "Interesting thing, that." He considered a bit longer, then looked back at Acair. "What do you make of that spot of shadow?"

"I'm not entirely sure yet," Acair said slowly, "but I will tell you that when I put my foot in one in Sàraichte just to see what it was about, it ripped off a piece of me somehow."

"Flesh?"

Acair shook his head. "I would say it was part of my soul, but that seems too poetic, even for me."

"Was it painful?"

"Excruciating."

"Good," Hearn said. "You deserve it." He considered, then glanced at Acair. "You can leave her here, you know. If you can convince her to stay."

"I'm not sure it would take much convincing," Acair said, "and I appreciate the offer more than you'll know. She has a mind of her own, though. I've tried to tell her what to do and she's told me to go to hell."

Hearn smiled. "I like her." He rubbed his hands together. "Clean up, my boy, and come inside for supper. Your lady will be taking her ease there."

"She's not—"

He didn't bother to finish his protestation. Hearn never lingered anywhere, or so it seemed, and the present moment was no exception. He had walked off with a purpose before Acair could properly formulate a denial of anything of a romantic nature.

Acair sighed, then went to seek out water for himself. He didn't imagine he would be allowed to use what was reserved for the horses, but he managed to find something that seemed clean. He dried his face on his shirt, dragged his hands through his hair, and wished quite desperately for a decent bath, but that was obviously out of reach at the moment. Truly, he was operating under reduced circumstances in many things.

He walked out into the twilight and looked up at the sky. He wasn't sure what sort of magic Hearn possessed, if any, and his clandestine foray into the man's solar all those many years ago hadn't provided him with any answers. There was definitely something there, though, some sort of something that draped itself over the keep. 'Twas hardly noticeable but seemed to keep at least a storm brewing to the east at bay. Perhaps that was all Hearn wanted, to keep his horses dry and warm. There were worse uses for a spell, and Acair considered himself one who would know.

He shrugged his shoulders to work out a bit of stiffness, then walked across the courtyard to the great hall. At least he wouldn't be shoveling in the rain.

Things could have been much, much worse.

Seventeen

Léirsinn thought she might never be able to catch her breath again.

It had nothing to do with the work, which was less like work and more like an endless bit of wonderment, and more to do with the fact that she had spent the morning inside Aherin itself, working horse after horse, each one more spectacular than the last. Patterns, jumps, simple canters about Lord Hearn's arena, there had been nothing those horses wouldn't do—couldn't do. After a bit, she'd honestly lost track of how many hours had passed and how many horses she'd worked. It had felt as though she'd been trapped in a dream filled with beasts only a consummate storyteller could envision.

She'd woken from that dream only to realize that it was noon and she had been riding for hours. She'd been exhausted.

And then Hearn had bought her another horse.

"We call him the Grey," he had said, "but that's because we have no imagination here. His true name is Turasadhair. I'll let you figure out what that means."

Léirsinn had accepted the Grey's reins with a hesitancy she had never once felt since she'd come into herself and known what she could do. Hearn had only smiled at her and walked with her to the front gates.

"He will eventually go white, as this breed tends to do," he had remarked as the guards had opened the gates, "though I imagine his mane and tail will keep a touch of silver. He's young yet, but I think you'll manage him well enough."

"Any suggestions?" she'd asked.

"He likes to go fast," had been the lord of Angesand's only comment, made in such an offhand fashion, Léirsinn had hardly known what to make of it.

Or at least she had until she had realized exactly what Turasadhair could do.

His speed across the grasslands surrounding Aherin had been breathtaking. She had understood then why Hearn had put such a light saddle on him. She had leaned low over his neck and given him his head. She had realized at one point that she'd been laughing as tears had been streaming down her cheeks.

And then she had asked him for more.

It was as if he'd become not an arrow from a longbow, but a bolt shot from a crossbow. Where he had dredged up more speed she hadn't known; all she'd been able to do was cling to both the reins and his mane and trust he wouldn't lose her off his back.

He had then asked her if *she* could bear more.

It had been as she'd realized they were twenty feet off the ground that she'd noticed he had acquired wings. They had been gossamer bits of business, though, only a hint of something there. Her mind had been so empty of anything but flight, she'd been unable to determine if those wings were only useful in keeping them aloft or perhaps had a different purpose. In truth, she hadn't cared enough to discover the truth. His hooves had clawed at the air as if it had been solid ground, but his gait had been so smooth it felt as if they were the ones who were still and a fierce, endless wind blew the ground past them.

She had no idea, now that she was walking with him back up the way to the front gates of Hearn's hall, just how long they had been out chasing after a terrible amount of speed. The sun was turning toward the west, so surely the better part of the day. All she knew was that she was less exhausted than simply drained.

Hearn was leaning against a gatehouse wall, waiting for her. She stopped in front of him, then smiled.

"Did you watch?" she asked.

"Of course," he said pleasantly. "Have a good ride, missy?"

She could only stand there and laugh. Hearn chuckled, then nodded at the horse.

"He must like you," he remarked. "He doesn't fly for very many. Indeed, I can only think of one other person, but I think the experience was so terrifying, that lad might never sit a horse again. I suspect you wouldn't have that problem."

"I wouldn't." She stroked the Grey's nose for a moment or two, then looked at Aherin's lord. "He must be very valuable."

"Priceless," Hearn said. "Don't think I'd ever sell him. You feel free to come ride him anytime you like, though."

"Thank you, my lord."

He nodded up the way. "Let's put him away and then you can tell me what your plans are for Falaire and what mischief he's been combining."

Léirsinn nodded and walked with him back to his stables, waving away the lad who came to take the Grey from her. She untacked him herself, though she wasn't above handing things off to others for them to clean and put away. She brushed Turasadhair until his coat gleamed and his mane and tail were waterfalls of silver, glowing in the afternoon sunlight that streamed in from the windows set high in the walls.

She put the combs and brushes away, then left the stall. She closed the door, looked at that glorious horse who looked as if he'd been cast in silver, then at Hearn.

"Priceless," she agreed.

"If I ever find a price, I'll let you know."

"I won't be able to afford it, though I'd be tempted to rob every nobleman I could find to manage it."

Hearn smiled faintly. "Now you understand what drives that blasted Acair, I imagine."

She leaned against the stall door. "Do you think that's it?"

He sighed. "What do I know of men and mages? His father is an arrogant, merciless bastard and his mother one of the most terrifying women I've ever met. His brothers are every last one of them the sorts of lads you absolutely wouldn't want to meet without a gaggle of mages at your heels to keep you safe. Where Acair fits into all that, I couldn't say. You would do better to ask someone who knows his family. Miach of Neroche is wed to his half-sister, though I'm not sure how well either of them knows him. I suppose Prince Soilléir would have his opinions, if you're that curious."

She shook her head slowly. "I prefer to judge men on my own." She looked at Hearn. "I don't believe he's all that evil."

"That's because you've never seen him with magic to hand," Hearn said seriously. "Then again, who am I to judge? If someone tried to hurt one of my horses—actually, the things I've done to keep them safe . . ." He blew out his breath. "As I said, I'm not one to judge. I will tell you this much, though: he's fearless. The places that boy has gone? Not in my worst nightmares and I don't mind admitting that."

"All in the search of power?" she asked.

"And other things, no doubt." Hearn nodded at the Grey. "Where would you go for that one there?"

She smiled. "Don't ask."

He laughed a little. "I understand, believe me. Let's go have something to eat before the thought takes root and puts us off our feed."

"Where's Acair?"

"Moving a pile of manure from one spot to another," Hearn said without hesitation, "a completely useless exercise I put him to simply because I could."

"And of course you aren't enjoying that at all."

"The little fiend broke into my solar a few years back and

rummaged through not only my papers but my private collection of very rare, very *expensive* whisky that happened to be a gift from a buyer in Gairn. Damned if I didn't catch him just as he was preparing to open a bottle and have himself a taste."

She had to smile. "What did you do to him?"

"Took him by the scruff of the neck and threw him out my front gates."

"I'm surprised he didn't use a spell on you," she said, then she shook her head. "I can't believe those words just came out of my mouth."

"Too much time with the Grey. He will leave a lass thinking that all manner of impossible things are possible. As for the other, I am who I am. I think despite all his vile threatenings, your lad there simply couldn't bring himself to destroy a legend." He shrugged. "Or it could be my hall is protected by spells he suspected might come back to haunt him if he vexed me overmuch."

"He isn't my lad, but he does seem to have at least a bit of good sense from time to time."

"One could hope," Hearn agreed.

Léirsinn nodded and walked with him back to the hall. She tried not to gawk at her surroundings, but it was difficult not to. She was in a place that felt familiar, given that it was full of horses, yet so far above her uncle's stables that she felt as if she'd never been inside a barn before.

If only she could have perhaps convinced Hearn to take her on even as a lowly stable hand, it would have been more than she could have expected, truly.

He paused on the top step in front of the doorway to his hall and looked at her. "Come back and ride."

She looked at him seriously. "Not work?"

"I have the feeling, missy, that your destiny lies elsewhere." He hesitated, then shrugged. "If that changes and if you want a place, I will make one for you here."

She had to blink very rapidly for a moment or two. "Thank you, my lord."

He put his hand on her shoulder briefly. "You have a way with horses, Mistress Léirsinn." He opened the hall door. "Let's go fetch ourselves a mug of ale, then we'll go watch your lad finish up his work. That seems like a perfect use of the rest of the afternoon, aye?"

She had to agree it did. She couldn't say she wouldn't be happy for a place to sit down for a bit. It might give her a chance to recover from the day she'd had.

She was going to be a long time in forgetting the horse she'd ridden that afternoon.

I t was perhaps unsurprising that she found herself in his stall that evening, grooming him again. If she'd leapt at the chance to simply trot him about a small arena beforehand, well, how could anyone have expected her to refuse? He could do the same prancing movements that any exclusive cavalry horse could do and there wasn't a jump in Hearn's keep that he didn't leap over with grace.

"Take him outside if you like," Hearn had said at one point.

She hadn't argued. And she had to say that a spectacular sunset was even more enjoyable when viewed from the back of a spectacular horse.

All of which left her where she was at the moment, grooming his dark grey sides with his silver tail saved for very last.

"You know, Acair," Hearn said from where he was leaning on the stall door, "there are people in the East who are horse lovers."

"Are there indeed, my lord?"

"I take it you never travelled so far in your endless quest to nick things. Spells and whatnot."

"Nay, my lord," Acair said politely. "Their magic is strange and I find myself favoring that which my sparse wits can wrap themselves around. Besides, 'tis a bit of a journey, wouldn't you agree?"

"Aye, you lazy whelp, it is. Worth it, though."

"Is it? What is it about these horsemen that's intriguing?"

"Nothing for you to work yourself up over given that they have no magic that you could steal. Nay, what they have isn't in their blood, 'tis woven into their souls."

"Poetic."

"Isn't it, though?"

Léirsinn looked over Turasadhair's neck at the men who were standing there watching her work. "Don't you two have anything better to do than stand there yammering on?"

Acair looked at Hearn. "Red hair," he said knowingly. "Comes with a temper and a sharp tongue."

Hearn only smiled pleasantly. "May you feel the fire of it until it singes you to death, my lad. Now, as I was saying, there are horse people in the East. No magic that you would recognize, but there is something about them that is unusual."

"Their ability to shovel great amounts of horse sh—"

Hearn tsk-tsked him. "Mind your manners before I put you back to work moving that pile again."

"To an unnecessary location."

"Never said the work had to have a point to it, did I? And stop interrupting me. These horsemen have, from what I understand, developed a very keen eye. Not Seeing in the usual sense, but just regular seeing that the high and mighty ones tend to miss because they're so involved in their vaunted Looking About."

"I know the type," Acair said.

"You *are* the type," Hearn said.

Acair only laughed briefly. "Trust me, my lord, I've done a great deal of looking at all sorts of things I shouldn't have. Now, do they do anything else besides make everyone around them uncomfortable with their observations?"

"I daresay they know which end of a horse bites."

Acair snorted. "Even *I* know that."

"Now," Hearn said dryly. "I understand from Mistress Léirsinn's pony that such wasn't always the case. He finds it terribly amusing. And don't think he doesn't recount your misadventures with him to other horses as often as he can."

"That damned nag."

Hearn laughed. "I believe if you could ever come to an under-standing with him, you might like him. He's as fond of a well-executed piece of mischief as you are. As for what I was attempting to spew out before you interrupted me, I think it would be an interesting thing to see who is related to whom, wouldn't it? Your lass there, I mean."

"Aye," Acair said, "it would be."

Léirsinn thought it would be more interesting if they took them-selves off to cozy up to a keg in Hearn's cellar, but perhaps that would have been rude to suggest.

Hearn rubbed his hands together. "Offer to aid her in her work here if she asks, Acair, then we'll spend a pleasant evening together. You'll want to be on your way in the morning. Your gel there is welcome to come back anytime she likes."

"And me?"

"If she invites you, I'll always have things for you to shovel."

Léirsinn smiled to herself as she worked on Turasadhair's mane. She took longer at it likely than she needed to, but it was soothing work, work she knew how to do, and work that never left her facing anything she didn't anticipate.

Exactly the opposite of what her life was offering at present.

She finished eventually, then handed off her gear to one of the stable lads. She left the feeding of the Grey to lads whose business it was, admired him one more time, then let herself out of the stall. She looked at Acair who hadn't moved from his place.

"You lean a great deal, don't you?"

"How do you mean?" he asked.

"Against doorways," she said, "walls, pillars, mantels." She shrugged. "That sort of thing."

"It gives me the opportunity to display my profile, something you can't help but have admired more than once."

She smiled. "You are a showy pony, aren't you?"

"You should see me when I'm at liberty to shapechange," he said.

"Women swoon, mere mortals weep in fear, mages grind their teeth. I would suggest that it is very bad for my enormous ego, that sort of thing, but I will admit I enjoy it. Mainly the swooning, but there you have it. I can't turn my back on who I am."

She leaned against the stall door. "You say these things, yet I'm not sure you mean them."

"You don't think my ego is enormous?"

"I think your ego is colossal," she said, "and there are times I believe you almost take yourself seriously."

He sighed lightly as he joined her in her leaning. "I have the very fine example of my father to keep me from it, if you want the entire truth. He is so enamored of himself, I'm not sure he ever truly notices anyone else. Oh, he'll make you believe he does, for a time, but it never lasts."

"What does he want, then?"

"Power." He smiled briefly. "'Tis what every decent mage wants."

"Why?"

He nodded toward the spectacular horse with his nose as far into his grain bucket as it would go. "Why do you want that horse?"

She took an unsteady breath. "Hearn already forced me to acknowledge this."

Acair looked at her. "Wouldn't you have a dozen of his like if you had an endless amount of gold in your coffers?"

"You can only work so many horses," she said.

"But a dozen of that lad's ilk?" he said. "I would hazard a guess the prize might be worth all the work to have it. And so says every mage with a handful of wits rattling around in his head."

"But you're not trying to acquire more horses. Surely there's a limit to how much power you can use." She stopped and looked at him. "I can't believe I said those words."

"Don't make your pony take you outside and prove again what he's capable of." He nodded knowingly. "Magic, if you weren't clear on what I was referring to."

"I'm trying to convince myself I dreamed all of it," she said, then she breathed deeply. She gestured toward that magnificent, impossibly swift horse in front of them. "That is what I understand. The rest of it? I will continue to call it fanciful imaginings."

"Cling to that, my gel. Cling to it."

"I suspect I should."

He smiled and watched the Grey investigate the depths of his bucket a bit longer. "As for the acquisition of power, who knows why a mage wants more? Perhaps it comes from being afraid someone might have more of it than he does, or perhaps it simply comes from fear he won't have enough."

She looked at him in surprise. He was looking at her in almost the same way.

"Good hell," he said faintly. "I believe I have finally shoveled too much manure and lost my mind somewhere in the pile."

She smiled. "Stable work is good for the soul."

"Unless you are me, in which case it is very bad for whatever soul I have left." He shook his head slowly. "I have obviously had too much time on my hands for thinking ridiculous thoughts."

She shifted so she could still lean against the stall door yet face him. "Are you afraid you won't have enough power, Acair? And keep in mind I can't believe I'm saying those words without indulging in a snort of derision."

He watched the Grey for another moment or two, then shook his head with a weary smile. "I'm not sure I can give you the answer that question deserves," he said. "Perhaps there are only so many spells one can have, just as there are only so many horses one can ride. But how can you not wonder if there might be a horse in a stable down the way who might be the one pony in the world to take your breath away?"

She understood. She wasn't sure she wanted to examine whether or not she could bring herself to believe in magic, never mind what she'd seen and ridden, but she could understand the thrill of wondering what might lie around the corner.

Acair offered her his arm. "I can see you have taken a figurative step down that very dangerous path. I've been walking it for years, so allow me to point out the pitfalls. The first is not taking advantage of decent meals whenever they're offered, so off we go to supper before you plot a course to that horse haven in the East."

She could have told him she had no intention of traveling so far, but she hadn't intended to leave Sàraichte either. She sighed, took his arm, then walked with him out of the stables and into a beautiful, chilly twilight. She avoided that spot of shadow almost out of habit, then paused on the steps leading up to Hearn's great hall.

"If you have so much power," she said slowly, "why don't you just destroy that spell you say is following you?"

He lifted his eyebrows briefly. "An excellent question." He opened his mouth, then stopped. "I was going to pontificate, but I fear I might bore even myself."

"Be brief, then."

"Briefly, then," he agreed. "The magic I fear that spell is fashioned from is of a different and, frankly, unsettling sort."

"Worse than the spots?"

"*Worse* is relative," he said. "Most magic is a bit like a suit of clothes. You put it on, you put it on others, but underneath, you are still yourself and your victims—er, I mean those favored enough to enjoy your attentions—still remain who they were. But that thing there?" He shook his head. "I haven't had the stomach to have a look at it over tea, but given who fashioned it, I assume 'tis Cothromaichian rot. Even with as many things as I've seen and, I must admit, used myself, that magic gives me pause. It doesn't simply lay a spell over something whilst leaving the essence of the thing the same, it changes that thing into something else entirely."

She snorted before she could stop herself. "Ridiculous."

"The next time you see a birdbath that looks suspiciously as if it might have been a mage not a fortnight earlier, ask it for its opinion on the matter."

"And have everyone around me think me utterly daft? Never." She glanced at the spell that seemed to be never more than ten paces away from Acair. She had no way of judging what its purpose was and she hardly wanted to dignify its existence with a bit of a look, so she ignored it and looked at Acair. "Is this Soilléir person evil?"

He pursed his lips. "Unfortunately he isn't—and this is not a subject you want to bring up with my mother if ever you meet her. She will talk about his code of honor and what a stellar soul he is until you'll be tempted to look for anything to stuff in your ears to have relief from the torment." He shook his head. "Unless things have changed drastically, he would never use his spells for ill."

"Then why would he create something to slay you?"

He considered, then looked at her seriously. "Because I deserve it."

"For someone with your reputation, you're terribly contrite."

"It has been a very long few months," he said grimly. "I'm worn down by the sheer force of all the opportunities to do evil that I've missed. I'm sure I'll be right back to my old self when I'm finished with all this business of do-gooding."

"Do you know any of Soilléir's spells?" she asked, then she laughed a little at herself. "Spells. Can you believe I'm even using that word with any seriousness at all?"

"I might not be the right man to ask about that."

"I suppose not. So, do you?"

"Know any of those spells?" he asked. He shook his head. "Not a damned one of them."

"Something you would no doubt like to change."

He looked at her. "I would give a king's ransom for a single one."

"Have you offered a king's ransom for a single one?"

"Why do that when there is the challenge of trying to nick one whilst Soilléir is dozing off after supper?"

She couldn't help but smile. "You are a very bad man."

"As I said," he said cheerfully. He opened the door, then made her a slight bow. "After you, mistress."

"Bad man, good manners," she noted.

"Easier to invade kings' solars when you have decent manners and can make polite conversation at supper."

She imagined it was.

. . .

A pair of hours later, she was trying and failing to find any ease in a hayloft over the Grey's stall. Hearn had told Acair very sternly that he was welcome to join her there but he was to maintain a circumspect distance. Léirsinn had rolled her eyes. The very last thing she would ever expect from Acair of Ceangail was that he would look at her twice. Her hair, perhaps, but it seemed to unnerve him more than attract him, so she supposed she was safe enough.

That said, she found *him* rather more distracting than perhaps she should have. She finally sighed and turned on her side to look at him as he lay a few feet away from her. He was awake, staring up at the ceiling.

"You think too loudly," she said.

He smiled. She winced involuntarily. Admittedly, she had heard what she had to believe was a fairly limited list of his bad deeds, but she had a hard time reconciling all that nastiness with the man there. And when he smiled . . . well, she suspected that was all he needed to gain entrance to any solar he cared to frequent.

"You're watching me," he said, still not looking at her.

"I'm trying to decide how best to plunge you into senselessness so I can sleep."

His smile deepened, then he looked at her. "You are a very fierce wench."

"I'm accustomed to managing stallions," she said.

"Trust me, I've seen you at it." He turned back to his contemplation of the ceiling. "What did you think of that grey horse down below?"

"I might be tempted to steal a spell or two for him."

"Ah," he said in satisfaction, "now you see how it begins. First a little spell here, then a larger spell there, then you're beginning to look further afield to the odd, priceless treasure. Before we know it, you'll be sneaking back into Ehrne of Ainneamh's palace to pinch his crown and sell it to Sìle of Tòrr Dòrainn for an eye-watering price."

"Is that how it begins?" she asked.

"Either that or one starts out to impress one's father, realizes there is no hope, then one continues on because one is an ignorant ass."

She smiled. "Is *that* how it is?"

He sighed deeply. "Today, I don't know." He looked at her. "I think there might be an abundance of anger in me."

"You need a horse."

"The *last* thing I need is a horse."

"They're good for a man's soul."

"But very bad for his arse, which is where on me most of them seem to think their next meal is located."

She turned toward him and propped herself up on her elbow. "What do you think those shadows are?"

"Something very bad," he said seriously, "and I would know."

"Who do you think could have put them there?"

"The list is long," he said, "and not one I particularly care to make, though I suppose I should. I don't know that doing so would serve either of us given that I couldn't do a damned thing about it even if I knew who was behind that mischief."

"Which is why we're off to see Soilléir?"

"I," he corrected. "*I* am off to see Soilléir." He looked at her then. "In all seriousness, Léirsinn, I think you should stay here."

"And you think I'm going to argue?"

He looked at her in surprise, then scowled. "I am only surprised that you can spew out those words with any conviction at all. Surely you're planning on coming. The fairness of my face and the truly appalling nature of my reputation are simply too much to resist."

"Show pony."

"Red-haired harridan."

"Careful," she warned. "Too much more flattery such as that and I will become as insufferable as you are."

"I'm not sure you could," he said seriously, "and your hair is beautiful. As are you. Now, go to sleep so I can think. You're distracting me with all this feminine chatter. And I *will* leave you behind, just so you know."

"Nay, you won't."

He blew out his breath and turned back to his study of the roof, but he said nothing.

She watched him watch the ceiling for a bit longer, trying to ignore the appalling fairness of his face and the inescapable realization that he was who he apparently was.

"Acair?"

"Aye, Léirsinn."

"Are you afraid?"

"Me?" he scoffed. "Never."

"Never?"

He looked at her. "Do you think I would admit it if I were?"

She shook her head. He held out his hand and she put hers in it before she could think better of it.

"Go to sleep," he said quietly. "I'll have a bit of a think, then leave you to your peaceful dreams. And don't worry. I'll keep you safe."

"Harsh language?"

"*Very* harsh language and the dagger stuck down my boot."

She supposed others had done more with less. She nodded, then closed her eyes. She didn't want to believe what she had seen and done over the past several days, but it was impossible to deny what it meant.

Magic existed.

She felt as if she were being torn in two. She felt Acair's fingers laced with hers, his hand warm and quite ordinary save for the calluses he had no doubt earned by shoveling so much manure over the past fortnight. Yet if she were to believe what she'd heard, that hand was also capable of wielding mythical, unseen forces to do his bidding whenever he chose, and apparently he had done quite a bit of that sort of choosing over the course of his impossibly long life. She had ridden a horse with gossamer wings that day, a horse who had been nothing more than a horse when his grain had been brought and he'd plunged his soft nose into the bucket to inhale it in typical horse fashion.

Spots of shadow, flying horses, and a man who had seen things that she could see lurking in the back of his eyes. It was so thoroughly not what she'd expected to find filling her life. She wasn't sure she would trade what she had at the moment, though, for what she'd left behind, and that was perhaps the most alarming thing of all.

Sleep was long in coming.

Eighteen

❧

Acair stood inside the gates of Aherin at a far earlier hour than that which he usually preferred to count as the start of his day, looked at the lord of the keep, and wondered if how he could politely point out that they were, as shouldn't have surprised him at all, back where they'd started.

"My lord," Acair ventured, "about a horse—"

Hearn shot him an impatient look. "You don't give up, do you?"

"It isn't in my nature," Acair said. "'Tis what makes me a good mage."

"You are a *bad* mage, which you know very well." Hearn folded his arms over his chest. "How is it you can possibly think I would give you a horse?"

"Because I'm asking to *buy* a horse," Acair corrected. "Well, not with any gold that I have with me at present, but if you'll name your price, when I'm at my leisure to see to it—"

"In another year."

"Aye, in a year," he said, trying not to growl as he said it. "In a year, I will happily pay any price you ask."

"And what if my price is yet another year of your not using magic?" Hearn asked politely.

Acair was beginning to think he had been the topic of conversation at a dinner party with several souls he might or might not have given trouble to in the past. It had likely taken several bottles of wine for them to have come up with any useful thoughts, but he suspected his current straits were the result of all that inebriation. He looked at Hearn evenly.

"Any price but that one."

Hearn looked at him with that horse-sight that was past unnerving, then grunted. "I'll give it some thought. Let's discuss first what I've heard from both of you about Mistress Léirsinn's horse. He sees these things we don't particularly want to discuss, then he destroys them?"

Acair nodded, then heard himself describe in a fair amount of detail what had happened when Falaire had encountered one of those spots of shadow. He leaned back against a handy railing when Hearn and Léirsinn called for the horse to be brought to them, then fussed over him for so long that Acair found himself wondering why the hell Hearn never had any sorts of benches placed anywhere where a man might find them convenient.

"I'll walk him to the gates," Léirsinn said, startling Acair out of his stupor.

"Let one of the lads do that," Hearn suggested. "One of you at least needs to be awake to hear this."

Acair hid a yawn behind his hand and forced himself to concentrate on the lord of the hall. Hearn shot him a disgruntled look, which Acair shrugged off. Too much shoveling, not enough sleeping. 'Twas a potent combination.

"Any ideas where that pony came from?" Hearn asked seriously.

Léirsinn frowned. "He was brought to the barn as a yearling, but I didn't investigate his lineage. Why?"

"Because I am fairly certain he's from Sìle of Tòrr Dòrainn's stables," Hearn said. "There's a thread of elven magic running through his veins that is unmistakable. And that name? Too close to what they call their magic for coincidence, wouldn't you say?"

"I don't believe in coincidence," Acair said through another yawn.

"Neither do I." Hearn looked at Léirsinn. "I'm not sure it means anything, but it makes me wonder if his name is a message of sorts. I've now seen how fond he is of those shadows, but I don't think they're doing him any harm." He shrugged. "He might be of use to you if you could convince him to stay in his own shape long enough to tell you when he sees them."

"Is he strong enough to carry us both," Acair asked gingerly, "or do you think his encounters have weakened him?"

Hearn gave vent to a gusty sigh. "He can easily carry our gel here, but you and your enormous ego might just be too heavy for him. I suppose I'll have to send you off on something else."

"A horse for me?" he asked as casually as possible, trying not to sound anything like the ten-year-old lad he felt at present.

Hearn ignored him and motioned to one of his lads. "Go fetch that monster we discussed earlier."

Acair felt Léirsinn elbow him. "I think this will be interesting," she said with the enthusiasm of someone who had actually slept the night before.

Something to remind himself of periodically: never sleep next to a woman who bothered you whilst you were awake. He was a shameless rogue and a terrible womanizer so holding her hand for most of the night shouldn't have troubled him at all. That it had left him pacing in front of that grey demon's stall before the sun was up should have told him something. That he was a fool, perhaps, or that he needed to get hold of himself, no doubt.

He smiled weakly at Léirsinn, then fought not to show any reaction to what was brought to stand in front of Hearn. He supposed it was a horse, but he honestly wasn't sure. It bared its teeth at him, then tried to reach past its handler to bite him.

"Perfect," Hearn said, sounding perfectly pleased.

"He's spirited," Léirsinn said enthusiastically.

"He's a devil," Acair wheezed. "And he's already tried to bite me!"

They weren't listening to him, those two horse people who seemed to find nothing at all untoward about a horse that snarled at him every time it looked his way. He supposed he should have been extremely grateful that Hearn was deigning to sell him any-thing at all, but 'twas difficult to thank a man for giving him some-thing that Hell had obviously just recently vomited up on his front stoop.

"What's he called?" Léirsinn asked.

"Sianach, through several lines that I didn't investigate very far. He was sent to me by someone I won't name, and he is a particularly difficult case."

"Seems like a match to me," Léirsinn said. "They might be good for each other."

Hearn laughed. "I thought so too."

"I can't ride that monster," Acair said. "He'll kill me!"

"Or just do great amounts of damage to you," Hearn said. "If that happens, I suppose Mistress Léirsinn will just have to tie you to her saddle and drag you along wherever she goes."

"I don't like this," Acair said faintly.

"I would imagine many of your victims have said the same thing over the years."

"I made certain to render them mute before I did anything to them," Acair said without thinking.

"You might want to keep that sort of thing to yourself," Hearn suggested, "before you give that horse any ideas." He shrugged. "Take him or leave him behind. It's all the same to me."

Acair looked at the stallion, who looked as if his fondest wish was to kick the life out of him, then looked at Léirsinn. "What do you think?" he asked. "And pray let it be along the lines of, *this beast is not ridable.*"

"I would say he is a challenge," she said, charitably.

"Which means he frightens you."

She looked at him from clear green eyes. "Nothing frightens me."

He could only hope that would always be so. He didn't want to begin to think of all the ways she might be inspired to revisit that declaration.

She turned to Hearn. "Was he mistreated?" she asked.

"Perhaps less mistreated than simply ignored. He was rescued by someone who thought I might want to rehabilitate him."

"Can he *do* anything?" Acair asked in a last-ditch effort to perhaps hear something that would allow him to be very grateful for the offer of a horse but unfortunately forced to politely decline that same offer. "Do anything besides look at my arse as if he might like to take a piece out of it, that is. And what's his name again, if I'm allowed to ask."

"Sianach," Hearn said mildly. "Means *terror* in horsey speak. Or *screaming*, which is what everyone who rides him seems to do." He shrugged. "I forget which it is."

Acair imagined Hearn hadn't forgotten anything. "Did he name himself, then?"

"Your lady might ask him that after she's seen what he can do."

Acair would have said that his lady, who was assuredly not interested in being the like even if he had been—but was absolutely not—interested in a red-haired horse miss who ruined his sleep, was absolutely not going to get anywhere near that beast who had obviously just stepped from someone's worst nightmare, but he realized he wasn't going to have a chance to offer his opinion. Léirsinn was already tucking her hair up under a cap she had apparently borrowed from someone. The cap looked rather fresh, so perhaps Hearn had a selection of them for just such an exigency. Acair supposed he might not want to ask.

He also refrained from commenting on how Léirsinn led that damned horse away without trouble, but that might have been because he was preoccupied with not making an ass of himself by wringing his hands. She was a grown woman who knew her business very well. She didn't need his aid.

He had to remind himself of that several times.

Sianach followed her happily and seemed to be just as fascinated by a bit of her hair that had escaped her cap as any other lad with two good eyes. She stopped, turned, and gave him a look that had him backing up a pace. She tucked that snuffled lock under her cap, then clicked for the horse to follow her. He ducked his head and walked docilely behind her.

"And all is as it should be," Hearn murmured.

Acair shot him a look full of as much irritation as he dared use, then turned back to look at exactly what he was apparently about to saddle himself with. Léirsinn put a rope around the horse's neck and started to run him around her in the usual circles. Acair watched for a moment or two, then realized things were not going to go exactly as they usually did.

The pony reared, roared, then came back to earth as a dragon. He shot Acair a pointed look, snorted out a bit of fire in the same direction, then folded his wings up and trotted—well, waddled, actually—in that same circle around Léirsinn.

She only took a deep breath, then snapped a whip against the dirt behind his long, scaly tail.

From there, the shapes only became more outlandish and substantially more terrifying. Dragons, things that slithered, nightmares on four feet. Acair was actually fairly impressed—and a little unnerved, frankly—by what he was seeing.

"Ah, watch how she manages him," Hearn said, sounding pleased.

Acair shot him a dark look. "Don't suggest she's planning the same thing with me."

"Lad, I don't think she's planning *anything* with you, something which you would be mourning if you had the good sense the gods gave a cockroach."

"I think I should be offended."

"The truth can be painful."

Acair studied him, then nodded knowingly. "I see where you're going with this. I've heard you're a terrible matchmaker."

"Nay, I'm a very *good* matchmaker."

"My father would say I should wed a princess."

"Then why haven't you?"

Acair shrugged. "I have an unsavory past. Your average crown-wearing papa doesn't care for that sort of thing."

Hearn glanced his way. "You also have the ability to conjure up staggering riches at any time. For all I know, you have an enormous pile of things you've pinched from various places hiding in some hillside bolthole."

"That would be my father, and his collection collapsed in on itself," Acair corrected.

Hearn snorted. "And you're telling me you didn't liberate all the originals and puts forgeries in their places?"

Acair knew his mouth had fallen open, but he was powerless to do anything about it. He retrieved his jaw with difficulty. "You horse people frighten me."

"We should." Hearn tapped his forehead. "We have sight the lads from Cothromaiche dream about." He smirked. "You would think a princess of breeding would be tempted by your largesse, ill-gotten or not, and in spite of her father's wishes."

"You would think."

Hearn studied the horse in the arena who was still trying on the shapes of various mythical creatures apparently in an effort to see if any of them suited him. "He might have you for supper if you're not careful."

Acair looked at Hearn. "And yet you'll allow me to buy him?"

"Lad, I'm begging you to take him off my hands."

That perhaps should have been some sort of warning that all was not as it seemed, but Acair ignored it. "I must pay you something, truly."

Hearn studied him. "That's an interesting notion, coming from you."

"I'm not completely without honor, such as it is." He looked at the lord of Aherin seriously. "What will you take for him?"

Hearn blew out his breath. "I will tell you something, but it is strictly in confidence. Spread this about and I will kill you."

"I believe you."

Hearn looked about himself casually, then nodded for Acair to move closer. "Find out who creates those shadows."

Acair looked at him in surprise. "That's all? I was intending to do that just the same, for Léirsinn's sake."

"Do for mine as well." Hearn paused, then swore quite inventively for a bit before he seemingly ran out of vile things to say. "That lad I told you about?" he asked grimly. "The one who went mad?"

"Aye, I remember him," Acair said slowly. "And?"

"He's my son."

Acair had to shake his head a time or two, but that didn't aid him in ridding himself of his surprise. He settled finally for looking at Hearn in astonishment. "You're wed? I should say, I knew you had sons, rather, but, ah, I've never seen—"

"We don't live together any longer," Hearn said shortly. "We see each other now and again and I see that she lives a life of luxury, but the truth is, I drive her to drink. My youngest son is with her and has been for the past month. She fears he will simply sit still for so long that he'll stop breathing." He looked at Acair. "Find who creates those, stop him, then tell me how to heal my lad. That is my price."

Acair held out his hand. "Done."

"Say nothing—and if you give me your word as an honorable black mage, I will flatten you."

Acair smiled briefly. "My word as Sgath's grandson, then."

Hearn shook his hand, then nodded briskly. "I'll go speak to your mount."

"Thank you."

"You may regret that," Hearn said airily, as if they'd been discussing nothing of import but a moment or two before. "That one is a demon."

Acair watched Hearn walk off and supposed if he'd been paying less attention, he might have suspected he'd imagined the whole thing. He wasn't sure if he were more surprised that Hearn was wed or that one of his sons was the one who had gone mad.

There were foul things afoot in the Nine Kingdoms.

He was beginning to wonder why he seemed to be encountering them so often.

Their leave-taking was accomplished with absolutely no fanfare whatsoever. Hearn shook Acair's hand, patted Léirsinn fondly on the shoulder, then turned and walked back inside his gates as if he didn't know either of them. Off to do other things, perhaps.

"What now?" Léirsinn asked, holding Falaire's reins.

"Tor Neroche, if we can manage it," Acair said. "'Tis a fair distance, even in the air, but at least we're getting an early start."

"Acair, it's halfway to noon."

"As I said," he said. "Early."

She rolled her eyes, but she was smiling. He had to ruthlessly suppress the urge to smile back at her. He took the reins of his . . . well, the beast was a horse at the moment, but he supposed that wouldn't last. He fussed with reins, made a production of looking at stirrups and a saddle whilst having absolutely no idea if they were settled properly or not, then gave himself up for lost. The seventh bastard son of the worst black mage in history and his lover the witchwoman of Fàs finding himself smitten with a flame-haired stable lass?

He was in trouble.

But, hopeless romantic that he was, he couldn't help but think about it a bit more as they flew. Sianach was apparently on his best behavior, though Acair was sure that had nothing to do with him. Léirsinn had talked to him before they'd taken flight and she was obviously the sort of horsewoman a pony wanted to make a good impression on. He had to admit he understood.

What he didn't understand, as the morning turned into afternoon, was why the hell he'd spent so much time not paying any heed to his surroundings. He realized with a start that he should have been concentrating on what was going on behind him instead of who was riding beside him.

A clutch of black mages in flight. He recognized the type.

They were hardly past Chagailt, not that anyone there would have let him inside the doors anyway, but at least it would have been some sort of shelter. As it was, they were simply flying over the endless plains of Neroche, completely out in the open, perfectly visible to anyone who cared to look up.

Damn it anyway.

He looked at Léirsinn. "We're in trouble," he shouted over the wind.

"Why?" she asked, obviously startled.

He nodded back over his shoulder. He would have warned her not to look, but it was too late. He had no idea how many there were, but he would have guessed a dozen at least. That alone surprised him. It wasn't as if he had anything anyone wanted—

Was it?

Perhaps putting his foot in that shadow had stirred up a great deal more trouble than he'd thought.

Either that, or some busybody—Ehrne of Ainneamh came immediately to mind—had sent word to as many vile mages as he could that Acair was out in the open without his usual protections to hand.

Good hell, it was just impossible to move about as a normal mage with his past that trailed after him like sparks. Unfortunately what was trailing after those mesmerizing sparks was a burgeoning cloud of blackness that was rapidly darkening the sky.

It occurred to him with a startling flash of clarity that he had seen the beginnings of that storm the night before as he'd stood in Hearn's courtyard. More the fool was he for not having paid better heed to it.

"What are they doing?" Léirsinn exclaimed.

"Theatrics," Acair said succinctly.

He would know. He'd done the same thing hundreds of times. Black mages were pompous gits, there was no getting around that.

Unfortunately, whoever those lads behind him were, they were very good at several things not limited to a showy display. He might not have been able to use his magic, but he had two perfectly good eyes and a nose for all kinds of untoward things. That cloud of mage was gaining on him rapidly, more rapidly than a group of neophytes would have managed. He didn't have the patience to try to identify them, but he supposed that didn't matter. If they caught up, they would first slay Léirsinn, then they would take him off to places he wouldn't want to go, do things to him he wouldn't like, then watch him as he enjoyed a lingering, painful death.

He knew. He'd watched it be done. Whether or not he'd done it himself was something he didn't think was particularly useful to bring to mind at the moment.

He considered his mount, who was wearing a modest but rather fierce-looking pegasus shape, then wondered what else the horse might be willing to do. He wasn't quite sure how to communicate that query, so he thought perhaps a gentle suggestion might be a good place to start.

"We're going to have to go faster, you demon steed," he bellowed.

Sianach paused in mid-flap, leaving Acair wondering if the damned beast was in league with those lads behind him. Then his mount tossed his head and showed Acair a mental image of an evil intention speeding across countries as quickly as a piece of palace gossip.

"I'll be damned," Acair said in surprise. He looked at Léirsinn and held out his hand. "Jump."

"What?" she squeaked. "Are you mad?"

"Jump," he said impatiently. "Sianach will go very fast. Bring your horse along."

If there was one thing that could be said without reservation about that horse-mad gel, it was that she didn't lack courage. She pulled her feet out of her stirrups and jumped. She almost knocked him off his own mount, truth be told, but he managed to catch her and keep his seat. Barely. Falaire had to struggle to keep up with them, then he seemed to gather himself together for a final bit of a change. Léirsinn scarce managed to catch him as he flung himself toward them in the solid shape of a lovely little pewter pony. Eulasaid's influence, obviously. Well, if nothing else, they could throw him very hard at someone and perhaps leave a mark.

"Hold on," Acair managed as he felt Sianach gather himself for a bit of equine magic.

And that was the last thing he said for quite some time.

He would have to give Léirsinn as much credit as possible. She didn't scream or faint and she would have been justified with either. He had no idea what Sianach considered himself at present, but it was something only slightly more substantial than horse-shaped air. His speed was terrifying and Acair thought he might be qualified to judge that given that he was someone who had craved speed like another might crave sweet wine after supper. He shifted Léirsinn toward him and tried to wrap his cloak around her to cut some of the wind. It was hopeless, of course, but she didn't complain.

It turned into a perfectly horrible afternoon, even by his very low standards of comfort acceptable whilst being chased by mages with his death on their minds. Sianach was nothing short of spectacular and Acair supposed he might have to do more than what he'd promised Hearn in order to properly repay him.

"They're gaining on us!"

Acair looked over his shoulder and realized she spoke the truth. He swore, then looked down to see where they were. He could hardly believe they had come so far north so quickly, but there was no denying the lay of the land, as it were. He supposed *without words* was Sianach's preferred way of communications, so he asked—

And almost fell off backward from that hint of horse.

He clung with one hand to the reins, which looked as if they were attached to nothing more than a fond wish, clutched Léirsinn to him with the other arm, and tried to distract himself.

It was impossible. The truth was, he'd been watching Léirsinn ride that grey beast and he'd seen the speed that one had achieved. He'd been rather relieved it had been her riding the wind, as it were, and not him. But what Sianach was managing at the moment was much more than that. It was as if he'd become the bitterest of winter winds screaming across the plains of Ailean.

Acair laughed before he could stop himself. It shouldn't have been possible that he had forgotten so quickly what true flying felt like, but apparently it was.

It was, in a word, glorious.

"You're mad!" Léirsinn shouted.

Most likely was half torn from his mouth before he realized that his pleasure was going to be short-lived. The black cloud behind him that had become a terrible, terrifying storm was so close to them, he could feel the cold reaching for him. Sianach could obviously sense it as well for he suddenly fell from the sky like a bolt of lightning.

"We're going to die!"

Acair wasn't entirely sure she didn't have that right, but they were within Neroche's borders, which was something of a relief. He supposed he could point that out to Léirsinn later and tell her how it was he always kept a weather eye out for that silver-blue line that separated their soil from everyone else's, but at the moment, he was too busy being grateful for the spell that accompanied that thin line of border. He suspected most people came and went across that line and under the canopy of that spell without having any idea either existed. He knew, though, and he was, for a change, damned grateful for it.

Even so, the land north of the border was still an endless stretch of farmland, dotted with little hamlets and farms and other pedestrian though no doubt quite useful dwellings. Sianach was hurtling toward an enormous field that looked as if it might be just the right sort of place for a horse to wander over, eating its bloody head off.

In the midst of that expanse of prairie stood a lone figure.

Acair could only hope it was who he hoped it was and not his sire escaped from his prison in Shettlestoune.

The spell guarding Neroche parted long enough for them to

scamper through. Acair supposed he should have discussed with Sianach the need to slow down before he drove them straight into the ground, but thankfully that horse was as intelligent as he was deviously creative. He skidded through the air as he slowed, then he made a rather lazy, impudent circle around the figure in the field before he came to ground in front of the man standing there, simply watching.

Acair squawked as his mount dipped his head in something of a bow, went rolling arse over teakettle over the damned horse's neck, then landed with Léirsinn in an untidy heap in front of a lad who looked far too young to be wearing that hint of a massive crown atop his head.

Acair attempted to untangle himself from his companion, but he found himself too distracted to do more than push himself up far enough to sit, wrap his arms around Léirsinn, and watch as Mochriadhemiach of Neroche did what he did best. Acair had never faced him over spells, but he'd heard tales. He had to admit what he was seeing did the lad credit.

The spells that guarded Neroche kept out some of the rabble, but half a dozen very disreputable sorts had somehow managed to slip through the gates, as it were, and had taken up temporary residence fifty paces away. Acair watched in a good deal of surprise as Sianach turned himself into a barrier covered with a rather substantial spell of protection and set himself in front of them in an advantageous fashion.

Well, if that was how things were going to be, there was no point in not enjoying the rest of the entertainment.

Miach of Neroche was young, true, but the lad was nothing if not inventive and he obviously had a collection of spells that Acair realized he should have taken note of much sooner. Perhaps they could discuss that list over tea at their earliest opportunity.

He kept a running tally of the magics Miach used—one never knew when that sort of thing might come in handy when a spot of extortion was called for—but had to admit that the earliness of his hour of departure from Aherin was beginning to take its toll. He yawned, patted his mouth discreetly, then finally rested his chin on Léirsinn's shoulder. He suspected he might have closed his eyes for the briefest of moments, but he thought it wise not to admit to anything.

Léirsinn elbowed him at one point. "You're snoring."

"I never snore," he said, suspecting that might not be as true as he would have liked. He rubbed his eyes with the back of one of his wrists, then assessed the field of battle.

There was a pair of black mages still putting up a bit of resistance, but they soon gave in and departed with howls of outrage. He imagined they were rather glad to have preserved their anonymity in light of their ignominious defeat. All that was left was to collect the spoils.

Acair shifted a bit to look at Léirsinn, who was gaping at the man who had just, literally, saved their collective arses. She twisted around to look at Acair.

"Who is that?" she wheezed.

Acair heaved himself to his feet, helped her to hers, then made the other man a decent bow. No sense in not getting things off to a good start. He dusted off his best courtly manners and gestured where appropriate.

"Léirsinn of Sàraichte may I present you to Mochriadhemiach, king of Neroche. Your Majesty, Léirsinn of Sàraichte."

"Who don't you know?" Léirsinn whispered in surprise.

He supposed the present time was not the best one to be making that sort of list, so he gave her a look that promised details later, then turned his mind to keeping them alive, which he suspected would require a great deal of flattering the king. There were, as it happened, several things he thought little Miach of Neroche could perhaps toss onto a rubbish heap of past misdeeds too unimportant to remember the author of clearly.

He suppressed the urge to take a step to his right and use his companion as a shield, took instead a deep breath, and put on his most conciliatory smile.

"I believe," he said with as much contrition as he could manage, "that I might have some apologizing to do."

The words rolled off his tongue with an ease that he knew should have shaken him to his foundations, but there you had it. His life was no longer his own, his code likely corrupted past redemption, and his willingness to save his sweet neck leading him down paths he never would have trodden if he'd been in full command of his power.

He sighed. The things he did . . .

Nineteen

Léirsinn wondered if she were having a particularly long string of encounters with handsome men or if it was just that everyone in Sàraichte was ugly.

She had considered the possible truth of that for the whole of the way north, simply because she'd needed a distraction. The journey had been made very quickly on the back of Sianach, who had changed his shape into something she had been just too tired to try to identify. He was fast, she would give him that, and he seemed to have an unwholesome fascination with trying to surprise Acair, which she couldn't blame him for. She had heard Acair blurt out more curses in the past few hours than she had over the entire course of their acquaintance. She supposed he wasn't particularly happy about any of it, but what could he do? He had a horse with a sense of humor who was apparently enjoying himself thoroughly at his new master's expense.

She had to admit she was currently enjoying the fact that she was off any sort of winged beast and standing in the shadows of an enormous castle that looked as if it might offer not only a decent meal, but a safe place to sleep. She didn't care if she slept in the stables, indeed, she thought she might prefer it. All she knew was she didn't want to ever, *ever* look back over her shoulder and see a storm of that sort hard on her heels. It had been painfully obvious that it wasn't a storm of the normal sort, it had been a conglomeration of evil.

She had almost died of fright.

"Mistress Léirsinn, perhaps you would care to sit."

She looked at the king of Neroche and noted that he didn't look any older than she was. How he had come by such mighty magic she didn't know, but he certainly had it. She wished she could have said he was waving his arms and spewing out words in languages she didn't understand just to make a spectacle of himself, but unfortunately, she had to admit she knew better.

At least she had stopped trembling when thinking about magic, never mind trying to deny it existed. She had seen more of it than she cared to, but she suspected that was going to be her lot in life for at least the foreseeable future. She looked at her horse and Acair's grazing happily together fifty paces away. Shapechanging horses. Who would have thought it?

So many things she hadn't expected when she'd gotten on that little boat and floated up the river to Beinn òrain.

She took the king's proffered hand and didn't protest when he saw her seated on a log. She lifted an eyebrow at Acair when he blustered that he could have done that, then propped her elbows on her knees and her chin on her fists and settled in to watch what promised to be a goodly amount of entertainment.

She turned to the first player: the king of Neroche. He was, as she'd noted before, surely not old enough to be wearing a crown. Actually, he looked as if he spent most of his time in a barn or tromping about a farmer's field. He was undeniably handsome, very well-fashioned, and looked to be the comfortable kind of lad she could have discussed tack with.

As far as his magic went, there had been no sparks coming from his mouth or streaks of white lightning coming from his fingertips, things she would have expected based on the faery tales she'd so loved in her youth. She had, however and in no particular order, seen him light a fire with a word, listened to some fairly dire things spilling out of his mouth back on the plains, and watched him earlier turn himself into a swirling wind that had then sped off toward the place where they now were, leaving them to catch up with him.

Hard to deny any of those things.

She looked at Acair next. She'd been looking at him for quite some time, actually, partly because he was very easy on the eye and partly because she simply couldn't reconcile who she saw with what others said he was. He was as tall as the king of Neroche, easily, and equally well-fashioned. She couldn't say that one of them looked more jaded or world-weary than the other. She could tell, however, that there was something going on between the two of them that she had definitely missed during the past moment or two.

Too much traveling on a horse made of wind, perhaps. It was hard on a woman's wits.

"Don't hold her keeping company with me against her," Acair was saying seriously. "I didn't give her any choice."

The king studied him for a moment or two in silence. "Kidnapping lassies now, my lord Acair? In truth?"

"With all due respect," Léirsinn said, which she honestly had trouble mustering up much of given that the man standing to her right had mud on his boots and looked as if he'd just spent the morning mucking out stalls, "he is telling only part of the truth, no doubt to protect me."

"Well, that's new."

"I don't harm women," Acair said huffily.

"You make up for it with the men."

"And you don't?" Acair said sharply. "And whilst we're on the subject, what the bloody hell did I ever do to you? Well," he amended, "to you personally, rather. I may have done several nasty things to your father."

The king of Neroche shrugged. "Call it sympathy for the rest of the world."

"The rest of the world is faring well enough without your

concern. Besides, I've turned over a new leaf. All those lesser mages and weak-kneed monarchs who have nightmares about my appearing at their hearthfires can now sleep in peace."

"When you present yourself at Uachdaran of Léige's front gates and apologize to him," the king said with a faint smile, "then I'll believe you've changed."

"That will be when hell freezes over," Acair said crisply.

"I wouldn't wait that long if I were you. Uachdaran grows more impossible by the year." He looked at Acair again, smiled, then came to sit down next to Léirsinn. "That was a very lovely introduction my lord Acair managed, but let's do this differently." He held out his hand. "I'm Miach."

She shook his hand, finding it was callused in a reassuring way. "Léirsinn."

"Your friend there said you were from Sàraichte."

"Unfortunately."

Miach smiled. "I've been there, so I'm afraid I have to agree. The visits were mercifully short, which I'm guessing wasn't the case for you."

"Nay, I tended my uncle's stables for almost a score of years."

"My sympathies, truly," he said. "I'll see if I can't provide you with a bit more comfort and better food than is to be found there. If you don't mind, though, I would like to pepper that one over there with a few questions before I decide if I dare let him in my gates to enjoy those comforts with us."

Léirsinn couldn't do anything more than shrug helplessly. The king of Neroche had saved their lives, but perhaps he had some sort of axe to grind with the man standing across the fire from them. She wasn't opposed to jumping in to rescue Acair if necessary, but she supposed he could take care of himself.

"I cannot use my magic," Acair said grimly, "which ought to be a comfort to you."

"I know," Miach said, looking up at him with clear eyes, "but that doesn't satisfy my curiosity. And you know what a valuable trait that is in a mage."

Acair rolled his eyes and sighed gustily. "Very well. Satisfy away, but please do it quickly. Léirsinn is exhausted and I'm starving. I'll grovel however it pleases His Majesty if he will just let me inside the guardhouse where I might gamble my boots for something edible."

"Oh, I will at least feed you," Miach said, "but I do wonder about a thing or two. Any thoughts on who those lads were who were following you, or why? Something foul you stirred up?"

"A few black magelings," Acair said dismissively. "Troublesome, but not powerful enough for concern."

Miach leaned back on his hands and stretched his legs out in front of him. "Which is why you were flinging yourself along as something slightly more substantial than a petrified thought."

"Haste can be considered a virtue," Acair said, "especially when viewed in a particular light."

"Aye, when that light illuminates the possibility of a painful, lingering death."

"Exactly."

Léirsinn watched them as they discussed the difficulties of traveling without magic and the generally unpleasant nature of black mages, and wondered how she had gotten herself caught up in such madness. Miach of Neroche, king though he might have been, looked like an average, though extremely handsome, sort of bloke who might have frequented the local pub after a hard day's work in the field. Acair, while equally handsome, looked as if he'd just stepped from a fancy lord's hall and was waiting outside the front door for his carriage to arrive and take him home to his equally luxurious abode. They were actually quite different, if one were to look at them in that light.

But even so, she could sense something in the both of them that said quite clearly that they had seen things she might want to avoid having to look at. Miach, while looking terribly at his ease, was obviously not relaxed, and Acair, while looking less at his ease, was obviously trying very hard to not make an ass of himself.

"How long have you been forced to endure him?"

She realized Miach was asking her that question and dragged her attention away from Acair, who was standing on the other side of the fire with his arms folded over his chest. "Ah, a fortnight," she said, "but perhaps more. It seems much longer."

"And how has he been? Rude? Dismissive?"

"Quite charming, actually."

Miach glanced at Acair, raised his eyebrows briefly, then turned back to her. "He has done some terrible things, you know," he said seriously.

"Haven't we all?"

Miach smiled faintly. "Acair's level of terrible is quite a bit worse than the usual bit of misbehaving."

Acair glared at him. "And that is useful, how?"

"I just thought it needed to be said before I let you through the gates. I believe I'm the least of your worries once you find yourself with them locked behind you. Don't want you to be surprised by your lack of welcome. I'm not sure Morgan is terribly fond of you."

"She can name the slight and I'll apologize for it."

"Will you mean it, I wonder?"

Acair looked at him evenly. "It is difficult for a man to change when everyone around him continues to throw his past in his face."

"Do you want to change that past, I wonder?"

"Ye gads, nay," Acair said without hesitation. "I'm simply pointing out that 'tis difficult to change one's *future* when one is continually reminded of one's failings. If I ever wanted to change, which I do not, I would find this unwholesome habit from so many to be quite off-putting."

Miach looked at Léirsinn. "How have you managed to come this far with him? I think I would have smothered him in his sleep long before now."

"Willpower and a very strong stomach."

Miach laughed. "I daresay." He turned to Acair. "I suppose you will behave if I let you inside, won't you?"

"Wouldn't think to do otherwise."

Miach's look of skepticism was hard to miss. "I suppose we'll see, won't we? At the very least, I think we should see your lady inside the walls. You and I can then speak privately. "

"You may speak freely in front of her," Acair said, sitting down wearily on a stump across from them. "Ehrne gave her an exhaustive list of my adventures."

"Ehrne?" Miach repeated. "When did you see him?"

"We landed on the wrong side of his border and please don't force me to give you the details now. Let's just say that Léirsinn has heard more than she needed to and anything she didn't already hear is exactly the sort of thing you don't need to tell her."

Miach stared at him for several long minutes in silence, then looked at Léirsinn. "Has he been unkind to you?"

"Nay," she said, surprised at the question. "The epitome of chivalry. Well," she amended, "what he claims he can manage of it. I've little experience with it, so I'm taking his word that he's not very good at it. I haven't had any complaints about his behavior, though. He has bought me several meals, rescued me from what would surely have been my murder, and taken me to visit Hearn of Angesand. Heady stuff, that."

"But," Miach began slowly, "you realize he's toppled thrones, left realms in disarray, stolen priceless treasures, and generally wreaked havoc simply because he could, don't you?"

"Not recently, I don't think."

"That's because he doesn't have any magic he can use."

"I don't," Acair said crisply, "which is, again, why we have come to your humble abode to find the man who can change all that. If we could leave off with the chit-chat, I'll be about that, then we'll be on our way."

"Rùnach isn't here," Miach said mildly.

"I'm talking about Soilléir!"

"I knew that." Miach winked at Léirsinn. "I'm annoying him because I can. I'm the youngest, you know, so it comes quite naturally to me. Don't know why Acair doesn't feel a bond with me over that."

"You didn't have my brothers," Acair said darkly.

"You didn't spend your youth with Adhémar," Miach said dryly.

Acair paused, then nodded. "You're right. You had it worse. Now, to the material point, which is where is that damned Soilléir? I want to talk to him and the sooner the better."

"He's not here."

Léirsinn supposed that if he hadn't had a decent amount of balance, Acair would have simply fallen backward off the stump he was sitting on. He gaped at Miach, his mouth working for several moments with no sound issuing forth, as if he simply couldn't latch onto any useful thing to say.

"That bloody whoreson," he managed finally.

"I believe he had business elsewhere—"

"He didn't, damn him to hell," Acair growled. "That vaunted sight of his told him, I'm quite sure, that I was stumbling after him as best I could. He is doing this apurpose simply to make my life hell."

"Well, that might be possible," Miach agreed. "I think I can find him, if you can give me a few hours. You can sit in front of my fire and keep a weather eye out for any of my brothers who might want to murder you."

"At least I would have an idea who wants me dead," Acair said grimly. "I'm honestly at a loss about anyone else."

"I'll leave you with ink and paper," Miach said solemnly. "You can make a list. I think you can leave me off it, though."

"There's a mercy," Acair said with a sigh. "And I don't think I thanked you properly for the rescue. Very kind and, I will admit, rather unexpected."

"Hard to turn over a new leaf without a bit of help," Miach said with a faint smile. "You're welcome. Perhaps after a late supper, you can tell me what the hell you've been doing that stirred up that hornet's nest following you. There were at least a dozen of them and they were definitely not novices."

Léirsinn watched the fire burning between her and Acair and listened to discussions of things she had to admit she now had no trouble believing. Patches of shadow, mages who didn't care for having them stepped in, Droch of Saothair, supper at Sgath and Eulasaid's table, then an endless number of other things. She realized after a certain point that she had stopped paying any heed to what they were discussing. They were under the cover of spells and starlight and she was perfectly happy to watch the heavens and let talk of mages and magic wash over her.

"I think we've bored her past all endurance," Miach remarked.

Léirsinn came back to herself and realized they were both simply watching her. She smiled. "Forgive me. I was thinking of nothing."

"Acair does that often," Miach said.

"You could only wish to reach the superior quality of my thoughts," Acair said with a snort. "But don't trouble yourself overmuch, Miach my lad. Locked here in this rustic hovel of yours, you won't need them."

Miach only laughed. "And you think I'll let you inside my gates now?"

"If I were polite, you would suspect me of nefarious intentions," Acair said. "Insulting you is likely my only hope of having any supper."

Miach stared at him for several minutes in silence, then looked at Léirsinn. "Does he do that often?"

"Do what?"

"Blurt out those bits of uncomfortable truth?"

"He is blunt," Léirsinn conceded. She smiled faintly. "Is he right?"

"I'm embarrassed to say he is." Miach rose and looked at Acair. "My apologies."

Acair huffed a bit as he pushed himself to his feet, then pulled Léirsinn to hers.

"I believe my ears have failed me, but I won't make you repeat that for my benefit. Know that I fully intend to hide behind you if I manage to get past your front gates without them falling on me out of habit."

"Have you ever been inside Tar Neroche?"

Acair smiled. "Before you were born, my little mage king. Your honored sire and I had spirited words together in the garden. I only got off a few choice insults before your mother came out and frightened the hell straight from me."

Miach smiled. "I'd like to hear that tale in full. Over sour wine in my tower chamber later, perhaps?"

"I'm sure you would enjoy it," Acair said, "for she, as my father's father would say, took me to the woodshed and beat a few manners into me. A remarkable woman, Queen Desdhemar. I believe she even gave my father pause."

Léirsinn wondered if Acair knew he was endlessly keeping hold of her hand to tuck it under his arm or if that was just habit. Courtly manners, perhaps, beaten into him by Miach's mother.

She suspected he was going to need them.

"I would *definitely* like to hear that tale," Miach said with a smile, "as would several of my brothers. Let me feed you, then you can repay us with it. You might even manage to make it to dessert that way."

"One could hope," Acair said. He looked at her, then nodded toward the keep. "Safety."

"For me, at least," she conceded.

"I'll hide behind you," Acair said. "Miach too, if necessary."

"Perhaps your lovely manners will be enough to save you," she offered, then she lost her train of thought as they made their way to the castle.

The road there led past walls that seemed to tilt outward just the slightest bit, no doubt to intimidate and frighten. She understood completely.

In time, she walked through massive gates and into what she supposed was the main courtyard. She wondered if the time would ever come where she didn't feel like a rustic miss who had never seen anything more grand than an ordinary supper laid out on a table inside a manor house she wasn't free to enter.

She feared not.

Half an hour later, she realized that while she was perhaps a bit closer to a meal in a fine house than usual, it was going to take a bit of talking from her two escorts before she was going to be able to sit down to it.

She had been right about the need for courtly manners. She found herself in the private dining chamber of the palace of Neroche, a place that was far grander than anything she had ever seen in her life. She would have perhaps more successfully gaped at it, but she was standing with her nose pressed against Acair's back while he had his nose pressed against Miach's back. If he removed his nose, it was only to shout the occasional apology or bellow a prettily spoken compliment. Neither was being received very well.

"Are you daft?" someone shouted furiously. "What in the bloody hell are you thinking to allow that piece of refuse in here?"

"Thank you for your opinion, Rigaud," Miach said calmly. "I'll take responsibility for him."

"When?" that same man spat. "After he makes you too dead to watch him slay the rest of us?"

Léirsinn leaned up and looked over Acair's shoulder. He put his hand behind him and held her where she was.

"I wouldn't," he whispered.

She patted him, then stepped around his hand before he could stop her. She went to stand shoulder to shoulder with Miach so she

could better see what was going on in the pasture, as it were. Her
first thought was that, again, she would someday have to learn not
to gape at her surroundings with what she was certain was an
expression of utter astonishment.

She leaned closer to the king. "If this is the dining chamber,"
she whispered in awe, "I would hate to see the rest of this place."

He smiled at her briefly, then turned back to face several men
who were past furious. Léirsinn paused, then changed her mind
about that. There were five men facing her and of the five only one
seemed to be past reason. The remaining four were simply watching
one of their number as he thoroughly lost his temper. Some of them
were smiling, others were obviously attempting not to smile.

They were the king's brothers, or so she'd been warned as they
had made their way through the palace. Acair had also made a point
to warn her that his welcome, as usual, wouldn't be a warm one.
She had watched him be proven wrong both at his grandparents'
house and Aherin, so she hadn't been particularly worried.

Now, she was beginning to think she had let her guard down
too soon. Miach's brother Rigaud was absolutely beside himself
with fury and not shy about sharing his opinions. She suspected
Acair wouldn't even manage an apology before that one slew him
if given the chance. Then again, it wasn't as if she could have done
anything to save the man standing behind her, continuing to offer
the occasional kind word.

"He's turned over a new leaf," Miach shouted at one point.

"Aye, to find all the bodies of those he's slain when they wouldn't
give him their magic!"

Acair cleared his throat and leaned over Léirsinn's shoulder. "I
believe, Prince Rigaud, that you're confusing me with my illustrious
but admittedly morally impoverished sire—"

"Shut up!" Rigaud thundered.

"Well," Acair said, "there's no need to be unpleasant."

Miach laughed. Léirsinn watched Rigaud, definitely the best
dressed of the lot, offer a final warning in less-than-dulcet tones

before he stomped off, snarling curses at no one in particular. The rest of the men there didn't seem to be reaching for swords or spells, which she thought boded well. Miach looked at her.

"Introductions," he said. "These are my brothers: Cathar, Nemed, Mansourah, and Turah. Rigaud is the one who recently made such a graceful exit, hastening off to no doubt make plans to slay Acair in his sleep."

"No doubt," Acair muttered. "I'll sleep with one eye open, I daresay."

Miach winked at Léirsinn, then nodded in the direction of his brothers. "And that rabble there has now been joined by my lady wife, the princess Mhorghain of Tòrr Dòrainn, now queen of Neroche."

Léirsinn wondered how she hadn't noticed the queen before. She was so painfully beautiful that Léirsinn half wondered if she might be—well, of course she was. She couldn't say she was good with very many things, but she'd discovered in Sgath's library that she had no trouble memorizing maps. Tòrr Dòrainn was the elven land to the east of Ainneamh, which meant that if the queen of Neroche hailed from there, she was obviously of that elven bent.

She didn't look as arrogant as King Ehrne and his lads had been, though. She rolled her eyes at her husband and walked across the chamber to hold out her hand.

"I'm Morgan," she said with a smile.

"Ah," Léirsinn said, at something of a loss. Queen though the woman might have been, she somehow seemed a great deal like the comfortable sort of person her husband was. "I'm—"

"Léirsinn of Sàraichte," Morgan finished. "So I hear. I've never been to Sàraichte, but I hear it isn't a place to linger."

Léirsinn suspected she might be looking at a friend. "It's worse than you can imagine."

"Oh, I can imagine quite a few things," Morgan said. She looked over Léirsinn's shoulder. "And who do we have here?"

Léirsinn stepped aside, mostly because she couldn't imagine

that the queen would damage the man behind her. She looked at Acair to find him looking a bit winded, actually. He took a deep breath, then made the queen a low, sweeping bow.

"Your Majesty," he said. "A pleasure, truly."

Morgan pursed her lips at him. "Flattery, my lord Acair?"

He shrugged and smiled faintly. "I thought I would give it a try."

Morgan considered him for a moment or two, then looked at Léirsinn. "We share a father, you know, who I fortunately don't remember very well. They tell me that one there is nothing like him save for perhaps the fairness of his face. All I know of him is what I've heard thanks to an endless number of tales about his bad behavior. What do you know?"

Léirsinn wasn't sure she'd heard the queen correctly. "You share a father?" she asked blankly, feeling quite thoroughly as if she had indeed been raised in a barn. The twistings and turnings of the family trees she was encountering were truly something to behold. "Sgath is your grandfather, then?"

Morgan nodded. "So he is." She glanced at Acair, then looked at Léirsinn. "What do you think of my half-brother there?"

"He tucks my hand under his arm constantly," Léirsinn said, because it was the first thing she could think of. "He has also fed me when I couldn't afford to do so myself."

"Interesting," Morgan said. "I understand he's spent a goodly part of the past year groveling before various offended dignitaries. Sounds unpleasant, doesn't it?"

"Very," Léirsinn agreed.

Morgan looked at Acair for a moment or two longer, then seemed to come to some sort of decision about him. She smiled at Léirsinn. "Let's leave him to fend for himself. If he manages to survive the gauntlet that will form on his way to the table, I might just see him fed."

Léirsinn followed the queen across the chamber, noting that she had predicted things aright. The king's brothers seemed determined to perhaps have a bit of sport at Acair's expense. Well, save for one of those who deserted the rest without hesitation and hurried around the table to hold out a chair for her. She looked at the queen, but Morgan only smiled and shrugged.

Léirsinn was uncomfortable accepting aid from someone besides Acair, a rather alarming realization to be sure, but she sat where invited to just the same. She then looked at the man who plopped himself down next to her. He was terribly handsome, so much so that she had to admit she felt a little light-headed.

"Drink," Morgan said dryly, handing her a delicate glass of something. "Sourah, leave her alone."

"She's exquisite," the man said. "She obviously needs my protection."

"You realize that means you'll be fighting Acair of Ceangail for her, don't you?" Morgan asked seriously. "I don't imagine you'll win."

"I intend to give it my best effort. The prize would be worth it."

"Léirsinn, this is my brother-in-law, Mansourah," Morgan said. "Mansourah, leave her be before you ruin her appetite."

Mansourah of Neroche was polite and gallant, Léirsinn would give him that. She knew she had made some bit of conversation that was probably not as lofty as it should have been given her surroundings, but she was profoundly uncomfortable with the attention Morgan's brother-in-law was paying her and she wasn't sure quite how to avoid it.

"Move."

Léirsinn looked over her shoulder to find Acair standing behind her, his hand on her chair. Mansourah only looked at him coolly.

"I beg your pardon?"

"You may find that necessary at some point," Acair said in that posh accent he tended to use with royalty and other rich men. "As that might be unpleasant for you, I suggest you save yourself that pain and get up. Now."

"So we can brawl before supper?"

"I wouldn't make a nuisance of myself in such a manner," Acair said. "I assume you have the same level of decency."

Mansourah pursed his lips, then looked at Léirsinn. "I forget who he is far too often." He rose and inclined his head politely. "I concede the chair, but not the battle. Mistress Léirsinn, if you'll excuse me?"

Léirsinn kept her mouth shut and nodded, which she supposed was the best she could do under the circumstances. Acair exchanged places with the king's brother with a minimum of curses muttered, settled himself in the chair next to her, then looked at her.

"One skirmish won."

She hoped that would be the worst of it, but she hardly dared hope for it. She smiled weakly, then turned and watched the rest of Miach's family seat themselves around the table. They might have been sitting in a grand chamber, but when it came to supper, they were very much as she remembered her family having been before they'd had to leave their home. If she hadn't known better, she would have thought herself in a place no more grand than some minor landholder's kitchen with a table built for his robust collection of children to gather around each night. Morgan and Miach of Neroche were very fortunate indeed.

She had no idea what she ate, though she supposed it had been tasty enough. She wanted to believe she had no reason to be nervous, but she couldn't help but wonder if they would manage to finish dessert without someone flinging his pudding at Acair, accompanied no doubt by a barbed spell or two.

Supper ended unremarkably, though, and she soon found herself sitting with the company in front of a fire in a private gathering chamber that was no less lovely than the dining hall but definitely smaller. She was exhausted, but she couldn't not struggle to keep her eyes open lest she miss something important.

There was a great deal of abuse heaped on Acair's head, which he took with more grace than she would have managed herself. Prince Rigaud even unbent far enough to sit with them, though he made up for that with the looks he was sending Acair. Acair glanced at him occasionally with a look of such utter boredom that Léirsinn had to smile. That one there. She thought that he might deserve a few of the souls who didn't care for him.

"I think there is something going on."

Léirsinn looked at the queen. "I beg your pardon, Your Majesty?"

"Morgan," she said with a smile. "Call me Morgan. This whole business of crowns and such is a recent development. Most of my life, I've just been a soldier of fortune."

Léirsinn looked at her in astonishment. "I can't believe that."

"Sometimes the tales we hear about others don't tell the whole story," Morgan mused. "If you know what I'm getting at."

"I think I do." Léirsinn looked at Acair who was currently ignoring Prince Rigaud in favor of sending Mansourah of Neroche a selection of very cool looks. "I've heard a great deal about Acair's adventures, but I find it still difficult to believe." She looked at the queen. "Has he done all those things they claim, do you suppose?"

"I wouldn't be surprised, but you have to consider his past and what it contains." Morgan shrugged. "I won't admit to the number of times I slipped inside a keep in the middle of the night and whispered *boo* into a lord's ear before I put a knife to his back and forced him to open his gates to a different lord who had paid me to do the like."

Léirsinn looked at her in surprise. "Impossible."

"'Tis all too true." She glanced at Acair briefly. "I have only known him as someone to be avoided at all costs, but looking at him now, I wonder if perhaps the tales have been a bit exaggerated. He does clean up well, I suppose."

"He didn't throw food or knives at supper."

Morgan smiled at her. "I must admit that I did worry he and Mansourah would come to blows."

"What did Acair do to him?"

"It would seem the rub concerns what Mansourah would like to do, which is spend a night dancing with you. I imagine he's already sent a message to the musicians to prepare."

Léirsinn felt her mouth fall open. "But I don't dance."

"My brother-in-law won't care."

She couldn't imagine that, but she was hardly an authority on the doings of royalty. She decided it would be best to just leave Mansourah to his plans and Acair to his snarling. Perhaps she would escape to the stables and see how their horses were faring.

At the moment, that seemed like the safest place to be.

It was very late when she stumbled along with Acair behind a servant with the promise of her destination being a soft bed instead of a ballroom or a straw-filled stall. She wasn't one to keep royal hours, which seemed to include chatting far into the night, so she supposed she might not manage any presence at Tor Neroche's morning stables. Hopefully their ponies would forgive her.

She stopped in front of the door a young man indicated, listened to Acair thank and dismiss their escort, then looked blearily at the man who had survived supper and conversation.

"Where are they putting you?" she asked, hiding a yawn behind her hand.

"With any luck, somewhere besides the dungeons."

She couldn't even muster up any concern over that possibility. "Prince Mansourah doesn't seem to like you. If that isn't too rude to point out."

"It isn't, and the feeling is quite mutual." He pursed his lips. "He's preparing some sort of ball for tomorrow evening, which seems to be the limit of what he can do. Dancing and preparing to dance, that is."

"Can you dance?"

"Divinely."

She couldn't help but laugh. "You are without a doubt the most arrogant show pony I've ever encountered."

"One must keep up appearances." He opened her door, looked

inside, then pulled back. "No ogres, trolls, or black mages that I can see. I think you're safe."

She paused halfway across the threshold and looked at him. "They won't throw you in the dungeon in truth, will they?"

"Nay," he said. "Thanks to my half-sister and her strong-stomached husband, it seems I have been given the chamber next to yours. Knock on the wall if you need me. If you hear frantic pounding coming from my side, feel free to come execute a timely rescue."

"I would need something more than harsh language to use, I think," she said.

He smiled briefly. "You'll be perfectly safe here and, with any luck, so will I. But I will find you a dagger, if you like, and show you how to use it."

"Thank you, and for more than just that."

"Oh, it has been a glorious adventure thus far," he said with a wry smile. "I am breathless with anticipation over what lies around the corner."

She walked inside, then turned and held on to the door. "What should I do when I wake? I'm not sure of the proper comportment for a woman who is completely out of her depth."

"I would suggest a visit to the stables, if you like," he said, "then do what pleases you. I imagine there will be no shortage of Nerochian princes willing to aid you in that, damn them all."

"They seem very nice."

"Looks are deceiving."

She smiled. "And what will you be doing?"

"I'm going to hunt down that lazy mage who holds the key to my life," he said. "I'll return as quickly as I can. I wouldn't want to miss those delightful entertainments we have to look forward to courtesy of that empty-headed Mansourah of Neroche."

She started to shut the door, then paused. "Be careful."

He looked at her with absolutely no expression on his face. "I don't think another soul has ever said that to me before," he said quietly.

"Perhaps 'tis past time someone did."

He took a deep breath, then reached for her door. "Go to sleep, you red-haired vixen. Torment Mansourah properly whilst I'm away."

She let him shut her door, then stood there for several minutes with her hand on the wood before she looked over the chamber and tried to decide if she dared lay her head there. She was half tempted to see if she couldn't find an empty stall instead, which she suspected Morgan the queen might have understood.

But the bed looked softer than any bed had the right to look, someone had thoughtfully provided nightclothes for her, and she suspected she might never again have such a chance as that to sleep in luxury. Traveling with a mage apparently had its advantages, though perhaps she and Acair had simply had the good fortune to fall in with lovely people.

She didn't want to think about how quickly that might change when they continued on their journey.

Twenty

❧

Acair couldn't say he had ever been an early riser, but he also hadn't had a spell of death hounding him until he thought he would go mad. Getting an early start on seeing it consigned to the rubbish bin seemed only wise. Miach had sent him a message an hour ago telling him where Soilléir was to be found. No time like the present to make certain he had a future.

He walked out the front gates and into his, er, sister. Half-sister. The youngest legitimate child of his philandering father. Ah, rather.

"Mhorghain," he managed. "I mean, Your Majesty."

She looked at him seriously. "Call me Mhorghain if you like, Morgan if you care what I like, and Your Majesty only if you want me to stab you."

He blinked, then had to take a deep breath. "Morgan, then."

"Would our father hate that?"

"Profoundly, so I suppose Morgan it is." He supposed if he was going to call her that, he might as well dispense with qualifying what she was to him. A sister she would be, because it was simpler and because he rather liked her. He paused. "I don't want to seem rude, but why are you here?"

She turned to face him. He had to admit that it was a little startling to look at her. She couldn't have resembled Sarait of Tòrr Dòrainn any more if she had been Sarait herself. But there was something in her eye that was different, as though she hadn't been raised in beauty so painful that it had left an indelible mark on her soul.

He paused. Perhaps 'twas time to give up the business of black magery, retire to some exotic locale, and become a poet. He could think of worse ways to pass the time.

"Acair?"

"Sorry," he said. "I think too much."

"You asked why I'm here," she said, looking at him as if she very much doubted the quality of his wits. "I thought perhaps the youngest children of Gair's two broods should become better acquainted."

"Broods that we know about," he said before he stopped to consider that perhaps that wasn't the most politic thing to say.

She looked at him gravely. "I'm sorry that you saw so much."

If she only knew. He cleared his throat. "I offer the same condolences to you. We have had rather unique pasts, I daresay."

"My present is more than making up for it," she said with a half-smile. "And yours?"

"I'm not enjoying mine terribly much at the moment, but I think others are finding it rather amusing."

"If you only knew how true that is."

He held open his arms. "They may do their worst."

"You certainly have?"

"I wasn't going to admit that, but you're free to say what you like."

She smiled. "I'm not sure I want to know any more than I already do about your exploits."

"I suggest avoiding Prince Rigaud then."

"What did you do to him?" she asked. "He can't stand you."

"Ah, where to begin?" he asked with a light sigh. "I'm afraid our tastes run to a similar sort of brittle, unpleasant noblewoman, one dripping with jewels and highly skilled at cutting verbal repartee. 'Tis possible we might even have attempted to dance with the same woman on more than one occasion. Add to that the occasional argument over cards, differences of opinion on the proper way to tie one's neckwear, and the odd invitation to duels I couldn't be bothered to arrive on time for, if at all, and it makes our relationship rather prickly, I daresay."

She looked at him in disgust. "You're one of those, aren't you?"

"A well-dressed gentleman of modest means?"

"Aye, all but the last part," she said. "I understand you haven't just pilfered spells."

"Laboring with one's hands is so pedestrian."

She shook her head, then laughed, apparently in spite of herself. "You're vile. Weger wouldn't let you on his front stoop, never mind inside his gates."

"I loitered outside his gates for a bit last year," Acair admitted, and admittedly it was one of the less pleasant experiences of that year. "Not for the first time, it should be noted. I can safely say that Gobhann is the very last place on earth I would ever willingly go." He looked at her. "Magic sink and all that."

"Pointy swords and all that."

He shivered. "That as well."

"Yet here you are without magic just the same."

"Because I cannot use it at the moment doesn't mean I don't still have it," he corrected. "A distinction Soilléir of that damned place on the other side of the mountains that I will definitely be giving a closer look to in the future knows very well."

She pulled on a pair of gloves. "I'll pretend I didn't hear that." She shot him a look. "Miach knows all his spells, you know."

"Hence the idea I've been toying with for several months now of waylaying your husband some evening on his way home from the pub and torturing those spells out of him."

She smiled. "They won't let him go to the pub by himself anymore."

"Do you honestly believe his ministers frighten me?"

"Does Miach frighten you?"

He straightened the collar of his cloak and followed her away from the gates. "I don't want to answer that."

"Should your magic frighten him?"

He clasped his hands behind his back as they walked, then looked at her. "Are we riding or walking?"

"I had horses prepared, but you might prefer to fly."

"I would, but obviously I can't indulge."

"I'll change your shape for you, if you like."

"That would be terribly kind of you."

She looked at him, then laughed. "You do this all day, don't you? And so you don't have to ask what I'm getting at, I mean you avoid questions you don't like and spew out courtly pleasantries without thinking."

"Bad habit, I'm afraid."

"No doubt." She paused, then considered. "Dragonshape or something else?"

"Dragonshape," he said, "and if you give me wee wings that leave me gasping for air as I flap along behind you like a fat little pig, I will never forgive you for it."

She looked at him seriously. "Nothing more dire than that?"

"You are a woman, half-sister or not. I do not damage women."

"Men?"

"Don't ask."

She smiled and suddenly she was gone. In her place was a sleek, unadorned, black dragon. It was something he would have chosen for her himself if he'd been about the choosing, so he approved thoroughly of her taste in fire-breathing creatures.

He stretched his own wings out only to find they were approximately two feet long. The laughter at his expense from the gates was everything he'd expected it would be.

To his sister's credit, however, once he had attempted a pair of unsuccessful leaps up into the air—accompanied, of course, by more guffaws from lads he would have a year ago repaid with dire things indeed—on the third try, his wings stretched out to a proper length and he leapt up into the air as what he had to admit was one of the most impressive beasts he had wished for a still lake in which to admire.

He contemplated taking a bit of a detour over the heads of those lads who had mocked him, but two things stopped him. One, they were quite suddenly all looking at him in slack-jawed astonishment; and two, Mhorghain's voice whispered over his mind with a very firm, *don't you dare*.

He sighed in resignation. If he snorted out a bit of fire that sent the more vocal lads scrambling for cover as he rose majestically into the sky, what could he do but vow to offer his most sincere regrets later?

You are incorrigible.

Indeed he was, but he was also off the ground under his own power and damned grateful for the pleasure. He followed after his sister and decided that she was rather a sterling lass in spite of her heritage of gilded elven magic. Her time had obviously been well spent in that pit of swords and terrible food on the Island of Melksham.

A pair of hours later, he was standing on the edge of a road in his own shape, pushing his hair out of his eyes and hoping he looked as fierce and unyielding as he felt. He hoped Mhorghain wouldn't mind if he was a bit more rumpled in his dress than usual.

"He's waiting for us in the inn through those trees," she said.

"Are you coming too?" he asked her in surprise.

"If you don't mind," she said. "Miach thought I should keep the pair of you from killing each other."

"Don't you have a bairn to see to?" he asked in an effort to get rid of her.

"Young Hearn is with his father," she said, "so not to worry. I'm here to keep you company the entire time."

That was exactly what he was trying to avoid. He tried another tack. "I don't think you'll want to watch what I'm going to do to him," he warned.

"I think I'll survive it."

He imagined she would. He also imagined that she had spent her share of time intimidating the rich and powerful, so perhaps she had little room to criticize him.

Which she didn't seem to be doing, oddly enough.

He walked with her up the road and stopped her just before she reached for the door. "As for your question back at the palace, if I had any sense I would be afraid of your husband, especially on his own soil. His power is staggering."

"And yours?"

"My father's blood runs through my veins," he said, "just as it does yours. As does my mother's, which should give us all pause." He considered, then shook his head. "I'm not sure I either can or want to answer your question. My magic is . . . dark."

She studied him for a moment or two. "And yet you are not Gair."

"Nay, but I would have every damned one of his spells in a heartbeat," Acair said honestly. "More particularly, Diminishing, but what decent mage wouldn't say the same thing?"

"Ruith has them all."

"I know."

"And yet you haven't ransacked his solar."

Acair started to speak, then shook his head. "I haven't."

"Yet."

"I didn't say that," he said. "I didn't *not* say that, either, but what else can you expect from me?"

"More," she said simply, then she reached for the door. "After you, brother."

He caught the door over her head and nodded for her to go inside. "Don't think familial obligation or the sort of gentle guilting you're attempting will work on me. I'm a black-hearted bastard to my very innards. Dangerous. Merciless. Men cower and mages scamper when they know I'm coming through."

She only smiled at him and ducked under his arm. He sighed and followed her inside. Obviously he had lost his touch. She should have been weeping with fear, not looking at him as if she might at some point in the future experience a fond feeling or two for him.

The inn was rather nice as inns in Neroche went, though he supposed he was less concerned about the accommodations than he was the souls taking advantage of them. He spotted Soilléir immediately, relaxing in a choice spot by the fire, looking as if he didn't have a damned thing to do besides enjoy a decent mug of ale. He reminded himself that he needed that one alive, so he swallowed all the nasty threats he wanted to blurt out, fixed a pleasant expression to his face, and followed Mhorghain across the gathering chamber.

Soilléir rose as they approached, but that was obviously strictly for Mhorghain's benefit.

"Morgan," he said, leaning over to kiss her cheek. "How are you?"

"Exactly as I was two days ago," she said with a smile. "You?"

Soilléir saw her seated, then resumed his lazy pose on his own chair. "Ah, one does what one must to keep busy." He looked at Acair from languid eyes. "As you would say, that is."

Acair drew out a chair and sat down because it gave him something to do besides leap across the table and wrap his hands around Soilléir's throat. He was further distracted by the mug of ale Soilléir pushed across the table to him.

"Poisoned?" Acair asked suspiciously.

"Not by me," Soilléir said, "which is all I can guarantee."

"Your guarantees mean nothing," Acair groused. He paused for a sip of only marginally drinkable ale, then fixed Soilléir with a steely look. "Permit me to get right to the business of the morning. Take off that damned spell and do it now."

Soilléir looked at him blankly. "What spell?"

Acair didn't have to look over his shoulder to know that his constant companion was standing post by the door. "*That* spell. The one you put on me that promises death should I use any sort of magic."

Soilléir looked across the gathering room, frowned as if he struggled to find a useful thought, then finally looked at Mhorghain. "Would it bother you, my dear, if I were to draw a spell of un-noticing over us? I believe we have serious matters to discuss."

"You're damned right we—" Acair began. He would have finished, but he was distracted by the spell Soilléir was using. It wasn't essence changing, but it was something very much like it. "What was that?" he asked.

"Something I dug up out of one of my grandfather's books," Soilléir said mildly. "Interesting, isn't it?"

"Have the book with you?"

Soilléir looked at him with perhaps what passed with him for a smile. "What do you think?"

"I think you probably returned it to its spot and hoped Seannair wouldn't notice, what with all the dust disturbed, that you'd been nosing about his solar."

"Library," Soilléir corrected.

"How interesting," Acair said smoothly. "I'll remember that."

Soilléir did smile then. "You'll never get past the front gates."

"I can certainly try."

Soilléir looked at Mhorghain. "He is impossible, you know."

"I think he's just like you," Mhorghain said seriously. "All you mages are always on the hunt for the next spell. Never satisfied with what you have."

Soilléir raised his eyebrows briefly at her, then set his cup aside and looked at Acair. "You sent out a call for help and I've come. What do you need?"

Acair realized he was spluttering and it took him more time than it should have to control it. "Help," he gasped. "I never asked you for *help*. I want you to get rid of that damned spell over there so I can be about my business without *dying*."

"Whom did you offend this time?"

"I could have offended the entire world and it wouldn't change the fact that I need to use my magic without being slain for the same!"

"Humor me."

Acair would have preferred to do damage to him, but there were many reasons why Soilléir couldn't aid him if he were dead, so he had another fortifying drink of his ale and dredged up the last remaining shreds of his patience.

"I'll be brief," he said, lest Soilléir think they were going to be chatting all day. "I stepped in a spot of shadow, apparently stirred up a hornet's nest, and I've been trying to keep myself alive ever since by running from an ever-increasing collection of black mages. Is that clear enough for you?"

Soilléir only lifted an eyebrow. "I'd prefer to have a few more details, actually. If you wouldn't mind."

Acair minded very much, but he was also a realist. He would have nothing out of the fool sitting across from him until the man had satisfied his curiosity. But if he knew what was good for him, he would consider that curiosity satisfied sooner rather than later.

"Léirsinn," Acair said, "the lass running the stables where you sent me to serve out my hellish sentence, had been seeing spots on the ground, things that are only shadows of shadows. I found them unusual, so I thought I would investigate the same by stepping in one, just to see what it would do to me."

"Of course you did," Soilléir said mildly. "Your curiosity, Acair, will someday be the last thing you indulge. Very well, what happened then?"

"It assaulted me," he said, "and I'm still trying to forget the great tussle I had trying to rip myself out of its midst. I'm not too proud to say I believe I left a part of myself behind."

"Flesh?"

"Soul."

Soilléir considered the depths of his cup for a moment or two, then looked up. "Did you see these spots anywhere besides Sàraichte?"

"Lake Cladach and Aherin. I believe there was one in Beinn òrain as well, but my memory fails me about the particulars of that. I was rather occupied at the time."

"Busy being chased by Droch?" Soilléir asked politely.

"Aye, and finding that you'd done the unthinkable and flitted off on a bloody holiday," Acair said pointedly. "Who do you think you are taking days of leisure when there is evil afoot in the world?"

Soilléir looked at him for a moment or two in silence, then glanced at Mhorghain. "There are times I don't think he listens to what comes out of his mouth."

Acair cursed him. "I'm not talking about *my* sort of evil—and aye, I hear everything that comes out of my mouth. Sometimes I repeat the pithier statements to myself at bedtime to send me off properly into a blissful slumber, but that isn't the point here. Those spots are in places I wouldn't expect them to be. Why would anyone put anything untoward in Aherin?" He looked at Mhorghain. "Have you seen anything like them at Tor Neroche?"

She shook her head, wide-eyed. "I haven't. I'm not sure I would have thought to be looking for them, though."

"Well, if you do see any, I suggest not stepping in them. I am no woman when it comes to pain, but pulling myself free from that damned thing was quite possibly the worst thing I've ever felt."

"And then what?" Soilléir asked.

Acair looked at him narrowly. "And then, as I said, I found my life in peril, beginning with a pair of mages trying to murder me in my sleep in Sàraichte. If Léirsinn hadn't put crossbow bolts in them, I would be dead. I wasn't at my leisure to examine those bolts and we unfortunately left them behind in our haste to flee that damned barn, but I suspect they were enspelled." He blew out his breath in frustration. "Who knows who has them now."

"That was ill-advised," Soilléir offered. "Leaving them behind, that is."

"And you almost got me killed, which was perhaps just as ill-advised," Acair shot back. "You and your vaunted Seeing. Did you not see this coming down the road toward you? Nay, toward *me*, rather?"

"'Tis possible to make mistakes."

Acair wasn't entirely sure Soilléir wasn't mocking him, but he was quite certain he didn't care for where those words might be leading. "I wish you wouldn't admit that. It leaves me a little uneasy about the fate of the world, if you must know."

"I suppose you'll have to shoulder a bit of the burden."

"Me?" Acair hardly knew how to respond to that. "Thank you, but nay. I am utterly uninterested in any more do-gooding—"

"Why not you?" Soilléir interrupted. "Your ancestors are noble. Your father's are, definitely. And I think you might give your mother too little credit."

"I give my mother just as much credit as she deserves, the old harridan," Acair said with a snort. "If you think she longs for a happy, peaceful world, she has beguiled you as thoroughly as she does most everyone who walks through her door."

"I think she has perhaps stepped back from the issues of good and evil," Soilléir conceded, "which leaves her in a unique position to simply watch the world as it unfolds before her. She is, as you well know, a very committed diarist."

"With a collection of spells that would make you wince," Acair said, "which perhaps you didn't know."

"Oh, I know," Soilléir said. "We've discussed them more than once over tea. And speaking of things discussed over tea, you should know that she's enormously proud of you."

"She has reason, I suppose."

Mhorghain laughed. Acair wasn't sure he shouldn't have been offended, but he was finding that he quite liked a grown-up Mhorghain of Tòrr Dòrainn, her choice of husbands aside. He watched her lean closer to Soilléir.

"He's not exactly what he likes people to think, is he?"

"He is a mystery," Soilléir said. "Conflicted, I daresay, but absolutely fearless, if one must begin a list of his finer points."

"I am," Acair agreed, "which is why your grandfather had best send a diligent maidservant in to dust his library, that he might know when I've come to pay a call to investigate his most treasured and hidden of spellbooks. Now, before I find myself dazzled beyond measure by that thought, let's get back to the matter at hand."

"Those spots," Soilléir agreed slowly. "Any ideas on what they are?"

Acair almost threw up his hands in frustration. "I don't give a bloody damn about those spots. I'm talking about that spell over there in the corner! I want to be free of it so I can find out why I'm not seeing the usual suspects trailing after me with my murder at the top of their hastily scrawled lists of things to do before supper. Is that clear enough for you?"

Soilléir frowned. Acair didn't care for the look at all mostly because it contained an alarming amount of something that might have been termed *I haven't a bloody clue* if the look had been worn by someone else.

"Don't tell me you don't know what that spell is," Acair said, because he couldn't not say it.

"I haven't a bloody clue."

Acair realized he was halfway across the table only because his sister's hand was suddenly there against the middle of his chest, holding him still in mid-lunge. She was, he had to admit, rather strong for a wench. She looked him in the eye.

"Don't."

"But I want to so badly."

"You cannot fight him in your present state," she reminded him.

"In any state," Soilléir offered, then smiled. "Just thought you ought to remember that."

Acair sat back down with a curse, then glared at Soilléir. "You know, for someone who paints himself as always above the fray, you can be a great whacking bastard from time to time."

Soilléir sighed. "I know. I think I need a change."

"Fine, let me help you with that," Acair said. "I'll give you my spells and you give me yours. We'll meet back up in a year and see where we are."

Soilléir laughed reluctantly. "Heaven forbid." He considered, then sighed. "I must tell you, Acair, that this whole thing is odd."

"Then take off that bloody spell and let me see to it in the normal way!"

"I'll go have a look at it." Soilléir rose and looked at Mhorghain. "If Her Majesty will excuse me?"

She only smiled and waved him on. Acair watched him go, then looked back at his sister.

"I don't know how you endure him so often."

"You like him," she remarked.

"I can't bloody stand him. Now, if he were to break into his grandfather's solar library with me, then step aside as I helped myself to the most potent of those Cothromaichian spells, well, then we might have something."

"He never would."

"See? Doomed from the start." He paused and looked at her. "Don't suppose you know any of those spells of his."

"Don't suppose I would share if I did."

"You, my wee sisterling, have spent far too much time in Weger's company." He shook his head. "Hard-hearted wench."

She only smiled, so he supposed she knew he wasn't completely in earnest. He waited, considered a quick game of cards to refill his purse, contemplated with even more seriousness lifting the purse of a fat lord in the corner, then watched as Soilléir came back into the gathering hall. He looked perplexed, which Acair just couldn't believe was a good thing.

Soilléir sat, drank, then simply stared at him.

"Well?" Acair demanded finally.

"That's not my spell."

Acair retrieved his jaw from where it had fallen to his chest. "But . . . well, then 'tis something of Rùnach's that he made using your spells. You can remove his spell just as easily."

"It doesn't belong to either of us," Soilléir said. "Honestly, I have absolutely no idea how it came to be."

Acair felt his mouth working. He would have attempted to force a few choice insults out whilst he was flapping his lips, as it were, but he was simply too astonished for words. He shook his head, then realized he was sitting there, shaking his head as if he couldn't latch onto anything else useful to say.

"But that can't be," he managed finally.

"Unfortunately, it is. 'Tis a very elegant thing, though. I've never seen its like before." Soilléir shrugged. "I have no idea—"

"Stop saying that!" Acair exclaimed. "Good hell, Soilléir, what am I to do now?"

"Be careful?"

He exchanged a look with Mhorghain, which resulted in his not bothering to lean over the table and strangle that damned mage sitting there. He blew out his breath, then tossed a pair of coins on the table.

"For myself and the feisty one there," he said. "You can pay for your own drink, you useless whoreson."

"I think I should—"

"Consider how greatly you'll mourn the loss of your spells?" Acair finished for him, bitterly. "Aye, you should, for when I have my magic back to hand, you will find yourself missing them." He rose. "Come along, Morgan, and we'll leave this fool to his excuses."

He walked out of the door, snarling at his spellish companion as it left the inn with them. He walked a goodly distance away—no sense in terrifying the locals with a robust bit of shapechanging—then looked at his sister. "Well."

"I'm sorry, Acair," she said quietly. "I'm not sure what else to say. There is dancing to look forward to tonight, if that helps."

He shot her a look, but realized immediately that she was only trying to distract him out of pity. "Perfect," he said, trying to match her light tone. "And perhaps I'll kill Mansourah before supper, just to pass the time."

"I'm sure he would enjoy that." She paused, considered, then looked at him gravely. "We could fly for a bit, if you think better that way."

He looked at her in a fair bit of surprise. "You wouldn't mind?"

"I'm not an inventive shapechanger," she admitted, "but if you give me a spell you like, I'll see what I can do."

He wasn't one given to astonishment, but he could hardly believe what he'd just heard. "You would trust me that far," he said, almost unable to spew the words out. "To use one of my spells."

"Shouldn't I?"

"That isn't an answer, I don't think. I'm too off balance to properly judge, though."

She smiled. "What's your pleasure? Wind? Hummingbirds? An evil intention?"

"Heaven preserve me should I teach you that shape," he said faintly. "But a brisk wind? Aye, that might do. Just don't leave me strewn about the plains, if you don't mind."

"I won't—"

"Acair, wait."

He shut his mouth around the spell he was going to give Mhorghain when he found that Soilléir had come to stand next to them. He had appeared rather suddenly, which Acair supposed should have left him wanting to curse the man for his ability to change his shape into a swift thought, but in truth, he was simply too frustrated to do anything but snap at him.

"What do *you* want?" he demanded.

Soilléir looked hesitant. Of all the things Acair had seen and heard in the past pair of hours, that was the thing that unsettled him the most.

"I may have details you should hear," Soilléir said.

Acair realized that Mhorghain had come to stand shoulder to shoulder with him. He would have told her he didn't need protection, but the truth was, he wasn't sure he didn't. He raised an eyebrow at her briefly, then looked at the mage in front of him.

"Do tell," he said coolly.

Soilléir looked at Mhorghain. "You may not want to hear this."

"She's a strong-stomached wench," Acair said promptly. That and he thought he might want to use her shoulder as a handy place to lay his head and weep when he heard what he was certain would be Soilléir admitting that that damned spell of death was his but he'd forgotten how to destroy it. "She needn't leave on my account."

"Very well, if she likes," Soilléir said slowly. He seemed to gather his thoughts for far longer than it should have taken him before he spoke. "Why do you think we sent you to Sàraichte?" he asked.

"To shovel manure," Acair said without hesitation, then he rolled his eyes at the look of disbelief on Soilléir's face. "How the bloody hell should I know why you sent . . . me . . ."

He stopped speaking because he had to.

A stillness had descended over their little tableau there in the clearing, a stillness unlike anything he'd ever experienced before and his life was not without its memorable moments. Those had been confined generally to his irrevocably changing the lives of those he had chosen to vex, but there it was. He was not an elven prince, sprinkling his sparkling spells over everything in sight like so much faery dust. He was a ruthless, powerful mage, wreaking havoc and altering the course of kingdoms.

He didn't like thinking that his *own* life was about to be changed past all recognition.

A numbness started at the top of his head and spread rapidly downward. He was afraid he might be fainting. Perhaps that was more obvious than he cared it to be because Mhorghain had quite suddenly pulled his arm over her shoulders. The wench was strong, he would give her that, and ignored him when he made a sound of protest.

He forced himself to take a deep, even breath. "Why did you send me to Sàraichte?" he managed.

"To walk where I cannot."

"Walk?" Acair echoed with as much disdain as he could drape over the word. "Aye, all I can do is walk because I can't bloody shapechange—and apparently you can't make that any different for me!"

The faintest of smiles crossed the man's face. "You know what I mean."

Acair looked at him and felt as though he were looking at him for the first time. He leaned on his sister for a moment or two, then felt some of his old enthusiasm and strength return. He ceased holding on to her as if she were the only thing keeping him on his feet—which she had been, he had to admit—and simply kept his arm around her shoulders in a casual sort of brotherly way. "I vow I haven't a clue what you're talking about," he said, attempting a yawn.

If he'd sounded as if he were choking, so be it. He was not at his best and he was hearing things he didn't like.

"You will."

"Without putting too fine a point on it, Your Highness, I don't *want* to know what you're talking about. That, and I would very much like to take my sharpest spell of death and plunge it into your chest."

"I don't doubt that."

He considered several things, wished more desperately than he had ever in the whole of his life for a spell of Diminishing so he could have rid Soilléir of all his magic and schemes, then stepped away from the proverbial edge of the abyss and tried to make sense of what he was hearing.

He could walk where that one there could not?

"Are you saying," he began slowly and very quietly, "that you sent me on a quest?"

Soilléir nodded.

"To places you can't go . . . or you won't go?"

Soilléir only looked at him in that way he had, as if he could see things that truly should remain unseen.

"You underestimate who you are," he said quietly, "and what you can do. Discovering that is your work, not mine."

Soilléir then flipped a coin up in the air. Acair realized he was meant to catch it only because he was forced to stop it from clouting him on the nose. He looked at it, expecting it to be a sovereign, only to find it was something else entirely. He gaped at it for a moment or two, then looked at the man standing there.

"What is this?" he asked.

"Tòrr Dòrainn isn't the only place with magic and Sìle not the only one with runes to dole out," Soilléir said quietly. "That, my friend, is something of mine, fashioned from my own magic."

"And what in the bloody hell am I to do with it?" Acair said, holding it gingerly between his thumb and pointer finger. "Well, besides try to pull it apart and see what sort of spell you used to fashion it."

"Put it in your purse for the moment. When you need aid that only I can offer, use it."

Acair would have protested that the damned thing would surely collapse under the weight of all the coppers in the purse at his belt, but he could see already that it wasn't so fragile. What it was made of, he couldn't have said, but he would certainly do everything within his power to find out.

He watched Soilléir embrace Mhorghain briefly, shoot him one more look full of meanings he didn't want to try to identify, then turn himself into a bit of swirling wind that didn't waste any time scampering off.

Acair stood there in that bit of clearing near the inn and considered what he'd heard. It had rocked him to his very foundations, truth be told, but he would be damned if he let anyone see as much. He took a deep breath and looked at his sister.

"What a ridiculous bit of drama that was," he said patting her on the shoulder before he settled his cloak. "I vow I don't know what he was getting at with that business."

"Don't you?" she asked.

He considered, then shook his head. "It's not coming to me and I've no interest in investigating. Let's turn for your castle. I fancy a journey as a bit of brisk autumn wind. What say you?"

"As you will."

He could scarce believe he was trusting another soul with such a change in his own sweet self, but he thought he might almost be past surprise where his own actions were concerned. He gave his sister the spell and hoped he would remember to thank her for not simply slamming the words into him and leaving him in pieces. If she added a few Fadairian sparkles to him, well, what could he do?

Well, he could face the fact that those bits of heart-stoppingly beautiful glamour hadn't come from Mhorghain, they had come from inside him. Damn that Rùnach of Tòrr Dòrainn. That spell was going to be the death of him.

He spared one final thought for things that made him uncomfortable. So, Soilléir had sent him south because he hadn't wanted to send himself. Obviously, he'd had business that needed to be seen to that he hadn't bloody wanted to face, no matter the reason he'd given, and he'd tasked Acair with seeing to that business whilst not having the common courtesy to tell him what he was walking into.

Literally, apparently.

He didn't want to admit it, but he was absolutely shattered by the thought. There were things afoot in the Nine Kingdoms that were past evil and he'd just been told how unwittingly embroiled he was in those things. Dangerous things. Things he absolutely wasn't going to allow Léirsinn of Sàraichte to be any closer to than she had been already.

He turned his mind away from that unhappy thought and forced himself to concentrate on following his sister back to Tor Neroche instead of getting lost in all that glittering elven rot.

It was harder than he'd thought it would be.

Twenty-one

❦

Léirsinn held a dagger in her hand and wondered if that might be what landed her in a dungeon for good.

Of course, the potential for that had everything to do with the fact that the man she was facing over daggers was Mansourah of Neroche. She didn't imagine stabbing a prince of a royal house was looked upon with any sort of leniency. Then again, the whole morning of madness had been his idea, so perhaps if he walked away bloodied, he had no one to blame but himself.

It wasn't as if she'd woken that morning with the intention of facing a prince over daggers. Her day had started out in a fairly normal fashion with a trip to the barn, a bit of exercising not only her horse but Acair's, and a happy discussion with the stable master about the excellent accommodations enjoyed by a collection of horses she could readily see contained a handful of beasts from Hearn's stables. Falaire's right front leg was giving him a bit of trouble, but the king's horse master promised him all the healing they could put into him in the time they had. She had known that wasn't much more than she could have done herself and she'd left her horse to his care.

She'd then had a late breakfast with a pair of Miach's older brothers, Cathar and Turah, during which she'd been told more about the state of the world than she'd wanted to hear. She'd made her escape at noon after having been assured she was at liberty to wander where she cared to. She hadn't been sure she would ever accustom herself to scores of servants, a handful of whom had seemingly been assigned to see to her needs, but she'd supposed she would never have to.

It had been as she'd been wandering the passageways, trying not to gape at her surroundings as she was trailed by a handful of pages and maidservants, that she had encountered Mansourah of Neroche. He had wondered if she might care to learn to use the dagger he had found for her in the armory that morning.

"On Acair?" she'd asked.

"Now that you mention it," he had replied, "aye."

That had been at least a pair of hours ago. Since then, she had learned how to use a knife for more than cutting the string that held bales of hay together. Whether or not she could use a blade on another person was something else entirely.

She looked at the knife in her hand, then looked at Miach's older brother. He was as handsome as the rest of the litter, though she sensed a restlessness in him that made her wonder what he was still doing at the palace instead of wandering the Nine Kingdoms. If he'd been a horse, she would have sold him to an adventurer in need of a fearless pony not prone to shying at the unexpected.

"Mistress Léirsinn?"

"Just Léirsinn," she said, "and as such, I must be honest with you. I'm just not sure I could ever stab someone."

"Not even if they were trying to kill you?" he asked.

"Who would want to kill me?"

Mansourah only looked at her pointedly.

She returned his look. "Acair wouldn't, no matter what you think of him. And anyone else would likely have magic, which would be far more deadly than any knife I could use."

He sighed, then nodded reluctantly. "I must admit that is likely true," he agreed. "Why don't we then try something less sharp? You never know when a well-placed elbow or a judicious use of a curled fist will be what saves the day."

She smiled. "You have brothers, obviously."

"Each more irritating than the last," he agreed. "Save Miach, unfortunately. He's a lovely wee fellow."

"I'm sure he appreciates the compliment," she said dryly, handing him her knife.

"What he appreciates more, I imagine, is my ability to guard his back when the need arises. Let me show you what might be useful for you in such a situation."

She looked at him and shook her head. "I appreciate it, truly I do, but I'm just not sure I can do this."

He looked at her thoughtfully for a moment or two, then tossed her knife and his onto a chair near the fire. He returned to stand before her.

"I vex Acair of Ceangail because I can," he said slowly, "and because he deserves it. He has a terrible reputation, one he's earned, and he uses magic that most shy away from out of simple good taste if nothing else. But whatever else his failings, he is a gentleman and if he were able, he would protect you, I daresay, with his life."

"But?" she asked.

He looked at her seriously. "But there may come a time when he is not there to keep you safe and you must protect yourself by yourself. If you can at least give yourself time to flee, you should learn how to do so. And for all you know, you might be able to aid him, ruthless bastard that he is. For your sake, of course, not his."

She didn't have to give it any more thought. "Very well. Thank you."

"You might feel differently in an hour."

"So might you."

He only smiled. "Let's begin, then."

It wasn't an hour later, but several hours later that she had left Mansourah of Neroche limping off to dress for supper and found herself standing in her chamber, a chamber that was far larger than even her uncle's study, looking at herself in a polished glass and wondering how she had come to be where she was. She had wished for a change.

She thought she might want to be more careful what she wished for in the future.

It was odd to be in the midst of a flock of maidservants who were attending to things she didn't normally think about, such as her fingernails and whether or not her hair curled to the right or the left, never mind all the rest of the fussing and arranging of her person that was going on.

Her hair. She looked at it and wondered if it could possibly be called anything but red.

"Nay, you silly gel, not yellow. Let's hold up the red again."

Léirsinn identified the woman speaking with such authority as the Mistress of the Wardrobe. She would rather have been facing a dozen stallions with tempers than that one, but that was obviously not going to be her lot that night.

"What do you think, Your Majesty? This one, or shall it be the emerald green that I have already suggested?"

"I do believe, Mistress Wardrobe," Morgan said, nodding slowly, "that you have yet again made the right choice. The green is spectacular."

Léirsinn looked at the queen and had a sly wink as her reward. It might have cheered her, but she was still standing there in underclothing she was fairly certain had been fashioned by some black mage for a former lover he intended to torment. She allowed herself to be dressed in the aforementioned emerald gown, opened her eyes when her head had emerged from the neckline, then looked at herself in the mirror.

"Oh," she said weakly.

Mistress Wardrobe directed her assistants to put on the finishing touches, as it were, then clapped her hands and beamed. "Perfect. We're finished here." She made Morgan a crisp bow. "My duty is accomplished and quite successfully, as always." She shot Léirsinn a look. "Don't spill anything on your gown and leave your hair alone."

Léirsinn nodded and suspected she wouldn't dare do anything else. She watched the Mistress of the Wardrobe herd her flock of helpers out the door, then found herself vastly relieved to be left with just the queen of Neroche. She looked at Morgan.

"Well."

"She terrifies most," Morgan agreed with a half laugh. "The boys scamper when they see her coming. She and I, however, have come to an understanding: She leaves off with commenting on my training clothes and I wear whatever she tells me to for state events. An uneasy truce, but hard won. You look lovely, by the way."

"But my hair—"

"Is absolutely stunning," Morgan said seriously. "Don't change it."

"How would I change it?"

Morgan looked at her and sighed. "That is a sorry comment on the state of my life, isn't it? I've become all too used to having magic. Life is simpler without it, I think."

"Is it?" Léirsinn asked. She shrugged at the look Morgan sent her way. "I'm just curious. Acair seems to miss it. I've never had it, so I have nothing to miss. I just wonder what it feels like to have it."

Morgan paused, then nodded at the little table that had been placed a distance from the fire that Léirsinn supposed was the right distance to keep her from becoming too hot. "Let's rest for a moment or two and I'll tell you."

Léirsinn followed the queen over to a chair, sat, and happily accepted a glass of wine. Whatever else went on at the keep, they certainly had a decent lad manning the cellars.

"When I first realized I had it, I would have cut it from my very veins if I'd been able," Morgan said with a sigh. "Miach was the one who showed me that it could be a beautiful thing, but he does that." She shrugged. "I have what Acair has from my father and I have elven magic from my mother. Sometimes I feel as though it wars within me, though I suppose Gair's magic comes from elven sources as well doesn't it?"

"From his father, I gather," Léirsinn agreed. She had given up trying to deny what she had seen or found difficult to believe. She still felt a little as if she were in a play where she was just repeating lines about magic and elves and other unbelievable things, but she wasn't sure what else to do. No sense in wasting energy trying to deny what she couldn't any longer. "Very lovely, Prince Sgath and the lady Eulasaid."

"They are," Morgan said. "And so are you. Acair will be gob-smacked, I'll tell you that."

"He won't notice me."

Morgan looked at her, laughed, then shook her head with a final smile. "If you don't *want* him to notice you, then that's one thing. But I think the choice will be yours. He won't have a bloody thing to say about it."

Léirsinn sipped her wine, then set it aside. "And what do you think of him?"

"He is not our father," Morgan said. "Anything else? I think he's handsome, charming, and has too much time on his hands. He should spend more time mucking out stalls and less time at the gaming table."

"But evil?"

"I've seen evil," Morgan said quietly, "and he is not it. Whether or not he believes that is something I wouldn't presume to guess. What do you think?"

"He makes me laugh."

"Many marriages were begun with less."

"Marriage," Léirsinn echoed, choking. "To me? Surely not."

"Miach fell in love with me when he thought I was a soldier of fortune," Morgan said with a smile, then she laughed again. "Listen to me. Motherhood has turned my mind in directions it doesn't usually go." She set her own glass aside and rose. "Enjoy the eve-ning, Léirsinn, and leave the rest for the morning. For all we know, Sourah and Acair will fight a duel over you and we'll be rid of them both."

"Would that be a good thing?" Léirsinn asked, trying not to

wipe her hands on her dress. She had never in her life been nervous. She wasn't sure how she should feel about experiencing the same at the moment.

"Rigaud would happily be rid of them both, but he's not overly fond of Acair. I suppose the best we can hope for tonight is avoiding bloodshed." She smiled. "I'll go see that my wee son is settled, then see you for supper, aye?"

Léirsinn nodded because it was expected. She would have preferred to have been looking around her for somewhere to hide, but she suspected Morgan knew that. The queen gave her another encouraging smile, then left the chamber.

She wondered how long she could reasonably stay behind before she was missed, or if it might be possible to plead a headache and miss the evening altogether. She stopped in front of the polished glass and looked at herself reflected there. It was difficult to believe what she was seeing, but then again, she had only seen herself a pair of times in her uncle's house and that mirror hadn't been nearly so fine. Perhaps a horse trough full of still water was of less use than she'd believed.

She took a deep breath, smoothed down her skirts that didn't need smoothing, then turned and faced the door. It was simply supper and dancing. She could plead ignorance about the latter and ignore the fact that Mansourah of Neroche had taken the time to teach her a pair of patterns so she wouldn't look the fool. Supper, she thought she could manage all on her own.

She left her chamber and pulled the door shut behind her. A page stood across from her chamber door, apparently waiting for her. He made her a polite bow, then smiled.

"After me, if you will, my lady."

She didn't bother to correct his form of address and instead simply followed him down the passageway, around a corner, and into disaster.

Prince Mansourah was standing there. So was Acair. Léirsinn skidded to a halt, almost twisting her ankle in the damned shoes

Mistress Wardrobe had insisted that she wear. She would have fallen on her face if she hadn't latched onto the first arm thrust out in front of her.

"Don't."

She had supposed that had been directed at her, but once she regained her footing and caught the breath she'd lost in a terrified rush, she realized she was holding on to Mansourah's forearm and Acair was definitely not talking to her.

"I believe—"

"That you won't live till sunrise if you don't compliment this stunning woman on her gown, then take yourself off to the safety of a seat behind your brother the king? A quite useful thought, I daresay, and one I suggest you pursue with all diligence."

Léirsinn gingerly released Mansourah's arm and eased backward a step. If there was one thing she knew very well, it was never to step between two stallions in the midst of the usual business of asserting their positions. She smiled briefly at Mansourah, noting his very elegant suit of clothes, then looked at the man who had absolutely no business mucking out stalls to earn his bread. Acair of Ceangail was, she had to admit in a way that left her feeling as if she'd never done anything more substantial in her life besides admire handsome men, absolutely stunning.

It was no wonder he spent so much time hobnobbing with nobility. If she'd had a crown hiding in the back of her tack room, she would have issued him a standing invitation to supper herself.

He reached for her hand and tucked it under his elbow in his accustomed way, then looked at Mansourah and flicked at him as if he'd been an annoying fly.

"Begone. Live another day."

Mansourah only pursed his lips. "You, my friend, have absolutely nothing to use to enforce your threats."

"I won't embarrass your brother by breaking your nose before supper with my fists alone," Acair said shortly.

Mansourah looked at him, smirked briefly, then turned to

Léirsinn and made her a low bow. "A dance later, if milady would be so inclined. Thank you for a lovely afternoon. And you are stunning in that gown."

Léirsinn caught the look Acair sent Mansourah and would have smiled but there was something about him that was . . . changed. She waited until the prince of Neroche had departed for safer ground before she turned to another lad with royal blood in his veins and studied him.

"What happened?" she asked bluntly.

He smiled, but it was the sort of polite smile she'd watched him give to others without truly meaning it. "Nothing."

"You don't lie."

He blew hair out of his eyes. "Please don't ask."

"Did you see Prince Soilléir?"

"Aye."

She looked behind him to find the spell that followed him standing there, obviously still following him. She met Acair's eyes quickly. "Oh."

He took a deep breath, turned toward her, then put his hands lightly on her shoulders. He very carefully leaned forward and rested his forehead against hers.

"You are the most beautiful woman I have ever seen."

She would have smiled, but she could feel his hands trembling as they rested on her shoulders. "I'm sure that isn't the case, but I appreciate the compliment just the same." She reached up and covered his hands with hers. "What can I do?"

"Stop being kind to me before you drive me to tears."

"Put the whip to you instead, is that it?"

"If you have any pity in you at all, aye." He straightened and smiled, but he wasn't entirely successful. "If you would."

She supposed he would tell her what had befallen him earlier or he wouldn't. She wasn't going to force it out of him. She released his hands, then reached out and brushed a few stray bangs out of

his eyes before she thought better of it. He caught her hand before
she pulled away.

"Thank you."

"You look a little scattered."

He tucked her hand under his elbow again and nodded at the
page to carry on before he looked at her. "My sister did me the
honor of turning me into a bitter wind on our way back. I'm still
feeling the effects of it."

"Pleasant?"

"Today, I'm not sure," he said quietly. "I'll let you know later."

She had the feeling that was the last thing he would do, which
meant he intended to leave her behind, which meant she was going
to have to watch him very closely before he slipped out without her.
She looked at him pointedly.

"Don't go without me."

"And why would I do that?" he asked. "The most beautiful
woman in the hall on my arm and an evening stretching ahead of
me in which to admire her? You must be mad. I have no intention
of going anywhere but to table with you, then spending the evening
begging you to dance with me."

Which wasn't, as she was well aware, any sort of answer or
promise.

She didn't suppose she could have expected anything else.

She remembered very little of supper save that she thought she
might just have to thank Acair of Ceangail for his very lovely
manners and his ability to discreetly indicate which fork should be
used when without drawing attention to the same. What she ate she
couldn't have said, but she was confident she'd eaten it with the right
piece of silverware.

The dancing was planned for what she understood was the
grand audience chamber. She walked into the place and felt as if

she were walking into a dream. The floor was made of some blue stone that looked as if it still lay in the bed of a river with water flowing over it, the walls were hung with tapestries finer than anything she'd ever imagined, and she was fairly certain she couldn't see the ceiling. Behind the lord's high table was an enormous hearth and over that hearth hung two swords, crossed. She knew nothing about blades save what Mansourah had taught her that morning, but she wondered about that steel there.

She wasn't able to wonder about it for more than a moment or two before she realized Prince Cathar was asking her for a dance.

"I only know two patterns," she warned him.

"That's one more than I know," he said gallantly. "I'll attempt not to embarrass you. I don't know where Mansourah collected all these guests, but tell me if they bother you overmuch. I know the fastest way to the kitchen."

"I'll remember that," she managed. "Thank you."

And that was, quite honestly, the last bit of conversation she had with anyone past commenting on the weather, the refreshments, and the quality of the players. A good hour passed before she managed to plead weariness and escape to the high table and hide behind Miach who was leaning there, chatting up some well-dressed nobleman. She accepted the glass of wine he handed her, drank, then wished for somewhere more permanent to hide. She set her glass down on the table, turned, then ran bodily into Acair.

He held out his hand to steady her, then made her a low bow. "If you'll permit me?"

She looked at him blankly. "To do what?"

"Claim this dance."

"I only know two patterns," she warned him as she had Cathar. "I might embarrass you."

"I only know three."

She smiled in spite of herself. "You're lying."

"But 'tis a white lie," he said seriously. "I don't think they count."

She wasn't about to offer an opinion on that, so she accepted his hand and walked with him out to the middle of the floor. They had been seated together at supper, but she hadn't seen him once they'd adjourned to the great hall for the entertainments. Perhaps he'd been off brooding somewhere or picking locks on the king's private chambers or stirring up some other sort of trouble. With Acair, one just never knew.

What she did know, however, was that when he had said he danced divinely, he hadn't been exaggerating. It was no wonder he managed to get in high places so easily. Whether he managed to get back out of them as easily was perhaps debatable, but she suspected he didn't have much trouble with it.

She had no idea how long she danced with him. All she knew was that when he invited her to take a bit of air by way of the stables, she didn't argue. Finery, lovely music, and decent food were all very good things, but she suspected that if she ever had to exist on a steady diet of the three, she would need to season them liberally with an equal amount of time in the stables. It was no wonder Morgan spent so much time in the lists.

"My shoes," she managed as they walked through the kitchens. "Mistress Wardrobe will scold me if I get them dirty."

"They keep extra boots by the back door."

She looked at him in surprise. "How do you know that?"

"Miach's mother kicked me in the arse with a pair of them," he said with a weary smile. "Then she made me polish the manure off the bloody lot of them—and there were many pairs—then put them all back where they'd come from. Your kind of woman, that Queen Desdhemar."

Léirsinn supposed that might be the case, accepted a pair of boots in exchange for her shoes, then happily walked through the gardens and to the stables with a man who seemed to know where he was going.

Falaire was quietly dozing in his stall and Sianach celebrated Acair's arrival by trying to reach out his stall window and bite him.

"And all is right with the world," Acair said with a sigh. "Bad horse."

She supposed Sianach would take that personally, but perhaps that was an observation better made at a different time. She held up her skirts with one hand, held Acair's hand with the other, then walked out with him into the courtyard. The moon was waxing toward full, which she appreciated, and there were torches lit that made the pathways easily marked.

It also revealed that they weren't alone.

If she'd been able to do something besides try to keep from tripping on her gown as she was yanked behind her escort, she might have found words to comment on the handiness of being able to see where she was hopping. When Acair snarled at her to run, she thought she might have to find Miach's gardener and apologize for the plants she was currently trampling in her haste to do just that.

She stopped after a pace or two because she wasn't about to run away, no matter what Acair had told her to do. She turned around to watch him catch a rapier that Rigaud had flung at him.

"You have no spells," Rigaud spat, "so I'll kill you in a more gentlemanlike way."

"You might try," Acair said, looking at the sword casually. He leveled a very cool look at Miach's brother. "I imagine you won't succeed."

Léirsinn wondered if she would have time to run back to the hall and fetch help before something dire happened, but couldn't force herself to move. She was trapped by her fear of what might befall Acair, a fear that left her standing in the midst of brittle leaves and the last of autumn's flowers.

In time, she realized that the middle of a battlefield wasn't a wise place to be. Before she could decide which way she should bolt, Acair lost his sword. She had to admit that Prince Rigaud looked as surprised as Acair over that turn of events, but he wasted no time in weaving a spell that gave her chills just to listen to it. She had no idea what language the prince was using; she only knew that the magic was not of a pleasant sort.

Rigaud continued to weave his spell slowly and distinctly, no doubt so Acair would know exactly what was coming his way. It seemed as if he were creating a blanket meant to smother a fire. She suspected it was intended to smother Acair's ability to breathe, but what did she know? She could do nothing but stand there and watch Rigaud draw himself up, then step forward, no doubt to intimidate a bit more as he flung his spell toward his enemy.

Unfortunately, he caught his foot in a bit of garden foliage. She would have considered that a fortuitous turn of events except that what he had been directing at Acair had gone off course and was currently coming her way. Acair leapt toward her, though she wasn't sure what he thought he was going to accomplish by that. She took a step backward, trying to find her footing beneath her, but then she realized what she had stepped into.

A spot of shadow.

Time slowed to a crawl and her heart seemed to slow right along with it. She tried to hold up her hands to ward off that spell coming toward her or reach for Acair's hands he was holding out to her to pull her out of the way, but she found she could do neither. All she could do was stand there, motionless, and try to keep breathing. Her astonishment at what was happening to her was so great, she wasn't sure she would manage that last bit for very long.

She could *see*. It was as if until that exact moment she had lived her entire life in a chamber with nothing in it. No windows, no paintings, nothing on the floor, nothing but bland, colorless wood. All of that had disappeared, leaving her standing in the midst of a garden, dumbfounded by the sight of flowers, trees, stone pathways—even the air was alive with a sparkling awareness she had never imagined, never *could* have imagined . . .

Miach was suddenly there in front of her, holding off with his hand and will alone a spell that was so full of horrors, she wept just looking at it. Death, but death only after agony and a despair that would have brought her to her knees if she'd been able to move. The path that contained that despair was so bleak and so relentlessly beguiling that it was all she could do not to set foot to it and hope that the torment would end eventually. The agony was so sharp and clear that it took whatever willpower she had left not to reach out toward it as well and see if it might be cool against her hands, quenching the pain that seemed to burn within her with a heat she thought might soon consume her.

And all those things were wrapped up in the magic that Rigaud had thrown at Acair to slay him, a magic that seemed to have no end . . .

She let out a breath that was as unsteady as her knees beneath her.

Magic existed. She could no longer even pretend to deny it.

Rigaud's power was great, she could see that. *See* it, rather, in a way that left her wondering if she had ever looked at anything real before in her lifetime. The prince's power was part of him, locked in his veins, drawn from his forebearers, simply waiting for him to use it or not as he willed.

She looked away, but finding Miach in her sights was worse. Whatever it meant to be king of Neroche in practical terms was nothing when compared to what it meant for him to be a mage king in that realm. He was Neroche and Neroche was him and she couldn't begin to separate the two or find the words to describe what she saw in him. She fancied he could have cracked the world in two with a word if he'd so chosen, but she knew just as surely that he would never consider it. He held Rigaud's spell of death at bay with very little effort, then caused it to disappear with a single word.

Rigaud was full of a white-hot rage that should have singed anyone who dared come near him, but he cursed his brother, shot Acair a murderous look, then turned and strode away.

Léirsinn watched Acair turn to face her, then saw realization dawn as he understood where she was standing. And in the trio of heartbeats it took him to reach her, she saw *him*.

How she had ever thought him anything but what he was, she couldn't have said. He wasn't a cultured man with a deliciously posh accent and perfect table manners, he was a mage with power to rival the king of Neroche's. He might not have been able to use it, but it coursed through his veins and drenched his soul, enough power to have brought kingdoms to ruin. She half wondered how he managed to live inside himself. The light and the dark were perfectly balanced in him, something she had the presence of mind to assume he wouldn't want to hear.

He held out his hand to her as if he feared to touch her. She almost feared she wouldn't be able to reach him, but the moment she touched his skin, he jerked her out of the circle she'd stepped in and into his arms.

"Léirsinn," he said urgently.

"I'm fine," she managed.

"You were screaming."

She looked up at him, then felt her eyes closing. She surrendered, because she simply couldn't look at anything else. Everything she'd seen whilst standing in that shadow was gone. Miach and Acair were just men, the garden was nothing more than dirt and leaves, and the moon shone down with nothing more than an ordinary and quite pedestrian light.

She thought she just might weep.

She closed her eyes and saw no more.

Twenty-two

❧

It was useful, Acair decided, to periodically take stock of one's life and examine it for strengths and weaknesses, and occasionally simply for things that were so odd as to be scarce believed. Such as, for instance, sitting in the solar of the king of a realm full of magic ripe for the picking and not having any desire to bean the man over the head and make off with as many spoils as possible before he woke.

He paused. Well, perhaps he wasn't entirely free of that desire, but he was who he was after all. Old habits died hard.

"I'm afraid my selection of libations isn't vast," Miach said solemnly, "though I do have some Durialian bitter ale you might want to accustom yourself to."

"On the off chance I actually set foot inside that irascible old fool's borders and find myself in his dungeon?"

Miach smiled. "It might soften his heart to watch you toss back without flinching something that generally brings lesser men to their knees."

Acair took a deep breath. "Pour away, then. I like to be prepared."

"I'll return posthaste. Don't poach any spells whilst I'm away."

Acair smiled wearily. "Too tired tonight, though don't think the thought hasn't already crossed my mind."

"I would be disappointed by anything else."

Acair listened to him close the door behind him, then looked around himself in something he might have called consternation if he'd been prone to that sort of emotion. The archmage-now-king of Neroche's private tower chamber was the last place he would have ever thought to find himself. Well, find himself unfettered, that was. He was torn between walking over to Miach's table and rifling through papers there, or pulling the exceptionally lovely and fierce Léirsinn of Sàraichte up out of her chair and kissing the hell out of her.

Dire were his straits indeed.

He walked over to toast his arse against the fire and looked at the woman sitting in a chair next to that fire. She had regained her senses true, but she looked easily as devastated as he felt, though obviously for different reasons.

He had caught her as she'd fallen, after he'd pulled her free of that accursed spot of darkness. He knew Miach had covered that patch with a spell so it wouldn't cause anyone else trouble, been grateful for the king's aid, then accepted the sanctuary of that same monarch's private solar. Léirsinn had come back to herself after only a few moments and she hadn't looked terribly upset, but it wasn't as if she would have blurted out her fears right there in front of the company that had gathered to watch the spectacle of Rigaud of Neroche attempting to slay him.

He clasped his hands behind his back and studied his companion. She was simply sitting there, staring into the fire as if she saw things she didn't like.

"Léirsinn?"

She looked up at him. "Aye?"

He wasn't quite sure how to broach the subject of what she'd experienced, so he simply stared at her, mute. Foolish, aye, but there it was. She was completely out of his experience and he was definitely not at his best.

"Are you unwell?" she asked.

He looked at that remarkable woman sitting there in that glorious emerald gown and found himself without a single useful thing to say.

"Speechless," she noted. "An interesting development."

"Just trying not to distract you from your admiring of the very fine figure I cut in evening garb," he managed.

She only smiled at him as if she found him somewhat tolerable. He didn't dare hope for anything else, never mind that he shouldn't have been hoping for anything else—

Ah, hell. There was no hope for it. He was, he had to admit, rather lost. He shook his head. A horse gel. Who would have thought it? He was tempted to linger with that very pleasant thought for a bit longer, but he knew he couldn't. He struggled to drag his thoughts back to where they should have been—namely focused on the business of those damned pieces of shadow—but he was interrupted by the king of Neroche returning with glasses and a bottle or two. He sighed, then walked over to shut the door behind his sister's husband.

From there, things proceeded on the usual course that polite after-entertainment parleys generally took. He stood—well, he leaned, actually—against the hearth and listened to Léirsinn and Miach converse on subjects that he expected Miach assumed would interest her.

"I am ignorant of the world outside Sàraichte," Léirsinn said. "I would prefer to remedy that, but I have no idea where to start."

Acair realized Miach was pointing at him and wondered what in blazes he'd muttered before he thought better of it.

"Acair is a treasure trove of anything you would ever want to know, though I'm not sure you would want to wade through all his opinions to get to the facts."

"But I imagine he knows most of the players, wouldn't you say?" Léirsinn asked.

"Knows what the insides of their private solars look like, rather,"

Miach said wryly, "but aye, I imagine he's at least had a glass of wine with them before ransacking their treasures."

"I am being maligned," Acair managed. "I don't rob *everyone* I meet. Your solar here has remained unmolested."

Miach smiled. "There is that. Léirsinn, when you've the time for it, come stay with us for a bit. You're welcome to take your choice of my private library."

"Thank you, Your Majesty."

Miach only laughed. "Flattery will get you everywhere, as Acair could likely attest to. Now, I understand you were most recently in Angesand. What is Hearn breeding these days besides envy for his very fine steeds?"

Acair listened to them discuss horses and lines and prospects as he tried to sip Uachdaran of Léige's most bitter brew. It was absolutely vile and he wasn't sure it wasn't going to dissolve his innards before he finished the glass, but he feared Miach might have a point. There might come a time when tossing back a cup of the vile bilge whilst coming up smacking his lips might be what saved his sorry arse.

He tried to distract himself by listening to the conversation going on in front of him, but it was difficult. If Miach were curious about the night's events, he didn't show it. If Léirsinn were suffering any lingering damage from her encounter with darkness, she didn't mention it.

There were times social niceties were damned frustrating.

But he watched Léirsinn by the light of the fire just the same until his glass was empty, she was asleep, and his heart was utterly lost. He looked at the king of Neroche to find Miach watching him.

"What?" he asked crossly.

"Just enjoying your journey."

"To where, might I ask?"

"If you don't know, Acair, I have absolutely no hope to offer you."

Acair shook his head. "A gentleman doesn't discuss matters of the heart in front of the woman in question."

"She's asleep."

"She could be pretending." He set his glass on the mantel and looked at his brother-in-law—something he never thought to have, truth be told—purposefully. "I am, for lack of a better word, doomed."

"Why?"

"Because that spell that hounds me wasn't, I learned this morning, fashioned by Soilléir."

Miach frowned thoughtfully. "Rùnach, then?"

"Nay, or so Soilléir claims." He gestured inelegantly toward the woman—ah, hell. He gestured toward *his* lady, ignored the way even thinking such a thing rendered him off-balance, then looked at the king. "Did you see what—well, of course you saw. I have no idea what that patch of shadow did to her and I daren't ask. All I know is I can't do a damned thing about them and they're starting to affect people I lo—er, I mean, people I am responsible for."

Miach started to rise, then looked at him. "Do you mind if I have a look at your shadowy companion over there?"

"I would be most grateful, actually. It doesn't seem to care for my peering into its innards, but you go right ahead."

Miach smiled faintly. "A mystery. You should be enjoying this."

"Ask me how I feel after the mystery is solved," Acair said grimly, "something that would be far more easily accomplished with magic than without."

"I agree," Miach said, setting aside his cup. "Let's see what we can."

Acair approached the spell with the king of Neroche and tried not to spend more time than necessary thinking about how odd the whole situation was. He had never thought to stand on the same side of a battlefield with Mochriadhemiach of Neroche, never mind standing with the man in his own solar, accepting his aid.

His life had become very strange indeed.

The spell was standing in the corner—well, slouching there, actually, as seemed to be its habit. It straightened at Miach's approach. Acair would have warned the king not to get too close to it, but decided the lad was wise enough to determine for himself where to draw the line, as it were. For himself, he decided that keeping a decent distance was the best course of action, lest his irritation prove to be more than he could reasonably control.

"What do you think?" Acair asked, after Miach had done nothing but stare at the bloody thing for far longer than Acair thought necessary.

Miach looked at him. "Have you looked at it closely?"

"I haven't," Acair said. "I was under the impression it had been created by Soilléir and I could see immediately what its purpose was. What was the point of poking it in the ribs, as it were, to see what it was made of?"

Miach leaned against the edge of his worktable and studied the spell that stood there, looking back at him with the belligerence of a cheeky ten-year-old lad. Acair wondered just who in the hell had possibly created such an obnoxious thing.

"Not Soilléir's," Miach said. He looked at Acair. "Nor Rùnach's, aye?"

"So Soilléir claims, though I'm tempted to believe he's lying."

"'Tis an elegant thing," Miach offered. "For a spell of such power. But it doesn't look like something Soilléir would do. In truth, Acair, I have no idea who fashioned it."

"But its purpose is to slay me if I use magic."

"That seems to be the case."

Acair dragged his hands through his hair, then sighed. "I'm not sure how to describe how much I despise the place in which I find myself."

"No magic, mages with your death on their minds, and a lovely, defenseless woman to protect?"

"That sums it up nicely." He looked at the spell in the corner. "And that thing there . . . if I could destroy it, I would, but in destroying it, I destroy myself." He looked at Miach. "A bit of a tangle there, wouldn't you say?"

Miach shook his head slowly. "I've a strong stomach, but I'm not above admitting it makes me a little uneasy." He paused, then

looked at Acair. "Since we're speaking of things that make us
uneasy, I have something for you."

"An invitation from Rigaud to another duel? I believe I'll pass."
He looked at his host. "But don't think I don't appreciate the rescue
tonight."

Miach smiled briefly. "My pleasure, of course." He reached
behind him, then handed Acair a folded sheaf of paper. "This was
handed to a lad at the gates before dawn this morning."

Acair took it, though he was the first to admit he suddenly didn't
think he wanted to read it. It was a single line.

I'm watching you.

He looked at Miach. "A poor jest," he said dismissively.

"Which is why I pressed Cathar into watching my son so I could
watch over you and Morgan earlier as you traveled to find Soilléir,"
Miach said seriously, "then again tonight as you and Léirsinn
walked in the garden. I don't think it is a jest, Acair. Read it again."

Acair didn't want to tell his brother-in-law that he was mad, so
he humored him.

I'm watching her.

He looked at Miach, more startled than he should have been.
"What's this rubbish?"

"Try again."

"I don't think I want to."

"I think you should."

Acair looked again.

I'm watching you both. Always.

"Droch," Acair croaked, "at his least imaginative."

"I don't think so."

"Then one of the lads at Buidseachd," Acair said, grasping for the first thing that came to mind. "Some lad with more time than sense."

"Do you think so?" Miach asked seriously.

"'Tis a simple trick," Acair said dismissively. "Overly theatrical, but there you have it. If I didn't know better, I would say my spell-ish companion over there in the corner had written it just to vex me. Besides, 'tis in a woman's hand."

"Or a scholar's hand," Miach said.

"Or the hand of someone forced to write it whilst the creator—a student, I'm sure—slipped quite happily into his cups at the end of a long term at the schools of wizardry."

"There is magic infused into the parchment," Miach said slowly, "don't you think?"

"Impossible," Acair said immediately, then he paused. "A change of essence, perhaps?"

"I would agree, but 'tis impossible to animate something that has no soul." Miach looked at him. "You can turn a living being into a rock, but not a rock into a living being, if you appreciate the difference which I'm sure you do."

"Then this is not a spell of Soilléir's."

Miach shook his head slowly. "Not one I know."

Acair sat. He supposed he was fortunate that there was a chair beneath his arse and supposed it had been Miach to shove it there. He looked at the paper in his hands—his trembling hands, it had to be said—and thought things he didn't care for.

Soilléir's spell of un-noticing had been odd, hadn't it? And Soilléir had denied having fashioned the spell now looking over his shoulder at the sheaf barely in his hands, hadn't he?

Had the man gone mad?

Or had someone else nipped into Seannair of Cothromaiche's library and had a look in spell books that obviously needed better locks on them?

He folded the sheaf of parchment back into quarters and tucked it inside a pocket. He rose, brushed off his jacket, and looked at Miach.

"My most heartfelt thanks for the safe haven and that vile ale. Both have been very enjoyable."

Miach only looked at him with eyes that saw far too much. "Off hunting, are we?"

"Hunting what?" Acair scoffed. "The scribbler of that note and the maker of that spell? I wouldn't stir myself to even entertain the thought. Nay, I think I'll pop around to some of my old haunts and see what's on the fire. One must keep up social calls, you know."

Miach didn't move. "If you need aid," he said very quietly, "send word."

"You're a capital fellow," Acair said. He smiled pleasantly. "I'll rouse our horse miss over there, then I believe I should perhaps be on my way. If you wouldn't mind giving her an escort to wherever she wants to go? I believe she would be safer very far away from me."

"As you will, of course," Miach said, nodding.

Acair nodded in return, woke a woman who he supposed was accustomed to not having the chance to rub the sleep from her eyes before she needed to be about her business, then left the king's solar. That was preferable to plopping himself down on Miach's lap and begging the king to spot him a spell or two to keep him from being slain until he could solve his own tangle.

"I didn't mean to sleep," Léirsinn said.

"It was likely better that way," Acair said. "Long night and all that."

She said nothing else, which he considered a mercy. If he'd looked at him with those knowing green eyes of hers, he likely would have broken down and spewed out everything he knew before he could stop himself.

He walked her to her door, made her a low bow, then pulled the door shut once she'd gone inside. If he'd bid her goodnight, he honestly didn't remember it. He did come back to himself in time to realize he was facing Mansourah of Neroche and the man wasn't smiling. At least it wasn't Prince Rigaud.

Mansourah looked down his nose at him. "I believe I could have escorted her to her chamber."

Acair smiled pleasantly. "And I believe that if you don't leave her be, I will kill you."

"You forget I have magic as well."

"Is that what you call it?"

Mansourah looked primed to say something nasty, then suddenly sighed instead. "I find my heart is lost."

"I believe they breed excellent hounds in Darbyford," Acair said. "Hire a couple of those pups and put them on the scent. And stay away from Léirsinn."

"You flatter yourself if you think she wants you."

"What I can tell you is that she wouldn't want *you*."

"Don't you think she should have that choice?"

Acair spluttered. "You've known her less than a day. 'Tisn't possible to fall in love in that short a time."

"How long did it take you?"

Acair started to speak, then decided that didn't merit an answer. He glared at Miach's older brother. "I'm finished with this conversation."

"And with that spectacular woman as well, one could hope."

Acair glared at the man, then turned away. Aye, Mansourah had it aright. He needed to be finished because he couldn't ask her to go where he suspected he was going to need to go. He had no means of keeping her safe. He didn't even have a bloody sword to hoist in her defense.

All he had was his wits, various caches of gold scattered all over the Nine Kingdoms, and a nose for sniffing out unpleasant spells. He had the feeling the sooner he got to using all three, the better.

He shut himself inside his own chamber, ignoring the fact that nothing but a wall separated him from the woman he lo—er, the woman he was somewhat fond of. If he went and pressed his hand against that wall to be closer to her, well, there wasn't a damned person who was watching him, which meant he could make as great an ass of himself as he liked.

He was going to have to somehow lock her into her chamber by rather normal means, then be on his way before she woke in the morning. If he didn't, she would follow him, and then where would he be?

He stood there with his hand pressed against that damask-covered wall for a very long time indeed.

He walked out the front gates of the palace at dawn only to find his sister standing there, waiting for him. He shot her a warning look.

"You're not coming with me."

She shook her head. "I hadn't planned on it. Just thought I should send you off with your horse and a little rucksack of food." She shrugged. "I might have raided Rigaud's closet for clothes and his desk drawer for a few coins. I forget now exactly what it was."

He imagined she hadn't forgotten anything. "Thank you, Morgan."

"My pleasure. Any messages for your lady?"

"You could tell her that I think her hair is glorious," he said, "and that I left to keep her safe. She'll understand."

"She won't like it."

"But she'll understand."

Mhorghain nodded and handed him Sianach's reins. "Off you go, then."

He took the reins, then paused. "There's something you should know."

She looked at him sharply. "If you tell me you are my father instead of Gair, I will stab you."

He attempted a smile, but he feared it hadn't come out very well.

"Nothing so dire." He blew out his breath because he had never told a soul what he was about to vomit all over his sister. He shook his head. Bloody hell, if anything else untoward happened to him that day, he would simply . . . well, he would stomp about a great deal and rage, because that was what he did. He took a deep breath and looked at his sister. "About the well."

"The well?" she asked uneasily.

"Ruamharaiche's well," he clarified.

"I didn't realize it had a name."

"It does."

She looked a little pale. "Did you know what he planned?"

He nodded.

"And you didn't try to stop it?"

"My sire, the soulless bastard, has the spell of Diminishing," Acair said grimly. "There is no fighting that. Or at least there wasn't for me at the time. And if you must know, I was off at the time, making mischief."

"I see." She looked at him from clear eyes that were Sarait's eyes. "And?"

"We all knew what he planned," he said carefully. "My mother, if you can believe this, tried to convince your mother to not go forward, but I'm guessing she saw no other path."

"I think that is true," Mhorghain said very quietly.

"I felt him loose the well's power," Acair said. He looked about him, then looked at her. "This won't mean anything to you, I suppose, but I came as quickly as I could."

She didn't move. "You?"

"My life has been full of black mages and their ilk," he said, "but that doesn't mean I don't have the occasional impulse for good sneak up on me like bad eggs once or twice a century."

She didn't smile. "Am I going to want to be seated for the rest of this?"

"I'd prefer that you be relieved of your weapons and don't think

I haven't heard about how many you tend to wear," he said, looking at her pointedly, "but you can look for a bench, if you like."

"Perhaps I should stand."

"Easier to stab me that way?"

"Something like that."

He looked for the right words. "I won't tell you too much, for I can't fathom what you—" He had to take a deep breath. "I just wanted you to know that I did what I could."

"And what was that, Acair?"

"I told the mercenaries where to find you and paid them to watch over you."

She blinked. "I thought Nicholas of Diarmailt did so."

"I thought it might go badly if anyone knew the truth. King Nicholas agreed."

"You know *Nicholas*?" she asked in surprise.

"Well, we don't have tea often," he said stiffly, "but aye, of course I know him. I've nicked several of his books over the years."

"He can't be pleased with you over that."

"I always bring them back," Acair admitted, "but don't noise that about." He shrugged. "'Tis just for the sport of it and a bit of pleasant conversation."

"I don't think you're nearly as awful as you want people to believe."

"Definitely please don't noise *that* about."

She looked at him for so long, he flirted with the idea of turning and bolting.

"I've lost several of my brothers," she said finally.

"Well, you surely don't want any of mine."

She conceded that with a nod. "Nay, but I think I'll take you."

It was his turn to blink rapidly. Damned dusty roads. "You should have your men see to these byways more often. Hard to keep one's eyes clear, as you can plainly tell with me at the moment."

She smiled faintly. "Of course. And I won't tell a soul anything but that you are the worst black mage in history."

"Stop," he pleaded, "lest you drive me to tears."

"We wouldn't want that," she said. She looked at him seriously. "You can count on at least one safe haven with us. Well, Rigaud will kill you if he can, but you likely expect that most everywhere you go, don't you?"

"I do." He paused. "Thank you, Morgan."

"You're welcome. And the number is seventeen."

"Seventeen?"

"The number of blades I could have stabbed you with before you'd seen me draw them." She smiled. "State secret. Don't noise it about." She leaned up and kissed him on the cheek. "Send word if you need aid."

Damn the wench if she wasn't about to reduce him to tears again. He nodded, though he suspected that where he was going, no aid could follow.

He watched his sister go back inside her husband's fortress, then turned his face toward the sunrise and hoped it wouldn't be the last one he saw.

Twenty-three

※

Léirsinn stood in the courtyard of Tor Neroche and looked off into the late morning sun. It had been a horrible night's sleep, but that was perhaps all a woman could hope for when she knew that the man she suspected she might love was about to abandon her and go off alone into the Deepening Gloom to chase after evil things.

She had missed catching Acair before he left, but that was because he had stuffed those damned coppers he'd earned in Sàraichte between her door and its frame, effectively locking her in. It had taken a solid hour of shouting before someone had finally come to her aid, then more time still for them to determine what was keeping her inside, then yet more time to remedy the situation because obviously there wasn't a damned person in all of Tor Neroche with enough magic to simply make those coppers disappear as if they'd never been there.

She had suspected everyone was in league with Acair to keep her from following him.

She wondered if they might have it aright. If she'd had any sense, she would have asked Miach for an escort back to Angesand and left Acair to his own devices.

Only she didn't have any sense, apparently.

She hadn't been asleep the night before in Miach's solar. Well, she had been asleep for a bit, but she'd been awake enough to hear several things she honestly wished she hadn't.

Who in the hell had written that note?

It seemed like something her uncle would have done, but she didn't think Fuadain had magic and she was certain he had no idea where they were. She wasn't sure who that left on a list of mages who might want both her and Acair dead. All she knew was that the thought of someone watching them both terrified her. She wasn't sure how Acair carried on from day to day, if that was the sort of thing he faced with regularity.

As she had told Miach the day before, she didn't know nearly enough about the world in general and nothing about the world she was suddenly moving in. Gair had been terrible, reputedly, but surely he hadn't been the only mage in the history of the Nine Kingdoms to have had the idea of making others miserable. Where that left Acair, she didn't know.

She had seriously considered, as she'd been pounding on her door for aid that morning, simply going back to Sàraichte to take her chances with her uncle. She could return to what she knew and understood. Horses, stable lads, the routine of caring for noble beasts; that was the sort of thing she could count on. There was peace and safety in things she could rely on to never change. Even the buyers who would come to look at horses weren't unexpected and she knew how her uncle would behave.

Only the truth was, nothing was as it had been before. Some of it had to do with her uncle, some of it with Acair, and some of it with what stepping in that shadow the night before had done to her soul.

The inescapable truth was, she couldn't go back to where she had been because *she* had changed. She might manage to convince her uncle not to slay her, she might avoid an angry Droch of Saothair, who was likely wondering where his magical pony had gotten to, and she might even manage to learn to play cards well enough to afford to liberate her grandfather and find a place for them both to live out their lives in peace. But she would never forget the sight of

Acair of Ceangail standing in the gardens of Tor Neroche with his soul drenched with magic and his face full of fear that he wouldn't be able to save her.

Nay, she couldn't go back.

She could only go forward, which was exactly what she intended to do. Exactly where that was going to lead her was something she still had to decide.

She pulled her cloak more closely around her and knew very well that she had Morgan to thank for it. She also could likely tender more thanks to Morgan for the pack she'd found just outside her door that morning, a rucksack full of, among other things, light but very well-made clothing that would see her in and out of places with a minimum of fuss and in absolute stealth. She wasn't sure how that would possibly serve her in the future, but perhaps Morgan knew more than she did.

She walked over to her horse and attached her pack to his saddle. She put her hand on his neck, looked at him, then shook her head. It was an astonishing thing to think he could fly.

"He can do more than fly, but I suspect you already know that."

She squeaked, then looked over Falaire's neck to find Miach standing there. "Do you think?" she managed.

"I do." He smiled at her. "He's a beautiful horse."

"I'm afraid he's about to pull up lame," she said seriously. She paused, then leaned around Falaire's nose. "It has been a difficult journey here," she said slowly. "Difficult for him to be chased by things, if you know what I mean."

His smile faded. "Clouds of black mages?" he asked.

"As you saw," she agreed. "I'm not sure how that bodes for the future."

He studied her. "That's an interesting thought."

"I wasn't asleep last night, you know."

He smiled briefly. "I suspected as much. I'm sorry you had to hear our discussion."

She stroked Falaire's mane for some time in silence, trying to decide what to say. How was it a woman with no magic moved about in a world with mages? What if she took the chance to follow Acair and he hadn't just been leaving her behind out of a sense of chivalry? What if he simply wanted nothing to do with her and rushing off alone had been a convenient way to get that across without having to say it?

What if she had lost her mind somewhere along the journey from Sàraichte and she hadn't noticed?

"Has he gone off to find the writer of that missive, do you think?" she asked casually.

"I daresay," Miach said.

She met the king's eyes. She wasn't coming face-to-face with the might of his magic, as it were, but she found she could still see hints of it surrounding him. Hard to believe he was what he was, but she couldn't deny it.

She shook her head, mostly to herself. The things that she had never before considered . . . it made her feel just exactly what she was: a rustic horsewoman from quite possibly the ugliest place in the Nine Kingdoms. If she'd had any sense, she would have taken her magical horse and run off to some equally rustic locale to hide—

Leaving her grandfather in Sàraichte, which she absolutely couldn't do.

She sighed deeply. Life was so much easier in a barn.

She looked at Miach. "I'm honestly not sure I want to follow him."

"I know," he said quietly. "I could escort you to Hearn's instead, if you'd rather. That was what Acair was thinking, I imagine."

"Was it?" she asked in surprise. "Did he lock me in my chamber to keep me from following him, do you think?"

Miach smiled faintly. "Aye, of course. He is, and I can scarce get the words past my teeth, trying to exercise a bit of chivalry. I'm not sure he knows how to do it very well, not having had to do anything like it in the past."

"He's never plied any chivalry on anyone?" she asked.

"Oh, he has very fine manners when it comes to being

presentable at a state dinner," Miach said, "but as for the other sort? I'm not sure he's had much call for it."

"Are you telling me that he's trying to protect me?"

Miach looked at her with eyes she suspected saw far more than he would ever admit. "He is trying to protect you," he agreed.

"And he told you this."

"He told me several things very early this morning, most having to do with my either staying out of his way or going to hell. But amongst the rubble of his conversation, aye, there was a very pointed mention about what he preferred that I do for you."

"And that was to send me to Angesand?" she asked.

"Or offer you shelter here, which we would have done just the same. Just until he's finished with his business. Then I suppose you'll need to decide where you go from there and if you care to have him along for that journey."

She nodded. Regardless of the fact that she had her horse saddled, she had a decision to make about her future that couldn't be put off any longer.

Sàraichte was closed to her, so that took that off her list. She could go to Angesand and ask Hearn for a place. She was good with a manure fork and perhaps in time she could work off whatever care she was certain Falaire was going to need, as well as put aside enough money to go rescue her grandfather.

Or she could stay at Tor Neroche and offer the stable master her services in the barn, then wring her hands until she knew if Acair had survived a quest he surely hadn't asked for.

She reminded herself that it wasn't as if he needed her aid with it. He had seen—and no doubt done—things she couldn't imagine. He was a black mage; she was a red-haired, unsophisticated stable gel. He knew fancy manners; she knew how to look for thrush in her horses' hooves. He could likely produce the proper titles for any nobleman without thinking; she could do nothing besides hope not to get horse droppings on their boots if those noblemen walked past her at an inopportune moment.

Besides, he had left her behind. Not only had he left her behind, he'd gone out of his way to keep her from following after him. He was leagues away, no doubt, well on his way to finding out things she was certain she wasn't going to want to know. He would discover who had made those patches of shadow and see it dealt with. She would go . . . well, she couldn't go home, but she would find somewhere else to go after she'd saved her grandfather, and she would enjoy a very ordinary, very mortal life.

The small silver dragon that lay against her heart seemed to grow warm. She put her hand over her tunic and was surprised to find that was indeed the case.

And as she had heard, dragons didn't particularly care to stay at home and burn up their hay with their snores.

"You could head south," Miach said slowly. "Toward Angesand."

She made a decision. She realized it was a decision she had made long before the current moment, but perhaps that was something she could admit later. She looked at Miach. "Angesand is, I believe, the wrong direction."

He smiled gravely. "I won't stop you, of course, but I will say that I'm not sure this is the wisest course of action for you."

"What else am I to do?" she asked seriously. "Let him go off into the darkness on his own? I know I don't have any magic, but I can see those spots of shadow."

"Can't he?"

"Not while he's concentrating on other things." She supposed Miach knew exactly what Acair could and couldn't see for himself, so there was no reason not to be honest. "He doesn't need me," she admitted, "but I could be at least of that much use to him. As another pair of eyes."

"I think you're of far more value to him than just that, but perhaps we can argue that later."

Léirsinn wasn't sure there would be anything to argue over, but there was no point in saying as much. And as much as she thought well of the man standing across her horse from her, she couldn't ask him to rid the world of those shadows, stop whoever was sending them, or rescue her grandfather. There were some things, she supposed, that she would simply have to see to herself.

She and Acair, rather.

"He's in the pub a league up the way, if you're curious."

She looked at Miach in surprise. "He is?"

"I bought him breakfast an hour ago." He shrugged. "He accepted, but only after he'd called me a meddler and several other unkind names."

She wasn't surprised. "Were you watching over him?"

"He is my brother-in-law, as it happens. I thought if he were going off on a mighty quest, he might as well put his foot to that path whilst well-fed." He stroked Falaire's nose. "I asked him why he wasn't farther away."

"What did he say?"

"Why don't you go ask him?"

She shook her head. "I'm not sure I want to." She forced herself to meet his eyes. "On the off chance that he doesn't want me."

"Perhaps the more important thing to find out is if you want him."

"Him?" she scoffed. "Why, he's . . . well, he is definitely . . ." She attempted a handful of other things that ended up getting stuck quite firmly in her throat. "He's a bad mage. I have that on good authority."

"Unfortunately, he's a very *good* mage at bad magic," Miach said with a smile, "but even that might change with the right inducement."

"I think his mouth would catch on fire if he attempted anything like it."

Miach laughed. "Probably." He patted Falaire's neck. "I could see your pony to Hearn's stables, if you like."

"I couldn't ask it," she demurred, though the saying of that almost killed her. His front right hock was warm, which had concerned her very much, but she had supposed a bit of shapechanging might keep it from worsening. But to send him off where he might be well cared-for? It was too much to hope for.

"I'll trade Hearn a spell for your pony's care," Miach said, sounding as if he'd already made the decision for her. "That and a bit of gossip will likely suit."

She nodded. "Droch paid for Falaire, just so you know."

"All the more reason to leave a spell or two behind with Lord Hearn," he said pleasantly. He lifted his eyebrows briefly. "And the opportunity to vex Droch of Saothair? I should be paying you for the privilege."

She smiled, but she honestly didn't want to know what Miach's interactions with the man had been. She'd seen enough for herself. She nodded, unhooked her pack, then looked at him. "I will repay you someday."

"Of course you won't," he said with a smile. "'Tis my pleasure. And my library is still open to you, remember. You can even bring your lad with you, if you like." He pointed down the hill. "He's that way."

"I hope I don't regret this."

"I hope not, either."

She slung her pack over her shoulder, then paused and rested her cheek against Falaire's nose. Stallion though he might have been, he simply stood there and permitted it, as if he knew what was in her heart and didn't want to disturb it. She stroked his nose a final time, then looked at Miach.

"Thank you."

"I think I should be thanking you," he said quietly. "I said this to Acair, but I'll say as much to you as well. If you need aid, send word. I'll do what I can for you."

She nodded because she didn't trust herself to speak. She took a deep breath, then turned and walked away from the gates into morning sunlight streaming onto her face.

She could only hope she wasn't making the worst mistake of her life.

Twenty-four

❧

It wasn't often that Acair found himself a seedy, disgusting pub, surrounded by his sort of disreputable lads, and felt completely out of place. Uncomfortable. Ill-at-ease. Things were not as they should have been in his life.

That he was even wallowing in such maudlin sentiments was testament enough of the disaster that had become his very existence. He had been sitting in the same place for the whole of the morning, waiting for he knew not what. It was becoming apparent to him that he was going to be continuing to wait, alone.

He toyed with an almost drinkable mug of dark ale and examined all the reasons why he should have been thrilled with that. He was in a truly vile little village, in the worst part of that village, and a cursory glance about the pub in which he found himself told him that there were foul deeds going on. Indeed, he had every reason to kick up his heels and dance the proverbial jig. He had a dull dagger down his boot—something he definitely needed to remedy at his earliest opportunity—he had a fairly straight course laid out before him, and he has his health.

Oh, and he wasn't lingering in some mouldy part of a decrepit old forest in the depths of Shettlestoune where he was trapped behind impenetrable spells of essence changing, admiring all his power that had, by those same spells, been tossed down a well and locked there for eternity.

He also was again flying unencumbered, as it were. No one to worry about but himself, which was just how he preferred things. No need to always be making sure a companion was safe and warm and fed. That damned spell, which had turned out to be of someone's make besides Soilléir's, could certainly see to itself. He was free. Full of vim and good humor over the evil he would get right to as soon as he was at liberty to do so.

He applied himself to a goodly quaff of ale. It should have cured what ailed him, as it were, but all it did was leave him just as uncomfortable as he had been before. He eyed his cup suspiciously, but there was no magic adorning it that he could see and no poison garnishing it that he could smell.

He considered.

It wasn't possible that he was . . . well . . . *missing* her. Was it?

There was a commotion at the door. He sat up in surprise. Surely that wasn't—

Well, he would be damned. It was.

He started to rise, then decided that perhaps it was best that he not become part of the carnage there. A slender figure paused, looked at the trio of lads in various states of incapacitation around herself as if she could scarce believe she had felled them with such a judicious use of her elbows, then brushed her hands off before she walked over to the innkeeper and apologized politely for the necessity of teaching them manners.

The man laughed and promised her luncheon.

Acair watched as the woman—and it was indeed a woman— walked over to his table and sat down. She was dressed in black, which he supposed might have been intimidating if it hadn't been for that flame-red hair that had apparently escaped her cap during her, er, instruction.

Very well, so she was beautiful. He had to admit it. He admitted it a bit reluctantly, to be sure, for she wasn't his usual sort of woman.

"What is your usual sort of woman?"

He blinked, then looked at her. "Was I muttering?"

"Oh, nay, you were quite clear."

He would have flushed if he'd been a different sort of lad, but he didn't flush. He didn't cause others to flush either, as it happened, he caused them to faint or shriek or feign death to escape his notice.

"I was thinking aloud," he said.

"So I see," she noted. "If it eases you any, you aren't my usual sort of lad, either."

"Do you have a usual sort of lad?" he asked.

"I do, and you aren't it."

He nodded to the barmaid and indicated his companion was missing a mug of something drinkable. The girl sprang into action, prodded there no doubt by the innkeeper who had just finished directing his lads to clean up the pile of refuse Léirsinn had left just inside the door. Acair half suspected that the majority of them had simply fallen into a faint over the sight of her hair, but perhaps that was something better kept to himself.

He waited until Léirsinn had something to drink, then wrapped his hands around his own mug. "Tell me more about your usual sort of lad."

She looked at him from clear green eyes that he realized with a start were seeing things in him he wasn't sure he cared for. He hadn't had a chance to talk to her about her journey into the center of that spot of shadow, but perhaps that would need to be put on his list, near the top.

"I don't like lads with dodgy pasts," she said firmly.

"Understandable," he noted. "One never knows what sorts of unpleasant things might crop up from that past."

"One certainly doesn't," she agreed. "And I don't care for lads without a decent amount of chivalry."

He nodded. "One never knows when a large helping of chivalry or a robust display of courtly manners will be what turns the tide of battle, as it were."

"I would imagine that is indeed the case." She propped her chin up on her fist as if she strove not to nod off. "Now, what of you?"

He couldn't say he wasn't highly tempted to have a nap right there near the fire with her. It had been a long night that had been but one in a succession of very long nights. What they both needed, he supposed, was a safe haven that might welcome them for more than just a single night. More was the pity that he supposed that wasn't going to be in their future for quite some time to come.

"Oh," he said, dragging himself back to the matter at hand, "I prefer a brittle, unpleasant sort of woman who is accustomed to snubbing royalty and putting servants in their places. I daresay she should possess an encyclopedic knowledge of ways to poison visiting mages without their having seen it coming."

"That is quite a list."

"Perfected over decades of associating with just such shrews," he assured her.

She looked at him thoughtfully. "I think I might like a kind, honorable sort of lad who isn't afraid to show his feelings."

He felt a little queasy. "Show his feelings?"

"Daily."

"Ye gads, woman, are you mad?"

She smiled and he thought he might like to sit down. He realized he *was* sitting down.

What he needed, perhaps, was indeed a nap.

"And what," he said, grasping at the first thing to come to mind, "if the man—let's be serious here, woman, and speak of men, not lads—what if the man is more comfortable with dragons than horses?"

She sipped at her ale. "An interesting change of pace, I suppose."

"If you were interested in a man."

"Which I'm not."

"Well, I'm not interested in a woman, so I suppose that makes us equal in that regard."

She nodded, then her expression of fierceness faded. "I am rather frightened by this whole idea," she said quietly. "Magic and shadows and not having any way to fight either."

He understood completely. "Why did you come, then? Well, apart from no doubt being overcome by the desire to spend copious amounts of time gazing upon my admittedly spectacular visage."

She smiled faintly. "You are impossible."

"And you're impossibly beautiful," he said honestly. "Not brittle and beastly enough to suit me, of course, but very easy to look upon."

"Was that a compliment?"

"I think so," he said. He paused. "Does it need work?"

"Copious amounts," she said dryly.

"I'll work on it later." He sipped his ale. "So, in truth, what sent you scampering after me before I could scamper away?"

"When you say scamper, do you mean *sit here until Léirsinn comes after me*," she said slowly, "or something else?"

He pursed his lips. "We'll discuss that later, perhaps."

She considered, then pulled a necklace out from under her tunic. She held it out slightly and looked down as the firelight danced against the form of a dragon.

"That is interesting," he said thoughtfully. "Where did you come by it?"

"Your great-aunt Cailleach gave it to me several years ago."

He blinked. "She did? Has it magical properties?"

"I don't think so." She looked at him. "'Tis a bit like me, I suppose."

"I have enough for the both of us, I daresay."

"Magic you can't use."

"A temporary condition, I assure you." He had another sip of ale. "And the answer to my question?"

She looked at him very seriously. "I didn't want you to go without me."

He finished his ale because it was either that or break down and weep, hard-hearted bastard that he was. He made a production of complaining about the smoke in the room as well, because that seemed prudent. And once he'd gotten himself and his traitorous heart under control, he looked at his companion. "Let's go, fire-breather."

"Are you buying?"

"As if I would allow a woman to pay for my ale," he said, tossing coins on the table and taking her hand. "I'll teach you to play cards if we have the odd moment where we aren't being chased by mages with our deaths on their minds. I daresay you would be very good at fleecing lads who might find themselves completely overcome by the color of your hair. Then you can pay for us both."

She only sighed and walked with him. He hazarded a look, though, and found that she was smiling a bit.

The heavens were no doubt weeping over how far lost he was.

He paused on the front stoop of that very seedy pub and looked across the courtyard. He would have gaped, but he was too tired to. "Is that Mansourah of Neroche over there, guarding my horse?" he said grimly.

"It seems to be."

"So, you're taking up with him, now?"

She elbowed him rather sharply in the ribs. "I'm not taking up with anyone. He found me and volunteered to escort me to find you so I could guard your back. He suggested I do that because he thought your defense skills were lacking. He offered to come along on our quest and aid you in bettering them."

"I am utterly unsurprised." And he was. If there existed a family disagreement, political conundrum, or blossoming romance that Mansourah of Neroche could ruin by inserting himself into, he did. He walked with his lady across the way and stopped a handful of paces away from the man he had the feeling he was going to do damage to very soon. "Your Highness," he said stiffly.

"Bastard."

"I have a very long memory," Acair warned, "and no liking for insults. Never mind that I am a bastard *and* a bastard, if you appreciate the distinction."

Mansourah snorted. "I do and I have no fear of you given that you apparently have no ability to use your puny powers."

"That won't last forever."

Mansourah shrugged. "One can hope you'll meet your end before that time."

"Planning on helping whoever attempts to send me off to Hell?"

"I thought I might."

Acair looked at him narrowly. "Mhorghain asked you to come along, didn't she?"

"You're stupid, but I'm surprised to find you're fairly bright."

Acair wondered if he should send along a note to his sister thanking her or cursing her. "Did Mhorghain also tell you what we're about?"

"She thought I might like to hear the tale from our charming lady here."

Acair tucked Léirsinn's hand under his arm. "She's not *our* charming lady."

"Well, she's not yours."

"She's definitely not *yours*."

"Could you both please stop?" Léirsinn asked. "Not that I'm not enjoying this more than I thought I would, but it seems a little silly at the moment, doesn't it?"

Acair thought that *silly* might cover anything worthwhile about Mansourah of Neroche, but refrained from saying as much. He elbowed Mansourah out of his way and walked over to where he'd left his horse. Mansourah followed, something Acair realized he was going to have to accustom himself to. That, he admitted without any hesitation at all, didn't set well with him.

"Where are we going?" Mansourah asked.

"The library at Diarmailt."

"Are we?" Léirsinn asked in surprise. "Why?"

"I need to fetch a book," Acair said. He wasn't going to be able to use his damned book even if he could fetch it, but perhaps that wasn't a useful thing to admit at the moment. It was full of his own scribblings, true, but also a list of spells he'd either hidden in other places or thought he might like to liberate from their owners who were residing in other places. That was the sort of thing he didn't particularly care to have cluttering up his mind on a daily basis, which was why he'd written it all down and hidden it so well.

Mansourah looked at him as if he'd lost his wits. "But Rùnach has the book you left behind there."

Acair despaired for the success of the enterprise, truly he did. He looked at Mansourah evenly. "Do you honestly believe I left that there by accident?"

Mansourah's mouth fell open. "But—"

Acair tapped his forehead. "Think, lad, before you embarrass yourself."

Mansourah looked at Léirsinn. "How do you bear him?"

"If I were looking for a man, which I'm not, I would have to say that I like him." She smiled. "He's honest."

Mansourah took a deep breath and let it out slowly. "An honest black mage."

"Just that."

He shook his head, as if he simply couldn't wrap his mind around what he was faced with. He looked at them. "I'll need to give that some thought. If you don't mind, though, I think I'll go ahead and find lodgings. I do have my standards."

Acair imagined he did and he supposed hell would see its first frost before he bunked with that meddling old woman.

"See you there," Acair said cheerfully, waving him off. "Don't dawdle."

Mansourah grumbled a half-hearted curse at him, spoke a handful of words, then disappeared.

Acair realized that whilst he was no doubt not on Mansourah's list of favorite people, Léirsinn apparently was. He looked at the spell that had been cast up over them, then realized Léirsinn was turning in a circle, staring at it in astonishment. She stopped and looked at him.

"What is that?"

"Safety for the journey."

She smiled. "He is very kind."

"My sister told him to do it."

"Most likely."

"Besides," Acair said, taking her pack from her and attaching it with his own to Sianach's saddle, "he just wants to come along to see how black magery is properly done. Obviously all that prissy magic he's accustomed to putting on display simply isn't attracting the sort of women he would like to aspire to."

She put her hand on Sianach's withers. "And what sort of woman does a black mage attract?"

He looked at her seriously. "Red-haired, dragon-loving, fire-breathing horse gels who have more courage than most men I know."

Her smile faded. "I don't have any courage, Acair."

He considered, then reached out and pulled her into his arms. He wasn't entirely sure that her squawk hadn't come from his tangling a button from his cloak in her hair, but she seemed to find him not objectionable enough to not embrace in return.

"I have an abundance of the stuff," he said, with as much bluster as he could. "I'll share."

"Will we die?"

"Not today. Not tomorrow, either, if I can manage it. We'll worry about the day after when it comes."

He didn't want to think about that day after. He was off to do impossible things. He needed to locate the maker of those spots of shadow, discover what they meant, and eradicate them before they took over the world. He had to save Léirsinn's grandfather and Hearn's son. He had to find out who had created that spell that was following him before he did some unthinking piece of magic and it fell upon him and slew him.

And all of that whilst someone he couldn't name was watching him.

But the most daunting task of all was that he had to accomplish all that with a woman in tow, a woman he was still trying to convince himself he wasn't fond of, a woman without so much as a breath of magic to her name. A woman he thought he just might die to keep safe.

He was mad.

But he kept his arms around Léirsinn of Sàraichte just the same and was damned grateful for that red-haired gel who was willing to follow him into that madness. It was absolutely not what he'd expected and far more goodness than he deserved, but he wasn't going to look a gift horse in the mouth. They would do what needed to be done with whatever wit and cleverness they could both muster.

"Should we go?" she asked, finally.

"Probably so," he agreed. He released her, then waited for her to settle herself in the saddle before he tried to swing up behind her. He had to jump aside to avoid being bitten by his horse. And all was as it should have been.

Bad horse, astonishing woman, no magic.

He supposed many important quests had begun with far less.

The next Nine Kingdoms novel featuring Acair and Léirsinn is coming in the summer of 2017. In the meantime, turn the page for a sneak peek at the next Lynn Kurland novel,

Ever My Love,

due out in early 2017.

There were, Emma Barton had to admit, several benefits to learning how to drive on the left while in Scotland: fewer cars; fewer pedestrians; and more sheep who seemed to have absolutely no compunction about sunning themselves on tarmac.

Also, more room for almost having driven off the road while being distracted by the scenery.

She felt very fortunate that she'd eased off to the left instead of to the right, which would have left her in a long, winding river. She took a moment to indulge in a bit of deep breathing, then righted her car and continued on her way up the road toward the forest in front of her.

She paused, then considered. The forest road didn't have any *no trespassing* signs posted, but she wondered if it might be wise to figure out where she was before she wandered onto someone's private property and found herself mistaken for a grouse and shot on sight.

She pulled off the road, such as it was, and checked her phone. She had no signal, so she was obviously going to have to settle for physical maps. At least that way she could very reasonably claim ignorance if she wandered where she shouldn't have. She mapped out a route in her head, tossed the map in the passenger seat, then opened her door. She promptly stepped into a puddle that had to have been at least a foot deep.

Hopefully that wasn't a sign.

She took a deep breath, climbed out of that puddle and her car both, then locked the door. She put her phone in her pocket and set off in the vague direction she had chosen to go.

The forest, once she entered it, was a bit more dense than she'd expected it to be, but she supposed that had more to do with the cloudiness of the day than it did the number of trees. She zipped her slicker up and continued on, undaunted. No self-respecting Seattleite would have paid any attention to what was falling through the trees and she was nothing if not seasoned when it came to rain.

Unfortunately, having nothing to do but walk gave her far more time to think than she wanted. She'd put on a good face as she'd been bolting from her life, but now she had no choice but to have a good look at it.

The truth was, she was uneasy. She had walked away from everything because she had to. She was almost thirty years old, recently friend-zoned by her boyfriend of two years, and staring at the ruins of a business she'd built from scratch. What of her savings she hadn't been forced to give to her unscrupulous business partner—better not to think about that, she decided firmly—she had used to buy a ticket to Scotland and pay in advance for the first week of her stay. She had two months' worth of expenses in an account she had managed to keep separate from any business entanglements, but once that was gone, she was out of money and out of options. She had to come up with a solution and fast.

The solutions she didn't consider were insolvency, piracy, and moving back in with her high-brow parents, who would look her up and down and sigh lightly every time they saw her.

She had to pause and take several deep, strengthening breaths. She would manage it. All she had to do was put one foot in front of the other. She had come to Scotland for inspiration for not only her life, but for a new business direction as well. She just needed some peace and quiet to get her head together and start a new chapter in her life.

Because the truth was, she didn't have a choice. She had stepped away from a bad situation, she had paid a steep price for her exit, and now she had no choice but to go forward.

She took a deep breath and pushed aside her unhelpful thoughts. She could have been living eight hundred years earlier and on her way to the Tower of London. She could have been missing her shoes. She could have had a lifetime of the same sort of truly awful tea and stale cookies she'd made a breakfast of back in her room. When she looked at it that way, her life was looking pretty good.

In the end, where she found herself was her choice. She had chosen to take a step out into the darkness without knowing whether her foot would find solid ground or thin air.

She really wanted it to be the former.

That seemed to be the case at the moment. The ground was solid if not a little damp, the air was clean and crisp, and she had on warm clothes. Things were very good.

She continued to wander through woods that felt more like a church than just trees and sky and rain. She walked until she found herself standing on the edge of a lake. She watched the water for quite some time, hoping she wasn't trespassing. The tracks she had begun to follow were definitely not on the map she'd left back in the car and her phone was still useless.

There was a house sitting on the shore, actually not far from where she stood. It didn't look particularly inhabited, but maybe it was a holiday rental. She supposed she might ask around in the village and see if it was for rent. She could think of much more uncomfortable places to pass the winter.

She turned back and walked through the forest. It was only as she paused to catch her breath that she heard the ringing. It wasn't her phone; it was more a metal on metal sort of sound. Blacksmith? Fellow jewelry designer looking for the same sort of inspiration she was? She pulled her phone out of her pocket and looked at it just to be sure, but that wasn't what she was hearing.

She looked around herself and considered. She couldn't see anyone nearby, but what did she know? She supposed she could at least do a bit of careful investigation. For all she knew, she might make a friend. If she found something odd, she would just turn and run like hell. That useful plan made, she continued on silently, then stopped at the edge of a clearing with far less grace than she might have hoped for on another day.

No, it hadn't been her phone making that ringing noise.

It had been the guys with swords in front of her.

She had to reach out and put her hand on a tree, not necessarily because she wanted to lean on something but because she was having a difficult time trying to decide what she was seeing and she needed something real to hold on to. Was that a movie set? A re-enactment group taking things way too far?

A waking nightmare?

There was a mist surrounding the men fighting there, as if they were truly part of some sort of group that existed only in her dreams.

Scotland in my dreams. She'd actually thought that, hadn't she? Maybe she needed to be more careful with what went on inside her head.

The battle, if battle it was, was nothing like she'd ever seen in a movie, only because what she was seeing looked thoroughly unscripted and she could see men dying. Actually, the filthy clansmen shouting, the men dying, and the metal screeching against metal were everything she'd ever seen in a movie only this was a hundred times more intense.

That might have been because it looked real.

She couldn't move. She could only stand there, her fingers digging into the damp bark of the tree, and wish she could move so she could flee.

And then a dark-haired man stumbled out of the fog. He caught sight of her, then skidded to a halt. He was covered in what looked like blood, but she assumed it wasn't his own. Surely it was just some sort of stage stuff, or something he'd bought down at the local costume shop. It looked real, though, and so did he.

But it couldn't be real. She was obviously having a hallucination, but she found she didn't want to disturb it. She stood, frozen in place, and tried not to breathe. She might have been imagining things, but she was nothing if not pragmatic. Maybe if she kept very still, she might get a decent look at that guy before he disappeared.

He was beautiful; there was no other way to describe him. His face was planes and angles but in such perfect symmetry that she almost took her phone out and grabbed a picture so she could have reproduced his face perfectly when she'd had a pencil to hand. He was much taller than she was, likely a trio of inches over six feet. He looked as though he spent a fair amount of time working out—though she supposed that was less time spent at the gym and more time spent with, well, a sword.

Good heavens, she was losing her mind.

And his eyes were green. She could see that from where she stood.

He looked as if he'd just run into a wall, but perhaps that expression of surprise was what most hallucinations wore when they escaped from a dream and found themselves facing a human. It was the only explanation she could come up with on short notice and it seemed reasonable enough to her.

"Damn it to hell," he blurted out, adding several other things she didn't quite catch, though she had to admit he had a very lovely accent.

He stepped backward, then ducked. She knew why because she'd heard the whistle of sword coming his way as well.

She put her hands over her eyes, rubbed them, then looked again.

There was nothing else in the glade there, nothing but a bit of mist and the sound of rain falling lightly against the last of fall's leaves. She hovered there for a moment or two, her fingers digging into the bark of that tree, hearing that man's accent ringing in her ears.

Then she turned and ran.

It was certainly the most sensible thing she'd done all year. She ran until she stumbled out of the forest, then she kept running until she had flung herself inside her car. She turned that car around, then drove like a bat out of hell back to the village.

It had been nothing. Just a waking dream brought on by truly the worst cup of tea she'd ever had in her life. And those things that she'd found to accompany that tea? Awful. She wasn't sure what to call them, but she suspected that not even smothering them in chocolate would have redeemed them from their resemblance to sawdust. She suspected they had been sitting on that tray for months.

She reached the village without getting lost, no mean feat considering her state of mind but perhaps less impressive than it might have been if there had been more than one road leading in and out of the village. She parked, locked her car, then walked straight up to the turret room in her hotel. She locked the door, stumbled over to stand in the middle of that room, and shook.

She shook until she thought maybe her trembles came less from terror and more from a serious dip in her blood sugar. She reached for her phone to see what time it was only to realize she didn't have her phone. She looked around her frantically, then looked out her window to see if she'd dropped it in the front garden.

She thought back. She'd had it on her way into the forest, but she'd had it in her hand, not in her coat pocket. She remembered reaching for that tree, but couldn't remember the last time she'd had her phone in her hand.

She walked downstairs and looked carefully at the ground on the way to her car. She searched inside her car, even the backseat. She finally straightened, stood next to her car and let out a deep, shuddering breath. There was absolutely no way in hell she was going to go back and look for it now. Not when it was starting to get dark. Not in that haunted forest.

Highland magic.

Well, if that was what they wanted to call it, more power to them. She leaned back against her car and considered her next move. She was starving, cold, and more than a little freaked out. Well, the first thing she could solve was food, so she locked her car, then headed for the pub she'd walked past the day before. At least there she might find the company of real, live people.

Fifteen minutes later she was sitting in a corner near a fireplace with a comforting cup of tea. She sipped, then leaned her head back against the wall and tried to forget what she'd seen.

"I won't speak ill of them, but you do what you like."

"'Tisn't ill-speaking to speculate," said another voice. "And you must admit, odd things go on up in those woods."

"Aye, and goodly amounts of money come flowing down into the village to benefit the likes of you, so don't blather on about what you think you know."

Fortunately for her, Emma supposed, that old-timer didn't seem to take his companion's injunctions very seriously. He seemed perfectly happy to dish with the rest of his buddies. That worked for her, because she was perfectly happy to eavesdrop.

Though after a few minutes, she wondered why.

Highland magic was, apparently, just the beginning of the odd things that went on in the area. Ghosts, bogles, an influx of gold-diggers from down south: those were all examined at length with judgments passed on them accordingly.

But then their voices lowered and the juicy stuff was brought out and presented for speculation.

Emma listened through a lovely dinner of chicken, a jacket potato, and peas, though she had to admit after a few bites, she was only chewing out of sheer habit. The things she was hearing really couldn't be taken seriously, but she couldn't stop listening.

Time-traveling lairds? Money dug up from gardens? Murder and mayhem that stretched through the centuries and found itself solved in times and places not her own and with pointy medieval implements of death?

She had to have another gulp of tea. All that was starting to sound uncomfortably more possible than she would have wanted to believe, especially that last part about swords.

Good grief, what had she gotten herself into?

She was actually rather glad she'd already finished her dinner because she had certainly lost her appetite. She grabbed her coat and made her way as inconspicuously as possible to the door. She paused outside on the sidewalk and wondered if she might be losing her mind. It sounded reasonable. Actually, it sounded like the most reasonable thing she'd thought all day.

She pulled her slicker more closely around herself, gave herself a good mental shake, then walked off back toward her hotel. Jetlag. It had to be jetlag. She thought she had that crazy time change handled, but it was obvious she had been more affected by it than she'd feared.

It couldn't be that she'd signed herself up for a couple of months in a place where *magic* really meant what it sounded like it meant.

She would go back to her temporary home and get some sleep. Before she did, she would consign her day's events to the receptacle entitled *Jetlag Hallucinations*, then she would get back to her very sensible way of doing business, which included finding her phone in the bright light of day.

Unfortunately, she thought it might be quite a while before she managed to forget the sight of that green-eyed man in the ratty kilt.

Highland magic, indeed.

Photo by Lynn Rowley

Lynn Kurland is the *New York Times* bestselling author *of Stars In Your Eyes, Dreams of Lilacs, All for You, One Magic Moment,* and the Novels of the Nine Kingdoms, as well as numerous other novels and short stories. Visit her online at lynnkurland.com.